Praise for the novels
of Martha Grimes

The Grave Maurice
A *New York Times* Bestseller

"Sure to please. . . . Grimes's writing has rarely been more lovely." —*Chicago Tribune*

"Wickedly clever. . . . Fans will rejoice."
—*Chattanooga Times–Free Press*

The Blue Last
A *New York Times* Bestseller

"Grimes's best . . . a cliffhanger ending." —*USA Today*

"Explosive . . . ranks among the best of its creator's distinguished work." —*The Richmond Times-Dispatch*

The Lamorna Wink
A *New York Times* Bestseller

"Atmospheric . . . an elegantly styled series."
—*The New York Times Book Review*

"Swift and satisfying . . . grafts the old-fashioned 'Golden Age' amateur-detective story to the contemporary police procedural . . . real charm."
—*The Wall Street Journal*

The Stargazey
A *New York Times* Bestseller

"Wondrously eccentric characters. . . . The details are divine." —*The New York Times Book Review*

"The literary equivalent of a box of Godiva truffles . . . wonderful." —*Los Angeles Times*

continued . . .

The Case Has Altered
A *New York Times* Bestseller

"The way Martha Grimes tells it, there is no more atmospheric setting for murder in all of England than the Lincolnshire fens. . . . Richly textured."
—*The New York Times Book Review*

"Grimes is dazzling in this deftly plotted Richard Jury mystery. . . . Psychologically complex. . . . The novel also boasts Grimes's delicious wit. . . . [She] brings Jury triumphantly back where he belongs."
—*Publishers Weekly*

The Anodyne Necklace

"Not to be missed." —*San Francisco Chronicle*

"A comedy of manners with characters that delight and a mystery that confounds." —*UPI*

I Am the Only Running Footman

"Everything about Miss Grimes's new novel shows her at her best . . . [She] gets our immediate attention. . . . She holds it, however, with something more than mere suspense." —*The New Yorker*

"Literate, witty, and stylishly crafted."
—*The Washington Post*

The Five Bells and Bladebone

"[Grimes's] best . . . as moving as it is entertaining."
—*USA Today*

"Blends almost Dickensian sketches of character and social class with glimpses of a ferocious marriage."
—*Time*

"Holds the attention throughout."
—*The New York Times Book Review*

The Old Fox Deceiv'd

"A good puzzle . . . unusually well written."
—*The Boston Globe*

"Affectionately witty characterizations . . . give her writing the Dickensian touch that makes it glow."
—*The Philadelphia Inquirer*

The Man with a Load of Mischief
The first Richard Jury novel

"For readers who value wit, atmosphere, and charm in their mysteries . . . Grimes has soaked up the atmosphere of English villages and pubs in her travels. She has learned her sleight-of-hand from Christie and delights in the rich characterizations of Marsh."
—*The Washington Post Book World*

"[Grimes's novel] is cast in the mold of the great British mysteries and comes complete with all the classic elements."
—*The San Diego Union*

ALSO BY MARTHA GRIMES

Richard Jury Novels

The Man with a Load of Mischief
The Old Fox Deceiv'd
The Anodyne Necklace
Jerusalem Inn
The Deer Leap
I Am the Only Running Footman
The Five Bells and Bladebone
The Old Silent
The Old Contemptibles
The Horse You Came In On
Rainbow's End
The Case Has Altered
The Stargazey
The Lamorna Wink
The Blue Last
The Grave Maurice
The Winds of Change

Other Works

The End of the Pier
Hotel Paradise
Biting the Moon
The Train Now Departing
Cold Flat Junction
Foul Matter

Poetry

Send Bygraves

Help the Poor Struggler

A Richard Jury Novel

MARTHA GRIMES

AN ONYX BOOK

ONYX
Published by New American Library, a division of
Penguin Group (USA) Inc., 375 Hudson Street,
New York, New York 10014, USA
Penguin Group (Canada), 10 Alcorn Avenue, Toronto,
Ontario M4V 3B2, Canada (a division of Pearson Penguin Canada Inc.)
Penguin Books Ltd., 80 Strand, London WC2R 0RL, England
Penguin Ireland, 25 St. Stephen's Green, Dublin 2,
Ireland (a division of Penguin Books Ltd.)
Penguin Group (Australia), 250 Camberwell Road, Camberwell, Victoria 3124,
Australia (a division of Pearson Australia Group Pty. Ltd.)
Penguin Books India Pvt. Ltd., 11 Community Centre, Panchsheel Park,
New Delhi - 110 017, India
Penguin Group (NZ), cnr Airborne and Rosedale Roads, Albany,
Auckland 1310, New Zealand (a division of Pearson New Zealand Ltd.)
Penguin Books (South Africa) (Pty.) Ltd., 24 Sturdee Avenue,
Rosebank, Johannesburg 2196, South Africa

Penguin Books Ltd., Registered Offices:
80 Strand, London WC2R 0RL, England

Published by Onyx, an imprint of New American Library, a division of Penguin
Group (USA) Inc. Previously published in Little, Brown and Dell editions.

First Onyx Printing, February 2005
10 9 8 7 6 5 4 3 2 1

Copyright © Martha Grimes, 1985
The author is grateful for permission to quote from "Interior" by Dorothy Parker,
from *The Portable Dorothy Parker*, edited by Brendan Gill. Copyright 1928, re-
newed © 1956 by Dorothy Parker. Reprinted by permission of Viking Penguin,
a division of Penguin Group (USA) Inc., and Gerald Duckworth and Company
Limited, London.
All rights reserved

 REGISTERED TRADEMARK—MARCA REGISTRADA

Printed in the United States of America

Without limiting the rights under copyright reserved above, no part of this
publication may be reproduced, stored in or introduced into a retrieval system,
or transmitted, in any form, or by any means (electronic, mechanical, photocopying, recording, or otherwise), without the prior written permission of both the
copyright owner and the above publisher of this book.

PUBLISHER'S NOTE
This is a work of fiction. Names, characters, places, and incidents either are the
product of the author's imagination or are used fictitiously, and any resemblance
to actual persons, living or dead, business establishments, events, or locales is
entirely coincidental.

If you purchased this book without a cover you should be aware that this book
is stolen property. It was reported as "unsold and destroyed" to the publisher
and neither the author nor the publisher has received any payment for this
"stripped book."

The scanning, uploading, and distribution of this book via the Internet or via any
other means without the permission of the publisher is illegal and punishable by
law. Please purchase only authorized electronic editions, and do not participate
in or encourage electronic piracy of copyrighted materials. Your support of the
author's rights is appreciated.

To Leon Duke,
who leant a hand

and Mike Mattil,
who helped a poor struggler

Her mind lives tidily, apart
  From cold and noise and pain,
And bolts the door against her heart,
  Out wailing in the rain.

—Dorothy Parker

O, man, dear, did ya never hear
  Of pretty Molly Brannigan?
She's gone away and left me
  And I'll never be a man again;
Not a spot on me hide
  Will the summer sun e'er tan again,
Now that Molly's gone and left me
  Here for to die.

—Irish folk song

CONTENTS

PROLOGUE

The little girl stood in her flannel nightdress holding the telephone receiver. She carefully dialed the numbers her mother always did when she wanted the operator.

A silky-haired cat at her feet arched its back, yawned, and began washing its paw as the little girl waited through several *brr-brr*'s for the operator to answer. Maybe they didn't wake up until late, the little girl thought. Her mum always said they were lazy. She looked out the leaded glass window almost lost under its thatch collar to see it just pearling over with early-morning light and the moorland beyond floating in morning mist. There was a spiderweb with beads of dew between the thatch and the window. The *brr-brr* went on. She counted ten of them

1

and then hung up and picked up the phone again. The cat leapt to the table to sit and watch the spider painstakingly finish its web.

Bloody operators. That was what her mum always said, sitting here at the table, looking out like the cat, over the blank face of the moor that surrounded their hamlet. The phone kept *brr*-ing. The veil of gray light lifted like a delicate curtain drawn back showing the far horizon where a line of gold spun like the spiderweb.

There was a click, and someone answered. Her voice seemed to come from a great distance, as if she were calling across the moor out there.

The little girl held the black receiver with tight hands and tried to speak very clearly because if they didn't like you they'd just hang up. That's what her mother'd always said. *The cheek of them. Think they're the bloody Queen, some of them.* Her mother spent a lot of time on the telephone and slammed it down a lot.

"My mum's dead," she said.

There was a silence and she was afraid the operator was going to hang up, like the Queen. But she didn't. The operator asked her to repeat what she'd just said.

"My mum's dead," the little girl said patiently, despite her fright. "She never died before."

Now the operator sounded much closer—not way off across the moor—and was asking her questions in a nice tone of voice. What was her name and where did she live?

"My name's Tess. We live in the moor." *This bloody moor*, her mother had always said. She'd hated where they lived. "My mum's in the kitchen. She's dead."

Last name?

"Mulvanney."

The cat's white fur gleamed in the newly risen sun. The spiderweb was spangled with diamond-dew, and as Tess tried to answer the operator's questions the web broke and the spider—it was a tiny brown spider—hung on a silver thread. The cat's tail twitched. The operator was saying they must live in a certain *place* in the moor. A village? And what was their telephone number?

"Clerihew Marsh," said Tess, looking down at the dial. She told the operator the number there. "She's in the kitchen and she won't get up. I thought she was playing. Are you going to call the hospital and will the ambulance come?"

The operator was very nice and said, Yes, of course. She told Tess maybe her mum wasn't dead at all, just sick, and they'd get the doctor. The operator told her very clearly *not* to hang up, that she'd call someone and get back to Tess straightaway.

Silence again. The operator was being very nice, but the operator hadn't been in the kitchen and didn't understand. The cat wore a halo of light, and the spider was repairing its web with infinite patience.

When Tess heard the operator's voice again, she tried to explain: "I thought she was playing with my fingerpaints. We have paints at school. I thought she got the red pot." The operator asked her what she meant. "There's red all over the kitchen. She's cut. It's blood. It's on her dress and in her hair."

Quickly, the operator told her again not to hang up, that she had to call someone else. Soon she was back and talking to Tess in a soothing voice about things like school. Yes, said Tess, she went to school. They called it babies' school, but she wasn't a baby. She was five years old. She told the operator about her teacher, who looked like a toad. They talked a long time and Tess figured out why the operators hardly ever answered. They were talking to people.

The cat yawned and jumped from the table, and Tess knew it wanted its breakfast and would wander into the kitchen. "I've got to hang up. I don't want Sandy—that's our cat—to go into the kitchen." Tess hung up.

Rose Mulvanney lay beneath the kitchen table, her legs jackknifed, her dress blood-besotted. Blood had splattered the kitchen floor, the white daub walls, and even the low, dark beam of the ceiling.

Teresa Mulvanney wondered how it had got up

4

there. She shook and shook her head, forgetting everything as her mind drifted and filmed over. She closed her eyes and scratched her elbows. What must be happening was that she was having one of her "bad" nights; she was dreaming. It must all be paint, after all, or tomato ketchup. Her mother, Rose, had said that in films they used that. Tess, with her eyes still closed, told her mother it was all right and she could get up now. It was a game and it was all a dream anyway. Even the *brr*-ing of the telephone and the far-off double note that made her think of ambulances came as dark figures in fog. She began to hum a song that Rose Mulvanney used to sing when Teresa was a baby.

She forgot to feed the cat.

When Detective Inspector Nicholson and Sergeant Brian Macalvie of the Devon-Cornwall constabulary got to the small cottage in Clerihew Marsh, Teresa Mulvanney was humming and writing her name on the white wall in her mother's blood.

Brian Macalvie had never seen anything like it and he never forgot it. At this time he was twenty-three years old and was generally thought to be the best CID man in the whole Devon-Cornwall constabulary. It was an opinion held by practically everyone, even Macalvie's enemies—also practically everyone. He was not fond of taking orders; he was always talking about his Scots-Irish-American ancestry and dying to get out of England; he was always getting promoted.

He worked on the murder of Rose Mulvanney even after the file had been officially closed. Three months after the Mulvanney murder, they'd arrested (according to Macalvie) the wrong man—a young medical student who lived in Clerihew Marsh and went to Exeter University. He'd been arrested on flimsy, circumstantial evidence—he'd had a heavy crush on Rose Mulvanney, fifteen years older, and, being a medical student, he knew how to use a knife. The motive was unrequited love; the evidence (said Macalvie), Nil.

During the same period, he moved in on six other cases that he felt the department was snailing along on and solved those, so that it was difficult for the divisional commander to tell him to get off the Mulvanney case. Macalvie was his own police force. When he walked into the lab, the pathologists and technicians clung to their microscopes. It was Macalvie's contention their fingerprint expert couldn't find a bootprint on a hospital sheet. If it came down to it, the whole department couldn't find a Rolls-Royce if it was parked in front of the Moorcombe headquarters on Christmas Day.

Thus when the divisional commander told him to get off the Mulvanney case, that the case was closed, Macalvie dropped his ID on the table and said, "Macalvie, six; Devon-Cornwall, Nil." He wasn't halfway across the room before his superior's tone changed. As long as Macalvie didn't let the Mulvanney business interfere with his other duties . . .

"Tell that to Sam Waterhouse," said Macalvie, and walked out.

Sam Waterhouse was the medical student who had been sent to Dartmoor prison. It was a life sentence with the possibility of parole, since there were no prior convictions and the murder of Rose Mulvanney was judged a *crime passionel*.

Macalvie had not hesitated to let the Devon-Cornwall constabulary feel the full weight of his personal displeasure. They had ruined the kid's life and, possibly, a brilliant career.

And if there was one person who knew about brilliant careers, it was Brian Macalvie.

The tiny hamlet of Clerihew Marsh was nothing more than a few fat cottages huddled on either side of a curving road, giving the distorted image of dwellings reflected in a pier glass or a fun-house mirror. After the first clump of houses, so stuck together they looked as if they shared the same thatched roof, the cottages straggled a little, like a sleeve unraveling. The Mulvanney cottage was the last in the fringe. It sat by itself, windows on every side, quite visible to anyone passing.

7

But apparently no one had been when Rose Mulvanney was being cut with a knife. No one had seen anyone go in or out. No one had seen any strangers about. No one had heard anything. No one who knew him believed Sam Waterhouse could do such a thing.

Macalvie followed every conceivable lead—there were few enough—down to the milk-float man, and had the little wren of a woman who ran the sub–post office chirping nearly daily about the way Rose bought her food. Macalvie had browbeaten the teacher of the Infant's School into delivering up her small quota of information about Teresa Mulvanney. Nor was he beyond using the same tactics with the odd school chum if he could collar one. The headmistress finally complained to the Devon-Cornwall police.

One of the most important persons in the case, one he had not questioned initially, was Rose's older daughter. She'd been away on a school trip when the little sister had made the awful discovery.

She'd come bursting into Macalvie's office, a lanky kid of fifteen with toothpick arms and no breasts and long hair. She'd stood there with fire in her eyes and yelling at him, spattering obscenities like blood on his office walls. Her baby sister, Teresa, had been taken to hospital. Teresa was catatonic. All she did was lie on her cot, curled up like a baby, sucking her thumb.

It was as though Macalvie had been sitting in a warm bath of his own infallibility (it never occurred to him he wouldn't come up with the answers), and this kid had come along and pulled the plug. She got so hysterical she slammed her arm across the stuff on his desk, sending papers, pens, and sour coffee cups all over the floor.

He never solved the case; he never forgave himself; he never saw the kid again.

Her name was Mary Mulvanney.

I

The Alley by
the Five Alls

Twenty Years Later . . .

ONE

Simon Riley never knew what hit him.

That was, at least, the opinion of the medical examiner called to the scene by the Dorset police. The wound in the boy's back had been administered very quickly and very efficiently by a knife honed to razor sharpness. The pathologist agreed and added that, given the angle of the downward thrust, the knife had been wielded by someone considerably taller than Simon. That didn't help the Dorset police greatly, since Simon had been a twelve-year-old schoolboy and was wearing, at the time of his death, the black jacket and tie which constituted the school uniform. That the killer was at least a foot taller would not be particularly helpful in establishing identity.

The boy lay face downward in the alley by the Five Alls pub, crumpled in fetal position against the blind wall which was the pub's side facing the alley. Scattered around the body were a ten-packet of John Players Specials and a copy of *Playboy*. Simon had been indulging in every schoolboy's twin sins— smoking fags and looking at naked women—when the killer had come up behind him. This was the construction of Detective Inspector Neal of the Dorset police, and there was no reason to think it inaccurate.

It was the kitchen girl at the pub, opening the side door of the Five Alls to toss a bag in the dustbin, who had been unlucky enough to find him on that awful evening of February tenth. She had come in for some stiff questioning and had had to be sedated.

The Five Alls was a tucked-away place on a Dorchester side street. The squinty little alley where the boy had been found dead-ended on a blank wall. For Simon Riley's secretive pastimes, it was well located. Unfortunately for Simon, it was just as well located for murder.

TWO

I

Riley's. Fine Meat and Game. Superintendent Richard Jury and Detective Sergeant Alfred Wiggins looked through the shop window at their own reflections superimposed over the hanging pheasants. The shop was (a sign announced) licensed to sell game. A young man and an older one were serving a queue of women who were armed with wicker baskets and string bags. From the description given Jury, he took the older man to be Albert Riley himself, the boy's father. It was two days after Simon's body had been found and one day before his funeral. Jury was a little surprised to see the boy's father working.

Apparently, best British beef was in strong demand and short supply, given the way the drill-sergeant eyes of the line of women followed Jury's and Wiggins's progress to the front of the queue. There were mutterings and one or two astringent voices telling these two interlopers where the end of the line was just in case they were blind.

When Jury produced his identification, the young man's face went as white as that part of his apron which was still unblotched. Then he turned to the master-butcher, who was defatting some pork chops with swift and measured strokes. It was an unpleasant reminder of the autopsy performed on his son. Riley's knife stopped in midair when his underling turned him toward the Scotland Yard policemen.

Riley handed over the pork chops to the youth as the women behind Jury and Wiggins passed the information along like buckets of water in a fire brigade. Scotland Yard. Jury realized that Riley's fine meat and game might be even more popular today; murder usually had that effect.

Simon's father wiped his hands on a cloth and removed his apron. His thick spectacles magnified his small eyes and made his round face rounder. He was soft-spoken and apologetic, clearly embarrassed at being caught working in such dreadful circumstances. The authority with which he'd used the knife was completely lost when he put it down.

"Shop was closed yesterday," he said. "But I thought I'd go mad, what with pacing up and down and the wife—that's Simon's stepmother—yelling her head off." While saying this, he was leading them to a door at the rear of the shop. "Suppose you think it's cold-blooded, me working—"

Wiggins, seldom given to irony, said, "Not our business to wonder whether it's hot or cold, sir. Just that it's blood."

Riley winced as he led them up a twisting staircase. "Scotland Yard. I told the wife to leave off with that Queen's Counsel person of hers. Told her Dorset police could handle—" Then, seeming to feel he'd made a blunder, he quickly added, "Expect they need all the help they can get. We keep this flat over the shop. Have another house, but this is handy. The wife'll make a cuppa. I could do with something stronger myself."

The "something stronger" was Jameson's and the wife was not at all inclined to make a cuppa. Although it was lunchtime, she was more interested in whiskey than in lunch or tea. Her own hand didn't shake as she downed her drop, but her husband's did, as if he had palsy. When Riley took off his glasses to pinch the bridge of his nose, Jury saw the eyes were red-rimmed—from tears, probably. Mrs. Riley's were red, too, but Jury supposed that was owing more to the bottle than to bereavement. Since she was not the natural mother, she might have thought that released her from weepy demonstrations.

Beth Riley was a big, brassy woman; her face would have done better with a simple hairstyle than with the florid waves, red-rinsed, that framed the head. She was better-spoken than her husband, even given her lubricated voice. The Jameson's had already got a workout.

"Beth insisted on getting that Q.C. in London to call you people—"

"It's just as well *one* of us knows someone in high places." She turned to Jury. "Leonard Matching, Q.C. He's to stand for Parliament in Brixton." From the vague reports Jury had got of mealymouthed Matching, he doubted very much if Brixton would stand for him. The only reason Jury and Wiggins were here was that an assistant commissioner was a personal friend and had handed the request down the line to Chief Superintendent Racer, who had wasted no time in deploying Jury to the provinces. Too bad (Jury imagined Racer thinking) it was only a hundred and sixty-odd miles from London and the old market town of Dorchester rather than Belfast. Jury could just guess how much Inspector Neal enjoyed having his authority presumed upon, but Neal was too much of a gentleman to make Jury's life hell. Many would have.

". . . and not two decent relations to rub together," Beth Riley was saying in a shocking display of acrimony. The child was dead. What had family connections to do with it?

"All right, all right, pet," said Riley, in some attempt to shush her. Though why the father should have to minister to the totally unfeeling stepmother, Jury couldn't say. Indeed, he couldn't see the two of them together at all, if it came to that. She lost no chance to remind him of her superior education, and Jury simply let her get it out of her system as his eye traveled the room. Over the fireplace were photographs that might bear out her claim, for all its coldness. There was even one of those mahogany coats-of-arms that tourists seemed forever gathering in the race for their roots; there were also framed documents, one with a seal.

"I'm sorry to intrude upon your grief," said Jury to Mrs. Riley. His tone was icy. "But there are a few questions."

Beth Riley sat back, said nothing, left the question-and-answer period up to her husband. Simon had been (she reminded Jury) *Albert's* son.

"Had you remembered anything at all since you talked to Inspector Neal, Mr. Riley? About your son's friends . . . or enemies?" Predictably, Riley disclaimed any enemies—how could a lad of twelve have enemies? It was true the Dorset police had established to their satisfaction that Simon Riley had neither. He was not popular with his schoolmates, but neither was he hated. Nor did anyone seriously believe a schoolboy would be carrying the sort of knife around Dorchester that had inflicted the wound.

19

Inspector Neal had looked almost unhappier than the father himself when Neal had said *psychopath.* What else could it be? *You know what that means, Superintendent. Child-killer. In Dorchester?*

I wouldn't like it much in London, either, Jury had thought.

". . . psychopath." Albert Riley echoed the word of Inspector Neal. He was wiping his eyes with a much-used handkerchief. Jury's feeling about Riley had changed when he realized that the man probably did have to work to keep from crumbling. Certainly, he was getting no support from his wife.

But with Neal's and Riley's verdict upon who killed Simon, Jury did not agree. The single wound in the boy's back was clean, neat, quick—not the multiple stab-wounds one might have expected from a person who was out for blood or boys. There had been no molesting of the body. This was all Jury had to go on, but he still thought the murder was probably premeditated and that it was Simon—not just any child—the killer had been tracking. According to Neal's report, Simon's mates—though not close ones—hadn't known he stopped in that alley to smoke fags and look at dirty pictures. Thinking of it that way, the wrong questions were perhaps being asked. Certainly, it was possible the boy had an "enemy." It was also possible that the Rileys themselves had.

He did not pose that question at the moment. All

he said to Riley was that he wasn't convinced the boy's death was the work of a deranged mind.

Riley looked utterly astonished. "What other reason could there be? You sound like you think someone wanted to—murder *Simon*."

"I could think of half a dozen, Mr. Riley. They could all be wrong, of course." Jury allowed Mrs. Riley to give him another shot of Jameson's, more to keep her in a comradely mood than because he wanted a drink. Beth seemed actually curious about other reasons. She perked up a bit. Jury found her curiosity and perkiness as depressing as the gray weight of the sky beyond the window. "One is that someone actually meant to kill your son—I'm sorry," he added, when Riley flinched at the suggestion. Jury took a sip of the whiskey under the approving eye of Beth Riley. Approving what? That the law drank on duty? Or that someone had meant to kill her stepson? "Another is that Simon might have known something that someone didn't want him to know. Seen something that someone hadn't wanted him to see. Simon could have had knowledge he didn't even *know* he had, too. The thing is that he was in an alley that none of his schoolmates seemed to know about. It's not on his way home from school. And school had been out over an hour, if the medical examiner fixed the time correctly. Somewhere between five and perhaps eight o'clock. It might make one think that someone had been, possibly, following him—"

Riley was into his third whiskey, drinking with blind eyes, the handkerchief wadded against his face. "He could have been dragged there—"

Jury was already shaking his head. "No. There'd be—signs, if that were the case." Bloodstains, marks—Jury didn't elaborate.

The Rileys exchanged glances, but shook their heads.

"Could he have been meeting someone?"

They looked blank.

"Kids get up to things—"

Riley was out of his chair like a shot. Wasn't it enough the boy was dead? Did police have to go about ruining his character, too? Even Beth got in on this scene. She mightn't have missed Simon, but the family name was something else again.

Jury rose and apologized for intruding upon them, as he took another look at the pictures, the memorabilia over the fireplace. Beth as a young girl, Beth as a young woman. Nothing of Riley that he could see. Wiggins stood beside him, notebook clapped shut, pocketing his pen, taking out his lozenges.

February was hell this close to the sea. Dorchester was ten miles from it, but that was close enough for Wiggins.

They stopped outside and Jury lit a cigarette. "We wouldn't have got any more out of them. And the boy's funeral is tomorrow. Leave it for now."

The queue of shoppers had disappeared, but Jury saw in the faces of passersby more fear than curiosity. They walked at the edge of the pavement, as if coming nearer the scene of such a tragedy might contaminate them, might spread danger to their own children.

The Closed sign hung a little askew. Wiggins was studying a brace of pheasant, feet trussed up, heads dangling down. "No need to cause more suffering." Jury thought he was referring to the Rileys, until he added, "That's why I've been thinking of going vegetarian."

Jury tried to drag his mind from the man whose son was dead and the son himself, to say, "No more plaice and chips, Wiggins? Hard to imagine."

Wiggins considered. "I think I'd still eat fish. But not flesh, sir."

"No more missionaries, that it?"

"Pardon?"

"Never mind." Jury smiled bleakly. "There's Judge Jeffries restaurant just down the road. You hungry? Nothing like eating under the eye of the Hanging Judge." Jury looked at the pheasant.

Man, beast, bird. Life is cheap.

II

And he knew just how cheap when they got back to Wynfield, where the Dorset police had its headquarters.

"There's been another one," said Inspector Neal, looking a little grayer than when Jury had last seen him. "In Wynchcoombe. Another boy: name, Davey White. Choirboy." Neal's voice broke and he did not look at all pleased that his theory was probably being proved correct. At the same time he looked slightly relieved, and guilty for the relief. "Not ours, though. This is the Devon-Cornwall constabulary's manor. Wynchcoombe's in Dartmoor." He was interrupted by the telephone—a call, apparently, from his superior, for he kept nodding. "Yes, yes, yes. We've got every man on it we can spare . . . yes, I *know* the town's in a panic . . ." After more from the other end, Neal hung up, shaking his head.

Jury said nothing except, "How far's Wynchcoombe, then?"

Neal looked a little surprised. "Forty miles, about."

A police constable—a pleasant-looking young man—showed Jury the map on the wall. "You'll want to go to headquarters first, I expect. That's just outside Exeter—"

"Why do I want to go there? What's the quickest way to Wynchcoombe?"

"Well, I was just thinking you'd want to check with headquarters. Sir," he added weakly.

"It'd only waste time."

Neal was making a fuss over some papers on his desk seemingly in desperate need of rearrangement. "That's Divisional Commander Macalvie's patch, Mr. Jury."

"I don't much care if it's Dirty Harry Callahan's.

We've got a boy murdered in Dorchester and now another one in Wynchcoombe. So I'd like to get there as soon as possible. The divisional commander will understand."

The constable just looked at Jury. Then he said, "I worked with him once. Right cock-up I made of something and—" He pulled back the corners of his mouth. In a distorted voice he said, "I loss ta teeth. Crowns, these are."

Jury picked up the map the constable had marked the route on as Wiggins leaned closer and peered at his teeth. "I only wish I had your dentist."

II

The Church in the Moor

THREE

I

The silver chalice lay on the floor of the choir vestry, staining it darker with the wine that had been mixed with water now mixed with blood. Before the Scene of Crimes man had come, no one could touch it. After he had finished with it, no one wanted to. The lab crew of the Devon-Cornwall constabulary seemed to be avoiding it, superstitiously. As for the pictures, the police photographer had apologized to the curate for the little bursts of light in Wynchcoombe Church.

Police, both uniformed branch and CID, were all over the church, searching the chancel aisles, the nave, the main vestry. Wiggins and several others were outside going over the Green, on which the church fronted, and the deserted church walk, leading to the vestry doors on the other side.

Dr. Sanford, the local practitioner, had finished up his examination and said the boy had probably been dead around ten hours. The curate couldn't believe that the boy could have been there all that time and no one found him until three or four hours ago.

It had surprised Jury, too, who was standing down by the altar with TDC Coogan. He looked up at the altar, his mind a blank. Wynchcoombe had a beautiful church here. Even with its high spire, it appeared smaller on the outside than inside. The chancel and nave together measured over a hundred feet.

He could think of nothing to say to Betty Coogan, who was crying. She couldn't help herself, she said; she'd known Davey and his granddad, the vicar of Wynchcoombe Church. "Whoever'd want to do this to Davey White?"

In any other circumstances, Policewoman Coogan would have been a gift with her red hair and good legs. But not now.

It was the expression on the clear face of Davey White that had struck Jury most—a look not of terror but more of impish surprise, the mouth slightly open, smiling even, as if he'd thought it had been rather a wizard trick, this being struck without warning. Now here he lay, ten years old, another schoolboy, dead two days after Simon Riley.

Betty Coogan was talking about the boy in Dorchester, blowing her nose with Jury's handkerchief, voicing the opinion of the Dorset police: they had a psychopathic killer on their hands. Jury was more inclined to agree than he had been before, but he still withheld judgment. The method was the same. Simple. A knife in the back.

The fingerprint man came up to Jury and Coogan. "Where in hell's Macalvie?"

She shook her head, another bout of tears threatening. "In Exeter, on that robbery case. I tried to get him. Well, they must have got him by now—"

The print expert mumbled. "Ought to be here—"

He was. Divisional Commander—or Detective Chief Superintendent—Brian Macalvie came through the heavy oak doors of Wynchcoombe Church like the icy Dartmoor wind he brought with him. And he didn't tiptoe down the aisle.

The look he gave his TDC Betty Coogan did nothing at all to steady her. She seemed to sway a little, and Jury put his hand under her arm.

Chief Superintendent Macalvie looked briefly up at the altar and slightingly at them and said to Jury, "Who the hell are you?"

Jury took out his warrant card; Macalvie glanced at it and then at TDC Coogan (having dismissed Jury and all the credentials that went with him), saying, "You knew where I was. Why the bloody hell didn't you get to me sooner?"

She simply lowered her head.

"Where're you hiding the body, Betts? Might I have a wee look?"

There was a Scot's burr, probably put on when he felt like it. Macalvie's accent seemed to have got stuck somewhere in the mid-Atlantic. But the Scotch ancestry reigned at the moment: accent, coppery hair, blue eyes like tiny blowtorches. Jury could understand why Betty Coogan didn't snap back.

Still with head lowered, she said, "He's in the choir vestry."

Macalvie stood in the vestry, still with hands jammed in trouser pockets, holding back his raincoat—which was the way he had come in. "By now, fifty percent of anything I could use has washed down the Dart." It sounded as if he were privy to some invisible world of evidence from which mere, mortal cops (the Jurys of the world) were excluded. Macalvie had been standing and looking down at the body, looking round the vestry, looking out the vestry door. He was standing now at the door, still with his hands in his pockets, just like anyone who might have been speculating on a sudden change of weather.

To his back, a CID sergeant named Kendall said, "Nothing's been touched, sir. Except for Dr. Sanford's examination of the body."

"That's like saying an archaeologist left the digs as neat as my gran's front parlor," said Macalvie to the mist and the vestry walk lost in it.

Jury saw Dr. Sanford look at Macalvie with a wild sort of anger—at the man standing there communing with the trees. The doctor opened his mouth, but shut it again.

Constable Coogan, cheeks burning, decided to fight fire. "You'd think anyone else just *looking* at the crime scene before you got there erases clues—"

Macalvie turned those blowtorch eyes on her. "It does."

He nodded at the chalice. "What's that doing in the choir vestry?" Macalvie was down on one knee now, looking at the body of Davey White.

Dr. Sanford was an avuncular man who must have had an extensive National Health list of patients, as Wynchcoombe was an extensive parish. His smile—his first mistake—was condescending: "I assure you, Chief Superintendent, that the boy *wasn't* brained with the chalice. He was stabbed."

Macalvie favored Dr. Sanford with the same look he'd shot at TDC Coogan. "I didn't say he *was* 'brained', did I? I'm a simple, literal man. I asked a simple, literal question." He turned back to the body.

No one answered his question, so Dr. Sanford filled in the silence. "He's been dead, I'd judge, since about six o'clock this morning. Of course—"

"It could have been earlier or later." Macalvie finished the comment for him. "Not even you can tell the exact time of death. Not even me."

Dr. Sanford controlled himself and went on: "There's rigor, but the lividity—"

"You think it's hypostasis."

"Of course." Sanford continued his discourse on the blood's having drained and the darker patches of skin showing where the body had been in contact with the floor.

Macalvie, still with his eyes on Davey White's body, held out his hand as if he weren't paying any more attention to Sanford than a pew or a prayer-cushion. "Give me your scalpel."

Dr. Sanford was clearly shocked; his tone was frosty: "And did you intend to perform the autopsy here and now? You *do* have a pathologist—" He stopped and looked extremely uneasy. He might just as well not have been there at all, given the lack of response. Still, the doctor plowed the furrow: "I really don't think—"

Macalvie's hand was still outstretched. Jury imagined that when Macalvie was thinking himself, he didn't want those thoughts lost in the crossfire of underlings—TDCs, doctors, or even Scotland Yard.

Dr. Sanford reopened his bag and produced a scalpel.

Macalvie made a tiny incision in the center of one of the purplish stains and a bit of blood oozed and trickled. He returned the scalpel, pulled down the boy's vest, and said nothing.

Again, as if it were necessary to fill up silences Macalvie left in his wake, Sergeant Kendall said, "The curate couldn't understand how the lad could have been lying here for all that time—"

"Because the kid *wasn't* lying here all that time. That's a bruise, not hypostasis." He ignored Sanford and addressed himself to Jury, figuring, perhaps, since one nitwit had got it wrong, he wanted to hear if the other one would. It was the second time he'd spoken to Jury; Wiggins, he'd managed to neglect altogether. "What do you think?"

"I think you're right," said Jury. "He probably wasn't killed here and certainly hasn't been lying here for ten hours."

Macalvie continued to stare at Jury, but said nothing. Then he turned to his fingerprint man and indicated the silver chalice that had been carefully dusted and photographed. "You through with that?"

"Sir." He nearly clicked his heels and handed over the chalice.

In spite of its already having had a thorough going-over, Macalvie handled it with a handkerchief, holding it up to the light as if he were administering the sacraments.

Betty Coogan, completely unnerved by her divisional commander and (Jury supposed) sometime-lover, asked, "You think he was killed somewhere else and brought here? But why? That doesn't make sense."

"Really?" said Macalvie in his loquacious way.

Jury shook his head. "That's taking a hell of a chance, unless the murderer was making a point. The chalice wouldn't be in the choir vestry except for someone's wanting to smear it in the boy's blood. An act of desecration."

Macalvie nearly forgot himself and smiled. "Okay, let's go and have a talk with his dad."

"Grandfather. Davey's own father is dead," said Wiggins, sliding a cough drop into his mouth.

"Okay, grandfather." Macalvie held out his hand as he had for the doctor's scalpel. "Mind giving me one of those? I'm trying to quit smoking."

"Good," said Wiggins, promptly letting a few Fisherman's Friends drop into Macalvie's palm. "You won't regret it."

II

Although the housekeeper was weeping when she opened the door, the Reverend Linley White's eyes were as dry as his voice.

Wiggins had been dispatched to get what he could out of the housekeeper (which, if nothing else, would be a cup of tea), and Jury and Macalvie were seated in two ladderback chairs on the other side of Mr. White's large desk. Even with one less policeman in the room, the vicar appeared to think the ratio of two to one was unfair, though God was supposedly his ally. He could tell them absolutely nothing that would throw light on this "sad affair"—a favorite summing up, apparently; he used it several times.

"Sure, you can throw some light on things," said Macalvie, pleasantly. "Such as why you didn't like him."

The vicar was vehement in his denial of this charge, especially coming, as it did, before he could find a persona to fit it. "David has been living here for just a little over a year. My son and his wife, Mary"—the *Mary* called up someone he'd sooner forget, apparently—"died in a motorcycle accident and shortly after that, her aunt simply dropped David— quite literally—on my doorstep. It was supposed to be for a few days. I've not laid eyes on the woman since. I don't know why I was surprised." Under a gray cliff of eyebrow, the vicar's eyes burned with un-Christian-like feeling.

Jury wondered if, in the vicar's fight against feeling for Mary, he had won the battle but lost the war. The Reverend White could—as he went on to do— call Davey's mother "pig-track Irish," but Jury saw the tattered flag of emotion in all of this, and thought it probably sexual.

Macalvie said, "So you didn't like Mary. Either."

"Now listen, Superintendent—"

"Chief." It must have been almost unconscious.

37

Macalvie wasn't even looking at White; his eyes were raking over the room as they had been doing ever since he sat down.

"*Chief* Superintendent. This has been one of the worst experiences of my life."

Macalvie looked at him then. "What was the other one?"

"Pardon?"

"It must have been pretty bad if your grandson's murder is only one of them. I can't believe there were more than two. So what I gather is, since you hated the mother, you didn't much care for sight of Davey around the house. Constant reminder, right?" He had just stuck a Fisherman's Friend in his mouth and was sucking at it.

Color drained from the vicar's face until it matched the shade of the bisque statuette on his desk. "*Certainly* I was fond of David. What are you trying to say?"

"I never *try* to say anything. I just say it. So was his mother the only reason you didn't like Davey?"

The vicar was half out of his chair now. "You persist in this judgment—"

"Judgments I leave up to God. Sit down. He was killed sometime early this morning. Five, six. Why would he have been out at that hour and in Wynchcoombe Wood?"

Mr. White was astonished. "But he was killed in the *church!*"

Macalvie shook his head. "He was *put* in the church. Probably at that hour there was nobody about. And barely light. But would no one have been in the church this morning? A char? Anyone?"

The vicar shook his head. "Not necessarily. And no reason for anyone to go into the choir vestry."

"You don't keep a very sharp eye on your grandson, do you?"

Jury interrupted, much to Macalvie's displeasure. "Why would Davey have been out that early?"

Mr. White colored, smarting still under the bite of Macalvie's comment, probably, Jury thought, because it was true.

"Davey was a bit odd—"

Macalvie's impatient sigh told him how much he believed that excuse.

"I *only* mean that he occasionally liked to get out of the house before breakfast, before school, and go to the woods to, as he said, just 'think about things.' He hadn't many school chums . . ." The vicar's voice trailed away under Macalvie's blue gaze.

Jury was himself thinking about Simon Riley. "Thinking about things" could have meant smoking the odd cigarette. Or just getting away. Another lonely boy, perhaps, in a cold house. But he didn't voice his opinion.

Macalvie did. "Must have had a great life, your Davey. Didn't you worry about him, out in the dark or the dawn, alone in the wood?" He had got up to prowl the room and was now looking over the vicar's bookcases.

"Nothing's ever happened in Wynchcoombe Wood."

Macalvie raised his eyes from an old volume. "Something has now. And didn't you read about that kid in Dorchester, Mr. White?" he asked casually.

For the first time, the Reverend Linley White looked frightened. "I did. You're not saying there's a psychopathic killer loose?"

Macalvie's answer was another question. "Can you think of anyone who hated your grandson?"

"No. Absolutely not," he snapped.

"How about someone who might hate you?"

This time, the vicar had to stop and think.

III

What Wiggins had learned from the housekeeper verified the information they had got from the vicar. Except the housekeeper did wonder why Davey hadn't come back for his breakfast and his schoolbooks. Wiggins read his notes, and they were, as usual, thorough. Jury told him to go along to Wynchcoombe Wood. Macalvie cadged a few Fisherman's Friends and told Wiggins he wanted Kendall and his men to comb that vestry walk inch-by-inch. Davey could have stumbled, fallen, been dragged. That might account for the bruises.

Wiggins put away his notebook. "Yes, sir. You having an incidents room set up, sir?"

His yes was grudging. "Tell Kendall to get a portable unit and stick it in the middle of the damned Green." He nodded toward the clutch of villagers standing in front of the George and the tea room. Even from this distance, they seemed to pull back a bit, as if from fear, or, perhaps, the divisional commander's eye. "No, Wiggins," said Macalvie wearily, as the sergeant wrote it down. "Put it in that parking lot—" Macalvie nodded off to the right and a large lot, probably meant for the cars and caravans of summer tourists. "And tell Kendall to keep it staffed with the few men from headquarters who won't be stumbling all over their own feet. Much less mine."

The church had been cordoned off; now, perhaps to disengage themselves from the scene of the tragedy (or from Macalvie's stare), several of the villagers repaired to the pub, there to overhaul their former estimate of life in sleepy little Wynchcoombe.

"Pretty place," said Macalvie, qualifying it with, "if you like this sort of village."

It was indeed a pretty place, with its stone cottages huddled around the Green and the spire of Wynchcoombe Church rising above it. An enviable peal of bells told them it was six.

"I need a drink," said Macalvie.

"The George?" Its sign claimed it to be a fourteenth-century coaching inn.

He grunted. "You kidding? With all the regulars in there having a crack about what happened? There's a pub a couple miles away I go to when I feel especially masochistic. How Freddie—you'll love Freddie—gets any custom on that stretch of road beats me."

Macalvie looked off across a ground mist just beginning to rise. "It's not far from a village called Clerihew Marsh. I want to tell you a story, Jury."

FOUR

I

Help the Poor Struggler was the pub's full name, a wretched box of a building on a desolate stretch of road, whose ocher paint had dulled to the color of bracken from the smoke of its chimney pots. Its sign swung on an iron post over its door and the windows were so dirty they were opaque. The building listed from either dry rot or rising damp. Only the desolation of pub and traveler alike would tempt one to join the other.

There was no car park. What custom the pub got had to pull up by the side of the road. Two cars were there when Macalvie and Jury pulled in.

*   *   *

Brian Macalvie was now pursuing, with what Jury supposed was the customary Macalvie charm, a line of questioning directed at an arthritic, elderly woman who was swabbing down the bar. The "saloon" side was separated from the "public" side only by gentlemen's agreement. The public bar off to the left had most of the action: pool table, video game, Art Deco jukebox that was pummeling the customers with Elvis Presley's "Hound Dog."

"Where's Sam Waterhouse, Freddie?" Macalvie didn't so much ask for as demand an answer.

"I don't naw nort," said Freddie. "Y'm mazed as a brish stick, Mac. D'yuh niver quit?" She was wall-eyed, wattle-armed, and skinny, and with her stubby gray hair sitting in a lick on her head, she reminded Jury even more of a rooster. He guessed her sexual identity had been scratching with the chickens long enough to get lost.

"I never quit, Freddie. You treated Sam like you were his auld mum, the dear Lord help him."

"Ha! Yu'm a get vule, Mac, the divil hisself. Cider hisses when yu zwallers it."

"Hell, *this* cider'd hiss on a stone. You're thick as two boards and your right hand hasn't seen your left in forty years," said Macalvie, picking up his cider and moving to a table.

Freddie grinned at Jury. "What c'n I do ver 'ee, me anzum?"

Jury grinned back. "I'll try the cider. You're only young once."

"It was the stupidest arrest the Devon-Cornwall cops ever made." Macalvie was talking about the Rose Mulvanney case. "Here's this nineteen-year-old kid, Sam, who's living in Clerihew Marsh and indulging in fantasies, maybe about Cozy Rosie. Rose Mulvanney could start breathing heavy over anything in pants. In the U.S. she'd freak out in a cornfield over the scarecrows."

From what Macalvie had told Jury during their drive to the pub, it was certain the divisional commander's heart was in America—his mother was Irish-American—even if his body was in Devon. Obsessive as he was about police work, still he took his vacation every year and went to New York. His speech was littered with the old-fashioned, hard-boiled speech of a Bogart movie: *dames, broads*—that sort of thing.

"How do you know all this stuff about Rose Mulvanney?"

"Through extremely delicate questions put to the inhabitants of Clerihew Marsh," said Macalvie. "Like, did Rose screw around—"

"I'm sure that's the way you put it." Jury took a drink of cider and could believe in the sizzling throat of the devil.

"Be careful, Freddie makes it herself. My questions to the villagers were more disgustingly discreet. But what turned up when I collared the milkman and the old broad that runs the post office stores was that Rose Mulvanney, a couple of days before she died, started taking more milk and buying more bread. *This* even though her kid Mary was away on a school trip. The extra groceries went on for maybe five days. Now, she sure as hell wasn't doing that for Sammy Waterhouse. He lived right there in Clerihew Marsh."

"You're saying someone else was living with her?"

"Of course."

Jury tried not to smile. Macalvie was nothing if not certain of Macalvie. "I agree it's a possibility."

"Good. I can go on living." He popped another Fisherman's Friend into his mouth.

"So, assuming the Devon-Cornwall police picked on Waterhouse—why? Months went by before they arrested him, you said."

"It's expensive to mount a murder investigation; you know that. They wanted to get him a hell of a lot earlier, except I kept tossing spanners in the works, like trying to convince the effing Devon police that Sam Waterhouse couldn't have moved in with Rose."

"Aren't you making a lot out of extra bread and milk?"

"No. Rose wasn't buying bread for the church bazaar."

"There must have been evidence against Waterhouse. What was it?"

"That he was always mooning around Rose. He was *nineteen*, for God's sakes." Macalvie shoved the ashtray to the end of the table. "And the dame next door said she'd heard them having a king-sized row a few nights before Rose died. She saw Sam coming out of the house in a right blaze."

"And Waterhouse—what did he say?"

"He didn't deny it. He was furious Rose had been 'leading him on' and he really thought she cared. Told him she had another boyfriend, stuff like that."

"What did forensics turn up?"

"Their hands. They just shrugged. Of *course* there were prints. All over. Sam had admitted to being in the house. But on the knife? No. He'd have wiped that clean, said my learned superior. So I said to him, Then why didn't he wipe everything *else* clean he'd touched? And after the elimination prints—the two daughters and a couple of friends in Clerihew—there were still two sets left over. Could have been anybody, and certainly could have been the guy who did the job, if he'd been living there for a few days."

"The girls? The daughters? Where were they?"

"The fifteen-year-old was off on a school trip. The little one must have been in the house, except for the odd night or two she was sent to play with a little chum from her school."

"But that means she must have seen the man at some point—assuming you're right."

Macalvie's look sliced up Jury as good as any knife. Could there be any doubt about a Macalvie theory? "That's true. All she had to do was say, 'No, it wasn't Sammy.' And believe me, she would have if she could; she was crazy about Sam. Both girls were. He was very nice to them. So she could have said it wasn't him and maybe identify who it *was*. Only Teresa never spoke another word." Macalvie turned to stare into the inglenook fireplace, as if he too might never speak another word, a rare silence for him, Jury thought.

In the public bar off to the left, Freddie had mus-cled an anti-Elvis fan away from the jukebox to feed in her own coins. "Jailhouse Rock" made way for "Are You Lonesome Tonight?"

Jury saw Macalvie glance toward the jukebox and thought perhaps he was going to answer the question put by Elvis—and, for that matter, by Freddie, who was singing along: "D'ya miss me tooo-night?" in her cups and out of key. Macalvie snatched up both of their pints, saying, "It wouldn't be so bloody bad if Freddie'd shut up." He walked over to the bar, had his brief quarrel with her—their standard means of communication, Jury imagined—and was back and picking up the story of the Mulvanney family. He chronicled their lives as if he'd been a relation. The details he'd picked up during the investigation.

"It still seems like pretty shabby evidence," said Jury.

Macalvie drank his cider. "Oh, of course the prosecution had their witness. No, not someone who saw it. Just a friend of Sammy's."

"Friend? Doesn't sound like much of one."

"Ah, but in the interests of Justice, we must all do our bit. He was a student at Exeter, too. Law. Claimed Sam Waterhouse had said several times he'd kill her. Good old George, standing right there in the box saying Sam came in that night with what looked like blood on his clothes. Liar."

"What was Waterhouse's answer?"

"That if he ever said it, it was only a manner of speaking. And the blood came from cutting himself in the lab. Terrific. The prosecution made mincemeat of Sam."

Whether from the aftereffects of cider or the present effects of Elvis, Freddie was still singing along:

> *"Doon yer haaaart fill wit pain?*
> *Should ay COME beck a-GAAAIIN? . . ."*

wailed Freddie. Macalvie yelled at her to shut up. Freddie paid no attention.

"Christ, an Elvis song that doesn't bring down the walls and she's got to have a sing-along. The kid, Mary Mulvanney," Macalvie went on, "I saw her twice. Once at the inquest. She could hardly answer the questions."

He stopped, stared at the jukebox, then back at Jury.

"Unfortunately, I wasn't there. I wasn't in charge of the case. Bad luck for Devon. What I did, I did on my own. Didn't amount to much. A few questions here, a few bruises there." His blue eyes glinted with reflected firelight and he almost smiled. "That's supposed to be my style, you know. Threats, blackmail, bullets in knee-caps." He shrugged.

"I don't worry too much about style. When was the second time?"

Macalvie was staring into the fire again, shoving his foot against one of the huge logs sprawled on the hearth like an old dog. "For what?"

Jury knew Macalvie knew "for what." "The second time you saw Mary Mulvanney."

"Months later. After they tossed Sam Waterhouse in the nick. The kid storms in my office—fifteen, scrawny, and freckles—talk about scarecrows. But, man, did she let me have it. She knew some words even I didn't know; must have been some swell school she was going to. I never saw anyone so mad in my life."

"Why at you? You were the one person who kept the case open and did all the work."

"So to her that meant I was in charge, didn't it? She knew Waterhouse didn't do it. And she screamed at me, as she casually removed all the stuff from my desk with a delicate sweep of her skinny arm: *'That's my mum got killed and my baby sister's in hospital and you'd fucking well better get who did it or I will!'* My God, could that kid get mad."

But Macalvie, who had seemed determined not to temper bad humor with good, was actually smiling. It was probably a relief to him to find somebody who wasn't afraid of him, even if she was only a skinny young kid.

"And then she stormed out. I never saw her again." The look he gave Jury was woeful. "It was the only case I never solved."

He wanted Jury to think that was the source of the unhappy look. Jury didn't.

II

They had been sitting there for a couple of minutes, in a small pocket of silence not shared by the regulars who were being treated to the wonderful voice of Loretta Lynn. Unfortunately, the coalminer's daughter had to make way to the voice-over of Freddie, behind the bar wiping glasses and singing about how she too once had to go to the well to draw water.

Macalvie yelled at her, "The last time you ever drank anything but booze was when they tossed you in Cranmere Bog."

"What about the little one, Teresa?"

51

"What about her?"

"If you're right—"

Raised eyebrows. *If?*

"Then why in hell did the killer leave a witness behind?"

That this could be a hole in his theory did not seem to bother Macalvie at all. He could, apparently, plug it up like a finger in a dike. "Say because the guy was sure Teresa couldn't tie him to her mother. Maybe Teresa *didn't* see him, or at least didn't know his name, or for a dozen reasons she simply wouldn't be able to point a finger at him. And if it were a crime of passion, it's possible that he couldn't see his way to killing a five-year-old, too."

"And the five-year-old? Could she have gone after her mum with a knife? Did you ever suspect her?"

The look Macalvie gave Jury could have carved him in pieces. "No, I always do things by halves, Jury. I'm a sloppy cop. I didn't even notice the trail of blood she left all the way from the kitchen to the phone and all the blood over her nightie and on the phone—" He waved a dismissive hand "Don't be an asshole, will you? Of course, little kids can wig out. She didn't do it." He was silent for a while. Then he said, "I went to the hospital. It was obvious, at least in the mumbo-jumbo land of shrinkdom, that she didn't stand much chance of getting well. Her mind seemed to have split. Catatonic and curled up like a fetus. Anyway, they finally moved Teresa to Harbrick Hall. Ever heard of it? They call it 'Heart-break Hall.' "

Jury had heard of it. It was one of those places he wished he hadn't. "I was there once."

"And you're almost cured?"

Jury ignored the sarcasm, thinking of Harbrick Hall. One of those cozy, innocent-sounding names that in no way reflected its huge, understaffed, over-full hospital. Endless corridors, bolted doors, grilles. The sickly, sour smell of urine and ammonia, and the gray-garbed janitor with mop and pail in a corridor awash in hopelessness.

Macalvie went on: "The place is so big you could get lost just trying to find your way out. Anyway, Teresa Mulvanney supposedly had got a little better. No, she wasn't talking. She never talked. But at least she wasn't lying curled up like a baby. The Paki attendant 'very proud' of Teresa's 'progress.' Progress. You know what her progress was?"

From Macalvie's tone, Jury didn't think he wanted to know. Right now, he couldn't get the faces of Simon Riley and Davey White out of his mind. They seemed to merge and separate and break apart, like little faces behind mullioned and rained-on window-panes.

"Fingerpainting," said Macalvie. "The Paki couldn't understand why 'she only like the red pot.' "

"Drop it." He blotted out the image of fingerpaints by trying to concentrate on the Irish singer someone had mercifully found on the jukebox. Jury was sure his display of weakness would earn him a surly answer.

But all Macalvie said was, "I did." He looked at his watch. "But Mary, the sister, couldn't, could she?" He turned to look at the jukebox from which came the lovely and mournful dirge:

> *I love you as I never loved before,*
> *Since first I met you on the village green . . .*

Macalvie was taking money out of his wallet and was out of his chair as quick as a cat. In one long movement, he tossed the money on the table of the man who'd slotted the ten p in the box and then he walked over and pulled the plug before the singer could finish *"as I loved you, when . . ."*

Freddie tossed down her bar-towel and started over; the man who'd played the song was bigger than Macalvie and getting out of his chair. Knowing that Macalvie—outsized, outweighed, or outnumbered—wouldn't hesitate to shove the man right back down again, Jury started to get up. Damned idiot. Couldn't he remember he was a cop?

Apparently, he could. The jukebox was in the public bar and so were Macalvie and his newfound friends; Jury couldn't hear what he said, but Macalvie was shoving his wallet in the big one's face and smiling. Freddie was standing with her hands on her skinny hips. The party at the table got their coats together pretty quickly, and Macalvie turned to Freddie, who gave him a bar-towel in the face.

At least that pleased the regulars who were on their way out. Macalvie just shrugged and came back to sit down.

"Pulling rank? That could be dangerous down at headquarters," said Jury.

That earned him an uncomprehending stare. Dangerous for Macalvie? "I don't pull rank, buddy." His elbow on the table, he turned his watch so Jury could see it. "You never heard of the licensing laws? I just told them Freddie had to close early and asked if anyone was in a condition to drive, seeing all the cider they'd put down." He picked up his and Jury's pints and strolled across the pub, which they now had to themselves.

Except, of course, for Freddie, who was filling the pints and Macalvie's ear with her opinion of him. It followed him across the room, silenced only by his turning and saying—Elvis done with, he didn't have to yell—"I'd of run you into Princetown years ago, Freddie, except I've got a certain respect for the murderers and psychos there."

He slammed down the pints, waterfalling the cider down the glasses as Freddie went to answer the telephone. "Christ, what a stupid old broad. That 'Freddie' doesn't stand for 'Frederika,' or any girl's name.

55

Stands for 'Fred.' The mum and dad must've wanted a boy; they'd have settled for a girl; they got a mineral." He drank his cider.

"Telephone, me anzum," fluted Freddie.

"She must mean you, Jury. She'd never call me that."

It was Inspector Neal, who had tracked him down through Kendall. What he had to report about his end of the investigation was very little. But a Chief Superintendent Racer had called and asked—well, *demanded* was a better word—that Jury report to him. And how was he getting on with Divisional Commander Macalvie?

"Swell," said Jury. "Friendly guy."

"That's a first," said Neal, and hung up.

Jury went back to the table and started to collect his coat. "It's not that I don't enjoy sitting around with you, but we've got two murders on our hands."

"One's mine. Don't be greedy, Jury."

"One's yours. I'd never know it. You can sit here and drink the night away and yell at Freddie. I'm going back to Dorchester."

"Can you just sit down a minute and shut up. Do you think I'm relaxing in the Victorian splendor of this roach-ridden flashhouse because I want to? Why in hell do you think I've been talking about the Mulvanney murder?"

"Because you're obsessed with it, maybe?"

Macalvie didn't rise to the bait. "Because in my gut, I know there's a connection."

As Jury asked him what, the door of the Help the Poor Straggler opened and shut behind them.

"I think it just walked in."

He sounded sad.

FIVE

Jury would have recognized the prison pallor anywhere; he'd seen it often enough. It wasn't the pale skin of a man who'd not seen enough of the sun. It was more as if one had put a paintbrush to an emotion—despair, desolation, whatever—and tinged it in that sickly whitish-gray. The pallor was accentuated by the black clothes: chinos, roll-neck sweater, parka. Accentuated too by the dark hair and eyes. He was tall, understandably thin, handsome, and maybe in mourning for nineteen lost years.

"Hullo, Sam," said Macalvie.

"I wondered who the car belonged to. I should've known."

Freddie came out from some inner room as if her antennae had at last picked up a welcome presence.

"Sammy!" She flung herself against him so hard that Jury was surprised he didn't hear bones breaking. She stepped back and gave Macalvie an evil look. Then to Sam, she said, "How are yuh, me dear?"

"I'm fine, Freddie. Just waiting for the place to clear."

Macalvie, who always knew what everyone else was thinking, smiled. "I know. I cleared it. So sit down, Sammy." With his foot, he shoved out a chair. And, as if they were on the best of terms, he said to her, "Freddie, bring the man some cider and go play Elvis. Just don't play 'Jailhouse Rock,' okay? Or I'll break your knees. Where've you been, Sam? You got out four days ago."

"You keeping track, Inspector? But it couldn't be inspector now. You must be chief constable."

"I will be. Right now it's commander. Or chief superintendent."

"Where'd you trip up?" asked Sam, as Freddie put down his pint. "Not over me, I hope." But his smile was hopeless.

"Who tripped up? You think I'm ambitious?"

Sam Waterhouse's laugh was so hearty that Freddie came out to check on things. She disappeared again.

"What've you been doing?"

"Seeing Dartmoor. Sleeping in an old tin-working or on the rocks. I like the moor. The way the mist comes up, the whole damned world disappears. Ever been up on Hound Tor? Nice. On a clear day you can see Exeter and police headquarters forever. Why don't you forget it, Macalvie?"

"Read any papers lately, Sam?"

Sam Waterhouse shifted uncomfortably in his chair and drank off nearly half of his pint. "Sure. The newsboy was flogging the *Telegraph* all over Dartmoor."

"Meaning you have," said Macalvie. "Meet any other tourists?"

Jury both could and couldn't understand Sam Waterhouse's anger. If you'd been in a high-security lockup on a trumped-up charge. Except Macalvie was the one who'd always believed in Sam's innocence and who'd worked like hell to prove it.

"I saw the papers. A boy was killed in Dorchester. What's it to do with me?"

"And another kid was killed in Wynchcoombe. You wouldn't have read about that yet. Look. I'm not asking you for alibis."

"What are you asking for then?"

Macalvie shook his head. "Not sure."

Jury was surprised Macalvie could say it.

Sam Waterhouse took one of Jury's cigarettes. He had the hoarse voice of a heavy smoker. Jury didn't imagine nineteen years in Princetown would make a voice mellifluous.

"You're still trying to solve that case." Sam shook his head.

"It's a blot on my career." Macalvie's smile did its quick little disappearing act. "Incidentally, you're sitting next to a CID man from Scotland Yard."

"Richard Jury," said Jury, embellishing upon Macalvie's gracious introduction. He shook hands with Sam Waterhouse.

"You can't be working our mutual friend Macalvie's manor? It's mined."

"Jury's working on the Dorchester case. It just happened to spill over into Devon."

"Too bad. But neither of them has sod-all to do with me."

"Has anyone accused you of anything?"

"Where would I get that idea? I walk into Freddie's, and who do I find but you, lying in wait." He leaned closer. "Macalvie, doesn't it occur to you that I want to *forget* about Rose Mulvanney?"

"It had crossed my mind. That 'other boyfriend' she had—"

"I don't want to talk about it."

"She never mentioned any names?"

Sam Waterhouse closed his eyes in pain. "Don't you think I'd have damned well *said* if I knew of anyone else? I looked at her diary; I went through her desk. All that got me was a shadowy snapshot of some man. I asked her who it was and she said her uncle." Sam shrugged.

"Well, we didn't find anything like that. Uncle must have taken diary, photos, and papers."

Sam's eyes glittered with anger. "Look, all of this has been said and said again." His face took on the look of the chronic loser. "For God's sakes, haven't you had any murders in Devon in the last nineteen years so you want to hook these up with the Mulvanney case?" Macalvie shook his head. "Then why here and why now?"

"Revenge, Sam. At least, that's what the papers—"

Sam Waterhouse shook his head. "I don't know what you're talking about. You've got a psychopath on your hands—"

"I don't think so. At least not in the sense you mean—that there's no connection between the kids' murders."

Freddie stomped in with a steaming plate of mutton, boiled potatoes and vegetables. She plunked it down in front of Sam and gave Macalvie an evil look as if he'd been the prison cook. Sam went at the food with a vengeance.

Macalvie went on: "You've been out walking the moor for four days? Why?"

"Because I've been in the nick for nineteen years and wanted to see a little open space. As soon as I'm finished with this meal, you can slap the cuffs on me. I'll go quietly, Commander."

"Well, arresting you's not what I had in mind. You staying here?"

"Probably. Freddie's been like a mother to me."

Macalvie feigned surprise. "A mother? She's not

even female. What I was really waiting for was to talk to you. You could be helpful."

Waterhouse leaned back in his chair and laughed: it was a transforming laugh; Jury could see in his face the nineteen-year-old student of medicine. "Help the Devon-Cornwall constabulary? I think I'd go back to Princetown first." That incandescent look of youth fell away like a falling star. "Even if I *would* 'help,' I couldn't. I don't know any more now than I did then. And I didn't know anything then."

"How do you know?"

Sam looked up from his plate. "Meaning what?"

"You might know something that you didn't connect with Rose's murder, or you might know something you don't know—"

"I had nineteen years to think it over. Case closed."

"Let's say I just reopened it."

III

The Marine Parade

SIX

I

Angela Thorne had been told by her parents never to stay out after dark, never to miss her tea, never to walk along the Cobb, never to play along the shingle beach when the tide was coming in. Angela Thorne was presently engaged in doing them all, attended only by her dog, Mickey.

Dark had come by five o'clock, and she was still out in it two hours later. Some of that time had been spent wandering aimlessly in the well-tended gardens above the Marine Parade. A further half-hour she'd spent going up and down several little flights of steps along the Parade and moving backward toward the stone wall to beat the running tide.

She was presently breaking another injunction by walking along the dark arm of the Cobb that made a safe harbor for the little fishing boats, creaking out there in the wind and the water.

Mickey puffed along behind her. He was a terrier and too fat because Angela kept feeding him scraps of food from her plate, disgusting things like mashed swede or blood pudding or skate that always looked to her like the clipped wing of some big bird. All Mickey was supposed to eat was dried dog food. He was old, and her parents were afraid he'd have a heart attack.

She was tired of her parents and she hated her school. She hated nearly everything. Probably, it was because she wasn't pretty, and having to wear this long braid and hard shells of glasses. No one else at school had to wear thick glasses. Her classmates teased her constantly.

Angela stopped far out on the Cobb to look back at the lights of Lyme Regis along the Marine Parade. She had never seen Lyme at night from this distance. She liked that unearthly glow of the lamps. The little town seemed light-lifted above the black sea.

She wished it would fall in and drown. Angela didn't like Lyme, either.

The tattoo of Mickey's paws scraping stone continued as Angela walked on. Mickey loved the sea. When the tide was out, he'd tear away from her like a bit of white cloth in the wind and chase the ruffs of waves as if he'd never felt freedom before, as if he were having the time of his life.

II

She took off her cape and threw it over the little girl. Better to freeze than have to look at the blood-soaked dress of the body on the black rocks. The small dog was hysterical—running to nose at the cape, then back to Molly, going dog-crazy.

Standing on the high-piled rocks at the end of the Cobb, Molly Singer felt removed from the scene, a dream figure, looking down; a nonparticipant, the prying eye of some god.

In the seamless merging of sea and sky she could find no horizon. There was a chalky moon, and the sky was hammered with stars. And a distance off were the lights along the Parade.

Back and forth ran the dog. She would have to do something about the dog. Molly had a vision of the little girl and her dog, walking out along the Cobb, two dark silhouettes against the darker outline of the seawall.

She would have to get the dog back to shore. She was freezing, but at least she couldn't see the body now, which was the important thing.

Holding on to the dog, which struggled in her arms, she picked her way over the rocks and back to the seawall. On one of the dogtags was the name of its cottage.

She found Cobble Cottage and left the dog there, inside the gate.

Molly stood on the deserted Marine Parade, her own rented cottage at her back, the cold forgotten as she leaned against the railing where seaweed was tied like scarves, thrown up by the tide. The wooden groins along the shingle kept the sand from shifting. It would be nice if the mind could build itself such a protective wall.

She looked along the Cobb to the pile of rocks from which she had come.

All she could think of was the line from Jane Austen. *The young people were all wild to see Lyme.*

SEVEN

I

Eleven it might have been, but the manager of the White Lion didn't argue about the licensing laws any more than had Freddie's customers—though here it worked in reverse. The manager reopened the bar and smiled conspiratorially after Jury and Wiggins booked rooms. "Residents only," he said.

Wiggins, probably in some attempt to stay the awful effects of sea air, went straight to bed. It was the weather that had forced Jury and Wiggins to stop on the way back from Wynchcoombe. Rain and sleet that finally turned to hail. Each time a rock-sized chunk hit the windscreen, Wiggins veered. Jury imagined he was taking it personally, the weather.

Weather and seasons were judged only in reference to Wiggins's health: spring brought allergies; autumn, a bleak prognosis of pneumonia; winter (the killer season), colds and fevers and flu. Driving along the Dorchester Road, Jury knew what was going on in his sergeant's mind, though mind-reading wasn't necessary: Wiggins was always pleased to open his Pandora's box of physical complaints and enlighten Jury as to which one had just flown by.

Before that could happen, Jury pointed out the turn to Lyme Regis.

Wiggins wasn't any too happy about sea-frets, either.

Jury got his pint, asked for the phone, and called headquarters in Wynchcoombe to let them know where he was. On his way back to the bar, he noticed a thin, elderly woman in a floppy hat watching a television as antiquated as she was.

Jury was slotting ten-p pieces into a stupid video game when she passed behind him, saying, "You can put money in that thing all night and you won't get any back. It's rigged." She went up to the bar and knocked on it with her knuckles for service.

"Thanks for the advice," said Jury, smiling. "Buy you a drink?"

"I wouldn't mind."

The manager, coming from an inner room, didn't seem surprised to see her.

"You a resident, then?" asked Jury.

"Off and on." She was wearing spectacles with sunglasses attached on tiny hinges. Why she needed the sunglasses in the murky light of the saloon bar, Jury couldn't imagine. She flipped them up and squinted at Jury as if he were light that hurt her eyes. "What's your name?"

"Richard Jury."

She snapped the brown-tinted glasses down again. "Hazel Wing," she said. The manager had already set up a pint of Guinness for Hazel Wing. Jury bought a drink for the manager, too.

Hazel Wing raised her glass and said, "Here's to getting through another one."

"Another what?" asked Jury.

"Day." Up went the sunglasses again and she squinted. This time, probably, to see if he was a little on the dim side.

"I'll drink to that, certainly."

"What do you do, if I may be so bold?"

"I'm a cop."

This news did not seem to surprise her. She said, "Oh. I sort of thought so."

"Why? Do I look like one?"

"No. You're better-looking. I just supposed it was about the little girl."

He felt himself go cold. "What do you mean?"

"That girl that's gone missing. Don't know her. Young. Got all of Lyme in a panic. You know. After that boy in Dorchester." Hazel Wing, who seemed the sort to chop off emotions as she did her senten-ces, still allowed herself a shudder. "Kids. Parents keeping them in. Dorchester's not far."

And neither was Wynchcoombe. "Excuse me." Jury put down his pint and made for the telephone again.

He stared in silence at the telephone in the lobby of the hotel. Constable Green, in the Lyme police station, had finally to ask if Jury had got the message. "Yes. Don't move her." He hung up while the consta-ble was assuring him no one would touch her.

"Bad news," said Hazel Wing. It was a statement, not a question. News came only in one way to her.

"What's the quickest way to the Cobb Arms?"

"Walking or driving?"

"Whichever's faster."

Hazel Wing evaluated Jury's six-feet-two and de-cided, for him, walking. "Straight down the hill and right on the Marine Parade. That pub's at the other end. Ten minutes. If you're in a hurry."

"Thanks," he said.

"Good luck," she said, the words unconvincing. Luck, like news, was seldom good.

II

The little girl under the cape was lying as if she'd been stuffed like a small sack in the crevice of the rock.

"Hold the torch over here, will you?" Jury knelt down and picked the seaweed from her icy cheek. He knew he shouldn't have touched her at all before the doctor or Scene of Crimes expert got there, but he felt he had to get that stuff off her face. Bladder wrack. He remembered it from a seaside town he had gone to as a boy. It was the stuff that would pop if you squeezed it. A wave collapsed against the rocks, spewing foam in their faces. The wet rocks made standing difficult.

"Do you suppose she came out here," asked Constable Green on a hopeful note, "to get the dog and then was trapped by the waves . . . ?"

"No," said Jury. "It was a knife."

III

When Jury and Green got back to the Lyme Regis police station, Chief Superintendent Macalvie had been there for a quarter of an hour and ticking off every minute of it like a bomb.

Throughout Green's explanation of the anonymous telephone call and his finding the body, Macalvie sat in a chair tilted against the wall, sucking on a sourball. "So where's the body?"

"Hospital," said Green. "We got the local doctor—"

"Did he see her before she was moved?"

Green retreated into monosyllables. "Yes."

"About this woman, Molly Singer—" Macalvie was waiting for Green to embroider upon his description. Green didn't, so Macalvie went on. "Correct me if I'm wrong: you know the cape belongs to the Singer woman, you have a suspicion it was this woman who left the mutt at the Thornes' cottage, and you also suspect she was the one who rang up, and yet with all of this, you haven't brought her in for questioning."

"We went to her cottage, sir." Green looked from Jury to Macalvie, uncertain as to who had jurisdiction here: Dorset, Devon, or Scotland Yard? "But you don't know Molly Singer, sir—"

"Obviously I don't know her, Green. She isn't here, is she?" Macalvie looked around the room. Then he said to Wiggins, who had been dragged from under his eiderdown quilt around two A.M., "Give me one of those Fisherman's things, will you?"

Wiggins did so. He was presently trying to fend off something terminal, in a chair drawn up to a single-bar electric fire, where his feet competed with a large ginger cat snugly curled there.

Macalvie went on. "Because if she *was* here, then maybe the three of us could have a nice chin-wag and figure out what the hell she was doing on the end of the Cobb tonight."

Constable Green kept his expression as flat as the side of a slag heap and answered: "The Singer

woman has lived in that cottage facing the Parade
for nearly a year. No one in Lyme really knows her.
She doesn't chat up the neighbors. She isn't friendly.
She doesn't go out, except I've seen her sometimes
at night, walking my beat. You might say she's
eccentric—''

Jury interrupted. ''You might say she's phobic,
from what you told me earlier. Doesn't go out to the
shops; doesn't mix with people at all . . .''

''I wouldn't know about that.'' Green turned to
Jury with relief. ''I've seen her a few times when I
was making my rounds. I know that cape. Only, I
couldn't make up an Identikit on her. That's how
much she shows her face.''

Macalvie's chair slammed down. ''I don't believe
it, Green. I just don't *believe* it—that a person you
think could be a witness, could be even the chief
suspect—''

''I never meant to say that.'' Green's voice rose in
alarm. ''It's just she won't talk to police.''

Macalvie looked at Green and shook his head. He
leaned across the PC's desk and his blue eyes
sparked like matches. ''We're talking murder, and all
you can say is the chief witness is incommunicado.''
Macalvie got up. ''Come on,'' he said to Jury, heading for the door. He looked over his shoulder at Wiggins, who had now grown as sluggish as the orange
cat that had oozed its body straight out, paws fore

and aft, stomach to glowing bar. That it was lying across the feet of Scotland Yard did not impress it at all.

"Wiggins," said Macalvie. "You going to toast crumpets or move?"

"You think the three of us are going to the Singer woman's house?" asked Jury.

"Of course."

"Kick in the door? Is that it?" Jury was putting his coat on. Macalvie had never taken his off. "Try to browbeat someone who's agoraphobic and see how far you get, Macalvie. I'll go by myself, thanks. This is Dorset, remember? Not your patch; at the moment, it's mine."

Macalvie was still sucking on the Fisherman's Friend. "Pulling rank. Well. And would you mind if I went out on my own and had a word with the Thornes? The dad and mum? And as long as you're going on your own, can I borrow your sergeant?"

He didn't wait for permission. The door of the station slammed after Macalvie and Wiggins.

EIGHT

Jury's idea of eccentricity might have been Hazel Wing. It wasn't Molly Singer, in spite of her off-the-rack Oxfam clothes: a shapeless sweater, a long and equally shapeless skirt. Jury guessed she was in her thirties; he had expected someone much older.

The fire and a napping cat were the only things that gave the room a semblance of warmth. It was a typical holiday cottage, furnished with remnants that could have been washed up from a shipwreck—mismatched sling chairs, a small cabinet whose open shelf held several bottles of liquor, a lumpyish love seat now occupied by the cat. In front of the window was an all-purpose table. Nothing here but the bare essentials.

Probably she was following the drift of his

thoughts. "In the summer, this place costs the earth. It's right on the Parade, has an ocean view, and the landlord cleans up."

"I can imagine," said Jury.

"I even had to buy the lamp—" She nodded toward a small, blue-shaded lamp, useless for reading or anything but giving off a watery light. "I hope you don't mind the dark. I'm used to it by now."

Jury looked down at some books of poetry on the table and wondered if there was a double meaning in the comment. Emily Dickinson. Robert Lowell.

"You like poetry? I've always liked those lines of Lowell: 'The light at the end of the tunnel / Is the light of an oncoming train.'" She seemed to be talking out of sheer nervousness. "You could say I rent the cat, too. It wanders in every day and takes the best seat." The cat could have been mistaken for a black pillow, it was so motionless. It opened its topaz eyes, looked at Jury warily, and went back to dozing. Molly Singer's black hair and amber eyes were like the cat's.

They still had not sat down, and she was turning the card he had slipped under the door round and round in her fingers. "You took a chance, didn't you, writing this message? 'What fresh hell can this be?'" Her smile was strained. "Who said it?"

"Dorothy Parker. Whenever she heard the bell to her flat."

"Sit down, won't you?"

The cat glared at Jury as Molly Singer picked it up and put it on one of the cold sling chairs.

She offered him a drink and, when he accepted, reached down into the cabinet by the couch and brought out another glass and a whiskey bottle that was three-fourths empty. She gave him his and replenished her own glass.

Jury felt strange in this room that had housed so many guests, like a room full of ghosts. A log crumbled and the fire spurted up, one of the ghosts stirring the ashes.

"It's the cape, I guess."

Jury had been avoiding this sudden plunge into the death of Angela Thorne. He nodded. "Constable Green recognized it."

"Which puts me in the thick of it, doesn't it?"

"You must have known the cape would be traced to you. Why'd you do it?"

"You mean, kill her?" Her equanimity was more disturbing than a screaming denial would have been.

"I didn't say you killed Angela Thorne. It would be stupid to do that and leave that sort of evidence behind. What happened?"

"I was walking along the Cobb somewhere around ten or ten-thirty. I heard a dog barking. It sounded rather terrible, you know, panic-stricken. I followed the sound to the rocks and found her. I returned the dog; I couldn't return Angela," she said with some bitterness.

"Did you know her?"

Molly shook her head. "I think I saw her once or twice. I don't actually know anyone."

"How do you live?"

Her smile was no more happy than her laughter. "I bolt the door, Superintendent."

"You've lived here nearly a year. Why? Do you like the sea, then?"

"No. In a storm the waves crash over the walls; sometimes even drenching the cottages. Throwing up seaweed, rocks, whatever. It's all so elemental."

"So you found the body, covered her with your cape, took the dog to the Thorne cottage. Is that all?"

"Yes."

"But you rang up the police anonymously. Why?"

"I didn't want to get involved, I suppose."

"Then why did you leave your cape? You must have been freezing."

"I have another one," she said simply, as if that explained everything.

"Where did you live before?"

"London, different places. No fixed address. No job. I've got some money still. I used to be a photographer. My doctor advised me to find some nice little seaside town. I was taking pictures of Lyme."

Jury looked at two fine photos above the mantel: the Lyme coast, the Marine Parade, with its lonely strollers.

She left the couch and walked over to those pictures. "Don't bother looking; I'm not much good anymore. The sea, the sea—it's so elemental." Her glass was empty, and she poured herself another double. "I drink too much, you've noticed." She shrugged and went back to the mantel. The light from the fire suffused her face, sparked the strange dark gold eyes and gave her an almost daemonic look. He thought of the women of myths whom the ill-fated stranger— knight or country yokel—was constantly being warned to steer clear of.

"Have you been reading the papers?" Jury asked. She shook her head. "Where were you earlier today?"

"Here. I'm always here. Why?"

"There was a boy killed in Wynchcoombe. And two days ago, one killed in Dorchester. You didn't know about the Dorchester business?"

Her eyes had a drowned look. "My God, no. What are you saying—that there's a mass-murderer running round the countryside?"

"There could be. Look, there's no way you can avoid talking to police. You don't want to go to the station. Then come along to the White Lion in the morning." He was silent, looking at her, all sorts of sham comfort trying to form itself into words: *it won't be bad; Macalvie is a nice chap; there'll only be the three of us.* All of it lies. It *would* be bad; Macalvie was *not* a nice chap. And "only three of them" might as well be the whole Dorset police and Devon-

Cornwall constabulary together, as far as Molly Singer was concerned.

The silence waited on her. "Nine?" was all she said.

"All right."

Jury picked up his coat, once again dislodging the cat from its slumbers—and Molly went with him to the door.

She was still holding the card, folded and refolded, as if it were a message in a bottle that might give some report of land.

NINE

I

"George Thorne." In the dining room of the White Lion, Macalvie speared a sausage and shook his head. "One and the same. Witness for the prosecution."

"That doesn't make it look good for Sam Waterhouse, does it?"

"He didn't do it. Pass the butter, Wiggins."

Both Wiggins and Macalvie were having the full house. Jury, who couldn't stick looking at sausages and bacon and eggs, had ordered coffee and toast. "Who'd have a better motive?"

"Someone else," said Macalvie, with perfect assurance.

85

"But, sir—" Wiggins began and then stopped when Macalvie shot him a look.

"Both of you seem to have forgotten one salient detail. It wasn't Waterhouse that found the kid and tossed a cape over her. Oh, sure. Thorne was ranting on about Waterhouse out for revenge, et cetera. The guy looked like he'd just risen from the grave. Serves the bastard right. Big-deal solicitor." Macalvie was busy with bacon and a reappraisal of the waitress whose Edwardian looks—black hair rolled upward, slim figure in ruffled white blouse and black skirt, and porcelain skin—he had already commented upon. "Yesterday, Angela Thorne was 'acting up'— her mum's words—and trying to plead off school by saying she was sick to her stomach and being a pill nobody wants to swallow. Her teacher said the kid had got into a fight because some other girls were making fun of her. They made up this song: 'Angela Thorne, Angela Thorne, don't you wish you'd never been born?' Kids are so cute, aren't they?"

"It was after one when you talked to the Thornes. When did you get a chance to talk to the teacher, for God's sakes?" Jury imagined Macalvie was one of those cops who never slept.

"Afterwards. Let me tell you, the Thornes don't go down a treat. The teacher I knocked up around three—" Macalvie's blue eyes glinted "—you know what that means in American? Anyway Miss Elgin— Julie—didn't especially enjoy having her door busted down by the Devon-Cornwall constabulary, not with her dressed only in a flimsy wrapper—"

"You make it sound like a gang rape, Macalvie. Maybe Wiggins could just read the notes."

Disinclined as he was to stop eating his boiled egg, Wiggins put down his spoon and took out his notebook.

"Put that away, dammit," said Macalvie. "*I* know who said what. So, the kids made up this silly song, mostly, I imagine, because *The Thorn Birds* has been putting everybody to sleep for days now on the telly. You know; it's that mini-mind soap opera series. Julie—"

Macalvie could get on a first-name basis pretty quickly, Jury thought.

"—said Angela got a real going over with that pun on her name. None of the lads much liked Angela Thorne. Why?" Macalvie answered his own question. "Because she was sullen, bad-tempered, plain as pudding, wore thick glasses, and was so good at her lessons it even tired out the teachers. Julie said the headmistress just wished Angela'd take her O levels and get the hell out. Pretty funny." Whatever Macalvie was remembering from the night before obviously delighted him.

"Not very funny for Angela. Wasn't this Julie Elgin a little cut up over Angela's murder?"

"Sure. Scared witless, like everybody else. News travels fast. At midnight parents were calling her to say their kids wouldn't be going to school. But the point is, nobody liked Angela, including her parents."

Jury put down his coffee cup. "Her teacher said that?"

"No. And she didn't have to, did she?" Again he answered his rhetorical question. "Mummy's eyes were red, but more from booze than from tears. George was more worried about his own neck than his kid's death, though of course, he put up a front— but it was all pretense, no pain—and the older sister, the one who got the looks, kept talking about being in shock, as if she'd like to go into it for my sake, but couldn't get the electrodes in place. In other words, it was all an act. I asked them for a picture of Angela. Mum and Dad kind of looked at one another as if they couldn't quite place their youngest, and finally Carla—the sister—had to go off and *look* for a picture. Funny. There were certainly pictures of the bosomy rose Carla all over the mantel. But not even so much as a snapshot of Angela."

"Then she must have been a lonely little girl. Let's get back to your theory of what happened."

"Well, it's the dog, isn't it?" Macalvie watched Jury lighting a cigarette as if it were a daemonic act, meant to trap Macalvie into reaching for the packet.

"The dog? Macalvie, if you say something about the dog in the nighttime, I'll do just what you want— leave." Jury smiled.

Macalvie's hopeful look vanished when Jury didn't actually get up. Then he shrugged: stay or leave, it was all one to Macalvie. "The person who killed the kid must have had some connection with her or Lyme Regis. How the hell did he or she know where to drop the dog?"

"Dogtags, maybe."

Macalvie looked pained. "Oh, for Christ's sake, Jury. A perfect stranger wandering all over Lyme carrying a terrier looking for Cobble Cottage? No way. So it was either someone who befriended the Kid and the Poor Kid's dog" (Jury could just feel the sympathy welling up in Macalvie's breast), "someone not from Lyme, or someone who's been *living* in Lyme and knew the kid's habits."

"But Angela Thorne didn't habitually go against the rules, you led me to believe."

Impatiently, Macalvie stuffed a sourball in his mouth, sucked on it awhile as he hankered after Jury's cigarette, then tossed the candy in the ashtray. "Wonder how Kojak stood it. . . . Look at little Angela's feelings about Mum and Dad and school and so forth. Somebody could have befriended her and then hung around Lyme, waiting for a chance. What do you think?"

"I think no." Jury would have laughed had Macalvie not looked so serious. Disagree with Macalvie's theory?

"Why the hell *not?*"

"Aren't you overlooking the obvious?"

Macalvie gave Wiggins a *can-you-believe-this-guy?* look, got no reassurance from Jury's sergeant, and turned the sparking blue eyes back to Jury. "I never overlooked the *obvious* in my entire life, Jury."

"That's swell. You do think Angela was killed by the same person that murdered the other two, don't you?"

"Probably," said Macalvie, cautiously, like a man being led into a trap.

"Then you'd have to assume that the murderer was friendly with *all* of the victims. That's possible, but not very probable. I don't think the murders are indiscriminate or arbitrary, but at the same time, I don't think the killer took the chance of 'befriending' these children. Simply because it would have been a hell of a chance to take—"

"True. Especially for a man just out of prison."

And since Macalvie's theory left only one candidate for the string of murders, it was perhaps less than fortuitous for her that Molly Singer chose that moment to appear in the doorway of the White Lion's dining room.

II

It wasn't love at first sight when Molly Singer met Divisional Commander Macalvie.

The sparks between them made Jury think of a

high-speed train braking. She could sense Macalvie's hostility, even before he opened his mouth.

Jury offered her breakfast, and Macalvie offered her a grim-reaper smile, which was enough to kill anyone's appetite. Jury doubted she had one to begin with. She asked for coffee.

Today she looked different. Her eyes were less molten gold and more honey-colored. That might have been because of the gold cape she wore. Her dark hair was pulled back, but the shorter ends clung to her face as if they were wet with seaspray or rain.

"I just wanted to have a little talk with you about last night," said Macalvie. "Your handling of the situation was kind of odd."

"Yes, I suppose it was. Though at the time I wasn't thinking too clearly—"

"Did you panic, or something?" His tone was almost friendly.

"Panic. Yes, I suppose you could say that."

"That's why you threw your cape over the girl?"

She nodded and looked away.

"Not because you wanted to hide the body." The tone was simply matter-of-fact.

Quickly, she looked at him again. "That's ridiculous. If I'd killed her, I certainly wouldn't leave my cape behind to lead police right to my door."

Macalvie shrugged. "You're not the only one in Lyme or hereabouts who owns a cape."

"You think I'd take a chance like that?"

"I don't know. Do you know the Thornes?"

She shook her head, looking down at the coffee brought by the patrician waitress, but not drinking it.

"How did you know where to take the dog?"

"The name of their place was on the tag."

"Very humanitarian. There's a pub in Dorchester called the Five Alls. Ever been there?"

"No. I don't go to pubs."

"Not a drinker?"

"On the contrary, I drink a lot. But alone."

Wiggins, who seemed to have taken a liking to Molly Singer as another victim of life's vicissitudes, looked sad. Jury was afraid he might take them all for a stroll down Gin Lane.

"As I'd guess," Molly went on, "you already know."

Macalvie's eyes grew round as a cat's. "How would I know that?"

She looked at Jury. "The superintendent might have told you. More likely you've already been at the dustbin men."

Macalvie laughed. "You're pretty smart." He made it sound like an indictment. "Where were you early yesterday morning? Around six, say?"

"In my cottage. Asleep. Why?"

"And where the afternoon of the tenth?"

"In my cottage. Or walking on the Cobb."

"Like last night?"

"Yes."

"Anyone see you?"

"Probably not."

"You don't go out much."

"No."

"You don't see people."

"No."

"Funny way to act."

"I think I'm agoraphobic." What there was of an embarrassed smile was quickly erased when Macalvie slammed his fist on the table.

"I don't care sod-all about some phobia. If you've been to psychiatrists, I'll subpoena their records if I have to. You don't go out, don't see people, and yet—" Macalvie pointed toward the street "—in that short-stay parking lot by the ocean you've got a great little Lamborghini that's clocked up over sixty thousand on a 'C' registration. You do a hell of a lot of traveling, don't you? In that car you could make it to Dorchester and back in a little more than an hour and to Wynchcoombe in two, I'll bet—provided a cop didn't get in your way. What's a little stay-at-home like you doing with a Lamborghini?"

Molly Singer got up slowly. "I think I've answered your questions."

"No, you haven't. Sit down."

"Wouldn't you rather finish your breakfast?" Before anyone could stop her, she tipped her side of the table, sending plates, food, cutlery crashing and rolling, and most of it into Macalvie's lap. Then she walked out.

"God! What a temper." Macalvie seemed perversely pleased, looking at his stained suit and the wreckage all around them: cups, kippers, broken glass.

It even broke the porcelain pose of the waitress in black and white.

III

Lyme Regis was one of many coastal villages whose beauty was reckoned in proximity to the sea. It had been two centuries ago so much the object of Jane Austen's affections that it now had, where the Marine Parade ended in a narrow street, a pretty boutique called Persuasion. Thought Jury, If Stratford-upon-Avon wants to put Shakespeare on sugar cubes . . . why not?

Macalvie came out of the newsagent's at the top of the street, at the triangle where Broad Street and Silver Street ran together down to the sea, taking tearooms, greengrocers, Boots, and banks with them. Wiggins had been left to see to the wreckage at the White Lion.

Just as Macalvie appeared, a Mini went speed-boating down the narrow street. He wrote the registration number in his notebook. Macalvie would do dog's duty just so long as it gave him the pleasure of collaring some miscreant.

He slapped the notebook shut and said, "Nothing there. She knew Angela because Angela would stand around reading *Chips and Whizzer* without paying. The old broad in there hated her. She chased her off yesterday evening somewhere around six. She was closing up late."

Macalvie was turning a stile of postcards and removed one that showed the confluence of the streets they were on. He stuffed a stick of gum in his mouth, and said, "You're a minder, you know?"

Jury looked at Macalvie, who was frowning down at the postcard. "Meaning what?"

Macalvie shrugged. "A minder: kind of cop who watches over frails. Defenseless women."

Jury laughed. "You see too many American films, Macalvie."

Unoffended, Macalvie said, "No, I'm serious."

Indeed he did look it, staring from the picture-view of the street to the real thing. One would have thought he might be an artist, studying light and angles. "I'd like to know what she's doing in Lyme," he said, almost inconsequentially.

"Molly Singer?"

He shook his head. "Her name's not Molly Singer. It's Mary Mulvanney."

Macalvie slotted the card back in the rack and started up the street.

IV

*

The St. Valentine's
Day Massacre

TEN

I

The Lady Jessica Mary Allan-Ashcroft looked from blank square to blank square on the calendar hanging in the kitchen and with her black crayon, stood on tiptoe so she could reach FRIDAY: 14 FEBRUARY. She drew a giant X across that square, knowing she was cheating, since it was only tea-time and the awful day was not yet over. Another day as blank as the square. There were now five X's in a row. The picture above them showed some Dartmoor ponies doing what they always did—chewing grass. She looked at the picture for March. It showed the giant rock-formation of Vixen Tor and a few hardy pilgrims on their way up the rocks. Another stupid pile of rocks they walked for miles to see.

Just last August she had been driving out with Uncle Robert and had seen a lot of people with boots and back packs at one of those tourist centers, all kitted out to walk to one of those tors in the middle of Dartmoor. Jessie and her uncle were driving with the top down in his Zimmer, and she thought those people out there must be crazy, walking when they could be driving. She told him this and he burst out laughing.

"Eat your tea, my love," said Mrs. Mulchop. Her husband, Mulchop, served as groundskeeper and sometimes as butler and looked no more like one than he did the other. He sat now at the kitchen table eating a mess of something.

Mrs. Mulchop moved a pot in the huge inglenook fireplace, in the huge kitchen, in the huge house, in the huge grounds. . . .

Jessie's mind drifted like a veil of rain over all of this hugeness that was the Ashcroft house and grounds. "It's too big," she said, looking at the egg on toast on her plate. Its sickening yellow eye stared back at her.

"Your egg, lovey?"

"No. The house. I'm all alone." Jessie rested her chin in her hands.

Mrs. Mulchop raised her eyes heavenward and

shook her head. She did not realize that beneath this surface melodrama, a true drama of heartsickness was playing itself out. "You're ten years old, not a baby. Wouldn't your uncle be annoyed to see you so sorry for yourself?"

Jessie was shocked to think that anyone would believe Uncle Robert would ever be "annoyed" by Jessie. "No! He'd understand." Now Jessie felt the threat of real tears. Real tears she could not contend with.

"Your uncle's only been gone a few days, lass. No need to get fidgety about it—"

"*Four* days! Four and a *half*! See—" Jessie scraped her chair back and marched to the calendar. "He didn't leave me a note. He didn't give me a Valentine, either." She went back to her chair as if she'd just proven all theories of a clockwork universe defunct in the face of this outrage against reason. But what she felt was more worry than outrage.

"He's probably only gone up to London to see to another governess for you." Mrs. Mulchop glanced at her husband, but his face was too near his bowl to return the look.

Jessie heard the slight sharpness in that *another*. She ran through governesses like a shark through a salmon-fall.

"And you're not all alone. There's me and Mulchop and Miss Gray and Drucilla."

The Dreadful Drucilla, Miss Plunkett, the present

tutor-governess. Not a proper one, though. More of a minder Uncle Rob had settled for when he had discharged the Careless Carla, who was absolutely brilliant at maths, but a little absentminded about keys and spectacles. Out walking across the moor, she had lost Jessie one day, though there had been, in the confrontation with Robert Ashcroft, some doubt as to who had lost whom.

Battalions of governesses. How they sat so neatly and nicely when he was interviewing them. Uncle Rob questioned them closely about their former posts, their credentials, their ability to respond to emergencies; but now and then he would throw one in from left field, such as *And do you like rabbits?*

Jessie liked to see the corners of his mouth twitch and the bewildered look on the face of the prospective employee. *Well, yes. That is, I expect I've nothing against them. . . .* He had explained later to Jess that it was a matter of honesty, and Miss Whatever-her-name wasn't being honest. She was from Portland (where the Ashcroft stone had come from). *In Portland, one is never allowed to mention rabbits. They all hate them,* Uncle Rob had told her.

Thus that one had lost out on a very well paying post, as did most of the prospective women who applied. They sat there saying, *Oh, yes, Mr. Ashcroft,* when they meant No; or *Oh, no, Mr. Ashcroft,* when they meant Yes. And a lot of them would try to snuggle up to Jessica until they realized she wasn't much good for a snuggle, and call her stupid things like "Poppit," and pet her dog Henry, to show how much they liked animals.

Robert Ashcroft could not go on forever relentlessly pursuing the perfect governess, so in the end, he left it up to Jessie, as she was the one who would have to put up with the woman. Uncle Rob often asked her why it was she avoided the nicer ones and chose the worst. There was the Hopeless Helen (who kept the key to the drinks cabinet in more or less constant motion); the Mad Margaret, who had trembled during the interview with a severe case of stage fright, but ended up roaring like a lion, acting being her field of expertise; the Prudent Prucilla, who left rather quickly one night, along with the Crown Derby. Of all of them, the Dubious Desiree had lasted the longest because she had done nothing absolutely wrong, short of hating her pupil, a fact that she kept very well hidden from everyone but Jess herself. Jess put up with the cold-blooded treatment because she knew Desiree was going to do herself in anyway, eventually. In the meantime, she did make Jess a little nervous because of her looks: she was dark and sleek and always winding herself on the couch like a cobra when he was around. But Uncle Rob was not easily fooled; the Dubious Desiree lasted a month.

It seemed a great puzzle to Uncle Rob—his niece's choices. Why Miss Simpson instead of Miss James? *Miss Simpson seemed a bit stiff to me. But Sally James was, well, rather smashing,* he said, before he had returned to the reading of his morning paper, the jamming of his morning toast.

Jessie was not about to have any Smashing Sallys around.

Thus Jessie had never complained about any of them because she knew, every time one of them got sacked, there might be another just waiting in the wings. The Amiable Amy.

Jessie was an omnivorous reader—largely owing to Mad Margaret, who stuffed books and plays into her like sausage. Mad Margaret thought herself the heroine of all of them. Many was the rainy morning that found Jess curled up on the window seat in the library with Henry as a backrest, poring over *Jane Eyre* and *Rebecca.* Jessie knew just how sly some women could be: soft and kind and quiet-spoken and so sly (and amiable) they might even catch Jessie in their nets.

Her uncle had once been married—years and years ago—to a dazzling but false woman who had broken his heart, left him shattered with grief—or, at least, that was the way she put it to him at the breakfast table. "I know it must have left you shattered. You can never look at another woman, can you?"

He did not seem, as he slit open the morning post, terribly shattered. This was, unfortunately, confirmed when he said, "No—I mean to the 'shattered' part of your tale. As to the rest, I think I could bear to look at another woman again, yes. God knows I've looked at enough of them trying to find someone for you."

She had placed a consoling hand on his arm. "But she was beautiful, wasn't she?"

"Indeed she was. But she hated motorcars." He smiled.

"But she loved you madly."

"Not really." He went back to his paper.

All of those governesses over the four years they'd been at Ashcroft. Look what they would get: wealth, position, the glories of Ashcroft itself—to say nothing of one of the most eligible bachelors in the British Isles. And nine motor cars.

The only thing that stood between them and Heaven was Lady Jessica Allan-Ashcroft.

II

The funeral had been held in a parish, the body committed to the ground of a leaf-strewn cemetery in Chalfont St. Giles, where her father had been born and where Jessica's mother had died years ago. Her father had been the Earl of Curlew and Viscount Linley, James Whyte Ashcroft; her mother, plain Barbara Allan, but plain in name only. And between them they had passed on their names to Jessica.

When her father died, Jessie was six years old, and mere days before this she had been chasing her dog,

Henry, all over the grounds of the old home in Chalfont.

They had dressed her in mourning. An aunt with eager fingers had affixed the boater with its black ribbon to her head, placed the gloves in her hand. Jessie did not know the aunt, nor any of the cousins—a great ring of them around the grave—nor anyone except for a few of her father's old friends.

She was dead silent, but Jessie wanted to scream when the vicar went on about Heaven and Rewards. She did not think her father would be tempted by Rewards. He would rather be back here with Jessie.

All around her stood those odd friends and relations, as stark and unmoving as pollarded trees. All in black and dreadful, some with heavy veils, or, hats in hands, expressions frozen, like skaters on a dark lake. One hand fell on her shoulder. She shook it off. The fingers felt like claws. When she looked all round the grave-site again, she saw red-rimmed eyes, not sorrow-laden, but the eyes of wolves.

Jessica Allan-Ashcroft was worth four million pounds to them. And that didn't even include the family seat of Ashcroft.

Just as the service ended, she noticed a stranger in a light-colored Burberry. The mourners were going through the awful ritual of throwing a handful of earth on her father's grave. The stranger walked through the dark stalks of mourners, knelt down and brushed the blown strands of hair from her face. "*Cry,*" was all he said, but in such a tone that her mind split and the tears gushed out. In his own face, she saw something of her father's and even her own and she threw her arms around him and buried her face in his raincoat.

Solicitors were wandering everywhere, in and out of the house in Eaton Square, like dream figures. There were more relations to come, too, others whom Jessie didn't know, coming with long faces, bringing her things she didn't want and calling her "love" and "dear" and none of them meaning it, she knew.

The day after the funeral—to her it had seemed like months—she stood before the long window in the house in Eaton Square, wondering if the man in the raincoat would ever come back. The trees dripped rain and Henry looked up at her with red-rimmed eyes, a true mourner.

Everyone seemed to be keeping a vigil. The relations had gathered in the library with her father's solicitor, all of them coughing gently behind their hands.

When finally he did come, running across the road in the rain, Jessie ran to the door and listened. She heard voices in the hall, an exchange between the butler and the stranger, and then all was quiet again.

Until the will was read.

* * *

The solicitor, a plump man whose jowls reminded her of Henry, took her hands in his plump, perspiring ones and explained "the situation."

It was boring to Jessie, all of this talk about money and property. The important thing was who her guardian was to be. As if on cue, a large woman and her smaller husband came through the door. The woman was the same one who had laid her hand in such a proprietary way on Jessie's shoulder. Her fingers flashed with rings and the poor fox-fur around her neck flashed its glass eyes. Jessie could tell, with one look, she wasn't an animal-lover. "What about Henry?" she asked.

Mr. Mack, the solicitor, found that very funny. "Now you do understand, Jessie. All of your mother's property was left to you and your father. Now all of it goes to you. You must have someone to look after you."

The large, ring-studded cousin snorted, saying it should be her and Al to do the looking-after, and Mr. Mack asked her to leave. Her husband told her there was no use crying over spilt milk, and to come along.

Through the door then came the man from the cemetery.

Mr. Mack told her that this was her Uncle Robert, her father's brother, Robert Ashcroft. Her father had appointed him trustee of the estate and Jessica's guardian.

"Henry's, too," said Robert Ashcroft, winking.

Thus amongst the raised voices that seemed to be calling for Robert Ashcroft's blood, or at least his bona fides, after his ten-year absence in Australia, Jessie felt as if, on the verge of drowning, she had broken the water's surface, dazzled by sunlight. His hair was dark gold and his eyes were light brown. As the thunder of the others' voices receded, Jessie felt the sun falling in shafts across the room and that all those vaults were really full of gold.

ELEVEN

I

The "letters"—they were what prevented the relations, some inarticulate, some artful—from breaking the will. Her father had been clever enough to leave tiny bequests to those relations whom he disliked (which meant most of them), acknowledging that they were "family," but sorry they were his. It was a little like leaving a small tip for poor service.

It was a very large family, but not a close one. "When I left for Australia over ten years ago, I was thirty," her uncle had told her. "In all of those thirty years before, I can't remember seeing any of these relations who've descended like vultures."

The vultures had flown after months of talking

about "undue influence" and "unsound mind," and Jessie and Uncle Robert were sitting in the drawing room in Eaton Square, its furnishings flooded with April sunlight. "Undue influence." He laughed. "It would have been hard to have influenced your father in any case. So how was I supposed to have done it all the way from Australia? Ten years of letters." Robert had stopped and looked at his niece intently. "Jimmy—your father—in any event, how was I supposed to have done it all the way from Australia? Ten years of letters . . ." He had stopped and then said, "It doesn't make you sad, I hope, talking about your father?"

"No. I want to hear about him. And Mother, too." Henry was lying between them, being used as an armrest. "Go on."

"There must have been, over the course of ten years, hundreds of letters. Jimmy was having a hard time of it after your mother died." He paused, thinking back. "And before that, even. He was depressed . . . I don't know if it was because he felt some sort of prescience of Barbara's death, or what. I felt guilty leaving. But I had to."

"Why?"

He was quiet. "I just had to. Anyway, those letters showed we'd kept in touch. You know, when I was at a perfectly awful public school, when I was ten and Jimmy was twenty and my life was hell, he wrote to me three or four times a week. He knew

111

how miserable I was. That's really something for a chap of twenty to do for a boy of ten."

Jessie had managed to circumvent the baggage of Henry to lean across and put her head on her uncle's shoulder. "You were mates. I bet when you were six he got into fights because the boys teased you and threw things at your dog and made fun of you and called you names. Didn't he?" Her tone was hopeful.

"Absolutely."

"Tell me about Mother," she commanded.

"She was beautiful. Dark hair and eyes. You look just like her."

So that her uncle wouldn't see her blush, she busied herself in trying to tie Henry's ears together. A difficult job, since they were hard to find.

"Talk about getting teased over your name! 'Barbara Allan' is an old folk song," said Robert.

"What about?" Henry awoke and shook at his ears.

Robert didn't answer at first, and Jess poked him. She refused to let any important question—meaning any of hers—go unanswered.

"About Sweet William's dying because he loved her."

It was the way he said it. Jessie didn't like his silence. "I've got a picture!" She bounced up, unsettling the cushions and comfort, much to Henry's displeasure. "I keep it locked up."

"Locked up? But why?"

Because she had always had a secret fear that if too many eyes saw her mother's picture, her mother would grow less clear, less distinct, the outlines blurring into the background until the beautiful face of Barbara Allan disappeared altogether. The worst was that Jessie was one of them. If she looked too long, the face in the picture would go away, as her mother had done. But she couldn't tell *him* such a stupid, silly thing. Jess went over to the ebony desk and took a key from a vase and turned it in the bottom drawer. It was only a snapshot. The woman there was kneeling in long grass, gathering wildflowers. Peering through the long grass was a funny-looking puppy.

"That's Henry," she said with feigned disgust. "I wish he hadn't followed her around like that. He made her trip once—I saw it—and she fell down. It could've *killed* her. He was a bad dog." She looked quickly at Henry to see if he might contradict her. "But Henry's okay, now." It was with a growing horror that she saw the weight she'd been carrying for years. She was afraid she'd done something to her mother. Killed her by being born, maybe.

And Robert knew. He put his hands on her shoulders and said, harshly, "Listen to me! You didn't do anything to hurt your mother, Jess. She looked healthy and was much younger than your father. But she was still a sick woman."

Jessie looked down at her mother's picture, the awful weight lifted from her shoulders. She rubbed the glass carefully, delicately, with the hem of her skirt. Then she set the picture atop the desk. Her mother wouldn't disappear just because Jessie looked at her too long.

But she was still embarrassed that her uncle had figured all of this out about her when she'd only just found it out herself. "I think it's time for Henry's walk," she said, smoothly. *Henry's walk* would have been only an annual event, had exercising him been left to Jess.

"Mind if I come?"

"Oh, I guess not. But Henry will only listen to *me*. So it's no use you trying to make him catch sticks, or anything. He won't unless I command him."

It was no use *anyone's* trying to make Henry catch sticks, as Jess perfectly well knew.

II

Thus here she was, four years later, four years of picnics and open motor cars; and trains to London and Brighton; and Careless Clara and all the rest of the benighted ladies. Here she was musing over the past, while Mrs. Mulchop kept to the present, wrist-deep in dough.

Jessie leaned a cold cheek against her fist and punched the spoon down into the equally cold porridge with which Mrs. Mulchop had replaced the egg. And Jess let it sit there like the egg. It had hard-

ened to such a thickness, the spoon stuck straight up.
"He never goes off without leaving me a note or
something." It was the dozenth time she'd imparted
the same information in different ways.

"Well, lovey, he just forgot this time—"

Forgot? Was Mrs. Mulchop crazy?

"—and he has to have his bit of fun, now doesn't
he? Do you begrudge the man that, my lady? Think
of him, not yourself: a man in his forties always in
company of a ten-year-old—" The look in My Lady's
eye changed her tune quickly. "—not that you're not
fun. But your uncle should have a nice wife to look
after—"

"He doesn't *want* one. He already *had* one." Jess
had left the kitchen table and was taking down an
overall from a peg by the back door. "It left him a
broken man." She stuffed her legs into the overall.

" 'Broken man'? *Your* uncle? He's about as broke
as Mulchop here."

Mulchop looked up from his huge bowl. He was
bull-necked and stout-armed and had a spatulate
face, flat as the spades he used on the flowers and
shrubs. He seldom spoke and appeared to resent it
if others engaged in conversation. Words were
wasted on Mulchop.

"Where's the spanner?" Jessica leveled her eyes at
his thick brows.

The spoon, which had but an inch to travel from
bowl to mouth, stopped. "You not be foolin' with

115

them cars, Miss!" Mulchop also took care of the cars; he and Jessie spent what little time they spent together haggling over Uncle Robert's cars.

While Mrs. Mulchop went prattling on about Mr. Robert's sad marital status, Jessie took the spanner from Mulchop's tool box and stuck her tongue out at both of their backs.

". . . a nice wife, that's what he needs."

Not if the Lady Jessica Mary Allan-Ashcroft had anything to do with it.

She lay with the spanner and some old rags on a mechanic's creeper underneath the Zimmer Golden Spirit. It was a good car for thinking under; some of the others, like the Lotus and the Ferrari, were a little too close to the ground for her to get comfortable unless she jacked them up, and Mulchop would always come out and raise a fuss. The Zimmer was one of her favorites, an astonishingly long white convertible, for which Uncle Robert had paid over thirty thousand pounds. Or Jess had paid. It took a platoon of solicitors to keep account of her money. Not that it made any difference to her if Uncle Robert used up all of it on his cars.

Jessie saw a bolt that looked loose and she tried to tighten it. That's what happened when someone went away. . . . Everything just fell apart. Her eyes widened. Forgetting where she was she sat up and bumped her forehead on the exhaust pipe. The cars.

* * *

"Well, *I* don't know, do I?" the Dreadful Dru was saying, as Jess stood there in the drawing room in her oil-stained overall. "You been muckin' about with those cars?"

"They're all *there!*" Jessie shouted. In a sort of ritual chant, she ticked off each one of the nine on her fingers.

Drucilla Plunkett tossed aside the fashion magazine she'd been reading and stuffed another chocolate in her mouth. Drucilla knew her days were numbered, so she wasn't being at all careful about what she did with them. The box of chocolates— a huge heart—Drucilla had said she'd got from an "admirer" down the pub. Most of her spare time was spent with one or another mystery man "down the pub," as she put it. "What do I know about those old cars?" Her bowlike mouth bit into a chocolate truffle.

"If he went to London, how did he go?"

"Say it once again and I'll *scream!*"

Jessie said she could scream the house down. All she wanted to know was where Uncle Rob was. "He's missing." Jessie turned and leaned her forehead against the cold glass, saw the ghost of her face in the slanting rain.

The Dreadful Dru screamed. Not long and loud, but a shriek nonetheless. Having exhausted her eyes with the latest fashions, Drucilla was now exhausting her mind with a newspaper. "God!" She sat up

117

straight. "Look here, there's a prisoner let out of Princetown several days ago. The Ax-murderer—that's what they call him."

Drucilla's little scream might have come from the ghost out in the rain, trying to get in.

Nobody cared, that was clear.

Victoria Gray was a cousin educated well beyond the means of the jobs that might have come her way. Thus Jess's father had employed her in the ambiguous role of "housekeeper," and Victoria did perform what duties she could find. With Mrs. Mulchop, Mulchop, and Billy (the stable-lad), the household was top-heavy with servants. Victoria's servitude was minimal, the line between housekeeper and long-standing guest somewhat blurred.

"Wonder how old she is?" Uncle Robert had said one morning before they had moved from Eaton Square to Ashcroft. He was slitting open the morning post, letter after letter from banks and solicitors. "I believe we've inherited Victoria along with the heirlooms. Still, she's all right." He stopped in the act of opening a letter and said, reflectively, "Actually, she's quite attractive."

Because Victoria Gray had been around ever since Jessie could remember, she hadn't expected trouble from that quarter. "Fifty," she said, beheading her boiled egg smartly with the clipper.

Robert frowned. "Fifty? Surely not. She doesn't look forty to me. Did she tell you, then?"

Jessie had looked at him with cool eyes. "Would *you* tell if you were that old?" With her uncle looking at her that way, now she would have to come up with an explanation as to how she knew Victoria's age. Inspired by the letters lying on the table, she said, "It was a birthday card. She left it on a table. There was a great, big fifty—" Here Jess drew a 5 and 0 in the air, huge numbers, in case her uncle thought fifty wasn't all that much. Satisfied, she dipped a toast finger in her egg.

Uncle Robert was looking at her with his head slightly cocked. And then came that bemused smile that bothered her. "If that's so, she must take wonderful care of herself."

Jessie concentrated on dabbing tiny bits of plum preserve on her toast. "She does. Victoria has lots of those little pots of colors and jars of cream and stuff. Before she goes to bed she wears the cream and a hair net."

Instead of being put off by this odious picture, he was fascinated and completely forgot about his mail. "Well, she certainly has beautiful skin. It must all pay off."

"That's from the mud."

"Mud?"

"Sometimes ladies put it on their faces when they're old to make their skin tight." Here, Jess

119

pressed her fingers to the sides of her own flawless face, pulling the skin back.

Uncle Rob shook his head. "Poor Victoria. Paint, cream, mud."

Quickly, the *Times* came up in front of his face, but Jessie thought she might have seen just the beginning of a smile, snatched away.

She studied the beads of jam on her toast and wondered if she should have left out the mud.

That evening of the fourteenth, Victoria Gray broke into Jess's reflections on the weather, the fog, the condition of the roads. Night had descended on the moor like a black-gloved hand. But he hadn't taken a car—that was the trouble.

"You're being childish, Jess. Better you go to bed and stop all this morbid worrying."

"I *am* a child, aren't I?" A fact she denied most of the time, using it only when it suited her. She watched Victoria collect the balled-up wrappers that the Dreadful Dru had aimed at Henry, now napping on a chair by the fire. He was always napping. She supposed she loved Henry, but he was getting boring.

Victoria was going on about the Dreadful Dru: ". . . glad to see *that* one leave. The only thing she's good at is penmanship. Probably a forger in her youth."

None of them seemed to understand the monumental importance of what had happened. "Did you see him leave?"

Victoria sighed. "*No*, for the tenth time. No. He obviously left early in the morning—he's done it before—when we were all asleep. You know your uncle is impulsive."

But that didn't explain the absence of a Valentine, the lack of a note.

"Jessie, dear." Victoria stood directly behind her now, doubling the reflection in the window. "Go to bed and stop worrying. Can't you allow your uncle to forget just *once*—?"

"*No!* Come on, Henry!" Jessie ordered the dog before she ran from the room. Henry, looking tired and sad, had to obey this injunction, as it was usually the only one he ever got from his mistress.

But she didn't go to bed directly. First, she took down her yellow slicker from the peg beside the overall and jammed her arms in it before she opened the heavy door leading out to what used to be all horse-boxes.

The stable now provided room for garaging nine cars. There were two horses boxed on the other side. Victoria loved to ride; Jessica hated it. She'd told her uncle there were so many ponies on the moor, just looking at a pony made her want to throw up. And she certainly wasn't going to some stupid riding school, only to go round and round in a ring.

"I want a car," she had said, as his collection grew.

"A *car*? Jess, you're seven years old."

She sighed. How many times had she heard that? "In a month I'll be eight. I want a Mini Cooper. You know. The one Austin Rover made." She was rather proud of having come upon this minuscule bit of information.

"Police don't look kindly on eight-year-olds driving."

The Mini Cooper was there. Henry slogged behind her, stopping when she stopped. He yawned, unused to this nocturnal inspection of cars in the dark and the rain. Rain blew the hood of her slicker as Jessica walked round the old stables, beaming her torch on each one, touching the bonnet—almost *patting* the car, as if each were indeed a favorite horse.

TWELVE

I

Jessie lay in bed in the pre-dawn hours, with Henry like a heavy duvet at her feet. She stared up at the tracery of light that the blowing branches etched on the ceiling. Then she turned on her side. Instead of counting sheep (which was horribly dull), she started counting off the rooms at Ashcroft. Her thoughts lingered on the long, dark hall beyond her bedroom door, and on Uncle Rob's room, two doors down, full of leather and chairs and books and a high mahogany chest where he kept the pictures of her father and mother.

But she couldn't think of that room and sleep. Her

mind traveled on to Dreadful Dru's—the room on the other side of hers. Dru was living the life of Laura Ashley (which didn't fit her a bit)—tiny flowers on wallpaper, tiny sprigs on curtains that made Jessie think of thorn-thickets. Whenever she went into the Dreadful Dru's room, she felt trapped by stinging nettles. Next to Dru was Victoria Gray, whose room matched her perfectly. It was rather mysterious, with its silky velvet drapes that lay in heavy folds upon the floor.

None of this was helping her sleep. She counted the rooms in the servants' wing where Mr. and Mrs. Mulchop and Billy had their rooms. The other six rooms in that wing were empty.

Like a potential buyer viewing a property, her mind was led down the dark hall outside her room and down the sweeping Adam staircase to what was now a well of darkness: the big entry room that on sunny days was bright, its floor of Spanish tiles, its circular table in the center pungent with the smells of roses or jasmine.

She opened her eyes and saw that the black panes had lightened to purple. The casement windows rattled in rain. Jessie turned on her other side and took her mind through the tiled hall, into the morning room where, at the dreary age of twenty or so, she would most likely have to talk to people like the local vicar or Major Smythe. . . .

*   *   *

"I don't want to grow up," she had told Uncle Robert a year ago. "To get old like sixteen and have to go to some boring boarding school like All Hallows."

It was a misty September morning. They had taken the Zimmer and a basket of lunch to Haytor.

Jess had held her breath, waiting for him to say something like *But you must grow up,* or *You'll love school.* Only, he couldn't say that, could he? Not after his own awful schooldays.

What he did say was, "I don't see why you have to do anything before you feel like it."

She looked up at the sky that had changed from a sluggish gray to clear pearl. "But I *have* to."

"Go away? When you're ready. Otherwise, it just makes misery."

Now she felt adult and indignant at his lack of knowledge of the Real World. "Don't you know people are *always* having to do things they don't like to? Lucy Manners—she had to go to All Hallows whether she liked it or not."

"She's got spots, hasn't she?"

Jessica was trying to be serious. "What's that got to do with it?"

Uncle Rob was lying on the rock, an arm thrown over his face. "Don't they all have spots, the boarding school ones? Either spots or teeth that stick out?

I don't think you should go because you're much too pretty. I'd hate to see you with spots and stuck-out teeth."

And she began to think of school in more kindly terms. "Lucy Manners would have spots *anywhere*," she said reasonably.

II

Jessie lay on her back and watched the shadows of the branches comb the ceiling in the gathering light. She was still debating what to do. She got out of bed.

Although Henry had no desire to rout himself from the foot of the warm bed and follow, follow he did. *Come on, Henry*, were the three worst words in the language.

She could not reach the telephone in the kitchen because it was high up on the wall. Jess pulled over the cricket stool that Mulchop liked to sit on and smell the soup cooking.

The operator took forever to answer. Jess hung up twice, each time being careful to dial 100. Finally, she got one of them, frosty, far-off in her wired-up ice castle. Jess cleared her throat. "My name's Jessica Ashcroft and I live at Ashcroft. That's fifteen miles outside Exeter. My uncle's missing. I want the police."

The operator talked to her in that sort of slow, loud way that people used with deaf people and dumb children. When Jessie explained that her uncle had been missing five days, the operator asked her why she thought he was "missing."

"Because he isn't *here!*" Jessie hung up. It was hopeless. How could she ever make the operator understand that he'd never go anywhere without leaving a note—and, especially, a Valentine. Today—well, just yesterday, was St. Valentine's Day. Uncle Rob always remembered every holiday. And how could she make the operator understand about the cars? Jessie leaned against the black telephone and came close to crying. She gulped to stop the tears. Henry shook himself out of his lethargy and pawed at her leg and whined in sympathy. But his eyes closed like shutters and he dozed off again.

While she was sitting on the cricket stool, an image came back to Jessie. It was the Dreadful Dru on the couch, stuffing herself with chocs and trying to read the paper.

Jessie took down the receiver and dialed Emergency—999. A crisp, no-nonsense voice asked her what she wanted. Ambulance? Hospital? Police?

Jessie lowered her voice a notch, rounded her vowels, and enunciated clearly, in just the way Mad Margaret had taught her. "I am Lady Jessica Allan-Ashcroft." Dramatic pause. "I want Scotland Yard." The telephone nearly slipped from her hand because her palm was so sweaty. Her heart pounded. "That ax-murderer that was released from Dartmoor prison has been to this house and he's killed—" she looked down—"the Honorable Henry Allan-Ashcroft."

Nose on paws, Henry raised beleaguered eyes, unaware that his blood—according to Lady Jessica—was everywhere. Almost total dismemberment. Then he returned to his light doze, equally unaware that he had just been knighted.

All of the operator's questions she had answered coolly, almost indignantly, as if surprised that Lady Jessica Allan-Ashcroft should be questioned by such a menial. Directions were given. Times were given. Names were given. And she hung up, after being told to stay calm.

Calm? With blood running all over the kitchen floor? Was the woman *mad*?

She had begun to believe in her own fantasy until she looked at Henry, lying healthily by the hearth, and wondered how she was going to explain to police how he was so unbloody. And unbowed.

"Come on, Henry. We've got to think."

Henry showed as little inclination for thinking as for following. In the pantry, Jessie found a can of Chum, struggled with the can opener, and put some in a bowl. This she placed on the pantry floor and had no trouble getting Henry in there for his unexpected tea at dawn. She shut the door.

As she walked through the dining room into the drawing room, where morning light lay in splinters on oriental carpets and velvet couches, it occurred to Jessie that the Devonshire police didn't know Henry. And Henry certainly wouldn't talk.

But she, Jessie, would have to. How would she explain the lack of blood? Blood was not easy to come by, and she had no intention of sacrificing any of hers. She sat on the same sofa as had the Dreadful Dru, trying to be calm, trying to think. Jessie looked out the window and saw the cold, scabrous dawn slither up the grass like a snake and considered tomato sauce.

But where was the slaughtered body? Cold in only her nightdress, she still sat there, constructing and reconstructing her story. In the attic was a dressmaker's dummy. If she put it in a dark corner of the kitchen and tossed the tomato sauce all over, she could say she saw it and just went crazy. . . .

Yet, wouldn't that open up more questions? *Who* had put the dummy there and spilt the sauce all round?

At the same time she heard barking from the pantry, she heard the double-note of sirens coming up the gravel drive. The revolving lights, the noise, caused a lot of thumping from the rooms upstairs.

Footsteps coming down the stairs, footsteps coming up the gravel. She felt sorry for Henry, shut up in the pantry, and sorrier for herself. She was going to have a lot to answer for.

III

The Dreadful Dru came in holding a candlestick, like a leftover from the Mad Margaret's repertoire of characters. But the Dreadful Dru looked more like a blow-fly than she did Lady Macbeth, heavy with sleep in her black peignoir.

Mrs. Mulchop was dressed in her mobcap and brown felt slippers. Victoria Gray in a velvet dressing gown.

Police were everywhere, some in uniform and some in plain clothes; there were also men in white coats, and a doctor with his black bag.

Jessica was surrounded.

There was a torrent of questions and a few shocked answers from Mrs. Mulchop and Victoria Gray. No, they knew nothing. The questions were orchestrated by the insistent barking of Henry. Mrs. Mulchop went to the pantry to investigate.

Jessica scratched at her ear and looked up through squinty eyes as if she couldn't imagine what had brought all this crowd together. The salvo of questions seemed to confuse her awfully, and the man in charge—an Inspector Browne—waited while she gazed all over the ivory and damask splendor of the

Ashcroft drawing room. Finally, she asked, "Where am I?"

Drucilla Plunkett was wringing her hands as if to keep them away from Jessica's throat. "Where *are* you? Whatever are you going on about, you silly thing?"

Jessie rubbed her eyes and turned her troubled face to Inspector Browne. "I must've been walking in my sleep again."

Drucilla was yelling now: "You *never* walk in your sleep!"

Jessie considered for a moment. "Yes, I do. You just weren't around."

The logic of this escaped Drucilla, who, having put down the candlestick, raised it now as if she meant to bring it down on her little charge's head. Inspector Browne came between them. The house and grounds were swarming with police.

Nothing, was the report passed back along the line of the inspector's entourage. *Nil.* No body, no blood, no sign of forced entry or anything else. They all looked to Jessie.

"It was a nightmare," said Jessie. "I was having this awful dream about my Uncle Robert. He's been missing—" (and here she looked out of the window to calculate another dawn into the whole of it) "—six days."

Once again Drucilla raised the candlestick. Victoria Gray turned away, looking pained. And the playlet was interrupted by the return of Mrs. Mulchop, marching in with Henry. "And why was Henry closed up in my pantry, I'd like to know, Miss?"

One of Browne's men flipped through a small notebook. "Report was that a Henry Ashcroft had been the victim. The Honorable Henry Allan-Ashcroft."

Before Dru or Victoria or Mrs. Mulchop could react fully to this announcement, Jessie had jumped up from the couch. "*Henry!* You're all *right!*" She flung her arms about the massed wrinkles that were Henry.

They all looked down in wonder. A child and her dog.

THIRTEEN

I

Brian Macalvie seemed at first to be merely irritated by the telephone's ringing at four A.M. in the Lyme Regis station. He cradled the receiver like a bawling baby against his ear. Macalvie might, indeed, have been a new father, thought Jury; he didn't seem to need sleep. They had been all day in Dorchester and Exeter.

As he listened to the voice on the other end, Macalvie stopped sucking the Fisherman's Friend. Wiggins had left the packet before going back to the White Lion for some sleep. In slow motion, Macalvie's feet left the desk that had been supporting them; the chair

creaked with his weight as he sat up. He nodded
and said, "Yeah, I've got it." He hung up.

Then he put his head in his hands.

"What the hell is it?" asked Jury, surprised by Macalvie's look of remorse.

"Dartmoor. Bloody Dartmoor. It sounds like it's
happening all over again."

II

"Dartmoor." Wiggins said it with a shudder as they
drove off the A 35 toward Ashburton.

"You'll love it, Wiggins," said Macalvie, "it's got
a prison and ponies and it rains sideways."

He was right about the rain. Wiggins was huddled
down in his coat in the back seat. "You should slow
down a bit, sir. This road's posted as not being appropriate for caravans."

"So who's driving a caravan?" said Macalvie, taking what looked like a single-lane road between
hedges stout as stone walls at a good fifty miles per
hour. God help them or anyone coming from the
opposite direction.

It was seven in the morning but it looked like
dusk—the rain, the ground mist, the dark rock formations rising against the sky. When they got beyond the hedged-in road, Jury saw acres of heather

the color of port, crippled trees, the occasional huddled house.

Ashcroft was visible from a turning a half-mile
away, standing on its hill, a large and perfectly pro-
portioned house. As they turned into its long, sweeping gravel drive, Jury saw the grounds were partly
formal—well-groomed hedges, flower beds—and
partly wild, as if the gardener had dropped spade
and hoe in the middle of the job.

In front were two police cars.

"Nice little place," said Macalvie, braking hard
enough to spit up gravel.

"What the hell do you mean, a *ruse?*"

Detective Inspector Browne looked as if he'd like
to be anywhere but where he was now. "Sorry, sir.
The little girl, Jessica Ashcroft—or Lady Jessica, I
should say, I expect—"

"I don't care what you call her, Browne. Just tell
me what's going on."

Eyes averted from Macalvie's, Browne explained.
"And by the time we found out, you'd already left
Lyme Regis. . . ."

Jessica looked up at the three new ones. She was
still in her nightdress, as were the other members of
the household. She sat on the couch, ankles crossed,
patiently waiting for whatever scolding the new ones
had to dish out. There should be enough brains

135

among all of them to find her uncle, she thought. She did not particularly like the look of the copper-haired one who stood with his hands in his trouser pockets and had eyes like torches. The other, taller one had gray eyes and looked, somehow, comfortable. . . .

Macalvie looked over the lot of them. Victoria Gray was sitting patiently enough on the couch facing the girl. The older one was the cook and she wrung her hands. Then there was the rich pastry of a piece named Plunkett. Their backdrop, the drawing room itself, was heavy velvet and brocade, portraits and gilt. No one was hurting for money.

"This," said DI Browne, "is Lady Jessica Mary Allan-Ashcroft."

On facing sofas, Chief Superintendent Macalvie and Jessica Allan-Ashcroft squared off. Jury sat in a heavy brocade chair and Wiggins in a straight one by the fire.

"You can call me Jessica," she said, with extreme largesse.

"Thanks." Macalvie glared at her, took out a pack of gum, and stuffed a stick in his mouth.

"Can I have some?"

Jury was glad to see Macalvie managed to keep from throwing it at her.

They both sat there, taking each other's measure, chewing away.

"Start talking," said Macalvie.

"My uncle's missing."

That statement seemed to bring housekeeper, cook, and governess to the edge of hysteria. Victoria Gray, the most controlled, stepped back from it and said to Macalvie, "Robert Ashcroft. Her uncle. He left several days ago, probably for London, but she's convinced he's missing. It's ridiculous; Mr. Ashcroft goes to London now and again."

Macalvie's eyes snapped from Victoria back to Jessica. He chewed and stared. "You know, there's kind of a difference between an uncle going missing and a friendly call from an ax-murderer. That occur to you?"

Jury broke in. "What makes you think he's missing, Jessica?"

"Because he didn't leave a note and he didn't leave a Valentine present."

"For a box of candy," said Macalvie, "you got half the Devon-Cornwall constabulary running across this godforsaken, bloody moor with some cock-and-bull story about a murderer. You know that, don't you?"

To that deadly voice, Jessie sighed and said, "I'm sorry."

"You're sorry."

She smoothed the skirt of her nightdress, folded her hands, and said gravely, "Yes. I'm sorry you're so disappointed that there wasn't a lot of blood and torn-up bodies and we weren't all murdered, includ-

137

ing Henry." She took out her gum, inspected the pink wad, and put it back in her mouth.

Macalvie's eyes were like lasers. He opened his mouth but was interrupted.

"Don't forget about that man that got out of Dartmoor." As if police weren't keeping abreast of the news, she handed Macalvie a neatly folded paper. It contained the clipping that Drucilla had read earlier.

Macalvie tossed the paper aside, angrily. "That *man* was *released* on good behavior. Your behavior I'm not so sure I could say the same about. Not only the Devon-Cornwall police, but the person sitting over there"—and he nodded in Jury's direction—"just happens to be a Scotland Yard CID superintendent."

"Then why isn't he asking the questions?" Jessica directed her attention to Jury. "My uncle disappeared five days ago, six, counting today." She was pleased the thin one was making notes of what she said. At least *someone* was taking her seriously. "He never forgets any holiday and he always lets me know if he has to go somewhere. Besides that, all of his cars are out there." She pointed in the direction of the stable-yard.

"What do you mean, 'all,' Miss?" asked Wiggins.

"All nine. The Zimmer, the Porsche, the Lotus Elite, the Mini Cooper—that's really mine—the Ferrari, the Jaguar XJ-S that goes from zero to sixty in under seven seconds, the 1967 Maserati, and the Aston Martin." She sat back.

Wiggins cleared his throat. "That's only eight, Miss." He counted with his lips again.

Jury thought Macalvie was going to belt one of them; he wasn't sure which.

Jessica looked for a thoughtful moment at the ceiling. "Did I say the Benz? I don't like it that much."

Wiggins wrote it down. "Your uncle's a collector, is that it?" He wet the tip of his pencil.

"Yes. He's five-feet-eleven with gold hair and light brown eyes." She looked back at Jury. "He's handsome. He took me in when my father died four years ago."

There was a slight laugh from Victoria Gray: "Wasn't it more like your taking *him* in?"

Jury looked more closely at her: good-looking, eyes heavy-lidded, as if she preferred not to have her thoughts read in her eyes. She seemed embarrassed now, having given voice to one of those thoughts. "Pardon me, but I'd like to get dressed." She drew the velvet wrapper more closely around her.

"Go ahead," said Macalvie. "Except for missing uncles there's no reason for us to be here."

Jessie looked around the room. "You're not even going to look for him, are you?"

Jury was impressed with the little girl's conviction that something was really wrong. Her uncle must be a very dependable person. "We will."

Macalvie was standing now, hands in pockets, turning the blowtorch look on Jury. "Isn't there enough on your platter already?"

"I just thought I'd ask Lady Jessica a few questions."

"Hell, ask away. I'm going down to Freddie's. Browne can drop me off and you can bring the car along whenever you're finished fooling around here. Come on, Wiggins. One drink of Freddie's cider and you'll never be sick a day in your life. You'll be paralytic."

Wiggins looked at Jury; Jury nodded. It amused him that Wiggins—or the pharmacy Wiggins carried with him—had become indispensable to Macalvie.

III

There in the drawing room, Jury listened patiently to the fabrication of faithless loves and deaths from broken hearts attributed to her mother. She had gone to a table on which stood some framed pictures and brought back the one of Barbara Allan Ashcroft. The woman in the picture, even squinting and half-blinded by the sun, Jury could see was herself blindingly beautiful. She might indeed have broken many of the hearts Jessica claimed she had.

The second picture was of her father: he was an older and more wasted version of the man in the portrait above the fireplace; a grave illness would explain it.

"She's pretty, isn't she?"

"She's more than pretty. She's quite beautiful. You look like her, you know." The woman was probably in her twenties, at any rate she was a good twenty years younger than her husband. Jury could almost believe the tale of woe and heartbreak Jessica had spun. Unfortunately, though, Jessica suffered from the Scheherazade syndrome. Whenever there came a pause in her tale of gloom and doom and Jury made to get up, Jessie would spin out an even richer thread. Scheherazade or Hephaestus—Jury wasn't sure which. He would start to rise and *plunk*, the golden net would fall and toss him back once more onto the couch. Her contriving the ax-murderer's visit was small potatoes, compared with the tragedy of Barbara Allan. If as many suitors had died for love of Jessica's mother as Jessica would have him believe, the population of London W1, Devon and Chalfont St. Giles would have been considerably diminished. Jessie was careful to assure Jury, however, that her mother would never have deliberately hurt whatever Sweet William happened to be in love with her at a given moment.

Barbara Ashcroft had died a few months after Jessie was born. When her Uncle Robert had gone off to Australia, Jessie had not yet been born. Victoria Gray (according to Jessie) had come to her mother's funeral and, being a cousin, had been urged to stay on by her father. There was an old cook who was especially fond of Lady Ashcroft and who had preferred to leave once she was dead. Thus, Mrs. Mulchop had come on the job afterwards. And so had the string of governesses.

No one in the present household had known Robert Ashcroft before he came back from Australia.

Jessie went on about her father, her uncle, her other relatives (all of whom were very distant). "After the will was read, they kept coming and calling, until Uncle Rob got rid of them."

"Do you know who your family solicitor is, Jessie?" asked Jury. They were out in the stableyard now, behind the house, a handsomely converted stableyard.

"It's Mr. Mack. Or, at least, he's one of them. We have—" She seemed uncertain as to how much they had. "—trunks full of money. Do you like cars?"

"How long has he been with the family?"

She frowned. "Who?"

"Your solicitor, Mr. Mack."

"Forever. Do you like *cars?*"

He felt an odd presentiment. Wynchcoombe, Clerihew Marsh, Lyme Regis, Dorchester. Only the last was outside a forty-mile radius. But the Ashcroft place was certainly within it. And she was ten years old.

"Yes. I like cars," said Jury.

They had come to the last of the nine—one of Jessie's favorites—the Lotus Elite. "Nineteen fifty-seven," she solemnly pronounced. Then she went on to interweave fact and fiction, using expressions like "stroke dimension" and "wishbone front" with all the assurance of an expert.

It was during this recital that there came a rush of footsteps and raised voices and a man striding across the courtyard toward the old horse-boxes. "Jess! What the devil's going on?"

The look on her face made it clear to Jury that Uncle Robert was no longer missing.

FOURTEEN

He would have needed no introduction. The way Jessie hurled herself like a discus into his arms would have told Jury that this was Robert Ashcroft.

"But I *did* leave a note," he was saying as Jury walked up. "I slipped it under your door. Who's our visitor?" He looked from Jessie to Jury.

"Scotland Yard." Jury handed Ashcroft his card, smiling to show his was a friendly visit. "It seems Lady Jessica got a little worried and told police you'd gone missing. The Devon police have been and gone."

Ashcroft looked down at his niece, astonished. "Good God, Jess. You called in police—" He looked at Jury and down at Jury's card. "Scotland Yard? I can't believe it."

"Well, I happened to be working on another case and came along with the divisional commander—"

Again, amazement was stamped on Ashcroft's face. "A superintendent and a divisional commander, Jess? Where's the Prime Minister? You left her out? How in the name of heaven did Jess manage to drag you all out here on a missing person case?"

Jessica was studying an interesting cloud formation and saying maybe they should go in as it looked like rain. Inspired by another means of changing the subject, she called for Henry. "Where's Henry? He came out with us. *Henry!*"

The sad face of Henry appeared slowly, rising behind the windscreen of the Ferrari.

"He likes to go for rides," said Jessie, as she pulled away from her uncle and made Henry clamber down from the car.

Out of sight, out of mind, thought Jury, smiling. "Sorry about the police intrusion, Mr. Ashcroft. All a mare's nest. I've been working on a case in Dorchester—"

"I read about it. Terrible."

"What's more terrible is there've been two others since then."

Ashcroft looked at his niece and went a little white. "Children?"

Jury nodded.

Jessica was back with Henry in tow. "One got stuck with a knife and the other one got his head

145

bashed in, or something." She made a dreadful sound, apparently her version of bashing.

"It's nothing to be making light of, Jess," said her uncle, sharply.

"I wasn't. I was just showing you—it happened in the church, too."

Ashcroft looked puzzled. "What church?"

"Over in Wynchcoombe."

Her proximity to murder did not seem to faze her, but Ashcroft looked worried enough as he studied Jury's face for some reassurance. Jury doubted he wanted to go further into details in front of his niece, and said nothing.

Jessie, however, had garnered plenty of details: "It's Drucilla who told me. She likes to read me the worst part of the papers. An ax-murderer got out of the prison in Princetown—"

Jury laughed. "Hold it a minute. The man was *released*, Jessie. There was even some question whether he'd ever done that—business. And he certainly wasn't an 'ax-murderer'; the papers like blood and thunder."

Ashcroft was angry, though not at Jury. "Drucilla's days are numbered. She shouldn't have been reading you that sort of stuff. And didn't you get the candy I paid that stupid bloke she runs about with to deliver?"

"Drucilla said the chocolates *were for her!* She's been stuffing them in till she's bloated."

"I'll see to her. At any rate, I've found you a new governess. This one I think will finally do."

Jury could almost hear the *Oh, no* directed toward her uncle. Beseeching eyes. Down-turned mouth. "But you always let me choose before!"

"I'm sorry, Jess. But they've all turned out to be such a bad lot—well, anyway, this time I advertised in the London papers. That's why I went up to London. You'll like Sara. I'm sure of it. And if you don't—" Ashcroft shrugged. "—she goes. Okay? In the meantime, I think you might want to meet her. She's in the drawing room."

Jessie didn't answer. Her eyes were on the ground.

"If there are no further questions, Superintendent—?"

Jury was fascinated by Jessie's little act. She might have been going to a hanging. "Questions? No, Mr. Ashcroft. No questions." He looked back toward the boxes that housed not horses but cars. "I was wondering, though, if I could have another look at your collection—"

"Certainly. Help yourself."

Jessie held him back, saying, "That's another thing. Why didn't you take one of the cars? Why didn't you drive?"

Ashcroft smoothed back her dark hair. "Because there was an advert in the paper about a Rolls; I was sure I'd buy it and drive it back. But it wasn't what

I wanted. And as it turned out, Miss Millar—that's Sara—had her own car. So we drove back."

Looking at Jessie's face, Jury thought the news couldn't have been worse. He only hoped, for the niece's sake, Miss Millar's car was a beat-up Volkswagen.

Jessie and Ashcroft walked off, hand in hand. Jury doubted it would take much time for Jessie to sort out the new tutor.

He walked along the courtyard, looking at each of the expensive automobiles in turn: the Ferrari, the Porsche, the Aston Martin, the incredible Zimmer Golden Spirit (he whistled under his breath), the Mercedes-Benz (that probably didn't get much of a workout), the Jag—there was a fortune here.

His skin prickled. Jury took out his notebook and wrote down the name of the solicitor, Mack. Robert Ashcroft's explanation had been plausible enough: note slipped under the door (that Jury bet had been mistakenly tossed out by a maid); chocolates meant to be delivered by surprise—and clearly were, since Miss Plunkett had been eating them . . .

Yet there was that same reluctance to leave as there was when Jessica had been spinning her stories. He wished he had some legitimate reason for coming back—

He could suggest to Ashcroft that, with a killer loose nearby, his niece might need police protection.

But Robert Ashcroft would hire a personal body-guard and get a matched set of Alsatians if he thought his niece was a target for a killer.

Jury was standing in front of Jessie's car, the Mini Cooper. It might as well have been a police-issue Cortina for all of Jury's interest in cars.

But then he smiled and ground his cigarette out on the stone and left.

V

The Jack and Hammer

FIFTEEN

An air of somnolence hung over the Jack and
Hammer's saloon bar, an air not altogether
owing to the fly droning around the black beams
overhead, nor to Mrs. Withersby's dozing by the fire,
nor to the report of the latest takeover bid of another
shipyard, which was what Melrose Plant was reading
about in the *Times*. Indeed, the only thing moving—
and possibly responsible for the general heaviness—
was Lady Ardry's mouth.

"*Gout!* That is ridiculous, Melrose." She addressed
the London *Times*, behind which was the face of her
nephew. "It most certainly is *not* gout!" Now she
addressed the painful foot, elastic-bound and supported by the cricket stool that Mrs. Withersby ordi-
narily claimed for herself. On this occasion, the usual

Withersby enterprise had exchanged it for a double gin, compliments of Melrose Plant, the nephew Lady Ardry was now upbraiding. "And if it *is* gout, *you'd* have it, not I!"

He lowered the paper. "I'd have *your* gout, Agatha? That would be a first in the annals of medicine."

"Please do not try to be witty with *me*, my dear Plant."

"That would be difficult." Melrose turned to the book reviews, having exhausted global conflict.

"What I meant was, as you perfectly well know, that it's *you* who drinks the port, not *I*." She raised her glass of shooting sherry, toasting her own powers of deduction.

Melrose lowered his *Times* once again and turned his eyes to the beams above, wondering if the fly would fall like a bullet in the vacuum of their conversation. "Gout has many causes, Agatha. Perhaps you have fairy-cake-gout. Who knows but that if you eschew those rich pastries, your foot might become less inflamed, as the condition is not irreversible." He wondered if life were, though, when talking to his aunt. He continued. "Gout comes from the Latin *gutta*. It means 'clot' or 'drop.' Surely, you don't believe that every old pukka sahib drinking port beneath the palms wound up with gout? Gout is caused by uric acid. Sort of thing you get with too many sardines or smelts or offal. You haven't been at the offal again, have you?"

"This is just what I would have expected of you, Plant. No sympathy whatever."

"Then why did you come clumping into the Jack and Hammer on your cane, if you already knew?" Trying to change the subject from gout to books and thinking that Agatha might be interested (by some weird crossover of the stars) in American writers, as she herself was American, Melrose said, "Now, just look at this—"

Look at this might better have been said of the man coming through the Jack and Hammer's door—Long Piddleton's antiques dealer, Marshall Trueblood. Trueblood always managed to appear on any scene like a voyager on the deck of a departing ocean liner, all confetti and colored streamers. Nothing so much resembled one as the purple crepe scarf loosely knotted at his neck and trembling in the same wind that stirred the cape of his cashmere inverness.

Dick Scroggs, the publican, looked up from his paper, spread out on the bar, and with that welcome reserved for regulars said, "Close the bleedin' door, mate." He then returned to his paper.

"My *dear* Scroggs. How can you be so churlish when trade is this good? There are at least three— well two and a half" (he corrected himself, looking at Mrs. Withersby) "—customers. Plant, Agatha." He unwhirled his handsome coat and took a seat as close to Lady Ardry's lame foot as would allow for a little bit of pain.

She said *ouch* and glared at Trueblood, whom she loathed only slightly less than Mrs. Withersby. Trueblood, after all, had money. Not as much as her nephew, but money nonetheless.

Trueblood called to the publican for drinks all around, and included Mrs. Withersby with a helping of gin-and-it. He offered his Balkan Sobranies, lit up a lavender one (in tune with his scarf), and brushed a mite of cigarette coal from his sea-green shirt. Trueblood was the jewel in the crown of Long Piddleton, a dazzling little collection of cottages and shops in the hills of Northamptonshire. Scroggs brought the drinks and Trueblood asked Plant what he was so deep into reading about.

"Book reviews."

"How lovely. Anything useful?"

Trueblood, though certainly no tightwad, couldn't help but think of everything in terms of usury.

"I was going to read this review to Agatha, since she's American—"

"I *do* wish you would stop referring to me in that way, Plant." Tenderly she touched the bandage like a newborn baby's cheek. "You always seem to forget that I married your uncle, and that—"

She was always shaking relatives from his family tree, as if Melrose couldn't remember them on his own. He ignored her. "Listen. This tone of easy superiority can sometimes be grating, primarily because it is symptomatic of a culture in its imperial phase—' "

"Who are they reviewing?" asked Trueblood. "Gunga Din?"

"No. It's this collection of essays by John Updike. But what in hell does it mean? Even leaving off the 'imperial phase' stuff—I mean the U.S. And just what is Updike's 'easy superiority'?"

"It's probably what Withers has." Trueblood called over to Cinders-by-the-ashes. "Withers, old trout! Another gin-and-it?"

Mrs. Withersby spat in the fire at the same time she hobbled over to the bar for a refill.

Trueblood went on. "No, I'd say easy superiority is what Franco Giopinno has. Vivian's slippery Italian."

Vivian Rivington, a long-standing and (in some minds) beautiful friend, was off in Italy visiting her "slippery Italian."

"Ah, yes. That's it precisely," continued Trueblood, marveling yet once again at himself. "Do you suppose she's gone to Venice to break it off or put it on—oh, sorry, old trout—" He turned to Agatha with innocent eyes. "That did sound a bit off-color."

"You needn't apologize to *me*, Mr. Trueblood! I'm sure I can put it on with the best of them."

Trueblood and Melrose exchanged glances.

"But if she thinks herself a woman of such superiority—"

"Uh-uh. *Easy* superiority," Trueblood said. "It's

157

like easy virtue. What do you think, Melrose? I know how fond you are of Viv-viv."

It was deliberate. It always was with Trueblood when Lady Ardry was around. Melrose knew she would gladly have given Trueblood a crack with her cane, had it not been more important to divert Plant's attention away from Vivian into other and less attractive quarters.

"*I* find the review extremely un-American."

"Well, it's certainly anti-Updike," said Melrose. " 'An American confidence which can treat the whole world as a suitable province for its judgments.' " He could only shake his head. "For the British to talk imperialism . . . Cheap shot."

The only cheap shot Agatha was concerned about was where her next shooting sherry was coming from.

"And here's another American writer being gunned down. She's described as writing a book 'ladylike in an American way.' That only makes me want to meet American ladies, to find out in what way they're so differently ladylike." Melrose looked at Trueblood, but doubted he'd have much to offer on that point.

"As far as I am concerned," said Agatha, "I mean to stay right here in dear old England." She patted her upraised ankle. "You will never get *me* back to the United States."

That was a good reason for a mass exodus, thought Melrose. But, then, why *should* she go back to the States? She had everything here she could ever want. Unfortunately for her, all of it was up at Ardry End—the crystal, the Queen Anne furniture, the servants, grounds and jewels. . . . Well, perhaps not *all* of the jewels, for Melrose noticed that riding on her bosom this afternoon was a delicately chased silver brooch he had last seen in his mother's possession. The Countess of Caverness had been dead for a number of years; his aunt seemed set on slipping into her shoes, even though Agatha was not, properly speaking, a Lady in any sense of the term. She had been married to Melrose's uncle—the Honorable Robert Ardry. Agatha had decided to let the dead bury the dead, but not the title, and had long since wedded herself instead to the cake stand and the shooting sherry.

"I cannot imagine," said Melrose, "one's giving up America to come live in a country of amateurs."

Trueblood raised an eyebrow at that. "And do you include retreaders of furniture in that category?" His description of himself and his antiques was hardly accurate.

Agatha sighed loudly. "I don't know what you're talking about, Plant."

She seldom did. It inspired Melrose to dip into further shallows of conversation, even if it was like wasting a good fly on a dead fish. "I am referring to amateur shopkeepers, amateur publicans, amateur politicians, amateur butchers—"

Lady Ardry sat up a bit too sharply and winced with pain. It was all right for Melrose to toy with prime ministers, but certainly not with the source of her daily chop. "Amateur butchers! You'd insult Mr. Greeley—after that magnificent joint we had just last evening—?"

"I'm not insulting Mr. Greeley's joints. But he's back there with hatchets and cleavers and saws, for all I know." Perhaps it was this reference in the paper to the release of a prisoner from Dartmoor who had been dubbed the "ax-murderer" that had allowed him to see Mr. Greeley in that light.

"Melrose! You're putting me off my sherry."

Melrose continued reading. It was possible to talk to Agatha and read simultaneously. "What I'm talking about is this: I bet you don't find American butchers greeting their customers while wearing blood-smeared aprons with knives in their hands. Everytime I see your Mr. Greeley I'm reminded of the *Texas Chain Saw Murders* or whatever that execrable film was we saw on ITV. And there's another category, too—amateur criminals. You've got—meaning America has, or had—Al Capone and Scarface and the Godfather and Richard Nixon. All we've got is Brixton and the IRA."

"I must say, old bean," said Marshall Trueblood, "that's hardly a compliment to the U.S.A."

"Not meant to be. I'm merely saying that when the Americans do something—at least the professional criminals, it's a bang-up job. Not slapdash, like most of ours."

"You're mad as a hatter, Melrose. Right round the twist. I'd like another drink, if you would be so kind." Agatha was not in the habit of inspecting her bread closely to see on which side it was buttered.

Melrose continued with his thesis. "Don't you remember John McVicar, who escaped from Durham? That's a high-security lockup, just like Dartmoor. No one had done it before—"

"Which merely disproves your point, old chap." Trueblood rose to get the drinks, and Mrs. Withersby snapped to attention.

"No, it doesn't. Two of them got out. One broke his ankle going over the wall or something and the plan for the pickup had to be dished. Well, there goes John into the Wear or the Tyne—whichever river—and he swims for it. But now he's got the problem of making contact with his friends on the outside. Guess how he does it?"

Agatha sighed even more loudly because Melrose was keeping Trueblood away from the bar. "Can't imagine," said Trueblood.

"Goes into a public call box. I mean, for God's

sakes, can you imagine Capone or Scarface in a phone booth searching for a ten-p piece—?"

Scroggs interrupted by calling from the bar, "Phone for you, M'lord." Dick Scroggs had never been able to work his mind round to Melrose Plant's having given up his title.

"A call?" said Agatha. "Here? Who would be calling you at the Jack and Hammer? I find that odd. . . ." She kept on casting about for reasons all the time Melrose was making his way to the phone on the other side of the bar.

It was Ruthven, his butler. Melrose was so mystified by the message that Ruthven had to convince him that, Yes, those were Superintendent Jury's directions. He would very much appreciate Lord Ardry's motoring to Dartmoor in his Silver Ghost—"He was very specific on that point, My Lord." Superintendent Jury had left clear instructions as to what he would like Lord Ardry to do.

"Yes, all right," said Melrose. "Yes, yes, yes, Ruthven. Thank you." Melrose hung up.

His friend Jury might have asked for some odd things over the years of their acquaintance, but why would he want an earl with a Silver Ghost?

VI

The End of the Tunnel

SIXTEEN

Jessica stood in the doorway of the drawing room that morning, refusing to put her foot over the sill, as if she hoped that might spirit away the person to whom she was being introduced. She wouldn't look up and she wouldn't come forward despite her uncle's growing impatience. It was because she knew what she'd see.

The Amiable Amy.

In that wonderful catchall tone that Uncle Rob could use when he was cross with her, yet understood her dilemma (a common occurrence in the household), he said, "Miss Millar will think you are determined always to address her from the other side of the room, Jess."

With daggers in her eyes, she looked at her uncle,

and then quickly down again lest the eyes might meet Miss Millar's.

Now it was Miss Millar's voice—amiable as could be—saying, "I can remember once having to meet a new teacher. I can remember being very shy of her."

Shy? *Shy?* Jessica Mary Allan-Ashcroft? Never in her life—or, at least, in the life she had led after Uncle Robert had come along—had Jessie been called "shy." Her face colored with rage, which only made her more furious because now it would be taken as proof of her being shy.

"Come on, Jess," said her uncle. Seldom could she remember his sounding as if Jessie's behavior were an embarrassment to him. Now, that's just how he sounded.

Henry, hearing the *Come on*, drifted out of his light doze, even though he was on his feet.

"Not you," she murmured, giving him a little kick.

The amiable voice continued: "Well, then, perhaps we can talk at luncheon. Or dinner." Now there was amusement in the voice. "Breakfast? Though I might not last that long. . . ."

That was smart of the new governess. It was as if she were trying to make light of what even Jessie knew to be perfectly odious behavior on her own part. Of course, the Amiable Amy would have to have a sense of humor. Because Uncle Rob had a smashing sense of humor, and Jessie knew humor would make up for all other sorts of defects. Except, perhaps, absolute ugliness. If Amy looked like an ogre or gnome . . . Jessie hazarded a quick glance upward. The case was hopeless. The Amiable Amy was almost *pretty*. Hopeless. She also had patience. Patience on a monument, she was. Jessie knew a lot of Shakespeare because the Mad Margaret had shoveled it—play after play of it—down her throat, Margaret acting out scenes and bawling soliloquies. Margaret had always wanted to be an actress. She was good at Lady Macbeth.

"Jess." There was Uncle Rob again, being beastly. "What *are* you doing, standing there like a statue and wringing your hands?"

Eyes closed, Jessie said, "Not *wringing*. I'm *washing* them. I must wash my hands. Nothing will make them come clean. They're incar——" She couldn't remember that word. It was something like carburetor.

Uncle Robert was actually beginning to sound concerned. "Jessie. Are you ill? What's the matter?" He laughed uncertainly. "You seem to have gone a little mad."

Quite. She smiled to herself and turned and ran from the room.

Since the exit included no *Come on, Henry*, Henry continued to doze in the doorway.

SEVENTEEN

I

"So here's what happened," said Macalvie. They were sitting in the mobile unit in Wynchcoombe, Macalvie having cleared the place of the sergeant manning the telecom system, three constables going in and out, and TDC Coogan. The only person (besides Jury and Wiggins) who had held his ground was Detective Inspector Neal, calmly observing Macalvie over the rim of his coffee cup.

"You've solved it, Macalvie?" Neal's tone was wry.

"I sure as hell hope so. Because I don't seem to be getting anywhere. Our chief constable is a little upset. He keeps getting these calls from frightened parents."

Macalvie leaned back in his chair, hands laced behind his head. He gave Neal his laser-look. "That's too bad. Give Dorset my blessing and ask your chief if he'll grant me another twenty-four hours."

Neal smiled and dumped the rest of his coffee in the sink. "I'll do it straightaway. In the meantime, I better go back and look for the Riley boy's killer. Don't you think?"

Solemnly, Macalvie nodded. "It'd be a great kindness to Dorset police."

Neal left, shaking his head.

Macalvie started talking as if it hadn't been Neal, but Neal's wraith that had just floated out the door, part of a spirit-world set to drive him mad, since the forces of the real world couldn't dent him.

"Take the name of the pub where this string of killings started, the Five Alls: the sign is usually divided so you see these five figures representing authority. 'I pray for all'—that'd be a priest or other symbol of the church; 'I plead for all'—barrister or solicitor; 'I fight for all'—military, right? 'I rule all'— a lot of positions fit that; and 'I take all.' Interesting, that figure. Sometimes the Five Alls sign says, 'I pay for all,' meaning king, queen, and country. Other times the fifth figure is John Bull, who 'pays for all.' But in our Dorchester Five Alls, the fifth figure is the Devil, who 'takes all.' Like lives. Now, we've got George-bloody-Thorne, solicitor; we've got Davey White's granddad, vicar—"

Wiggins interrupted. "But you're forgetting Simon Riley's father is only a butcher."

Macalvie smiled slightly. "True, but his wife's got some family connection with a Q.C. who's running for Parliament—'I rule for all,' in other words. That's two figures left: the soldier and the Devil. The Devil's the killer. So that leaves one more murder." He looked at Jury. "Your expression tells me you don't like my theory. Disaster." Macalvie held out his hand to Wiggins, who rolled a lozenge into it.

"I'm sure you noticed the portrait of Jessica Ashcroft's father."

"Of course. He was a Grenadier. Military." Macalvie opened the top drawer of a desk and took out a pint of whiskey and a smudged glass. "I'm going to quit this lousy job, I swear to God. Go to America. The booze is cheaper." He looked up at the ceiling as if the geography of the United States were etched there, uncapped the bottle, took a drink, and handed the glass to Wiggins.

"We might have come to the same conclusion by different routes," said Jury. "That is, if you're thinking of Jessica Ashcroft."

"Yeah. I'm also thinking of Sam Waterhouse. He sat in a cell for nearly nineteen years, knowing he was railroaded." Macalvie shook his head. "I still say he's not the type. He wasn't once and he *still* isn't. Are you reading your fortune in the bottom of that glass, Wiggins, or are you going to pass it along?"

"Waterhouse would be a dead cert, given *your* reasoning. Hatred of authority. And he got out just before these murders were committed."

Macalvie lapped his hands round the glass and studied the ceiling. "I still don't think it's Sam."

"What about Robert Ashcroft?"

Macalvie stopped looking at the ceiling and took his feet off his desk. "Meaning?"

"Four million pounds. And being gone just over the days of the murders. No one in the present Ashcroft household had ever seen him before he returned from Australia. I'm going up to London to talk to the Ashcroft solicitor. But even if Ashcroft *is* the real brother, there's still—"

Macalvie interrupted. "The Campbell Soup Kid's money. Right?"

Jury nodded.

"Then why the other killings? A blind?"

Jury nodded again.

Macalvie shook his head as if he were trying to clear it, poured some more whiskey in the glass and handed it to Jury. "What's his story about taking BritRail to London?"

"That he thought he'd be buying a Roller advertised in the *Times*."

"I'll have somebody checking the paper on that one, to see if there *was* a car. And check to see if Ashcroft really went to see it. But let's assume—just for the sake of the argument—"

"I'm not trying to argue, Macalvie." Jury handed the whiskey glass to Wiggins, knowing he wouldn't drink from the same ditch. "I just think Jessica Ashcroft's in trouble."

Macalvie went on as if Jury hadn't interrupted. "—that Ashcroft's guilty. Ask again—why didn't he drive up to London? He stayed at the Ritz. The doorman would have noticed any of those cars of Ashcroft coming in and out. He couldn't have used his own cars. They'd attract too much attention. It's got to be either train, bus, rented car. No, renting's too risky. Probably train. Early morning train from Exeter to London on the tenth, and he has a talk with the stationmaster to make sure he's remembered *leaving* the area. He checks into the Ritz. Train back to Dorchester—it's only a three-hour trip—six hours coming and going. Or he could even have got off in Dorchester, killed the Riley boy, then gone on to London. On the twelfth, to Waterloo Station, late night train to Exeter—no, not Exeter. The stationmaster might remember him. Axminster. What about Axminster?"

Wiggins shook his head. "Why would he go to all of that trouble? Going back and forth? If he wants to put us on the trail of a psychopath—?"

"Because he's got to be *out* of the area the killings are done in," said Macalvie.

"Then what does he do," said Jury, "after he gets off your Axminster train? He can't *walk* to Wynchcoombe. How does he get there? And how does he get to Lyme Regis?"

"Not the train, then. So he doesn't rent a car. He *buys* one in London. Something fast and pricey that's already M.O.T.'d. Buys it from one of the sleazy grafters all over London. They don't give a damn what name you tell them. That gives Ashcroft the thirteenth to do his interviewing of tutors and allows her to pack up and they go back to Ashcroft on the fifteenth." He looked at Jury. "So what do you think?"

"Do you care?"

"Not particularly. We'll circulate pictures round the used-car lots. Pictures. But I don't want to breathe on Ashcroft hard enough to make him suspicious." Jury's theory had now become his. "I can't send a police photographer."

"We've got a photographer," said Jury.

Macalvie frowned. "Like who?"

"Molly Singer."

Macalvie smiled. "You mean Mary Mulvanney." He sat back and put his feet on his desk.

"Okay, just for the sake of argument, I'll go along with you. Let's say she *is* Mary Mulvanney. Given Sam Waterhouse, given Angela Thorne's father, that certainly adds up to a lot of coincidences. Too many. There's a connection between the murders. The old one and these new ones. The same theory that applies to Waterhouse might apply to her. Revenge.

Though the killing of the Riley boy and Davey White isn't clear. Anyway, we get Molly into Ashcroft as a photographer for some classy magazine about cars or the country gentleman. We can certainly work up some bona fides."

Macalvie took his feet off the desk and frowned. "Jury, you're saying you want to put your chief suspect in the *same house* with Jessica Ashcroft?"

"Who says she's my 'chief suspect'? And what about Waterhouse? Anyway, Jessica's living there right now with another suspect. Her uncle. If Molly Singer were guilty, she'd hardly try anything in the house on a photography assignment."

"Mary Mulvanney." From his wallet, Macalvie drew a snapshot. It was a smiling trio of a woman, a little girl, and an older girl with pale skin and dark hair who was the smiling center of the three.

Jury shook his head. "I don't see any more resemblance to Molly Singer than to any dark-haired girl."

Macalvie returned the picture to his wallet.

That's what got Jury. He'd been carrying it around for twenty years. "You'll never get over that fifteen-year-old kid walking into your office and telling you the law's scum, police are scum, and especially *you're* scum. She really got to you, didn't she?"

Macalvie didn't answer for a moment "No, Jury. She really got to *you*. Let's go talk to her, if that's the only way to convince you who she is."

"A little browbeating?"

"Who, *me?*"

"Just let me handle the photography business, will you? After a chat with you she might not feel like cooperating with police."

II

Macalvie had made himself at home in the chair by the fire, having picked up the black cat and dumped it on the floor. The cat sat like lead at his feet, its tail twitching.

They had appeared unannounced, Macalvie overriding Jury's objections. It had taken enough persuasion on Jury's part to keep the chief superintendent from dragging Molly Singer into the Lyme Regis station.

"I don't know what you're talking about," said Molly, looking from Macalvie to Jury.

"The hell you don't," Macalvie said, working the old Macalvie magic. "Twenty years ago your mother, Rose, was murdered in a little place called Clerihew Marsh—"

"I've never heard of it," said Molly.

"In Dartmoor, maybe forty miles from here."

Her face was a mask, unreadable; her body rigid, untouchable. But the emotion she was holding back seemed forcibly to spread through the room. Jury felt simultaneously drawn to her and held off.

What interested him was that Macalvie seemed totally unaffected. It wasn't that he was an unfeeling man; he just didn't seem bothered by the electricity in the air.

"Would you like to see my birth certificate to prove who I am?"

"Love to." He popped a hard candy in his mouth and leaned toward her. "Papers don't mean sod-all. You could bring in the priest who officiated at your baptism and all the rest you've made your weekly confession to—you *are* a Catholic, I suppose—and it wouldn't matter. You're still Mary Mulvanney. What the hell are you doing in Lyme?"

"Must I get a solicitor?"

Macalvie smiled slightly. "Of course *Singer* could be your married name. Is it?"

"No."

"Why don't you finish telling us just what happened in Clerihew?"

The question surprised Jury. It clearly surprised Molly Singer. And as he asked the question, he had taken the snapshot from his wallet and handed it to her.

She wouldn't take it, so he dropped it in her lap.

"I don't know what you're talking about."

"You really overwork that line, you know?"

Molly looked at Jury almost hopefully, as if he might untangle the web Macalvie was weaving. Jury said nothing, even though, strictly speaking, he had precedence. This was Dorset, not Devon. But there was a chemistry in the room, a delicate balance that he might upset if he intervened.

"Sam Waterhouse is out—but I expect you read about that."

"I've never heard of him." Her voice was flat; her expression bland.

Macalvie had played two aces in a row right off the bottom of the deck—showing her that picture and then suddenly bringing up Sam Waterhouse. Macalvie, for all of his surprises, didn't use cheap ones. He grew serious. Unless that too was a trick. Maybe Macalvie's pack didn't have a bottom. "Let's go over that story of what happened on the Cobb again."

Molly Singer merely shook her head. Still she hadn't touched the picture. "Why? You wouldn't believe it."

He slid down in the chair, crossed one leg over the other, and said, "You'd be surprised." He sounded almost friendly.

She told him. It was the same story she'd told Jury. And she had no explanation. Impulse, she said. To Jury, her story had the form of a dream . . . this woman out on those rocks, finding a dead child, carrying back the dog . . .

He saw Macalvie look at him, reading the expression. His smile was taut and his message clear: *Minder.*

Molly was talking again: "It's the truth, what I told you. I know you don't have sympathy for what might loosely be called 'neurosis'—"

"Try me."

He sounded perfectly sincere. But what did that mean? "When you walked into the hotel dining room, you recognized me, didn't you?"

"I never saw you before that day," she said.

"Well, I sure as hell knew you: the kid who walked into my office twenty years ago and took the place to pieces. You've got to watch that temper, Mary—excuse me, *Molly*—or someday you'll wind up killing somebody."

She stared at him. "So now I'm the chief suspect." She looked down at the picture and shook her head. "It's a poor picture. How could anyone say this girl and I are the same person?"

"I'm not going by the picture and you damned well know it." He reached out his hand for the snapshot.

"What motive would I ever have for killing Angela Thorne?"

"I'm no psychiatrist—"

Bitterly, she said, "That's obvious."

"—but I imagine it'd be very hard to think of your baby sister writing on the wall in her mother's blood. Hard going to that nut-house and seeing her catatonic. And what you screamed at me twenty years ago was that no matter how long it took you'd get

178

your revenge—against police, judges, God—anything responsible for not finding the real killer. Sam Waterhouse was a friend of yours. And you wouldn't look kindly on anyone who helped put him away. George Thorne. The kid's father."

Her face was blank. "I don't know her father *or* what he does or did. You're just determined to make a case up out of whole cloth—"

"The cloth's already cut to fit you, Mary."

She glared at him.

"Circumstantial evidence alone—" said Macalvie.

"It would have been pretty stupid of me, then, to leave my cape and bring the dog back."

"True. I haven't worked that out yet." There seemed to be no doubt in his mind that he would. "Like I say, I'm no psychiatrist."

Molly Singer got up. "And I'm not Mary Mulvanney."

As Macalvie rose, the black cat's tail twitched again, the inverted triangles of its pupils glaring up at him as if to ask, *What fresh hell can this be?*

EIGHTEEN

I

"Eat your soldiers, Jess."

Robert Ashcroft spoke absently from behind his newspaper. At the breakfast table now sat three where two had been perfectly comfortable before.

"I don't like my toast cut in strips," said Jessie, fingering a page of one of the books she had brought to the table.

Uncle Rob looked up from his paper. "Since when?"

"I don't like my egg topped, either. I like to peel it." Casually, she turned a page of *Rebecca*.

Sara Millar, the third of their party, cocked her

head. She was sitting with her back to the window, and the morning light made her pale hair glow.

(*Bleached*, thought Jessie.)

"I'm sorry, Jessica. I guess I just assumed . . ." The quiet voice trailed off. The Selfless Sara had undertaken the job of fixing Jessie's breakfast, thereby relieving the underworked Mrs. Mulchop of yet another chore.

"You're still angry with me, aren't you?" Robert Ashcroft looked unhappy.

Jess was sorry for the hurt look on his face and pained because she was its cause. But this was going to be a battle of wits, make no mistake. Thus she must harden her heart. She simply shrugged her indifference.

Of course, that worried her uncle more. "You're acting awfully—"

Sara Millar interrupted, thereby cleverly deflecting the thrust of Robert's words. "What are you reading, Jessie?"

She was clearly determined to be nice as ninepence. "*Rebecca* and *Jane Eyre*." Jess looked Sara straight in the eye. Sara had nice eyes, widely spaced and the same bluish-gray of the suit she had worn yesterday. The eyes were set in just the face that Jessie would have expected: clear-skinned and, if not absolutely *pretty*, it was far from plain, framed as it was by that ash-blond hair. Round her hair was a dusty-rose band that matched her jumper. All of her

181

clothes (Jessie bet) would have that dusty, subdued look—colors muted, makeup understated, just that bare hint of lipstick. The metamorphosis would come later, after she got her claws into Uncle Robert. Then would come trailing the plumy gowns, waterfalls of jewels (Barbara Allan's emeralds, maybe?), the blond hair coiled but with little tendrils struggling free as Sultry Sara swept down Ashcroft's magnificent staircase.

But as for now, Sara Millar was perfectly content to let her beauty lie skin deep.

She had been talking about the books during Jess's ruminations over her transformation: ". . . two of my favorites," said the Selfless Sara.

Jess looked up from the book she was only pretending to read. Uncle Robert had once told her it was rude to read in others' company, but she had merely taken him to task about his morning paper. Jessie was not disposed to bring books to the table, anyway, before now.

"Two of my favorites." Sara would have said that if Jess had brought *Beano* and *Chips and Whizzer* along.

Sara quoted, " 'Last night I dreamed I was at Manderley again . . . ,' " and she had the nerve to look around the dining room as if Ashcroft might give Manderley a run for its money. "Isn't that a smashing line? I only wish I could write one a quarter as good."

Robert Ashcroft looked at her, seeming pleased. "Do you write, then?"

Sara Miller laughed. "Nothing you'd want to read, I'm sure."

Jessie glared. If she was dreaming of Manderley, why didn't she go back to it? She gave a little kick under the table.

Sara lurched slightly. "What's that?"

Uncle Rob pulled up the tablecloth. "What's Henry doing there? Get him out, Jess."

"It's all right," said Sara, recovering quickly from the paw that had hit her silk-stockinged leg. "I was just surprised. Hullo, Henry."

Jessie watched the traitor Henry burrowing out and accepting a head-rub, all uncaring of the knives grinding in his mistress's mind. "May I be excused?" she asked in a determinedly polite manner.

"To go where?" asked Uncle Rob. "You have to begin lessons."

A look passed between Sara and Uncle Rob. Jessie could barely control her rage. But the Mad Margaret had taught her a lot about control. *"No, no, no, my dahling, No! You don't scream the line out—'Not all the perfumes of Arabia can ever make this little hand clean.'"*

"I'm going to sit on the wall."

"The wall?" Sara looked puzzled.

"Around the *grounds*," Jess answered, in a tone that suggested Sara must be a bit dim if she didn't know grounds had walls. "I like to sit and look way

183

off at the prison. Where the ax-murderer escaped from."

"Jess, for the umpteenth time, no one *escaped*."

She shrugged as if that made no difference. "Anyway, what about the murders?" This question was directed to Sara Millar. Jess hoped it might take the place of Rochester's crazy wife.

"Jessie, you oughtn't to be afraid—" Jessie's look stopped Sara.

Afraid? Jess wasn't afraid of anything except her uncle's getting married. With her two books clutched to her chest—and wishing Mrs. Mulchop would wear black and give Sara Millar evil looks, just as Mrs. Danvers did the mouse that married de Winter, she started toward the door.

Victoria Gray was coming in, dressed for riding.

The good-mornings were spoken. Victoria was welcome to share the table, but she stood instead at the sideboard, helping herself to coffee from the silver pot. Since Sara had turned back to her own coffee, she didn't see that dagger-like look that Victoria Gray planted in her back. Jess glanced from the one woman to the other. Although Victoria was better-looking, she was old. At least, nearly as old as Uncle Rob. Selfless Sara was young and dewy, maybe just the age of de Winter's mousy wife.

"Well, I'm off," said Victoria. "Do you ride?" she asked Sara, without enthusiasm.

"A little," Sara said, smiling.

Like she wrote. Probably she was the Brontë sisters and Dick Francis all rolled into one.

II

Don't talk to strangers, Jess, Uncle Robert had cautioned her. As if whole platoons of strangers were walking by the wall trying to engage her in conversation.

She was sitting on the part of the wall that abutted onto one of the end posts that formed Ashcroft's entrance to its long, tree-lined driveway, like a double-barricade against the drive's low, stone wall. On the post was a simple bronze plaque, saying ASHCROFT. Jess often sat here, hoping she'd see something interesting on the road, but she never saw anything except the occasional car or a drover with a bunch of sheep.

It was too high for Henry to clamber up, and she wasn't going to help him because he was doing penance for that head-rub he'd allowed Sara to give him. Henry didn't seem aware he was doing penance; his position was, as usual, prone.

The full horror of her situation was beginning to wash over Jess. Sara Millar had been sitting at breakfast as if she belonged there just as much as the egg cups and the teapot and the toast. A familiar fixture. Yet, there had been no hint at all of her having "taken over." She was merely—at ease.

Jess hit at the stone with her spanner and crumbled a bit of it that drifted dust down onto Henry. He didn't care. No one . . . What was that?

Down the road to her right a car was coming, coming very slowly. Probably tourists limping along, taking their time. Then her eyes opened wide. *What* a car! It was long, elegant—a classic. And it seemed to be in some sort of trouble.

The automobile drew abreast of her and stopped. The driver rolled down the window. "I beg your pardon. You wouldn't know of a garage around here?"

Jessie hopped from the wall and strolled over to the white car with its glistening finish. A dozen coats of lacquer, she bet. Red leather interior. And the winged hood ornament of a Rolls-Royce. She sighed. "No, there's nothing for miles and miles. What do you want one for?"

He smiled. If he was the ax-murderer, he was certainly a good-looking one. Green eyes and sort of straw-colored hair. "Something's wrong. It keeps cutting off—" On cue, the chariot of fire cut off.

"Let's have a look under the bonnet."

He laughed. "I'm not much of a mechanic." He got out.

Jessie squinted up at him. Rich. Good-looking and rich. She took the spanner from her pocket. "I am." She gestured with the spanner, a plan forming in her mind. Where Jessica's thoughts darted, lightning often followed.

Removing his driving gloves, he looked hopefully toward the long tunnel of trees. "Perhaps up there, at the house—"

"Open the bonnet."

III

The moment he saw her sitting on the wall, Melrose Plant swore. If there was one thing he didn't need at this juncture, it was this child. He knew about her; he knew about each member of the household, since Jury had given him details over the telephone. He just hadn't expected her to turn up in dirty overalls with a spanner in her hand.

The plan to get the Silver Ghost just far enough up the drive looked about to be scotched by Jessica Ashcroft. It had been Melrose's intention to let the Rolls rest peacefully on the Ashcroft drive so that he could walk to the house and summon Robert Ashcroft to the rescue. That *was* the plan.

And now here was this ten- or eleven-year-old with black hair and bangs and big brown eyes, with a damned spanner in her hand and a threat in her voice. She stood there, solid as the wall, obviously not about to make a spritely run to summon her elders and betters. He'd have to humor her.

Bonnet up, the two of them peered inside. She did a little clinking about with the spanner and, for one ghastly moment, Melrose was afraid that here might

187

be some mechanical wizard, some garage-prodigy who'd *fix* the damned car. Ah, but she couldn't. Not unless she had a fan belt (which he had removed a quarter of a mile back) to a Rolls in her pocket.

"Look, I wish you wouldn't go banging that thing about. I mean, the old Roller can't take too much of a beating."

She got her head out from under the bonnet and heaved a sigh. "Probably the carburetor. Only, I can't see why—not on a Rolls-Royce."

"Nothing's perfect."

Her eyes widened. *"That* is." She pointed the spanner at the car.

"Do you think the people in that house up there would just let me pull into the driveway and use the telephone? I think I can get it started again."

Her smile absolutely transformed the sullen little face that had glared from the wall. "I'm *sure* they would. It's *our* house. And my uncle knows lots about cars. He has nine, but not a Rolls-Royce."

"Nine! Imagine that!"

"I don't have to," she said, squinting up at him as if he might be a bit dim. But the tune changed again after she'd run behind the wall and come back with the strangest-looking animal Melrose had ever seen— a dog, he supposed. Though he wouldn't swear to it. "Do you mind if Henry sits with me? You won't get anything dirty, will you, Henry?" she fluted to the odd assortment of laps of skin. It sat on the seat like a wrinkled stump.

She got in; Melrose got in and turned the key. "That's an incredible dog you've got. Isn't it a Shar-pei?"

"Oh, it's only a stray. It might be Chinese." She glanced at Melrose. "It's got green eyes."

The engine turned over and Melrose said, "I can't see its eyes."

She sighed. "No one can."

Melrose got the Silver Ghost partway up the drive before it stopped.

"Don't worry," said Jessica. "My uncle can fix it. Unless he has to send to Exeter for parts. Come on, Henry!" The dog clambered down. "If he does, it'll take a couple of days, I expect." The expectation made her smile.

The house was magnificent—Palladian, made of Portland stone. Must be spare rooms all over. "Look, now. I don't want to put your uncle to any trouble."

Her answer rang with sincerity. "You won't! Really! My name's Jessie Ashcroft. What's yours?" And then she was skipping backwards like any ordinary ten-year-old. Happy, carefree.

"My name's Plant. The family name, that is." This was the part Melrose abhorred.

She stopped dead. "You mean you've got a title?"

189

Jessica Ashcroft would know about titles, given that her father had had one.

"Well, yes. Yes, as a matter of fact. Earl of Caverness."

Her eyes widened. "My *father* was an earl." And then her glance was a little wary. "I guess because you're expected home you're going to have to ring up the countess?"

"No. There is no Countess of Caverness. I'm not married, you see."

She saw. Her smile beamed at him again. As they ascended the broad steps of Ashcroft, she told him about her uncle and Mrs. Mulchop and Victoria Gray and her new governess, Miss Millar.

And she continued to paint the canvas of Sara Millar in the most astonishing colors. She was beautiful, beneficent, agreeable . . .

Melrose noticed Henry was not with them.

"Oh, him?" Jessie said to his question. "He likes to sleep in cars; he's probably climbed back in. Never mind him." And she put the last dab of color to the portrait of Miss Millar by saying, "Honestly, she's almost saintly."

IV

"Wonderful," said Robert Ashcroft, his head half-buried under the bonnet of the Rolls-Royce. "Absolutely terrific. Just look at the way . . ."

Thus had Mr. Ashcroft gone on, while Melrose shifted from one foot to another, bored to tears with the lesson he was getting in auto-mechanics.

"It's only the fan belt. Can't imagine one simply slipping off. But we can get one from London."

Jessie beamed up at Melrose.

"So please," said Ashcroft, "be my guest, won't you?"

"Oh. But I couldn't *possibly* impose . . ."

No one seemed to notice Plant was a few steps ahead of them as they started toward the house again.

NINETEEN

I

Why Sara Millar had been presented by Jessica Ashcroft as the well-wrought urn round which played all the lively virtues, Melrose could not imagine.

Sara Millar was not overly smooth, often clever in her conversation, and very nearly pretty. She seemed to just miss being all or any of those things completely. She wasn't so much the urn, but a very mixed bouquet done up quickly for the occasion. Melrose thought she might be somewhat too much of a soft touch for the likes of Lady Jessica. But then he thought he detected in Miss Millar's velvet glove something of an iron hand. He doubted that Jessica would welcome anyone's telling her what to do.

Other, that is, than her uncle, whom she clearly adored. The feeling seemed to be mutual: Robert Ashcroft thought the world of his niece.

But, then, if one is sitting next to four million pounds, one might not find it difficult to give it a loving pat on the head. Cynical of him. Yet, he had been sent here to be cynical—or, at least, objective. Who was it in the household Jury suspected if not Ashcroft himself? It was too bad that the man was so likable. He was unpretentious and hospitable, not particularly impressed by Melrose's titles. Yet Jury told him to trot out the whole batch of them. Agatha was missing a rare treat in not hearing all of that Earl of Caverness; Viscount of Nitherwold, Ross and Cromarty; Baron Mountardry stuff dragged out.

The introductions were handed round in the drawing room during a pleasant hour set aside for cocktails. There was Victoria Gray, who did not fit at all the role of housekeeper-secretary. In her background were culture and breeding, more so than in Sara Millar's. Victoria Gray was also better-looking, although a trifle witchlike. She was dressed in black, with a long-sleeved jacket of some sequined material. Her hair was black, turned under slightly—perhaps it was all of this that gave Melrose his impression. Perhaps his mind was tired, what with the drive itself, the trumped-up mechanical trouble, and Dartmoor.

As they had walked up to the house earlier, even though scarcely noon, their feet were buried in mist, which rose until the trees were gloved in fog.

"I like your dress, Victoria," said Jessica, who was herself quite dressed up in a blue frock.

Victoria Gray looked at Jessica with a frown. (It seemed compliments from Jessica were rare enough to be suspect.) "You do? Thank you."

"It's beautiful. All spangly. It makes you look ever so much younger."

Robert Ashcroft looked at his niece sharply and then laughed it off. His instinct was probably right. Calling attention to Jessica's rudeness might only have made the matter worse, though Victoria seemed to take it in stride.

"That's why I wore it," she said. "Takes at least a hundred years off my age. What about you, Jessica? It's the first time I've seen you out of your mechanic's outfit in ages. And what have you done to Henry? It looks like a ribbon in his collar."

Since it was difficult to see Henry's collar, buried as it was in his furled skin, the bow peeked out as a tiny ruff of green.

"I dressed him up for company. It matches his eyes."

Ashcroft was surprised. "Henry's eyes? Didn't know he had any."

"You *know* he has green eyes," Jess said, looking innocently into their guest's own.

194

*   *   *

However unprepared Mulchop was to be butler, Mrs. Mulchop certainly wasn't to be cook. Smoked salmon, double consommé and roast duckling with a mararet stuffing unlike anything Melrose had tasted before. He would like to have the recipe to give to his own cook, he said.

It was Sara Millar who told him: "Herbs and such, and mushrooms, anchovies and poached sweetbreads. Delicious, isn't it?"

Jessie, who had just taken a bite of this delicacy, stared at her plate. "Yuck! Why didn't somebody *tell* me?" She pushed the offending stuffing onto her small bread and butter dish and set it on the floor. "There, Henry," she said sweetly.

"No feeding Henry *at the table*, Jess," said Ashcroft.

Melrose had until then been unaware that Henry made one of their party. It also surprised him that, rather than Jessica's insisting she sit next to the fascinating stranger, she had allowed Sara that honor.

"You must forgive Jessie," said Victoria.

No one looked in less need of forgiveness.

"Poor Henry." Jessie sighed, as if the world were against him, and reached down to pat him in a lightning gesture that rid her plate of a particularly uninteresting turnip that had been lolling there. Then she set about eagerly eating her potatoes and making conversation before someone noticed the gap. "Lord Ardry . . ."

"Lady Jessica?"

"Oh, don't call me *that!*"

"All right, if you don't call me 'lord.' The family name is Plant. It's really horribly complicated, isn't it?"

"Yes. My father's name was Ashcroft. But he was also the Earl of Clerlew."

Ashcroft said, "You mean Curlew. Eat your dinner, Jess." Robert Ashcroft seemed disturbed by all of this talk of lineage.

"I can't eat, not after you told me about the *brains*." She readdressed herself to Melrose. "My mother's name was Barbara Allan." Pointing her fork at the wall opposite, she said, "That's her portrait. Wasn't she beautiful?"

The picture hung behind Robert Ashcroft, who, Melrose saw, had put down his fork. He also seemed to have lost his appetite.

The Countess of Ashcroft was indeed beautiful— slender, tall, dark and wearing a smile that implied having one's picture painted was silly.

"She was also very nice," said Victoria Gray. "So was James, her husband."

Undercurrents, thought Melrose. Or an actual undertow.

Jessica, however, was not going to let her mother's reputation hang by this slender thread of "goodness." "She had a very tragic life—"

Her uncle said, "Leave it alone, Jessie. *Mulchop*— stop lolling there and bring us some more wine!"

Melrose suspected that Ashcroft merely wanted to get their attention away from the Countess of Ashcroft.

It was no deterrent to Jessica. "Grandmother Ashcroft was mad because my mother was only a commoner and her family was in trade. My father always thought that was a good joke. 'In trade.' You can make a lot of money 'in trade,' he kept saying. Like being shopkeepers, if you have a lot of shops."

Robert interrupted. "I don't think our guest is interested in the family tree, Jess."

But Jessica continued to wash the dirty linen. "There was one of them that ran a pub. . . ." As she continued the Barbara Allan saga, it was clear that not only did the Allans have the money, but that hearts had shattered to smithereens wherever the woman walked.

Victoria told her to stop exaggerating and stubbed out her cigarette violently.

"I'm *not!* It's just like the song—isn't it, Uncle Rob. You told me."

Ashcroft smiled and clipped the end of a cigar. "I'm not sure who told who at this point. There seem to be a few frills and furbelows that I don't remember."

In her gossipy way, Jessica went on: "She was lots younger than my father. . . . Though there's nothing wrong with that. I think it's all awfully romantic. But Gran thought it was just to get the title and was furious about it—"

Sara Millar broke in: "I don't think all of this

should be trotted out in front of, well, *two* relative strangers, Jessica." Her voice was soft and pleasant.

Melrose wanted to laugh. In Jessica Ashcroft he had an unexpected ally. She would make sure he stayed and *stayed*, as long as he took Miss Millar when he left. Romantic things like that happened in Jessica's mind, he was sure. In this case, the romance would also be most fortuitous.

The subject of the recent murders came up—was brought up by Jessica, that is—when they were seated in the drawing room with coffee and cigars and cigarettes.

Robert Ashcroft and Sara Millar were seated side by side on the small sofa. Melrose regarded it as a marvel of logistics, the way Jessica worked herself round to sit between them. She was merely leaning against the arm of the sofa when she said, "The vicar's son. It was really grisly—"

While Jessica enjoyed the grisliness, Melrose studied the portrait of James Ashcroft, which hung above the marble fireplace. He only half-heard the conversation while he thought about James Ashcroft. Clerihew. Curlew. An easy enough error to make . . .

When Melrose turned his attention back to the conversation, he heard Jessica talking about the boy in Dorchester—

Magically, she was now sitting between the two grownups.

198

"Bed, Jessie," said Ashcroft.

"Very well." She sighed. "I only wish I could go for a ride tomorrow."

"That," said Victoria, "is one of the few positive things I think I've heard from you. It's about time I put you up on that horse—"

"*Horse?* Who said *horse?* I mean a motorcar. Sara and Mr. Plant haven't had any rides at all in your cars. Couldn't Mr. Plant drive your Aston?" She looked at Melrose. "It goes from zero to sixty in five-point-two seconds."

"It might, but I doubt *I* could go from zero to one in under an hour. Must be the Dartmoor air." He yawned.

"*You* want to ride around Dartmoor, Jess?" Ashcroft said. "You're always telling me how boring it is."

"That's only because we *live* here. It's always boring where you live. But they'd like it—" She looked from Sara to Melrose. "Just as long as we stay away from Wistman's Wood and the Hairy Hands. *Come on*, Henry."

And she and the dog walked slowly off to bed.

II

Victoria Gray was arranging flowers in a shallow cut-glass bowl for the circular table when Melrose came down for breakfast. She was dressed in riding togs.

"Good morning, Lord Ardry." She cut the stem of

one last chrysanthemum, stuck it in the center of her arrangement, and stepped back to look at it with a critical eye much like a painter evaluating his canvas. "Will it do?"

Melrose smiled. "Very nicely, I'd say. Am I the last one down?"

"Except for Jessie. She said she had a sickheadache, and asked to be excused from your excursion into the wilds of Dartmoor."

"I see. But she was to be our tour-guide."

Victoria smiled. "She told me to give you this map. As far as I can see, it's to be a grim tour. Wynchcoombe, Clerihew Marsh, Princetown. I'll have coffee with you, if you don't mind. All the food's still warm, though Mulchop did his best to wrestle it off the sideboard."

"Mind? Indeed not. One gets tired of breakfasting by oneself." Just as one, thought Melrose, gets tired of talking like a peer of the realm. Melrose was having difficulty with his earldom, a difficulty he had never had before he gave up his title. He was perfectly happy talking like a commoner *then*. He felt like someone Jury had dragged out of a ditch, dusted off, and said, "Okay. You'll do."

On the sideboard was a lavish display, all kept cozily warm in their silver dishes. He spooned up some kidney, took a portion of buttered eggs, layered on a couple of rashers of bacon, and helped himself to toast and butter. Then he frowned at his plate and wondered if a peer would gorge himself in this fashion.

Victoria Gray helped herself to toast and coffee. When she had settled at the table across from him, Melrose said, "If you don't mind my saying it—you don't fit the stereotype of 'housekeeper.' "

She laughed. "If you mean changing the linen and towels and wearing keys at my waist—no, I don't. This position is a sinecure. I do take care of the horses pretty much—Billy's a bit lazy—type the odd letter or two for Robert, and arrange flowers." She smiled. "Barbara—Lady Ashcroft—and I were first cousins, though she was born in Waterford. County Waterford. A typical Irish colleen, she was. We were also very good friends. Barbara made an excellent marriage—well, she deserved it, didn't she . . . ?"

She seemed to be talking to herself. Or in the manner of one who is addressing an intimate acquaintance.

"The late Lady Ashcroft was Irish? You mean her daughter's tale of gloom and doom is true?"

"Of course not. Barbara didn't leave a trail of fallen hearts behind her like petals in the dust." She paused. "At least not knowingly."

He wondered what she meant by that. Barbara Ashcroft's face looked down at him from the far wall. The smile was inscrutable, a Mona Lisa smile. "If that portrait doesn't flatter her—"

"Flatter—?" Victoria Gray turned to look. "Oh, not

at all. If anything it diminishes her beauty. Jessica will be that beautiful too, one day. You can see it when she isn't dressed in that oily overall she loves to wear and carrying tools around."

"She's quite the mechanic."

"Jessie? She doesn't know a battery from a silencer. I'll bet she told you it was your carburetor."

"Right."

"Her favorite word."

Melrose laughed. "Well, she needs some sort of occupational therapy, wouldn't you say?"

"Believe me, she's got an occupation—though I don't know how therapeutic it is. Keeping her beloved uncle from marrying." She picked up a piece of toast and munched it; then she said, "It's fortunate for Jess that Dartmoor isn't peopled with eligible women."

Seeing the faraway look on her face, Melrose wondered if the fortune weren't divided.

"Why do you think she's been through such a string of governesses?"

"Didn't know she had been." He accepted another cup of coffee from Victoria's hand. "Tell me: why did the Ashcrofts not make the obvious choice and have *you* take care of Jessica? You say your job is a sinecure: seems to me it'd simplify things all around."

Victoria laughed. "Precisely because I *would* take care of her. Did you ever see a child so indulged? I wondered when Robert would get wise and choose a tutor himself, like Sarah Millar."

But she did not look at all as if she felt the choice had been wise. She looked, indeed, inexpressibly sad. Melrose could read it in her face: if only Robert Ashcroft's feeling were as certain as this sinecure of a post she held.

III

He had asked Victoria if there was some writing-paper about, and was now sitting in the drawing room, looking up again at the portrait of the rather formidable Earl of Curlew. He then wrote no more than a couple of sentences on the rich, cream-laid Ashcroft stationery, took another sheet, and wrote the same sentences. Then, he addressed both to Jury—one to his flat in Islington; the other to him at the Devon-Cornwall headquarters. If he posted them today, Jury would be bound to get one tomorrow, whether in London or Devon.

Melrose stood beneath the portrait, holding out a finger length-wise, and squinted, in this way ridding James Ashcroft of his full mustache. There was a strong resemblance between the brothers. As Curlew resembled Clerihew.

TWENTY

I

At least, thank God, it was a closed car. The mist looked as if it meant to hang about all morning, making distances deceptive, bringing the giant tors closer than they actually were. The moorland ponies were huddled against the leeward wall with that instinct they had for an approaching storm.

And, thank God, she was not one to feel sorry for herself. It was only owing to Melrose's judicious questioning that Sara was telling him the story of her life, a life she had herself described as placid, at best; at worst, dull. To Melrose, however, it sounded like neither—more a Dickensian tale of abandonment and woe. There was the boardinghouse through whose portal she had been shepherded by the aunt into whose care she had been given when Sara's mother died. It was run by an iniquitous woman, Mrs. Strange, the embodiment of her name, said Sara.

"Fiery red hair she had that looked like a tent right after she'd washed it. I suppose, though, I ought to be grateful to her. Since she was lazy and I was older than the others, and hadn't much to say in the matter, the care of them often fell to me. So did my own education. I had to read a lot, as she kept me out of school. To take care of the children."

"Good Lord, why should you feel 'grateful'? You might have gone on to do something more suited to your intelligence than acting as overseer to other people's children."

"Thanks. I had only the one good reference, really. But as it came from a countess, Mr. Ashcroft seemed suitably impressed. I'm fond of children."

"I'm fond of ducks. It doesn't mean I want them running round under my feet all day."

Sara laughed. "With Jessica, it's not being underfoot that I'm in danger of; it's more in being undermined. She doesn't care for me too much."

"On the contrary," said Melrose, slowing to peer through the fog at a signpost, "as we were walking up to the house, she was singing your praises."

"That in itself's suspect, since I'd only just arrived the day before. I wonder how long I'll last? Mr. Ashcroft said his niece was running through tutors at the speed of, well, this car. There were three of us to be interviewed in London. I suppose he winnowed out the rest by mail. Given the salary he offered, he must have been deluged. It's a post anyone would give her eyeteeth for." She paused for a moment, and then went on. "It's rather odd, though . . ."

"Odd, how?"

"To do the interviews that way. It was rather like being cast for a role." She paused. "I only wish I knew the script." She sounded uneasy about her new post.

"Ashcroft strikes me as an amiable, informal chap. Unlikely he's reading from a script."

" 'Amiable'? He certainly is. And goes to no end of trouble for Jessica. I only meant I wonder why he held those interviews in London rather than at Ashcroft?"

"Perhaps because the Lady Jessica wasn't having too much luck herself in choosing the proper person." He slowed the car again to look at another signpost, trying to bury his question—"When was this unnerving interview? Sounds a bit Jamesian to me. Think I'll turn here"—in a comment about their direction.

"What do you mean by Jamesian?"

"The Turn of the Screw. The governess goes up to London and finds a handsome, prospective—" Melrose didn't go on. Probably, he was embarrassing her.

206

"When was the interview? Just a few days ago. The thirteenth. Why?"

"No reason. Will this mist never rise?"

As Melrose negotiated a sharp turn on the narrow road, she said, "Isn't this signposted for Wynchcoombe? And isn't that where the little boy was murdered?"

"Don't you want to go there?"

"Frankly, no." She shivered.

"Oh, come on. Be a sport. Can't we be just a couple of bloodthirsty thrill-seekers?"

Sara laughed. "Do you hang around accident sites?"

"Of course."

II

The vestry of Wynchcoombe Church was still sealed off. A constable stood on the walk outside as stiffly relentless as a horseguard at Buckingham Palace. The rest of the church, though, was open to worshippers and visitors.

"I don't know that I want to go in," said Sara, "now we're here."

"Superstitious?"

"No, afraid," she said quite simply.

Melrose would have made a burnt offering of his Silver Ghost to have a look in the choir vestry, but the presence of another policeman told him there'd be no joy there. The constable, however, seemed to be finding a bit of joy from a *Playboy* magazine, turning it sideways and upside down to get the full effect of a centerfold who must have managed an extremely acrobatic position for the photographer.

Nothing ventured, nothing gained, thought Melrose. At least this policeman looked a bit more human, lacking in the granite calm of the constable outside.

Thus, while Sara walked down the nave, Melrose moved to the vestry door, taking out his visiting-card case. He handed the P.C. his card. "Don't suppose there's a chance of getting in there . . . ?"

"About as much as getting into Buckingham Palace," said the P.C., pleased he had precedence over a peer.

Melrose went to join Sara Millar. She was studying a small picture of the sacrifice of Isaac.

"The God of the Old Testament didn't pull his punches, did he?" said Melrose. "Job, Abraham, voices from whirlwinds." He saw her fingering the silver cross she seemed always to wear. Filtered light from the stained-glass windows made a colored tracery over her pale rose jumper and paler skin. She looked delicate, almost otherworldly, and innocent, as if her youth were still unspent. So engrossed was she with the painting, he thought she hadn't heard him. But she answered, "It's beyond belief. I mean, outside conventional belief. It doesn't count for anything, I think."

Melrose was somewhat astonished at this interpretation of a father's being asked to murder his innocent son. " 'Doesn't count' . . . ? I'm sure Isaac would have felt you to be cold comfort." His smile, when she turned on him, was a little fixed.

She had looked angry; now she looked sad. A woman much like the Dartmoor weather, he thought. Forever changing. Interesting, though.

"I only meant," she said, "that the whole notion of God and Abraham must transcend human understanding."

As they walked over to the other wall, Melrose said, "Then what's the point? What's the point of a moral lesson that requires transcendent vision?" She was reading an account in a glassed-over case about the Devil honoring the church with a visit. "It seems someone who owed him his soul fell asleep in church and Satan simply took the roof off and collected him." Sara shook her head. Melrose was wondering if the vicar would ever appear, or whether this was simply not his day. He looked at his watch. Eleven. The pubs would be open. He was afraid if he didn't divert this discussion, she'd have them stopping here all day talking transcendentalism. "The only way I can justify God's way to man is by malt, as Houseman said."

She smiled slightly. "I take it you noticed the George."

Sara was, in spite of her transcendent streak, quick enough and a good sport. He looked around as the heavy door to the church opened and shut behind an elderly man, who then made his way down the aisle with a proprietary air. Melrose wondered if this might be the Reverend White. Certainly, the man paid no attention at all to the Devon-Cornwall constabulary, so Melrose assumed he was not just another pilgrim. This was borne out by the Devon-Cornwall constabulary's quickly closing his magazine and shoving it under the cushion of his chair.

Melrose told Sara he'd be back in a moment and walked down the aisle in the wake of this white-haired man, making up his excuse as he went.

"Terribly sorry to intrude upon your grief." This comfortless cliché embarrassed Melrose. "You *are* Mr. White?"

The vicar said he was, and appeared to be less grief-stricken than a grandfather might have been. Less than Abraham, certainly, and Abraham was only following orders. The vicar's eyes were stony-cold.

"What was it you wanted?"

Melrose removed a card from the gold case that had been his mother's (before Agatha had appropriated it); the cards had been his father's, the seventh Earl of Caverness, and Melrose, the eighth, simply thought what was one earl, more or less?

The vicar read it and handed it back. There was something about one's own card being given back to one that was extremely discouraging.

"Sorry, but should I know you? You're not local. I'm not aware of the family."

Melrose almost wished Agatha had been there to hear *that* judgment passed. He felt a lack of locality stamped on his face, much like the coat-of-arms stamped on the card. "No. My home is in Northamptonshire. The account of your grandson's death in the paper gave the mother's name as Mary O'Brian." Melrose looked up at the intricately painted ceiling-bosses, each one of them apparently different, and wondered what sum of money would entice the vicar to look at life in a more worldly fashion. "You see, years ago we had a Mary O'Brian employed at our home—Ardry End—as upstairs maid."

"Yes? But it's a common name."

Melrose realized he had stirred something in the vicar's breast, for the man's face colored somewhat and he added, "But, then, Mary was a common woman."

Even Melrose, no stickler for men of the cloth being more than human, was a little surprised by this. Apparently the Reverend Mr. White was not

211

worried about the roof caving in. "It's been some years since she was there. I've had a bit of a time tracking her down—"

"That doesn't surprise me—given Mary."

Melrose would have been happy to wander through the dark wood of the vicar's feelings about his daughter-in-law had the vicar shown any sign of wanting to lead him. But the remark simply fell and lay there like a tree across their path. Mr. White reminded Melrose of someone he couldn't quite place.

"This has to do with a small bequest in my father's will."

"Oh?"

"My father found her to be an especially dependable servant; she went to a great deal of trouble nursing my mother through a long illness—"

"Mary? It's the last thing I'd have expected. At any rate, Mary's dead. Didn't the account mention that?"

Melrose, having seen no obituary, could only say: "Yes, it did." He thought perhaps he shouldn't elaborate on what the "account" *did* tell the world.

"Both of them died in a motorcycle accident. Mary liked fast living. David was in divinity school before he met her. He would perhaps have followed in my footsteps. Then he met Mary." The vicar closed his eyes as if he were hearing the painful news for the first time. "Whatever gift your father wished to bestow upon her . . ." He shrugged.

They had been standing all this time in the aisle.

Melrose wished they could sit down, but a church pew seemed an unlikely place for such a conversation.

"Perhaps then you would accept it for the church? In memory of your grandson?"

"David?" One would think he had to be reacquainted with the name.

"I realize five hundred pounds is not all that much—"

The Reverend White looked Melrose up and down. Melrose felt conscious of the suit from his bespoke tailor, the handmade shoes, the silk shirt, the handsome overcoat.

"Well, Lord Ardry, if you consider five hundred pounds meager, you must be wealthy indeed." He managed to make inherited wealth sound like plunder.

"I am," said Melrose simply. "I'll see the bequest is sent to the church, if that's suitable."

"Thank you."

With what struck Melrose as a rather summary dismissal in the circumstances, Mr. White started to turn and leave. "Just one more thing, Mr. White. I was wondering about the Ashcroft family."

With five hundred pounds in the balance, the vicar must have felt something was due this Nosey Parker of an earl. "Wondering what?"

"Well, I've rather made a hobby of heraldry and that sort of thing. How long have the Ashcrofts been feudal overlords of Wynchcoombe and Clerihew Marsh?" The question, of course, would annoy the vicar.

"Feudalism is dead, Lord Ardry. At least the last I heard—"

Melrose smiled fatuously. "Dying, perhaps. But I sometimes wonder if the liberties the feudal barons took were not still being taken . . . ?"

"Sir, I have a very busy schedule."

He seemed willing to look a five-hundred-pound gift-horse in the mouth after all. "I'm sorry. It's just that the Ashcroft family appears to be much the most important family about. James Ashcroft was the Earl of Curlew, wasn't he?"

The vicar frowned. "Yes."

"I just wondered if perhaps 'Curlew' weren't some deviant spelling of 'Clerihew.' Or it would have been the other way round, I mean? 'Clerihew Marsh' ought really to be 'Curlew Marsh.' The curlew being a bird and the crest on the Ashcroft coat-of-arms."

"That is correct." Again he turned to go.

"And your first name, vicar. 'Linley.' James Ashcroft was the Viscount Linley and one of his other names was 'Whyte.' Spelled differently, of course."

"If you're wondering whether I'm a relation of the Ashcrofts, yes, I am. But certainly a very distant one. His bequest to the church was even more surprising than yours. But he was generous, I'll say that for him."

Melrose wondered what the vicar *wouldn't* say for James Ashcroft.

The vicar continued: "I was certainly surprised at his leaving fifty thousand pounds."

So was Melrose.

Sara had been patiently hovering in the shadows all of this time, reading the account of the storm that described a visit from the Devil knocking the spire off the church.

"Sorry," said Melrose.

"Oh, that's all right. Was that the vicar?"

"Yes. I'm thirsty. How about you?"

"I could do with a cup of tea. But I expect you prefer the pub?"

She was certainly agreeable. And attractive. And— well, quite the sort of young woman that a de Winter or a Rochester *might* marry.

No wonder Lady Jessica was trying to hand her over to Melrose.

After they left the church, they stood looking for some moments at the moss- and lichen-veiled headstones.

"Now I remember who the Reverend Mr. White reminds me of. Hester's Chillingworth."

Sara was puzzled. "Chillingworth?"

"You know. *The Scarlet Letter*. I wonder if he looked upon Davey as a benighted little Pearl."

"Whatever were you talking about all that time? You hadn't heard of him before, had you?"

Melrose paused to consider the question and decided two lies were no worse than one. "No. You don't see a post office about, do you? I need to post these letters."

They walked off in search of one. Melrose took the quiet walk as an opportunity to reflect.

TWENTY-ONE

I

The cat Cyril sat on Fiona Clingmore's typewriter watching the noonday ritual of the rejuvenation of Fiona's face. Powder, mascara, lip rouge, eyeliner. When Jury walked in, Cyril appeared to have entered into some symbiotic relation with Fiona, in his stately posture on the typewriter, drawing his paw across his face, the student testing the lesson of the master.

There had been a great deal of speculation about the cat's appearance in the halls of New Scotland Yard. It was generally thought that Cyril had discovered the tunnel originally meant for theatergoers to a theater that never materialized and where the headquarters of the Metropolitan Police now sat, owing to some misadventure over cash flow or architectural fault or need. In any event, the cat Cyril had been seen prowling the halls as if his antennae were searching out (like some medium's familiar) the office of Chief Superintendent Racer. With Racer, Cyril enjoyed a slightly different symbiotic relation from the one with Fiona; and in Racer's case, it was doubtful that the relation was of benefit to both. But it certainly seemed to go down a treat with Cyril, who could outwit and outmaneuver Chief Superintendent Racer any day.

It was testimony to Cyril's staying power that he had been hanging around Racer's office for upwards of a year (maybe even two), which was more than could be said of any member of the Met—uniformed, CID, or civilian. Except for Superintendent Jury, whose staying power (and, Jury suspected, slight masochistic streak) matched Cyril's. Fiona, of course, was made of such steely stuff she could have walked under falling ladders or falling bombs and still remained upright. Only such a woman could have stood it as Racer's secretary. She was constantly being told to get the mangy rat-catcher *out* from under Racer's eyes and feet or he'd fire her and kill Cyril. Fiona paid far more attention to refurbishing her eye makeup than she did to the exhortations of her boss. Racer himself had often tossed Cyril out in the hall. But Cyril always returned, like Melville's Bartleby, to sit on a convenient sill and stare from a window at the blind brick wall of another part of the Yard.

Thus both Fiona and Cyril were engaged in their pre-lunch ablutions when Jury walked into Racer's outer office. "Hullo, Fiona. Hullo, Cyril," said Jury.

Fiona returned the greeting while running her little finger around the corners of her mouth; Cyril's tail twitched. He always appeared happy to see Jury, perhaps out of admiration for a soul-brother, one who could stick it.

"You're early, for once," said Fiona, snapping her mirrored compact shut with a little click. Jury often wondered where she came by these pre-Second World War memorabilia: he hadn't seen a woman with one of those Art Deco compacts since he was a kid. Fiona herself was like an artifact: she had been and still was, in her way, pretty. Pretty like the old photos of movie starlets with cupid-bow mouths and upswept blond hairdos used to be. Jury suspected that Fiona's own yellow curls came from the bottle, neat. That there were some silver threads amongst the gold Fiona had attributed to a good job of frosting at her salon. "He's still at his club," she added.

Jury yawned and scrunched down in his chair. "White's? Boodles? The Turf?"

Fiona laughed and rested her newly primed face on her overlapped hands. "You think one of them would let him in?" She checked a gold circlet of a watch—also from prehistoric digs—and said, "Been gone two hours, so he ought to be popping in any minute."

"Thanks, I'll wait in his office—give him a fright, maybe." He winked at Fiona, who then asked him if he'd eaten yet. It was as much a ritual when Jury was there as the revamping of her face. Jury made his excuses. A policeman's life is full of grief, he told her. It was Racer's cautionary phrase that covered everything from being first on the rota to finding a mass-murderer in your closet.

He noticed as he stood up she was taking out her bottle of nail varnish—a Dracula-like deep purple, almost black. Fiona favored black. All of her outfits— sheer summer frocks, winter wools—were black. Maybe she wanted to be sure she was ready for Racer's funeral.

The cat Cyril, seeing his chance, followed Jury into Racer's *sanctum sanctorum* and plumped himself in the chief's swivel chair. Jury sat in the chair directly across from Cyril and the broad expanse of Racer's empty desk. If there was one thing the chief superintendent believed in, it was delegating authority. Seldom did Jury see folders, notepads, papers—the usual junk—defiling his chief's desk. Jury looked at Cyril, whose head alone could be seen over the top of the desk, and said, "What was it, sir, you wished to see me about? Oh? Yes . . . well, sorry. A policeman's life—"

He hadn't got the end of the old Racer shibboleth

out before his chief's spongy step came up behind him. "Talking to yourself again, Jury?" Racer hung his Savile Row overcoat on a coatrack and walked around to his swivel chair. Cyril had slipped like syrup from Racer's chair and was now under the desk to study (Jury was sure) the best avenue of attack.

Racer went on: "Well, it certainly can't be from over*work*, lad. Obviously, you haven't been doing much on the Dorchester case or you'd have *reported in*, now wouldn't you? Not to say anything of the two others murdered! I do not like the Commissioner breathing down my neck, Jury. So what have you got to report. Meaning: what progress have you made?"

Jury told him as much as he felt was necessary for Racer to get the Commissioner off his back. It was, as always, too little for Racer. He would only have been satisfied with Jury's actually producing the murderer right there, in his office.

"That's *all*, Jury?"

"Afraid so."

"As far as I'm concerned—what the hell's *that?*" Racer was looking under his desk. He punched the intercom and demanded Fiona's presence to get the beast out from under his desk. "This ball of mange has used up eight of its nine lives, Miss Clingmore! Swear to God," he muttered, leveling a glance at Jury that suggested Jury might have used up nine-out-of-nine.

Fiona swayed into the office and collected Cyril. Fiona was certainly in no danger of using up *her* lives. The black-patent-leather belt she wore to nip in her waist sent the flesh undulating up and undulating down. Racer's eyes always seemed undecided on which direction to take.

"So go on," said Racer, when Fiona had left.

"Nothing much to be going on with. Sir." Jury always hesitated a little before the sir.

And Racer always noticed it. Thus Jury was in for the "ever-since-you-made-superintendent" lecture, one that Racer must have practiced in his sleep, so refined had it become, so ornamental—like intaglio figurines around a priceless vase. There was always something new to comment on, regarding the skill of the artisan.

Jury yawned.

"Where the hell's Wiggins? What's he been up to, except contaminating the Dorset police?"

Jury made no comment other than to say Sergeant Wiggins was in Devon.

"You do realize, don't you, how this psycho has hit the press? Three kids dead, Jury, *three.*" He held up his fingers in case Jury didn't understand the word itself. "And you can't nail one of these suspects?"

"Not on the evidence we have now, no. I want to see the Ashcroft solicitor."

"Then get the hell out and go and see him. I've got

enough work to do as it is." The pristine condition of his desk did not attest to this.

II

"Robert Ashcroft? But I've known him as long as I've known—knew—his brother James." He got up from his chair to pace several yards of cushioned carpet.

Mr. Mack, Jury decided, was solicitor to more than one moneyed family, given his surroundings: thick carpet, good prints on the walls, mahogany furniture, including the desk that shimmered like a small dark lake beneath its coats of beeswax. Its principal ornament was an elegant bronze cat, probably some pricey Egyptian artifact.

What interested Jury was that Mack did not simply reject the idea of imposture out of hand. Perhaps he was simply a very cautious fellow who would see all of the facets of an argument, no matter how prismatic.

His pacing was interrupted by the entrance of his secretary bearing a number of documents. His glance strayed up to Jury occasionally, as if he were turning the idea over as he turned the pages before him, signing each with a flourish.

The young lady who was Mack's secretary was the antithesis of Fiona Clingmore. One could tell her dress was expensive, not by its showiness but by the cut of the cloth. She was herself—hair, skin, nails—as polished as the desk itself.

But she lacked that certain something—that nice seamy presence which was the Fiona *brio*. Indeed, Jury wondered, as he watched the solicitor signing papers, if, in his realm of Ideas, Plato wouldn't have plumped for Racer, Fiona and Cyril, instead of Mack, Miss Chivers and the bronze cat.

Mr. Mack recapped his pen and Miss Chivers gathered up the papers and slid softly out, hazarding another look at Jury as she left. He smiled. She blushed.

Mack returned to the question of the Ashcroft identity. "No, it's improbable, Mr. Jury, that this Robert Ashcroft is not the real one. As you say, there was no one in the household who had known him, and the relations were all distant ones—but, no. When the will was probated, we certainly asked for Robert's bona fides—indeed, we did that of everyone. Victoria Gray, for example."

"I wasn't aware she came into a part of the Ashcroft fortune."

"She certainly did. Not much as an outright legacy, but a very substantial legatee were something to happen to Jessica. Very substantial. And insofar as Robert himself is concerned, I'm quite satisfied." He had resumed his seat and rested his chin on the tips of his fingers, prayerfully.

"What about other bequests? Any other substantial ones?"

"Yes. There was one to a church. And also to his wife's former nurse, Elizabeth. She was a cousin of Lady Ashcroft's." He ran a finger over the bronze cat. "Not a very pleasant person, as I recall." A heave of shoulders here. After all, solicitors can't be choosers. "But the thing is, you see, none of these were outright bequests. I didn't care for it, but there it was. All of the money went to Jessica."

"You mean, that as long as Jessica Ashcroft is alive, no one gets anything?"

Mr. Mack shook his head. "James Ashcroft wanted everything to go to Jessie. She can, of course, when she comes of age, honor those bequests immediately. Until that time, Robert is executor of the will and receives a fair allowance—"

"What's 'fair'?"

"I believe in the neighborhood of five thousand pounds a year."

Jury shook his head. "That'd be a slum for Ashcroft. It certainly wouldn't do much by way of supporting his habit. No, no, Mr. Mack—" The solicitor's eyes had widened. "—not drugs. Motorcars. Vintage, classic, antique."

"Ah, yes. Well, Robert has access to Jessica's money, you see. All he need do is apply to me. If I think the expense suitable, I let him have it. You're quite right, those cars of his are pricey. But a drop in the bucket when we're talking millions of pounds. James and Robert were extremely close. Even when Robert went to Australia, they wrote to one another regularly. Those letters, you see, were paramount in establishing authenticity. Why are you suspicious of Robert Ashcroft, anyway?"

"No reason, except for the convenient arrangement of the household. Even the relations who came to the funeral hadn't seen him in a long time, if at all."

"Yes, that's true. When that much money and property's at stake, odd lots of relations come crawling out of the woodwork, some of them hoping to break a will unfair to them. Claiming what they consider their 'fair share,' or claiming the one who gets the lion's share isn't really the lion." Mr. Mack allowed himself a little purse-lipped smile.

"So the brother James more or less allowed Robert *carte blanche?*"

Mack frowned. "Yes. And I frankly don't approve of open-ended arrangements like that. Messy." He squared a cigarette box and adjusted the alignment of the bronze cat. "But James had the devil's own trust in Robert." There was another fussy little smile. "Not the best way of putting it, perhaps. But the other relations, by blood or by marriage, were rather a sorry lot. So far as I could see, they had absolutely no claim on the money, not to say upon James's affections. But he was—I advised him to do so—smart enough to leave small sums to the ones whom he felt would be the troublemakers."

"I'd like to see a copy of that will, Mr. Mack."

Mr. Mack rocked back in his chair. "Is that really necessary?"

Jury smiled. "I'd like to see it, necessary or not. The will's been probated. Public property now."

"Hmm. Very well. Miss Chivers can make you up a copy." He punched his intercom and gave his secretary directions.

"And I'd also like to see those letters."

"The ones from James? Well, Robert has them, of course." Mr. Mack frowned. "Are you suggesting an analysis of the handwriting?"

"Something like that, yes." Jury thought, really, that the Ashcroft solicitors would have done it themselves. He rose to go. "Thanks for your help, Mr. Mack."

On the way out he collected the copy of the Ashcroft will and another appraising glance from Miss Chivers.

Mr. Mack's office was in The City. Jury made his way to the Aldgate tube stop, wondering what was bothering him. Something he'd seen? Something he'd heard? James Ashcroft's will was thick. There was a great deal of property. The will had been signed by Ashcroft, witnessed by Mack and two other solicitors. One of the names was George Thorne.

George Thorne. Again.

Jury changed at Baker Street to get the Northern line and, as he waited for his train, looked over the tiled wall of the platform, where the profile of Sherlock Holmes had been wonderfully contrived during the station's renovation. It was a hard act to follow.

III

"So sad it is," said Mrs. Wasserman, who lived alone in the basement flat of the building in Islington. Jury's own flat was on the second floor, but he had stopped off to see how she was doing. To admit him, she had had to throw two bolts, release a chain, and turn the deadlock. There were grilles over her windows, too. Mrs. Wasserman could have slept with ease in the middle of the Brixton riots. But Mrs. Wasserman was never at ease, except when the superintendent was around who mercifully (for her) lived upstairs.

They were eating her homemade strudel and drinking coffee and she was talking about the case Jury was on. "I know you don't discuss," she said, "but it frightens me to death to see these children—" Unable to bring it out, she stopped, shook her head, drank her coffee. "I know you don't say, of course you can't, but this person, he must be crazy." And she made a tiny circle round her ear to demonstrate craziness.

"I expect so, Mrs. Wasserman. We don't know the motive."

"Motive? Who says motive? Crazies don't *have* them, Mr. Jury." Her smile was slight and forgiving, as if she couldn't expect this novice policeman to know everything, could she?

Indeed she was right on that count. "Psychotics do have motives, even if the motives are irrational and obscure. Or displaced."

"What is that, *displaced?*" She was suspicious of psychoanalytic jargon.

"Just that the killer's actual object isn't the person he kills."

She thought this over, chewing her strudel. "What a hideous waste of time." Mournfully, she glanced up at him. "The papers, Mr. Jury, are full of it."

Jury knew about the papers. And he also knew he had described, without consciously meaning to, Mrs. Wasserman's own phobia. How old had she been during the Second World War? Fifteen, sixteen perhaps. Whatever horrors she had suffered then had gone underground, submerged in her mind, but bonded to that scrap of memory she could stand—the Stranger who followed her, whose step behind her she could pick out of a hundred footsteps, whose description Jury had taken down in his notebook time and time again, knowing there was no such person. And it was Jury who had helped her with the locks, the chains, the bolts. Mrs. Wasserman could have written the book on agoraphobia.

Jury looked at her windows, grilles and shutters. He looked at her door, locked and bolted. "You bolt the door—" He really hadn't meant to say it aloud.

"Pardon? Of course I bolt the door." Her large breasts shook with laughter. "*You*, of all people! You helped me with the bolts." Then she grew concerned. "It's sleep you need, Mr. Jury. You never get enough. Sometimes it is not until two or three in the morning you get in."

Jury only half-heard her. His eye was still fixed on that impregnable door. "But what, exactly, does it keep out?"

She seemed puzzled, suspicious even—in the way one is suspicious that a dear friend might be going off the rails. "Why, Him, of course. As you know."

And she went back calmly to eating her strudel.

TWENTY-TWO

I

It was five miles on the other side of Dorchester, in Winterbourne Abbas, that it hit him—what had seemed insignificant at the time. Jury pulled into a petrol station, asked for a phone and was told there was one in the Little Chef next door.

The restaurant was almost antiseptically clean, right down to the starched uniforms of the waitresses. Jury asked for a coffee, said he'd be back in a moment. He put in a call to the Devon-Cornwall headquarters and was told that the divisional commander was in Wynchcoombe.

It was TDC Coogan in the mobile unit there who told Jury (testily, he thought) that Macalvie had taken

Sergeant Wiggins and gone to the Poor Struggler to make "inquiries." Jury smiled. Although Betty Coogan didn't believe it, Macalvie probably was doing just that. She gave him the number.

Jury could hear Elvis Presley in the background singing "Hound Dog" after someone answered the telephone at the Poor Struggler. Not Freddie, probably the regular who happened to be nearest the phone.

"Don't know him, mate. Mac-who?"

Jury could almost hear the phone being wrenched from the other's hand, along with a brief exchange that had Macalvie working the old Macalvie charm, complete with expletives. "Macalvie here." And he turned away to shout to Freddie to turn the damned music down or he'd have her license. "Macalvie," he said again.

"What are you doing there, Macalvie?"

"Oh, it's you." There was the usual lack of enthusiasm for New Scotland Yard. "Talking to your friend. The one passing himself off as a bloody earl. Seems okay, though."

Macalvie always seemed to like the very people Jury was sure he'd hate. He cut across the latest Macalvie theory by telling him what he'd learned from Mr. Mack.

"*Thorne?* He was one of the Ashcroft bunch. When? I mean for how long?"

"I don't know. Get one of your men to give him a call. Wiggins there?"

"Yeah, sure." Macalvie seemed to be carrying Wiggins around in his pocket. "For God's sakes, I should have known about Thorne."

"Why? You're not a mind reader."

There was a small pause, as if Macalvie were debating this point. "Yeah. What do you want to tell Wiggins?"

"Just let me talk to him."

"It's a secret between you two?"

"No. I want to check something. Stop pouting and put him on."

"Sir!" Wiggins was probably standing at attention.

Jury sighed. "As you were, Sergeant. Listen: when we were in the Rileys' flat, or as we were leaving, that is, you noticed a framed document above the mantel—"

"That's right. Mrs. Riley was a nurse. Had been, I mean."

"What name was on it?" Wiggins was not always spot-on when it came to sifting facts down to a solution, but he could usually be counted on to remember the facts themselves. A master of minutiae.

There was a silence on the other end of the telephone. Wiggins was thinking; Jury let him. Jury also thought he heard paper crackle. Opening another packet of Fisherman's Friends, probably. "Elizabeth Allan, sir."

"That's what I thought, Wiggins. Thanks. And thank Plant for his letter. I got it this morning." Jury hung up. He paid for his coffee but didn't bother drinking it.

II

"What's me being a nurse got to do with it?" asked Beth Riley. "What's it to do with Simon?"

"Maybe nothing, maybe a lot," said Jury, replenishing her glass with the bottle of Jameson's he'd the foresight to bring along. The glass in her hand welcomed the bottle in Jury's. She sat in the same cabbage rose chair she had the first time Jury had visited their lodgings. The husband wasn't here today, and she seemed to be trying to make up her mind whether she was flattered or a little frightened that it was she whom the superintendent wanted to see. "So given you were nurse to Lady Ashcroft before she died, and also her cousin, you knew Jessica and Robert Ashcroft."

Her answer was surly. "Yes. Not all that well. Jessica was only a baby, and the brother—I'd seen him at the Eaton Square house in London off and on. That was before Barbara got so sick she needed someone all the time."

"Is he much changed?"

"Changed? That's an odd question. Though I guess ten years in Australia's enough to change anyone."

"I mean, did he appear as you remembered him?"

Again, she frowned. "Well, yes—wait a tic." She leaned toward Jury, the flashy rhinestone brooch winking in the light of the lamp. "Are you telling me that's *not* Robert Ashcroft?" Obviously, no news could have pleased her more. Mrs. Riley had been the most adamant of the relatives who questioned James Ashcroft's will.

"No," said Jury, watching her hope dissipate along with the John Jameson's. He calculated that somewhere during the third drink she'd reach the confessional stage. "No, I'm stumbling in the dark, hoping I'll fall over the right answer." He smiled.

Beth Riley, cushioned by cabbage rose pillows and Jameson's, gave him a once-over that strongly suggested she wouldn't mind being what he fell over. Once again, she held out her glass. Self-pity would take over pretty soon, he knew. He was happy to help it along. He poured her a third drink and looked at the display over the mantel: the nursing degree with its gold seal, the family photographs, the mahogany-backed coat-of-arms. The same coat-of-arms, emblazoned here, that Jury had seen on the writing-paper, the note that Plant had sent him. It was the crest, the curlew embellished as carefully as some monk's Biblical illumination.

"They're none of us perfect," said Beth. "I made a mess of things, marrying as I did. Oh, not that Al's not a good *provider* . . ."

235

Jury wanted to steer clear of Riley's good points, which were certain to end with the bad. He was interested in facts, not in her soul-searching, the whys and wherefores of her marriage. "What was—or is—your relation to the Ashcroft family, Mrs. Riley?"

"You can call me Beth." Over the rim of her glass she looked at him coyly.

Jury assumed he'd damned well *better* call her Beth if he wanted information. He smiled a warm, insincere smile. "Beth. Your relation with the Ashcrofts?"

"To hear *him* talk—that Robert—I'd no more to do with them than the horses in the stableyard."

(Jury thought that Robert was probably right.)

"I was cousin to Barbara. *First* cousin." She made sure he understood that it was no fly-by-night relationship. "We were both born in County Waterford. I came to England when I was small, long before Barbara." She said it as if this gave her some proprietorial right over the country which Barbara lacked. "But I hardly ever saw them until she got sick. Just trust that kind of people to want your help, and then not to remember how much help you gave."

"But Ashcroft certainly did remember, Beth. You'd come into a sizable sum." He paused. "If anything happened to Jessica Ashcroft."

"What's likely to happen to *her?*" The whiskey hadn't softened her up enough, apparently. Nor did she respond to the implication of what Jury had said. "That's no way to leave an inheritance—you have to wait until somebody *dies.* It's Riley, that's what it is! Robert Ashcroft is too much of a snob to have us round. But then they always were the worst kind of snobs."

Jury was sympathetic as he topped off her glass. "That does seem a bit unfair."

She hooted. "Unfair? *I'll* say it's unfair. Listen: we were perfectly willing to take the girl in, to be mum and dad to her—"

(Like you were mum to Simon, Jury thought.)

"—but, no. She was handed over bag and baggage to him. As if he'd ever done a thing in his life for the child." She turned on Jury one of the most vindictive smiles he'd ever seen. "Though I wouldn't deny he might have done a good deal for the mother. Barbara."

The implication was clear. But Jury didn't want to give her the satisfaction, at the moment, of indulging her fantasies.

They were interrupted by her husband's coming into the sitting room, dazzled to see Jury there, as if he'd stepped into white light from the darkness of a theater. He blinked. "Superintendent?"

Jury rose. "Mr. Riley." They shook hands. "I was just asking your wife a few questions that I thought might be relevant to Simon's death. I've got to be going now."

Riley led him to the top of the stairs. He looked back over his shoulder, then whispered to Jury. "She gets a bit tearful after a drink. Not much of a drinker, is Beth. What about Simon?''

''Nothing new, I'm afraid. I was just trying to sort out the family connections. You see, I didn't know your wife was related to the Ashcroft family.''

He was not so far gone in sorrow that he couldn't laugh at this. ''You must be the only one in Dorchester who doesn't know it, then. What a row she made after the funeral.'' He sighed. ''Water under the bridge, why quarrel? Are you anywhere nearer finding out who did this?''

Jury debated his answer. ''Yes, I think so, Mr. Riley.''

''Dear God, I hope so. After reading about the other two—it's a dreadful thing to say, Mr. Jury,''—another confession—''but I'm glad Simon wasn't in it alone.'' He gave Jury a furtive look, as if there stood the messenger of God who would condemn him to the everlasting fire for such a thought. ''I can't help it.''

''I know. I only wish I could.''

And Jury went down the stairs and out of Riley's: Fine Meat and Game.

TWENTY-THREE

The black cat, tail twitching, sat on the stone balustrade tracking the progress of two seagulls on their unwary way toward half a discarded sandwich. When Jury's appearance disturbed this tableau—the oafish stranger walking between the tourist's camera and its vision of scenic wonders—the cat turned its yellow eyes on Jury as if any sacrificial victim were better than none. Then it jumped down and walked over to sit on the stone step and stare the door out of countenance. There was food in there somewhere.

Jury was surprised to see the curtains undrawn. And she must have been watching from a window, because the door opened as he raised his hand to knock. The cat marched straight in.

Molly looked down and up and smiled. "He'll

make straight for the kitchen and glare until I give him something. Come on in."

He felt an odd reluctance to put his foot over the sill. The sensation might have been something akin to what a medium feels when suddenly, across a sill, there's a cold spot. It only lasted a second or two, his hesitation, but she noticed it. Her smile now seemed almost left over, and she glanced at the windows as if she'd like to close the curtains, in the way she had just, in a flash, drawn one across her smile.

He had let her down, the last thing he wanted to do. But with Molly Singer he supposed it would be very difficult not to; it was not that she expected too much of the world, but that she expected too little.

She took his coat and went to feed the cat. From the kitchen she asked him if he'd like some coffee and, in an attempt at banter, told him he'd better take her up on the offer; it didn't come round often. He could not see her, only hear her. Her voice was strained as it hadn't been when he'd come to the door.

"Then you'd better bring it quick," he called back.

She must have had it ready, for she brought it in straightaway, after he'd heard dry food rattle into a bowl.

They went through the business of how much sugar and cream, and she had some toasted teacakes, which she cut with a knife that might have done them more service in cutting the tension. Finally, she said, "It was nice of you to send the message you were coming." She was studying her teacake. "I don't think Superintendent Macalvie would have."

Certainly, *that* couldn't have been truer. "You know police." He nodded toward the kitchen door where the black cat was washing its kingly self. "We're worse than *him*. Hell on wheels, beat down doors, storm right in." Jury mustered the best smile he could.

It was, apparently, good enough, for the invisible curtain opened and she said, "You didn't. You're not very frightening for a policeman, Mr. Jury."

"Richard. For God's sakes, don't tell Macalvie I don't scare people. He'll send me back to London."

"I doubt one just sends Scotland Yard 'back to London.'"

Jury laughed, and she sat back with her coffee and relaxed a little. Today, she had relinquished her Oxfam-special for what looked more like Jaeger—a wool dress in such a warm shade of gold she should have been able to cut through the cold spot, send the ghosts packing, tame the demons. She couldn't. Could anyone? "Macalvie—" He hadn't meant to say it aloud. He added quickly, laughing again. "You don't know Macalvie. . . ."

Although he hadn't meant to bring it up that way, or to make light of her dilemma, he knew it was as good a way as any. So he didn't retract when he saw the look on her face, a look of disappointment replaced quickly with a getting-down-to-business smile. He thought of that scene in the hotel. Molly could rise to an occasion. With a vengeance. That worried him.

"I didn't imagine," she said, "you'd come on a social call."

But one could always hope. Jury said nothing.

"Superintendent Macalvie will twist things into whatever shape suits his purposes."

"No. Macalvie's too good a cop; he doesn't twist things."

As the black cat positioned itself on the twin of Jury's chair and gave him a fiery-gold look, so did Molly Singer. "Well, he might not 'twist' them into shape, but he doesn't seem to mind battering them." She reached down to the bottom shelf of the table by the little couch and brought out a bottle of whiskey. She raised it slightly. "Want some in your coffee?"

Jury shook his head, watching her as she held the bottle on her knee. It was a fresh bottle, and she broke the seal. But she didn't uncap it; she stared at it as if the bottle were an old friend turned stranger. He did not think she really wanted a drink; he thought she wanted something to do for distraction. Her need for something no one was able to give her was so intense, it drained him to think that any comfort he could offer would be pretty cold comfort coming from a policeman.

That's a swell rationalization, Jury, he said to himself.

He could have given it. The truth was, there was something about Molly Singer that made him feel afraid of being drawn in.

"Why is Chief Superintendent Macalvie so certain I'm this Mary Mulvanney?"

"She was hard to forget." He smiled. "So would you be."

"Because we throw things?"

"No. You're afraid that Mary Mulvanney would be even more of a suspect?"

"She would be."

"Why?"

"Because Chief Superintendent Macalvie thinks so."

Jury smiled. "He could be wrong."

"Oh? Why don't you try telling him that? Because you value your life." She made a poor attempt at a smile, and then said, not looking at him, "Do you remember what it's like to be in love when you're sixteen?"

"Same thing as when you're forty, I guess." He looked at her long enough to force her to turn her eyes back to his. "Why?"

She sat forward on the couch, slowly, as if she were very tired and, even, very old. "Oh, Superintendent . . ."

You understand nothing. She didn't say it, but from her expression, she might as well have.

Mary Mulvanney would certainly have a reason to

243

hate the world. Indeed, Mary Mulvanney might have become obsessive. Like Molly Singer . . .

"You're thinking the same thing he is."

Jury looked up, surprised. She had been studying his face—carefully, he was sure—for hints of increased suspicions, and found them.

He tried to pass it off with a smile. "You read minds."

Leaning her head against her hand, she returned the smile. And her face had a tinge of the glow it had when he'd first come. "Faces."

That she thought Jury had a particularly nice one was pretty clear, and he looked away, toward the cricket stool where he imagined the house-ghost stirring the ashes. At least her reply brought him to the point: "You'd be pretty good at that, being a photographer." He looked back at her. "We'd like you to do us a favor."

Her head came up from her hand, and her body tensed. Even before he'd asked, she saw the red light of danger. "Me? I can't imagine what."

"There's a place in Dartmoor more or less equidistant from Princetown, Wynchcoombe and Clerihew Marsh." Her expression didn't change. "It's called Ashcroft. Quite a large manor house—"

"Go on." It was as if the suspense that clung to that word *favor*—which could only mean action of some sort—was pulling her from the couch. She was leaning forward, hands clasped so tightly the knuckles were white.

Jury simply brought it out. "We need a photographer—"

"No." She shook her head slowly, her eyes shut. "No."

"Say No, if you want, but let me finish. There's a little girl in that house; she's ten years old. She's the sole heir to the Ashcroft millions. Her father was a peer. There've already been three children murdered, Molly. We're not looking forward to a fourth."

Molly looked up then, astonishment stamped on her face. "Whatever it is you want from *me*—dear God, *why*? I'm your main *suspect*!"

"*A* suspect. Okay, I won't deny it, though I doubt you had anything to do with these killings." Doubt was not certainty; but the doubt was strong.

Astonishment gave way to something like hope and a half-smile. "You're outvoted."

"Macalvie?" Jury smiled. "Then it's one against one. Not outvoted."

"If Chief Superintendent Macalvie has the other vote, believe me, you're outvoted. But go on. I'll just say no at the end, but go on."

"We want pictures—photographs—of, well, everything. Your bona fides are all arranged. There's an expensive, sleek new magazine that specializes in classic and antique cars. You're their top photographer: and you know what a professional does because you've done it." He smiled. "Piece of cake."

"Dipped in cyanide. Are you crazy?" Her voice was going up a ladder of tension. "Richard—"

As she leaned toward him, he felt his name in her mouth as something strange, saltwater on the tongue. "Molly." Again he smiled.

Quickly she looked away, and for something to do, tried petting the black cat taking its ease beside her in this tension-filled room. It merely looked around and glared at her. "I don't even go out of the house here. And you think I'd have the nerve to gather up my Leica and go and do an *impersonation* in the manor house of a millionaire? God. I'd almost rather talk to the gracious Chief Superintendent Macalvie— don't tell me *he* expects me to do this?"

Jury nodded and offered her a cigarette, which she took, saying, "Thanks, it's an excuse for a drink. I don't suppose you'd care for one?"

"Try me."

Having poured the drinks into mismatched water tumblers, she sat back, raised her glass in a salute. "To your crazy idea. First of all, if you want a photographer, the Dorset police, the Devon constabulary—and Scotland Yard—must have darkrooms full of them. Why me?"

"Because they wouldn't be suspicious of you, Molly."

"I don't see why they would of a clever cop—you

are trained in the lively art of worming your way into people's confidence."

It wasn't anger but pain he heard in that remark. "The people at Ashcroft would sniff out a cop all the way across Dartmoor. At least one of them would, I'm sure."

In spite of herself she was curious. "Who?"

"Better you don't know, or you'd be falling all over your tripod every time the person said Boo."

The whiskey was relaxing her. "I'd be falling all over it *anyway*, you idiot." Her raised voice disturbed the black cat. It moved, recurled itself, and gave them both a squinty gold look. "And if I don't agree to this incredible scheme—I suppose you'll blackmail me into doing it: 'Go along with us, baby, and maybe we'll go easy on you—' "

Jury laughed. It was a perfect mimicry of Macalvie's hard-boiled-detective tone.

"Thinks he's Sam Spade." She took a drink. Two. "Photos of what? What are you looking for?"

"Given the mag and Ashcroft's collection, you'd be concentrating on the cars. And the people at Ashcroft. We need some photos for identification purposes—"

"You're *police*. Just go in and take the bloody things."

"We don't have any reason to: we don't have a bit of evidence that would get us in, and it would only put everybody on guard. You wouldn't, see."

247

"I know I wouldn't because I won't be there. But—out of curiosity—why?"

"Because you're running scared and that timidity is going to make Ashcroft—the girl's guardian—even more courtly, and the rest will be trying to put you at your ease."

"Thanks!" she snapped, downing some more whiskey. "That sort of person hardly sounds like one a high-powered magazine would be sending out on jobs."

"They would if she had your talent."

She lowered her head. There was no sarcasm in her voice, only defeat. "I can't do it. And I don't see any reason I should."

"I do."

"Oh, I know that old crap. 'Do it for yourself, Molly, it's what you need to—' " He could hear the tears beginning.

"No. Do it for me."

There was no sound but a log splitting and the waves beyond the window. She did not look up and did not move, but sat on the couch, feet drawn up, curled much like the cat, and just as silent.

Jury waited.

Looking not at him but at the glass she turned round and round in her hands, she said dully, "I'll need some film. I suppose this magazine wants color. Extracolor Professional or Extrachrome X." She smiled coldly. "Oh, I forgot. None of this is real, so I'll just use what I have."

"No. Treat it as if it were the real thing. Take along equipment you'd take if it *were* real."

She looked up at Jury then, still with that cold little smile, shaking her head. "Do you know the difference?" Her face turned toward the fire. "Then get me a haze filter."

He wrote it down, feeling rotten as he did.

Jury got up and went over to the couch. He leaned down, pushed back the black hair that had fallen across her face, and kissed her cheek. "Thanks, Molly."

It happened the way it had in the hotel. At one moment she was statue-still with her glass on her knee. At the next she was up and flinging it against the grate. She turned her back to him.

Jury made a move to get the glass out of the way. The cottage reeked not of whiskey, but of desolation.

"Don't bother trying to pick up the pieces."

TWENTY-FOUR

Even before Jess saw the passenger, she felt slightly ill just seeing the car. It was a Lamborghini. Besides the Ferrari, it was the best sports car there was. Uncle Robert had been trying to find one for years.

It was sleek, smooth, and silver. Almost the same thing could have been said about the woman who was getting out of the car, hiking an aluminum case over her shoulder. She looked so—*London*, Jessie thought. Annoyed enough about the car, must the person driving it be good-looking, too? Under the gray cape, which got in the way of the aluminum box, she wore a pearl-gray blouse and skirt and gray leather boots. It was almost as if she were choosing her clothes to match the car.

Her uncle and the rest were out. The photographer was supposed to get there at two o'clock and it was only a little past one. She was early. Jessie watched the woman come up the broad stairs and ring. Mrs. Mulchop and Jessie collided as both of them went for the door. "Now behave, for once," said Mrs. Mulchop, hand on door. "Don't be getting up to anything."

Jessie smiled benignly. The only thing she was considering getting up to was getting the photographer in and out as quick as she could. It shouldn't take long to take pictures of a few cars.

"Hello. I'm Molly Singer," the woman said.

Mrs. Mulchop said she was sorry that Mr. Ashcroft wasn't there at the moment. He hadn't expected her until two o'clock. Would she like a cup of tea?

"If she works for a magazine," said Jessie, "she's probably got a lot of things to do. She probably doesn't have time—"

"Be quiet, child." Mrs. Mulchop gave Jess a kiss-of-death glance and repeated her offer of tea. "Or coffee, perhaps?"

"That's very kind of you. But I suppose—if you don't think Mr. Ashcroft would mind—I could get to work straightaway."

"Oh, *he* wouldn't mind at all," said Jessie. "I'll just show you where the cars are. They're outside."

Mrs. Mulchop grumbled. "I don't expect Miss Singer thought they were in the drawing room."

251

Molly laughed. Besides having a nice, low voice, she had a nice laugh. Nicer than Sara's. And Sara only had that old Morris Minor. . . . Jess was beginning to feel sick again. "Come on, then."

"What's your name?" asked Molly as they walked through the expanse of marble hallway, through morning room, dining room, butler's pantry (where Mulchop was topping up his glass of sherry), and kitchen.

"Jessica Allan-Ashcroft. My mother's picture is in the dining room. She led a tragic life."

"Oh, dear. How sad."

"It was, really." Jessie had stopped and taken her overall from the peg. "I always wear this when I work on the cars." She looked this new woman up and down. "You wouldn't be able to get under them, not the way you're dressed."

"Well, I hadn't planned to, actually," said Molly as they went through a dark little hallway and out to the courtyard beyond.

"It won't take you long. I'll tell you what's what and you can snap your pictures and go. My uncle has always wanted a Lamborghini. Stable at one hundred and eighty mph," she added, casually.

"You certainly do know a lot about cars." Molly had taken her thirty-five-millimeter camera from the case.

"Yes. What you could do is just get them all together if you stand back far enough and you wouldn't be wasting film."

"Not to worry. I have plenty."

Jess was afraid of that.

"Let me look them over first—"

"That one's a Ferrari; that's a Jaguar XJ-S—silent as a Rolls and does zero to sixty in under seven seconds. That one's an Aston Martin—you know, the James Bond car; there's the Porsche; this is the Lotus; this is my Mini Cooper—"

"Yours? You mean you drive it?"

"No." Jess hurried on with her description, curtailing questions. "That one's a Mercedes two-eighty-SL, a convertible. That's a—"

Molly laughed. "Hold on, there! You're going much too fast for me to remember them all."

Jess kept going. "That's a Silver Ghost, and that one's—"

"My word, a Silver Ghost. That must have cost your uncle a mint."

Jess wished she'd stop commenting so she could get on with it. "It doesn't belong to him. It's our visitor's." And then she thought of bringing in the rear-guard action. "You'd *love* him. He's an earl, like my father was. Only, of course, not that *old*. He's handsome and rich. And very nice."

"Umm."

Jessie thought her description rated more than an *umm*. But some people just couldn't be pleased. "You don't really have to know the *names* of the cars, do you, if you're only taking pictures?"

Molly adjusted the lens of the camera. "Yes, I'm afraid I do. It wouldn't do the readers of the magazine much good to have the cars but not know what they were, would it?"

Frustrated, Jessie crossed her arms and scratched at both her elbows while she watched the photographer go about her business. She was being so careful with all of her equipment, at this rate they could be stopping here all afternoon. "What time is it?"

Molly looked at her watch. "One-thirty. If you have something you want to do, go ahead."

"No, that's all right. What about your husband? Does he take pictures too?"

"Haven't got one."

Glumly, Jessie looked her up and down again. No doubt about it, she was the best-looking one yet—all that glowing black hair and strange yellowish eyes with little flecks of brown. "Too bad."

"Not being married? You think being married's the best way to live?" Molly smiled.

"What? *No!* I think it's pretty dumb. Except for my mother and father—that was all right."

Molly fixed the camera to the unipod. "You sound like Hamlet. He said there should be no more marriages."

"I know." Mad Margaret had made an awfully fat Ophelia.

"You *do?* You must be going to a very good school if you already know Shakespeare."

"It's not school. There isn't one in spitting distance.

254

I have tutors. They don't last long. What's that? I thought it was a cane."

Molly laughed. "I'm not quite *that* old. It's a unipod. You use it to hold the camera steady." Going through the routine might help to steady *her*. She was beginning to feel the disorientation that triggered a panic-attack out here in this unfamiliar place.

"What's that thing?" asked Jessie. She sounded worried.

"Just a spot meter. So I don't have to unthread the camera to judge the lighting or if I want a close-up."

"It sounds complicated. It sounds like it's going to take a long time. I have a camera. All I have to do is point it."

"Do you want to take some pictures?"

"No, no," said Jessie, hurriedly. "It would waste your time."

Molly was beginning to feel beads of water on her forehead. With the hand that held the spot sensor, she wiped them away. Maybe she's right. *Just take the damned pictures and get the hell out*, she told herself. *Let them worry about Identikits*. She stiffened when something moved in the rear seat of the Ferrari. "What's *that*?"

"What's what? Oh, *Henry!* Don't worry, it's just Henry. He likes sleeping in cars. You look kind of pale. But Henry's safe, really. He never bit anything in his whole life. He doesn't even bite bones now, he's so old."

"I've never seen a dog like that in my entire life." Molly laughed, feeling the pressure in her mind ease up a little.

"It's just a stray we found." Jessie would never give Henry credit for his blue-blooded lineage. "He's funny-looking, isn't he?" She reached down into the Ferrari and heaved Henry out.

Molly looked up at the cirrus cloud scudding across the gray vault of endless sky and felt a wave of nausea. It always started like this, the panic-attacks. She found some tissues in her pocket and wiped the perspiration from her face.

"There's not going to be much light in a little bit. Maybe you'd rather leave and come back later. Anyway, you look kind of pale. You're not sick, are you?"

Molly had to smile over the little girl's attempt to get rid of her, though she didn't know what prompted it. The smile faded quickly, though, and she had to turn her face to the camera to keep it from cracking like a mirror. She had the unipod far enough back that she could see all ten cars together, each slotted into its *box*, like race-horses in their starting boxes. Irrational as it was—which made these attacks worse—she had the ugly feeling the head-lamps would switch on and come racing toward her. She felt she'd been dropped into one of those silly films in which a car takes on the human potential to kill. They looked diabolical.

In this open court there was no safe place to stand. No walls, ceilings—nothing. She felt as she always did a prescience of something awful.

"You *do* look sick."

"I'll be—all right. Just a moment . . ." Molly laid her head down on the arm supported by the unipod, and rested the other on Jessica's shoulder. The little girl put her hand over Molly's.

Even though she was out here in what seemed like an endless waste of sky and ground, Molly had the feeling of being shoved, stuffed into a dark closet where she would fall into a deep well. If only she could get back into her car—

And then she heard voices, people coming around the side of the house, laughter. People. The last thing she wanted. She was perilously near to blacking out.

Then she raised her head and saw the two men and the two women. One of the men started walking toward her, smiling. She looked at him, looked at the others, the man and the two women. Her eyes widened. She stared at this tableau vivant for a second before she felt the unipod slip beneath her weight. And she heard from what seemed a great distance, "It was Henry's fault. He scared her."

Molly Singer wanted to laugh. *Oh, the dog. The poor dog.*

257

* * *

When she came round, she was sitting in the Ashcroft library, being ministered to by Mrs. Mulchop with a cup of tea, Sara Millar with a cold towel, Robert Ashcroft and the other man looking concerned, and Jessica looking very guilty. It was as if her wish for release from the threat that Molly Singer represented had caused Molly's "bad spell."

Which was what Jessica was calling it as she patted her silk-sleeved arm.

"Sorry," said Molly. She put her head in her hand and tried to laugh. "It certainly wasn't Henry's fault." She smiled at Jessica.

The man standing by Jessica's uncle was introduced as Lord Ardry. "I nearly fainted myself when I saw the Ashcroft collection." He was offering her a snifter of brandy, which she took with far more gratitude than she had the cup of tea.

"Thanks. Yes. It's quite a stunning display, but—" She had been about to say it would be better if she came back another day, and watched with a sinking heart as they seemed to be settling into chairs for a relaxing chat. Again, gratefully, she took a cigarette offered by Lord Ardry, who seemed to be observing her with more acuity than she would have liked.

"What's your magazine, Miss Singer?" asked Ashcroft. "I've forgotten."

With mounting horror, Molly knew she'd forgotten too.

"*Executive Cars*, wasn't it?" said the Earl of Caverness.

Their eyes met. He smiled. It was almost conspiratorial. What on earth did this perfect stranger know?

"Yes, that's right." She leaned back, crossed her legs, tried her best to imitate herself—the old, fairly confident Molly Singer, photographer. And very good one, too. "It's a bimonthly. You've probably seen it."

"As a matter of fact, I haven't. I didn't think it would have much to do with the old ones. More modern-day stuff."

"No. It's got a misleading title. I keep telling them to change either the title or the image." She tried on a little laugh. It worked. Especially since the peer had given her a bit more cognac. "Let's try again, shall we. I shall try to remain upright this time."

"If you're sure—?" Ashcroft stubbed out his cigarette. "You want me in the picture?"

He asked the question shyly.

She smiled. "Of course. *And* you, young lady."

Jessica returned the smile. The scared look had vanished. Apparently, she was willing to let Miss Singer hang around as long as she wanted, now.

Indeed, Jess went all out: "*She* has a Lamborghini."

Robert Ashcroft laughed as they trailed out of the library "Believe me, I noticed."

Maybe, thought Molly, just maybe she'd get through it.

TWENTY-FIVE

I

The din from the jukebox would have paralyzed any but the worst of addicts, Jury thought, when he walked into the Poor Struggler that evening. Macalvie, Wiggins, and Melrose Plant were sitting at a table in the corner.

"You've been long enough," Macalvie said to Jury.

"For what?"

"For anything," said Macalvie. "The three of us have been sitting here putting two and two together and coming up with five. Well, four-and-a-half, maybe. I bet we did better than you, Jury."

"I didn't know we were running a marathon."

"Wiggins, get the guy a drink; he looks like he could use one." Macalvie held out his hand for the holy dispensation of another Fisherman's Friend. Wiggins slid one from the packet.

Plant shook his head. "Why do you suck on those things if you think they're so vile?"

Macalvie smiled. "I tell myself every time I take one that cigarettes taste even worse." He was waving away the fragrant smoke of Plant's hand-rolled Cuban cigar. "Plant took the new governess up at Ashcroft for a ride yesterday. They went to Wynchcoombe." He turned to Melrose. "Go on. Tell him." It didn't surprise Jury that Plant had dispensed with his earldom after a few hours with Macalvie. At any rate, London had very quickly sent the fan belt (Melrose told him), and he was on the road again.

"I already have. Some of it."

Jury took out Plant's letter, and read, " 'The Earl of Curlew was also Viscount Linley, James Whyte Ashcroft. The vicar of Wynchcoombe is named Linley White. And "Clerihew" might have been "Curlew." Any connection?' It sounds like it. What did you find out?"

"He said, yes, he was some distant relation of the Ashcroft family. James Ashcroft had left the church a generous bequest. The Reverend White was surprised."

Macalvie broke in. "Someone has it in for the Ashcrofts, then? But why kill the kids? The worst possible revenge? Let me see that will."

Jury handed it over to Macalvie. "I had a talk with Simon Riley's stepmother. Maiden name—Wiggins reminded me—Elizabeth Allan. Born in County Waterford, but not much Irish blood flows through her veins or her voice."

Macalvie was silent for a moment, combing through James Ashcroft's will. Then he turned to shout over the jukebox din that if Freddie liked "Jailhouse Rock" that much, he could arrange for her to hear it from the inside. "I told you these cases were related. And I told you about Mary Mulvanney, except you still don't believe it." He grinned. "Scotland Yard, two; Macalvie, two." He looked Plant up and down. "You, one."

"Thanks," said Melrose Plant, offering Macalvie a cigar, which (to Wiggins's fright) Macalvie took.

"Robert Ashcroft, Molly Singer—"

"Mary Mulvanney," Macalvie corrected Jury automatically, eyes closed so that he could enjoy the inhalation of smoke to the maximum.

"God, Macalvie," said Jury. "You're so damned *right* all the time."

Macalvie opened his eyes. "I know."

"Sam Waterhouse. Just assume for the moment he was guilty of Rose Mulvanney's murder—"

Macalvie shook his head.

"Where is he?"

Macalvie shrugged.

Jury almost laughed. "You're the only person I know who can lie with a shrug. You're worse than Freddie. No wonder you hang around here. Why the hell don't you stop trying to protect Sam Waterhouse?"

Macalvie studied the coal-end of his cigar. "Okay. He was in here."

Jury looked at Melrose Plant. "You met him?"

Plant nodded. "It does sound as if police were looking for a scapegoat. The evidence against him was pretty circumstantial. You think so, too, don't you?"

"I don't know. But I certainly think the evidence against Molly Singer is circumstantial."

"Mary Mulvanney." Macalvie's kneejerk response.

"How'd she do at Ashcroft?" Jury asked Melrose.

"Miss Singer? Incredibly well—"

"She's no more phobic than I am," said Macalvie generously.

Melrose Plant smiled. "I'd be careful with comparisons if I were you, Mr. Macalvie."

"So we've got the pictures, so what have we got? Yeah, there *was* an advert. Robert Ashcroft went to see a Roller in Hampstead Heath." Macalvie stuffed a couple of Plant's cigars in his pocket before he got up. "The hell with it. It's time we had a little talk with Robert Ashcroft."

On his way out, Macalvie kicked the jukebox and "Don't Be Cruel."

II

"Mr. Ashcroft," said Macalvie, "you usually interview potential tutors or governesses or whatever you call them at home, don't you?"

There was a decanter of whiskey at his elbow, and Macalvie had no hesitation in helping himself. It went down well with Plant's cigars.

"That's right." Robert Ashcroft looked from Macalvie to Jury to Wiggins taking notes. He frowned. "I'm sorry. I don't—"

Macalvie made a sign with his hand that Ashcroft didn't have to understand a damned thing. Yet. "But this time you went to London to interview the applicants."

Ashcroft smiled. It was an easy smile. "I decided it might be better. I believe I'd misjudged my niece's ability to make the final choice."

"The lady Jessica not being such a hot judge of character?"

Ashcroft's smile was even more disarming. "On the contrary, a wonderful judge. She always chose the one least suitable."

Macalvie frowned. "As a governess?"

"No. As a wife. Jess is afraid I'm going to be snagged by Jane Eyre."

"With you as Rochester," said Macalvie. "So you're not in danger of marriage, then?"

"I never thought of marriage as 'dangerous.' Are you suggesting some sexual leaning? That every couple of months I go up to London to indulge my perverse tastes?"

Macalvie turned the cigar round and round in his mouth. "We weren't thinking particularly of you down in your lab drinking something that would turn you into Hyde, no."

"Superintendent—"

"Chief." Macalvie smiled.

"I beg your pardon. Are you still upset about that crazy ruse of Jess's that brought you all out here?"

"Hell, no. Kids will be kids, won't they?" His smile flickered less like the flame than the moth. "You stayed at the Ritz, right? On the tenth to the fifteenth?"

"Yes. What's that—?"

"You interviewed several applicants for this post."

Robert Ashcroft nodded, frowning.

"What else did you do?"

"Nothing much. Went to see a Rolls-Royce in Hampstead. But it wasn't what I wanted."

"And—?"

Ashcroft had risen from the sofa and gone to toss

his cigarette into the fireplace. The picture of his brother hung over him. Jury wondered how heavily. "I went to the theater and the Tate. Walked round Regent's Park and Piccadilly. What's this all about?"

"What'd you see?"

Ashcroft's bewilderment turned to anger. "Pigeons."

"Funny. The play, I mean."

"*The Aspern Papers.* Vanessa Redgrave."

"Good?"

"No. I walked out."

Macalvie put on his surprised and innocent look. "You walked out on Vanessa Redgrave?"

"I didn't exactly throw her over for another woman."

"I don't imagine many people walked out."

"I wasn't checking. Except my coat," Ashcroft said, acidly.

"So since probably *no one* would walk out on Vanessa, I bet the cloakroom attendant would remember you."

Ashcroft was furious. "What in the hell is this about, Chief Superintendent Macalvie?"

"What was at the Tate?"

"Pictures."

It wasn't as easy to unnerve Ashcroft as Jury thought.

"Mr. Ashcroft, would you try not playing this for laughs? What was at the Tate?"

"The Pre-Raphaelites."

Macalvie was silent, turning the cigar.

"Ever heard of them?"

"Rossetti and that bunch. I've heard. Why didn't you drive to London with all those cars sitting around out there?"

"For the obvious reason. I thought I'd be buying a car—the Rolls."

Jury sat there, smoking, saying nothing.

Robert Ashcroft had an answer for everything. And Macalvie knew it.

TWENTY-SIX

I

"That's it for tonight, then." Sara slapped the book shut.

Jessie, whose bed they were lying on, since she refused her nightly story in the Laura Ashley room, had been getting so drowsy her head had nearly drifted onto Sara's arm. Quickly, she snapped out of it. To have Sara think she was actually cozying up to her would be dreadful. "You've left off at the best part. Where Heathcliff is carrying Cathy's dead body around."

"You do put things in the most morbid way."

"*I* didn't write it, did I?" said Jess, reasonably. She felt as if Sara had reprimanded her, no matter how mildly. Jess gave Henry (who was lying at the bottom of the bed) a little kick. If *she* was being scolded, then Henry would have to come in for his share of it. What was really bothering her was that, against her will—and *that* would require a strong force indeed—she was afraid she might begin to *like* Sara. The Selfless Sara. Jessie sighed. But she didn't think she liked her as much as that lady photographer. Maybe it was because the one named Molly had fears, just as Jess had, only they wouldn't admit it.

It was an awful dilemma, liking someone you wanted to hate, the worst dilemma since the ax-murderer call to police. All of that blood in her mind had become so vivid it might have been really running down the walls. She shuddered.

"What's the matter?" asked Sara.

"Nothing." Jessie picked up the glossy magazine Molly Singer had given her. *Executive Cars.*

Sara was saying something about Heathcliff. "I thought you thought he was so romantic."

Romance? How disgusting. Better to imagine murderers stalking her (and Henry) across the moor. Green, green bogs with liverworts and moss, like Cranmere Pool, and peat, and rush ground where you could be sucked down, your head just dangling, as if guillotined, your little hand (and Henry's paw), the last thing to disappear from the sight of all those gathered round, throwing ropes, calling to you. . . .

"Romance is stupid."

Sara hit her lightly over the head with the book. "You're the one asked me to read it." Sara sat up suddenly, her back rigid. "What was that?"

"What was what?" Jessie was looking at a picture of a Lamborghini, newer than Molly's. Twenty thousand pounds. Maybe Mr. Mack—

"It sounded like a car. Down the drive."

Jessie yawned, her eyes getting heavy. "Maybe it's Uncle Rob and Victoria coming back." She thought her uncle had been awfully moody at dinner. Victoria got him to go out for a drive and a drink at a new pub several miles away. Maybe Victoria would worm out of him what was wrong. Her eyes snapped open.

Victoria, Jessie realized suddenly, was rather good at getting her uncle in a better frame of mind. She frowned and thought about that.

"It's too early for them to be back," said Sara.

Now Sara looked moody and worried. What was the *matter* with everyone? "I want hot chocolate and toast. Come on, Henry."

Moody himself, Henry clambered down off the bed.

II

Jess sat at the kitchen table, turning the pages of *Executive Cars*, while the kettle for tea and the pan of milk for chocolate heated on the hob. Sara got out the granary loaf to cut and toast. "I wish the Mulchops were here," she said.

The Mulchops had gone to Okehampton to visit some relative or other. "Them? Whatever for?"

Sara shrugged. "I just feel—edgy."

Jess slapped over another page, annoyed. "Well, *they* wouldn't be any help. I mean if some ghost was walking around or something."

"Stop talking like that."

Jess shrugged. Sara was spoiling one of Jess's favorite times. The kitchen chill around the edges, but nice and warm right here by the fire, without Mrs. Mulchop bustling and kneading dough and Mulchop slopping down soup and giving Jessie evil looks. He didn't like her, she knew, because she got under the cars.

Probably because she was "edgy," Sara started humming to herself, and then singing while she sliced the bread. She must have thought ghosts and vampires and werewolves ran away when they heard old Irish tunes. Jess glanced up when she heard ". . . when she was dead, and laid in grave . . ."

"That's 'Barbara Allan.' "

Sara looked stricken. "Oh, I'm sorry. Really. I suppose it's because I hear so much about your mother—" She stopped, staring toward the kitchen door, the one that led out to the courtyard. "There *is* a noise out there."

This time Jess heard it too. A sort of scraping

sound. But the wind was getting higher, and one of the stable doors banged; the sound could have been anything. "It's just the horses." She really wished Sara weren't such a mouse about things. It was just like the wife in *Rebecca.* She thrust that thought from her mind.

Sara went back to cutting the bread, and just as suddenly stopped. "It sounds like footsteps." She listened intently, shook her head, went back to the bread.

Well, it *had* sounded like footsteps, but Jess refused to give in. "It's just Henry; sometimes he scrapes his paw in his sleep." Henry never moved *anything* in his sleep, as Jess knew perfectly well.

She went on looking at the cars. Daimlers, Rollers, Ferraris . . . next page, another Daimler and some cheaper cars, but still collector's items. Beside the black Daimler was a little Morris Minor, vintage.

The Daimler . . . she kept her eyes averted because they were filling with tears. Her father James had been taken to the cemetery in a Daimler. And once again the graveyard scene sprang up, as if it were yesterday, and she saw herself standing beside the grave. The mourners—thick-veiled women, black-suited men. Her uncle had been the only spot of light in that dark-shrouded world.

That Daimler had had a Y registration. Jess blushed from remembering having noticed, even in her grief, the registration on the funereal Daimler. And then her skin went cold.

She turned back to the page before. Morris Minor. Black. *R* registration. Jess's thoughts stopped suddenly, braking. It must be what an animal feels, maybe even Henry. The thoughts stop. Senses take over. You see, you hear, you feel fright. . . .

What she heard, and Sara, too, given the knife had stopped slicing bread, was the creaking in the kitchen entry. Sara's face was pale, looking toward the door that, when Jess had nerved herself to look around, was opening.

Molly Singer stood there in her silvery cape, white-faced, black-haired. In her fright, Jess almost thought she *was* seeing a ghost.

Except that this ghost was holding a gun in her black-gloved hand.

Despite all of this, the only thing that Jess could see in her mind's eye was a black Daimler and a Morris Minor. *R* registration. Not vintage.

She stared at Molly Singer and then back at the kitchen table, where an entire loaf of bread lay sliced, and wondered, what had Sara Millar's car been doing at her father's funeral?

III

Five miles away in the Help the Poor Struggler, Macalvie was still arguing that Ashcroft had gone about the whole interviewing business in a damned peculiar way.

Melrose Plant was drinking Old Peculier and smoking. And wondering about Robert Ashcroft's "interviews."

"He could have left that play *deliberately* so he'd establish that he'd been in London. How many people walk out on Vanessa?" asked Macalvie.

Wiggins said, "The cloakroom attendant recognized the picture immediately. No luck yet though with the car lots. But we've only had a few hours." He made a bit of a production of unzipping a box of lozenges to call the divisional commander's attention to the fact that Macalvie was smoking. Again.

"And why didn't he call home? Gone for five days and not a word back to his beloved niece," Macalvie went on, looking from Plant to Jury, irritated that he seemed to be arguing without an opponent.

"It was coincidence that the note to Jessica went under the rug. A coincidence with wretched consequences, unfortunately. Wasn't it the same thing Angel Clare did?" asked Jury.

"Who the hell's Angel Clare?" asked Macalvie.

Melrose Plant looked at him. "Commander, if you were hiring a tutor, you'd damned well make sure he or she was extremely well read, wouldn't you?"

Macalvie gave him an especially magical Macalvie-smile. "If you need a tutor, Plant, I'm sorry I don't come up to your standards."

"Ah, but you do. Superintendent Jury told me the

pre-Raphaelites held for you no horrors. Nor did *Jane Eyre*. What about Hester and Chillingworth?''

Macalvie cadged a cigar and looked at Plant as if he'd gone mad. "What the hell is this? A literary quiz?"

"In a way."

"The Scarlet Letter. So what?"

Plant shrugged. "I'd just think any tutor would—"

"Tess of the D'Urbervilles," said Jury, absently. He looked very pale and was getting out of his chair. "My God, all of this time and we forgot—"

He made for the telephone in the middle of the heartrending voice of Elvis singing "Heartbreak Hotel."

It was one of the last songs Elvis Presley had sung.

IV

At first, when Molly Singer said the name, Jess thought she was talking to her. But then she said it again.

"Let her go, Tess."

Jessie knew what real fear was as the arm tightened around her shoulders and the knife nearly bit into her throat. Sara—but was that her real name?—whispered, "Get out! *Who are you?"*

"Mary."

The arm moved up, nearly cutting off Jessica's

wind. She wanted to cry but she couldn't. Where, where, was everybody? She heard Henry whine. Henry knew she was in trouble.

The flat, now unfamiliar voice of the young woman choking her was saying, "I don't know you. I don't know you."

"But I know you, Tess." Molly's voice wavered, but the gun-hand didn't. "I took some pictures. Of the Marine Parade. I had one of them blown up because there was something familiar about the girl in the picture. It might be years since I've seen you, but I'd know you anywhere, anywhere. You always looked like Mum, even when you were little."

It was as though Sara didn't hear her. "Put down the gun or I'll cut her up right now, right here. I was waiting for him to come back, damn him and all the Ashcrofts. It has to be here in the kitchen. I'll write him a message in her blood. . . . *He killed Mum, don't you realize that?* They were there in the house together. And then I came down in the morning . . ."

This was coming out in gasps, and Jess felt tears on the top of her head, on her hair. But the knife was still there, sharply honed, edge now against her chest. "So you've got to put down the gun, Mary."

Jess could see the gun shake in the hand of Molly Singer. *Don't let her have it, please, please.* She would have cried it out, but the arm was like a steel band around her shoulders. And then, in despair, she watched Molly drop the gun. The sound when it hit the floor flooded Jess with terror.

Sara was shoving Jess toward the kitchen table, whispering to her, or to Molly, that it was just the sacrifice, you see, of Isaac. It had to be done. Like the others. "Only I didn't have to cut the others up."

"And you're not going to do it to Jessica, either."

It was another voice, a man's.

Jess felt the knife move away from her, the obstructing arm torn from her shoulders and the voice saying, *Run, Jess.*

She ran toward the little hall.

But then she remembered Henry. Jess ran back, bunched him in her arms, and flew out the door into the shielding darkness of the night.

The rage of Teresa Mulvanney made her faster than either of them. She was out of his grasp and sliding across the floor to grab at the gun before Molly's hand could get to it.

Tess Mulvanney whipped the gun around, and from where she lay on the floor she shot Sam Waterhouse.

Molly opened her mouth to scream. But she didn't. Instead, she tried to inch her way to the table where lay the knife and the loaf of cut-up bread. She tried to talk to her sister, while tears slid down her face. "Tess. That's Sammy. Don't you remember? You loved him—"

Teresa's eyes widened. "It's not." As she closed her eyes, as if in an effort of remembrance, Molly took another step nearer the table. "They put him away. I read about the trial a year ago. When I got out of hospital. Everybody lied—*don't touch that!*"

Molly had almost had her hand on the knife when her sister grabbed it up. She raised the gun and slowly lowered it again. The look of rage turned to emotions confused and more gentle. "Mary." Tears ran down her face. "Don't you understand that I should've saved her? I should've saved Mum. If only I'd been brave enough to stab him, but I didn't know what—" She looked at the knife in her hand and let it fall on the floor. Tess ran the hand holding the gun across her wet forehead, but when Molly edged toward her, she steadied the hand again and shook her head violently. "Good-bye, Mary."

And she was out the door, the same one Jess had run through carrying Henry.

Molly knelt by Sam. The bullet had caught him in the side. His eyes were closed and she was terrified. But then he came round. Blood was seeping through his fingers. "I'm okay. But for God's sakes, get Teresa. Or she'll be back—" Sam passed out.

Molly could see, through the kitchen window, a path of light cut by a torch. Then she heard a car door slam.

Teresa couldn't afford to stop to look for Jessie out there in the dark; Robert Ashcroft could come driving up at any moment—

And then she remembered the Lamborghini.

Molly ran through the house, out the front door, down the drive toward her car. She heard, way off behind her, the distant sound of another car starting up.

There was only one way out of Ashcroft.

V

"Heartbreak Hall," said Jury. "That's what you called it." Jury had his coat on.

Macalvie stared at him and got up. So did Plant and Wiggins.

It was the first time Divisional Commander Macalvie had looked ashen and unsure of himself. Or was at a loss for words. But he finally found them as the four men headed for the door. "God, Jury. Not *Teresa Mulvanney*. I forgot to check out Tess—"

"*We* forgot, Brian. The forgotten little girl. You told me about Mary Mulvanney coming into your office. She said she couldn't stand to go back there again. According to Harbrick Hall, Teresa Mulvanney appeared to be coming out of it, like someone coming out of a fugue state. That was six years ago. Over the next year her improvement was miraculous. They gave her jobs to do. She did them well. She was articulate, well-behaved, calm. And it was a Lady Pembroke, charitable old dame, who told them she'd take over the care of Teresa Mulvanney."

"Let's get the hell out of here." Macalvie turned to Melrose. "You mind if we use your car, pal? Mine won't go from zero to ten in under an hour."

There was an apprehensive glance from Wiggins when Melrose handed the keys over. "This one will go a little faster."

That was an understatement, or so Macalvie proved it to be. Wiggins was hunched down as far as possible in the back seat. The narrow road, the occasional thick hedges, the night, the murderous moor-mist, all contrived to make driving nearly impossible.

Macalvie didn't seem to notice as he careened the Rolls around a turn. "How did she know? How on earth could she hand-pick her victims like that?"

"Pitifully simple. As I said to Mr. Mack, a will that's been probated is in the public domain. Sara Millar–Teresa Mulvanney simply looked at the heirs to the Ashcroft fortune. As far as George Thorne was concerned, well, she might have thought of him as— who knows, a conspirator. And there was also the simple matter of geography. The final object was Jessica. The others she killed . . . on the way." Jury felt sick.

Macalvie scraped the left-hand fender cutting the curve of a stone wall too sharply. "Sorry, friend."

Melrose, smoking calmly in the back seat, said, "I can always get parts."

He hit the steering wheel again and again with the heel of his hand. "But goddamnit, Jury! They were kids! Why the hell didn't she just go after Ashcroft if he's the one who murdered Rose Mulvanney?"

"She couldn't."

Macalvie took his eyes off the road for a crucial second and the fender got it again. "What the hell do you mean?"

"He was already dead."

V

It was a long driveway, a drive like a tunnel, and Molly could hear the car, which must have been coming round the side of the house. She didn't yet see the headlamps.

She started to switch on the Lamborghini's lights, and paused. Tess could easily think it was Robert Ashcroft returning and head right into him. Molly found she had at least a little interest in living, which surprised her. There might be a way to stop Teresa without actually killing herself.

Something to take her by surprise, make her veer off into the thick trees, maybe an accident, but not a fatal one. The camera equipment. Flashbulbs? Not enough bulbs, not enough time. And now when she looked up she saw, at the end of the tunnel, far off, the headlamps of Tess's car.

The light at the end of the tunnel / Is the light of an

oncoming train. . . . The lines of Lowell suddenly came back to her. She snatched the unipod from the rear seat, smashed out the right-hand headlamp, tossed the thing in the back and got in. Was there anything more disconcerting to a driver than to see only one light coming toward him rather than two? What was it? Car? Motorbike? And the moment of confusion—

The other car was halfway down the drive, its lights hazy in the middle distance. Molly started the engine and headed up the drive. *Ah, hell. You only die once.*

They weren't more than a dozen yards apart, when the wheels of the Morris screeched and the car swerved and rammed into the wall. Then it went into a spin and rammed the front of the Lamborghini.

The Rolls was only a minute away from the Ashcroft drive when they heard the sound of tearing metal.

Macalvie jammed on the brakes at the entrance. The four of them piled out.

The Morris burst into flames as they ran.

Molly's car was a disaster, but it wasn't burning. It was a distance from the flaming Morris, and it was tougher.

And for the seconds it took Macalvie to pull her out of the wreckage, so was Molly Singer.

Blood trickled from her ear, and a tiny line of blood ran from the corner of her mouth. But she did not look bruised or broken. She looked up at Macalvie, who was holding her in his arms. She smiled. "Damnit. Why do you *always* have to be right, Mac——?" She didn't get out the last of it. The long fingers that clutched his shoulder slid down his coat as slowly as a hand playing a harp.

Macalvie started shaking her and shouting: *"Mary!"* He shouted the name until Jury pulled him away.

Melrose Plant took off his coat and put it under her head.

Jury took off his own coat and covered her with it.

A trickle of gas from the Morris reached the Lamborghini. All Jury could think of was the log falling and sparking in Molly Singer's cottage.

TWENTY-SEVEN

I

Jury found her on the mechanic's creeper under the Zimmer. She was holding on tight to Henry.

Jessica did not want to come out.

"Please, Jessie. It's all over. It's okay now."

Okay. It would never be okay, not for Divisional Commander Macalvie. He had disappeared into the trees and the fog.

"It's better here," said Jess. There was a silence. "I don't want to get cut up. And I don't want Henry to, either."

Jury sat down, there on the cold stone of the courtyard, cold as hell himself without his coat. She was silent. "Was Sara the ax-murderer?"

"No. There was never an ax-murderer, Jess. Sara—" He didn't know whether to tell her or not, then decided he might as well level. "Sara was sick, very sick. She was the one who killed the children."

"But why me? Was she their governess too?"

"No. No, she wasn't. Why you? Because she was confused. A long time ago, much longer than before you were born, someone hurt her and she wanted revenge. Someone killed her mother. You can see how terrible that would be."

"But *we* didn't do it—I mean me and Davey and that other boy and girl! Stop it, Henry! Henry doesn't like it under here, but I'm afraid something will happen to him."

She was crying, Jury could hear. "Nothing can possibly happen."

"Well, he'd rather be *in* the car than under it. So you put him up in the seat. But don't let him *go* anywhere." She said it pretty fiercely, as if she wanted to be sure, now Jury was there, that he stayed.

"Come on, Henry," said Jury. He lugged the dog out and put him in the front seat of the Zimmer. Henry shook himself and seemed to open his eyes. A new world. Strange, but new.

And strange and new for Jessica Ashcroft too. "Well?"

"Sorry. Well, what?"

"You didn't answer my question. We didn't kill her mother."

285

"I know."

"Well?"

Jury thought she must be getting better. She was certainly testier. "Let me tell you something that's very—difficult to understand, Jess. I think what was wrong with Sara was she felt guilty. She was only five when her mother died. And she *saw* it." Jury stopped for a moment. He remembered his conversation with Mrs. Wasserman, how he'd asked, without thinking, what the bolted door kept out. Him. To Mrs. Wasserman all the fears were focused on Him. Displacement, whatever a psychiatrist might have called it. "I think Sara felt, well, horribly guilty—"

From under the sanctuary of the dark car, Jessica said, "I know. She thought it was her fault. She thought she did it. And maybe she thought she was killing her own self when she killed Davey and that girl. And almost me."

He could hardly believe his ears. Until he heard her crying again, and then realized how much guilt she must have felt about the death of the most beautiful, the kindest woman Jessica had ever imagined, yet never known. And how she could easily have felt responsible. Barbara Allan had died so soon after her daughter was born.

Jury could think of nothing to say.

"How is that man who saved me?"

"He's fine; the ambulance just got here to take him to hospital."

She rolled out. She got off the creeper. Her night-dress, her face, her hair were smudged with oil and grease. "Come on, Henry," she said, her tone its usual testy self.

Henry clambered out of the car and followed them as they walked slowly across the courtyard. Jessie was holding Jury's hand.

"I'll tell you something," she said grumpily.

"Yes? What?"

"I hope I never run up against Jane Eyre."

II

When Robert Ashcroft and Victoria Gray were driving, a few minutes later, toward home, they heard the sirens, saw the whirring lights, saw the fire in the driveway.

"Oh, God, oh, God," whispered Victoria.

Robert Ashcroft gunned the Ferrari up to seventy.

He jumped out of the car, threaded his way through police and ambulance crew, and ran in the house calling for his niece.

Jury had never seen a man look so terrified, with one exception, and then so relieved. No exception there.

Jessica stood, hands on hips, grease-smudged face and oil-bedewed hair, glaring up at her uncle. "I don't want any more governesses. Until I go away to school, I want a bodyguard. I want that man that saved my life."

Ashcroft merely nodded. He had tears in his eyes.

"Come on, Henry." They climbed the stairs slowly. But halfway up she turned to deliver her parting shot.

"You're always away when the ax-murderers come." Then she and Henry continued their weary ascent.

VII

*

Pretty Molly Brannigan

TWENTY-EIGHT

I

The old char was singing in Wynchcoombe church and wringing her mop in a pail. Out of deference either to Jury or the vicar's lad who'd been buried only yesterday, she stopped singing and kept on swabbing the floor.

Death did not stop the stone from getting dirty or flowers from wilting, and the ones on the altar looked in need of changing. He watched her running the grubby mop over the stone floor and wondered how something that made such an enormous difference to so many—all of those deaths—could make little more than a dent in the daily round of cleaning.

The old woman with the mop and pail paid no

attention to him, one of the many who came to see this little marvel of a church that towered cathedral-like over its valley in the moor.

Jury dropped some money in the collection box, listening to the charwoman, who couldn't resist her bit of music, change to humming. He thought of Molly Singer and imagined that somewhere in Waterford or Clare or Donegal, a clear-voiced Irish girl might be doing her washing-up, maybe humming from the boredom of it.

Damn it, why are you always right, Mac?

Jury looked at the painting of Abraham and Isaac, the knife near the terrified boy's face. His father ready for the sacrifice. All God had to do was say *Go.*

To Macalvie, who had been right all along about her, she was Mary Mulvanney.

To Jury, she would always be Molly Singer.

He felt the old char watching him as he walked out of the church.

II

When he got to the Help the Poor Struggler, it was almost a relief to hear Divisional Commander Macalvie shouting over the noise of the jukebox that he'd tie Freddie to a tree in Wistman's Wood if she didn't stop singing along with Elvis. It was the version of "Are You Lonesome Tonight?" where Elvis forgot the words and was laughing at himself and the audience was joining in. What rapport, thought Jury, Elvis Presley had had with his audience. It was a song he must have sung a hundred times, yet he'd forgotten—probably because of his failing powers— the words. But his fans hadn't. They never would. There were some things people never forgot. Like his last concert.

"Y'r a rate trate, no mistake. He be dead, man. Hain't yuh got no respect fer the dead?"

Macalvie was silent for a moment. Then he shouted back, "If I did, Freddie, I'd have some respect for *you*. Hullo," he added grudgingly to Jury. Melrose Plant was sitting with Macalvie. It was a drunk Brian Macalvie. "How about one of your fancy cigars, friend?" he said to Plant. And to Wiggins, who had opened his mouth, Macalvie said, "Shut up."

Freddie, who must have heard something and was being halfway human to Macalvie, set his pint on the table and said to Wiggins—or all of them—"No use to argie-fy with Macalvie."

"How's Sam?" asked Jury.

"Fine. He's fine. Be out of hospital in a couple of weeks." Macalvie smoked and stared at his pint.

"How'd he know, Brian? That Jessica might be in danger?"

Turning his glass round and round, Macalvie said, "The bloody coat-of-arms. The letter Plant wrote to you. That and the picture. You remember, he went through her desk. The unidentified man. Sammy saw Robert Ashcroft at the George in Wynchcoombe. James and Robert looked a lot alike. At first he thought Robert was simply a man who looked a hell of a lot like the one in Rose's snap. It was seeing the coat-of-arms that he'd seen on a piece of notepaper in the desk that finally did it. Anyway, he thought he should keep an eye on Ashcroft."

"You were right. There *was* something he knew that hadn't surfaced. James Ashcroft was indiscreet, writing to Rose Mulvanney."

"To say the least. He let Sammy waste his life in prison. Bastard."

Plant said, "I think Robert Ashcroft will try and make up for that in some way."

Macalvie glared at him. "Buy him a car, maybe. Sam told me he watched that house from a spot on the moor where he set up camp. He figured something would happen." Another silence. "It happened."

A big, beefy man was plugging money into the jukebox. "Play a few Golden Oldies, or something, will you?" yelled Macalvie.

The perfect stranger looked around, and not in a friendly way. "Play what I like, mate." He rippled muscles as best he could under the leather jacket. "Who the hell you be, anyway?"

Macalvie started to get up.

Jury pulled him down. "Forget it, Brian."

Having to yell at someone, Macalvie turned again to Freddie. "Bring us four more and try and keep the tapwater out of it this time."

"A course, me 'anzum," said Freddie, over the double-din of the music and the casuals off the road. Considering the usual lack of custom, the pub was almost jumping. Even the dartboard was getting a workout.

And then an Irish voice from the jukebox, thin and silvery, was singing. Apparently, leather-jacket was a sentimentalist.

> *"O, man, dear, did ya never hear*
> *Of pretty Molly Brannigan—"*

The cigar stopped halfway to Macalvie's mouth. His expression was blank.

> *"She's gone away and left me,*
> *And I'll never be a man again—"*

Macalvie had taken out his wallet and checked the contents. "Being an earl," he said to Melrose, "and probably owning a big hunk of England, I don't suppose you'd be good for a loan of, say, eighty quid, would you?"

Without any questions, Melrose took out his money clip, peeled off four twenties, and handed them over.

> ". . . . *Now that Molly's gone and left me*
> *Here for to die.*"

Macalvie walked over to the bar where Freddie was singing along and spread a hundred and thirty pounds in front of her.

> "*Oh, the left side of me heart*
> *Is as weak as watered gruel, man;*
> *Won't ye come to me wake*
> *when I make that great meander, man . . . ?*"

Freddie, watching him, shouted, "'Ere, Mac, wot be yu on upon?"

Macalvie had already positioned himself, taken aim, and shoved his size ten straight into the jukebox.

The song splintered like a broken windscreen, flying into pieces, shivers of metal and glass. It caught the entire room in a freeze-frame. No one moved.

Except Macalvie, who walked back to his chair and snatched up his coat. He looked around the table and said, "Macalvie, nil. Mulvanney, nil."

Then he turned with his coat slung over his shoulder and walked out into the dark where, not far away, the prison rose through the mists of Dartmoor and hung over Princetown like a huge raven.

Don't miss Martha Grimes's new
Richard Jury novel

THE WINDS OF CHANGE

Available in hardcover
from Viking

DON'T MISS MARTHA GRIMES'S OTHER DAZZLING RICHARD JURY MYSTERIES . . .

The Man with a Load of Mischief

Introducing Scotland Yard's Richard Jury in Martha Grimes's intriguing first novel

At the Man with a Load of Mischief, a dead man is found with his head stuck in a beer keg. At the Jack and Hammer, another body was stuck out on the beam of the pub's sign, replacing the mechanical man who kept the time. Two pubs. Two murders. One Scotland Yard inspector called in to help. Detective Chief Inspector Richard Jury arrives in Long Piddleton and finds everyone in the postcard village looking outside of town for the killer. Except for Melrose Plant. A keen observer of human nature, he points Jury in the right direction: toward the darkest parts of his neighbors' hearts. . . .

"Grimes captures the flavor of British village life. . . . Long may she write Richard Jury mysteries."
—*Chicago Tribune*

The Old Fox Deceiv'd

Stacked against the cliffs on the shore of the North Sea and nearly hidden by fog, the town of Rackmoor seems a fitting place for murder. But the stabbing death of a costumed young woman has shocked the close-knit village. When Richard Jury arrives on the scene, he's pulled up short by the fact that no one is sure who the victim is, much less the killer. Her questionable ties to one of the most wealthy and influential families in town send Jury and Melrose Plant on a deadly hunt to track down a very wily murderer.

"A superior writer."

—*The New York Times Review*

"Warmth, humor, and great style . . . a thoroughly satisfying plot . . . one of the somoothest, richest traditional English mysteries ever to originate on this side of the Atlantic."　　　　—*Kirkus Reviews*

I Am the Only Running Footman

They were two women, strikingly similar in life . . . strikingly similar in death. Both were strangled with their own scarves—one in Devon, one outside a fashionable Mayfair pub called I Am the Only Running Footman. Richard Jury teams up with Devon's irascible local divisional commander, Brian Macalvie, to solve the murders. With nothing to tie the women together but the fatal scarves, Jury pursues his only suspect . . . and a trail of tragedy that just might lead to yet another victim—and her killer.

"Everything about Miss Grimes's new novel shows her at her best. . . . [She] gets our immediate attention. . . . She holds it, however, with something more than mere suspense."

—*The New Yorker*

"Literate, witty, and stylishly crafted."

—*The Washington Post*

The Five Bells and Bladebone

Richard Jury has yet to finish his first pint in the village of Long Piddleton when he finds a corpse inside a beautiful rosewood desk recently acquired by the local antiques dealer, Marshall Trueblood. The body belongs to Simon Lean, a notorious philanderer. An endless list of suspects leads Jury and his aristocratic sidekick, Melrose Plant, to the nearby country estate where Lean's long-suffering wife resides. But Jury's best clue comes in London at a pub called the Five Bells and Bladebone. There he learns about Lean's liaison with a disreputable woman named Sadie, who could have helped solve the case . . . if she wasn't already dead.

"Blends almost Dickensian sketches of character and social class with glimpses of a ferocious marriage."
—*Time*

"[Grimes's] best . . . as moving as it is entertaining."
—*USA Today*

The Case Has Altered

Timeless, peaceful, and remote, the watery Lincolnshire fens seem an unlikely setting for murder. But two women—a notorious actress and a servant girl—have been killed there in the space of two weeks. The Lincolnshire police are sure the murders are connected—and they think a friend of Richard Jury is responsible. Jury is anxious to clear Jenny Kennington's name. But the secretive suspects and tight-lipped locals are leading him nowhere. And with the help of his colleague Melrose Plant, he must struggle to navigate a series of untruths in the hope of stopping a very determined killer.

"Masterful writing, skillful plotting, shrewd characterizations, subtle humor, and an illuminating look at what makes us humans tick . . . [an] outstanding story from one of today's most talented writers . . . brilliant."

—*Booklist*

"Dazzling. Deftly plotted . . . psychologically complex . . . delicious wit."

—*Publishers Weekly*

The Stargazey

After a luminous blonde leaves, reboards, then leaves the double-decker bus Richard Jury is on, he follows her up to the gates of Fulham Palace . . . and goes no farther. Days later, when he hears of the death in the palace's walled garden, Jury will wonder if he could have averted it. But is the victim the same woman Jury saw? As he and Melrose Plant follow the complex case from the Crippsian depths of London's East End to the headier heights of Mayfair's art scene, Jury will realize that in this captivating woman—dead or alive—he may have finally met his match. . . .

"A delightfully entertaining blend of irony, danger, and intrigue, liberally laced with wit and charm. . . . A must have from one of today's most gifted and intelligent writers."

—*Booklist* (starred review)

"The literary equivalent of a box of Godiva truffles . . . wonderful."

—*Los Angeles Times*

The Lamorna Wink

With his good friend Richard Jury on a fool's errand
in Northern Ireland, Melrose Plant tries—in vain—
to escape his aunt and his Long Piddleton lethargy
by fleeing to Cornwall. There, high on a rocky prom-
ontory overlooking the sea, he rents a house—one
furnished with tragic memories. But his Cornwallian
reveries are tempered by the local waiter/cab driver/
amateur magician. The industrious Johnny Wells
seems unflappable—until his beloved aunt disappears. Now Plant is dragged into the disturbing pasts
of everyone involved—and a murder mystery that
only Richard Jury can solve. . . .

"Swift and satisfying . . . grafts the old-fashioned
'Golden Age' amateur-detective story to the contem-
porary police procedural . . . real charm."
—*The Wall Street Journal*

"Entrancing. Grimes makes her own mark on du
Maurier country."
—*The Orlando Sentinel*

The Blue Last

Mickey Haggerty, a DCI with the City police, has asked for Richard Jury's help. Two skeletons have been unearthed during the excavation of London's last bomb site, where once stood a pub called the Blue Last. The grandchild of brewery magnate Oliver Tynedale supposedly survived that December 1940 bombing . . . but did she? Then the son of the one-time owner of the Blue Last is found shot to death—the book he was writing about London during the German blitzkrieg . . . gone. A stolen life, a stolen book? Or is any of this what it seems? With Melrose Plant sent undercover, Jury calls into question identity, memory, and provenance in a case that resurrects his own hauntingly sad past. . . .

"Grimes's best . . . a cliffhanger ending."

—*USA Today*

"Explosive . . . ranks among the best of its creator's distinguished work."

—*Richmond Times-Dispatch*

Martha Grimes

The Richard Jury Novels

Available wherever books are sold or at
www.penguin.com

New York Times bestselling author
MARTHA GRIMES

Foul Matter

Author Paul Giverney is between publishers.
Despite stratospheric sales of his last book
and frenzied competition to sign him, he
lives modestly in New York City's
East Village and nurses a secret ambition of
a very different sort.

"IF YOU THOUGHT THERE WERE STRANGE, AMAZING
TWISTS AND WILDLY ECCENTRIC CHARACTERS IN
MARTHA GRIMES' RICHARD JURY NOVELS,
WAIT UNTIL YOU SEE WHAT HAPPENS WHEN SHE
TAKES ON THE WORLD OF PUBLISHING."
—ROBERT PARKER

0-451-21293-2

**Available wherever books are sold or at
www.penguin.com**

"Nell, I miss you." James gazed at her warmly.

"James, we can't do this. *I* can't do this."

"What exactly is this?" he asked quietly. "The fact that we like each other but shouldn't?"

"*Ja*, we shouldn't," she said and started to turn away.

He captured her arm. "Nell, I'm sorry. I know I have no right to ask anything of you, but please…consider us being friends if we can't be anything more."

"I don't know if I can," she whispered.

"Why not?"

She nodded. "'Tis too risky. I want more but it will never happen. So I'm sorry, James, but we can't be friends. *Ever.*" Nell turned back to the buggy and climbed in.

Her eyes slid over him as they drove away. She was a fool for loving him, but she couldn't help herself. Her resolve hardened—she needed to find an Amish husband and soon, so that she could forget that the price to pay for following her heart could be detrimental to her future.

Rebecca Kertz was first introduced to the Amish when her husband took a job with an Amish construction crew. She enjoyed watching the Amish foreman's children at play and swapping recipes with his wife. Rebecca resides in Delaware with her husband and dog. She has a strong faith in God and feels blessed to have family nearby. Besides writing, she enjoys reading, doing crafts and visiting Lancaster County.

Books by Rebecca Kertz

Love Inspired

Women of Lancaster County

A Secret Amish Love

Lancaster County Weddings

Noah's Sweetheart
Jedidiah's Bride
A Wife for Jacob
Elijah and the Widow
Loving Isaac

Lancaster Courtships

The Amish Mother

A Secret
Amish Love

Rebecca Kertz

HARLEQUIN® LOVE INSPIRED®

If you purchased this book without a cover you should be aware
that this book is stolen property. It was reported as "unsold and
destroyed" to the publisher, and neither the author nor the
publisher has received any payment for this "stripped book."

Recycling programs
for this product may
not exist in your area.

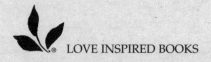

® LOVE INSPIRED BOOKS

ISBN-13: 978-0-373-62284-9

A Secret Amish Love

Copyright © 2017 by Candace McCarthy

All rights reserved. Except for use in any review, the reproduction
or utilization of this work in whole or in part in any form by any
electronic, mechanical or other means, now known or hereinafter
invented, including xerography, photocopying and recording, or in
any information storage or retrieval system, is forbidden without
the written permission of the editorial office, Love Inspired Books,
195 Broadway, New York, NY 10007 U.S.A.

This is a work of fiction. Names, characters, places and incidents are
either the product of the author's imagination or are used fictitiously, and
any resemblance to actual persons, living or dead, business establishments,
events or locales is entirely coincidental.

This edition published by arrangement with Love Inspired Books.

® and TM are trademarks of Love Inspired Books, used under license.
Trademarks indicated with ® are registered in the United States Patent
and Trademark Office, the Canadian Intellectual Property Office and in
other countries.

www.Harlequin.com

Printed in U.S.A.

And now these three remain: faith, hope and love. But the greatest of these is love.
—*1 Corinthians* 13:13

For my mother-in-law—my other Mom—with love

Chapter One

Lancaster County, Pennsylvania

Nell Stoltzfus opened the door to Pierce Veterinary Clinic and gaped as she stepped inside. Pandemonium reigned in the crowded waiting room. Dogs growled and barked as they strained at their leashes. Some owners spoke sharply while others murmured soothingly as they struggled to control their pets.

A cat in a carrier situated on a woman's lap meowed loudly in angry protest of the ear-splitting canine activity. An Amish man sat in the corner of the room with a she-goat. The animal bent her head as she tried to eat a magazine in the rack on the floor near the man's feet. The goat was haltered, and her owner tugged up on the rope lead to keep her from chewing on the glossy pages. The animal bleated loudly as she stubbornly fought to eat.

The goat's noisy discontent joined in the cacophony of human and animal sounds as the unfamiliar Amish man glanced at Nell briefly before returning his attention to his goat.

She searched the room and frowned. Every available seat was taken. There was no sign of Michelle, Dr. Pierce's receptionist, whose job it was to check in patients and, on occasion, bring them into the exam rooms when the veterinary assistant, Janie, was busy.

Nell narrowed her gaze, assessing. On most days, there were usually two or three people in the waiting room. At least, every time she'd brought her dog, Jonas, in, there had been only a few people with their pets waiting.

During her first visit to Pierce Veterinary Clinic, just shy of a month after it opened, she'd sought medical help for Jonas after he was cruelly tossed out of a moving car. The visit had been a memorable one.

She'd met Dr. James Pierce, who'd refused to charge her for taking care of Jonas, requesting instead that she spread word of his clinic to anyone who might benefit from his services. And he'd startled her by offering her a temporary job as his assistant, based on her ability to calm her injured rescue dog who had lain trustingly in her arms.

"You have a natural affinity with animals, Nell," he'd told her during her first visit. During her second and last visit to the clinic, she'd declined but thanked him for his offer, even though she would have liked nothing more than to have the opportunity to learn more about caring for animals since it was her dream to minister to those within her Amish community. But her strong attraction to Dr. Pierce made it wise to keep her distance from him.

Today, Nell had been on her way home after a morning spent with her aunt Katie when she'd decided to stop at the clinic to purchase heartworm medicine for Jonas. At the veterinarian's suggestion, she had waited to ensure that her dog was fully healed before introducing the medication.

I should go, she thought as she gazed around the room. Clearly, she'd chosen the worst time to come.

She turned to leave, then glanced back when her attention was drawn toward the sound of a door opening and voices. A woman exited from a back room with a tiny kitten.

Nell waited patiently, expecting to glimpse Janie following closely behind. But it wasn't the assistant she saw. It was Dr. Pierce who escorted the woman to the front desk.

Nell watched as he sat at the desk and keyed something into the computer. She heard the deep, indecipherable rumble of his voice as he spoke. The woman handed him a credit card, and Nell continued to watch as Dr. Pierce handled the transaction, then gave the woman a receipt stapled to a paper that she knew would be the animal's health summary.

Nell froze, and her heart beat wildly as Dr. Pierce stood. She sent up a silent prayer that she would remain unnoticed, but she was powerless to move or to keep her gaze from checking for any changes in the man since she last saw him over a month ago.

She released a shuddering breath. The veterinarian was still as handsome as ever, dressed in his white lab coat over a blue shirt and black slacks. His short hair, which was a little longer on the top, was tousled as if he'd recently combed his fingers through the dark brown locks. His features were chiseled, his chin firm. There was sharp intelligence in his dark eyes. She recalled the brightness she'd first noticed in them, and his kindness and compassion when he'd treated Jonas. He had a gentle and sincere smile that warmed her all the way from her head to her toes each time she'd seen him.

A shiver of something pleasurable yet frightening

slid down the length of her spine as she realized that she was attracted to him. Dr. Pierce still had the ability to affect her more than any other man since Michael, the man she'd loved and lost.

Nell stiffened and fought to banish the feelings. Dr. Pierce threatened her peace of mind. She drew a steadying breath as she struggled to pull herself together.

James. He'd told her at their first meeting to call him James. She shouldn't. But since that day, every time she saw him she immediately thought of him as James.

She closed her eyes briefly as she shifted farther into the corner of the room to stay unobtrusive. Nell swallowed hard. She didn't want the man to catch sight of her. As the eldest of five Stoltzfus sisters, she was expected to be the first to marry a faithful member of their Amish community. The last thing she needed was to fall for the English veterinarian. Being in James's company was dangerous. Even if he'd had feelings for her, there would have been no way for them to be anything other than polite acquaintances. Not that he felt the same attraction. It was all one-sided—her side.

The woman with the kitten turned to leave. On her way to the door, she walked past Nell, who froze. Nell knew that if she moved even a tiny bit, James might notice her.

Something shifted in his expression, as if alarmed at the number of patients in the waiting room.

Nell waited for him to call back the next patient. As soon as he left, she would go. She'd return when Michelle was in the office. Jonas could wait another week to start his medicine. Or she could play it safe and go somewhere else and escape the frightening, forbidden feelings she felt any time she was near James.

She sighed. She couldn't go elsewhere. It wouldn't be right after all James had done for Jonas.

Nell remained still but then released a sharp breath when James suddenly saw her. They locked gazes. Surprise and pleasure flashed in the depths of his dark eyes, and she felt an infusion of warmth.

She recognized the panic in his gaze. She sighed. He was lost without his assistant, and she was the only one available who might be able to help.

She had a moment of revelation. *The Lord wants me to stay.*

"Dr. Pierce?" She stepped forward with a tentative smile on her face. Her heart beat rapidly as she remained the focus of his dark gaze. "May I have a word with you?"

"Of course, Nell." He waited for her approach.

"No help today?" she asked softly so that the others within the room couldn't hear their conversation.

He shook his head. "Unfortunately, I'm alone today."

"I'll be happy to help if you'd like."

His eyes brightened as relief swept across his features. "I'd like that. Thank you."

James had never been happier to see Nell Stoltzfus. His receptionist, Michelle, was out sick, and Janie, his assistant, was on vacation, and he was swamped and alone dealing with a crowded waiting room.

As he'd watched Nell push out of the corner and approach, he'd been overcome with an immediate sense of calm. He'd never realized it before, but she had the same effect on him as she'd had on her injured rescue dog when she'd first brought Jonas in.

"Come into the back," he said, aware of the huskiness of his voice. He felt a jolt in his stomach as she smiled and followed him. Nell, a pretty young Amish woman, wore a spring-green dress with matching cape and apron. Her soft brown hair was covered by her white prayer *kapp*. Her nose was pert and perfectly formed, and her mouth was pink with a slight bow to her upper lip. He felt something shift inside him as he became the focus of her beautiful, brown gaze.

"Dr. Pierce, your waiting room seems unusually full." Her softly spoken words jerked him to awareness. She studied him with her head slightly tilted as if she were trying to gauge his thoughts. "I'd like to check your schedule."

They entered the reception area through a door off the hallway, and he showed her where to find the appointment book. "How long can you stay?"

"Through the afternoon." Her shy smile warmed him from the inside out. "May I use your phone?"

"Of course." She would need to get word to her family, he realized, so that they wouldn't worry about her absence. He waited while she made her phone call, trying not to listen as she explained the situation.

"*Ja*, Bob," he heard her say. "*Ja*, that would be *gut*. Thank you. Tell them that I shouldn't be too late." She glanced up to meet his gaze, and James instantly moved away to give her privacy.

He approached after Nell hung up the phone and stood. "Is everything all right?"

"*Ja*, 'tis fine." Her gaze met his, then slid away. He watched her study Michelle's appointment book. Her eyes narrowed. "You definitely don't have this many patients expected today," she murmured with a frown. "I'll have to do some rescheduling."

He started to leave, then turned. "Nell?"

She dragged her eyes away from the page to meet his gaze. *"Ja?"*

"Thank you." He spoke quietly so that no one would overhear him, but he knew immediately that she'd heard.

"You're *willkomm*," she breathed, and then she waved him away as she went back to studying the appointment book.

With a smile on his face, he opened the door to the back room.

"Dr. Pierce?"

He halted and faced her. "Yes?"

"Which exam rooms are available for patients?"

"One, three and four," he told her without hesitation. Then he entered the back of the clinic and went on to exam room two where his next patient waited.

James was examining the ear of a golden retriever when Nell knocked softly before opening the door.

"Dr. Pierce?"

"Yes, Nell?" he inquired without looking up.

"I've put Mrs. Rogan and Boots in exam room one and Mr. Jones with his dog Betsy in three. Mr. Yoder and his goat are in four. I rescheduled three patients for tomorrow because they didn't have appointments and your schedule could handle them then. Mrs. Pettyjohn is here with her poodle. She is your last appointment."

He straightened. "Already?" Amazed, he stared at her.

She gazed at him, her brown eyes filled with uncertainly. "Already?" she echoed.

"Are we really almost finished?" he asked. "Thank you for getting control of the situation so quickly." He looked sheepish. "I've been struggling about how to handle everyone for the last hour and a half." He rubbed his fingers through the dog's coat. "Bailey is going to be fine, Mrs. Martin."

The woman looked relieved as she glanced back and forth between them. "Thank you, Dr. Pierce."

"You're welcome." He turned toward Nell, pleased that she hadn't moved. "Nell, would you mind checking out Mrs. Martin and Bailey?"

"I'd be happy to," she said politely. She turned to the dog's owner. "Mrs. Martin, would you please follow me?"

James caught Nell's gaze as she waited for the woman and her dog to walk past her. He grinned in approval and was relieved to see her answering smile before she quickly followed Mrs. Martin.

Nell came into the back as he exited exam room two. "I forgot to tell you that Mrs. Rogan in exam room one had the next earliest appointment, then Mr. Jones, then Abraham Yoder."

He couldn't keep from studying her face. Nell Stoltzfus was genuinely lovely, with no need for artificial enhancement. He noted her smooth, unblemished skin, her pink lips, the reddish tinge to her cheeks. Since graduating from vet school, he'd had little time for a personal life, especially now that he was working hard to establish his new practice. He didn't know why, but there was something about her that made him long for something more. "Thank you, Nell."

"You're *willkomm*, Dr. Pierce."

He briefly met her gaze. "James, please," he invited. Again.

"James," she said then she blushed. "It was Mrs. Beggs, Mr. Merritt and Mrs. McDaniel whom I rescheduled."

"I appreciate your help," he told her, meaning it. "I didn't expect Michelle and Janie to both be out today. Janie asked for the week off, and Michelle is home with a stomach bug." He sighed. "I confess that I'm not good at juggling appointments."

Nell looked confused. "Juggling?"

He laughed. "Sorry, I'm not laughing at you but at myself. I don't know how Michelle does her job. She's good at what she does." He studied her thoughtfully, liking what he saw. "Apparently, you're good at it, too."

"At juggling appointments?" She arched her eyebrows.

"Yes." He chuckled, and the smile that came to Nell's pink lips had him mesmerized until he realized that he was staring. He stole one last glance at her as he opened the door to room one.

He heard her *"Ja"* before he closed the door.

The day passed quickly, and soon the last patient had been seen. Nell set aside the appointment book along with the checks, money and credit card transactions for the day. Fortunately, she'd quickly figured out how to use the credit card machine. She'd seen Bob Whittier of Whittier's Store use one often enough to recall how it was done.

She even had the opportunity to assist James with his last patient. Mrs. Pettyjohn's poodle, Roggs, had a lump above his right hind leg. James had determined it to be an abscess following a small injury. He'd asked for her help as he did minor surgery to open the wound.

"Will he be all right?" Nell asked as she handed him supplies and observed his work.

"He'll be fine. It looks as if he got into a rosebush. See this thorn?" He held up a tiny dark object that he'd removed with tweezers. "I'll prescribe an antibiotic for a couple of weeks. He'll have to wear a cone until his follow-up appointment."

Nell had enjoyed her afternoon at the clinic being his assistant. Too much. And she knew it had as much to do with the man as working with animals. Thankfully, the day was over, and after she helped to clean up, she'd be able to leave.

She cleaned the exam room floors with disinfectant. She was quiet as she mopped, her thoughts filled with what she'd seen and heard that day. When she was done, she emptied out the wash water and put away the bucket and mop.

"I'm finished with the floors, Doctor—James," she told him as he came into the reception area where she picked up her purse. "I'll be heading home now."

"Thank you so much for your help today," he said. "I don't know how I would have managed without you." He gazed at her a moment, then frowned. "Why did you come into the office today?"

"My dog, Jonas, is well and old enough to start his heartworm medicine."

"I'll get it for you." James retrieved a box from a cabinet and handed it to her. "Take it. No charge. If you come back tomorrow, I'll have cash for you."

"For what?" She frowned. "For helping out for a few hours? *Nay*, I'll not take your money."

"Nell…"

"*Nay*, James."

"But you'll take the medicine."

She opened her mouth to object but relented when she saw his expression. The man wasn't going to take no for an answer. *"Ja. Danki."* She gasped as she saw the time on the office wall clock. "I've got to go. *Mam* will be holding dinner for me." She hurried toward the door. *"Gut* night, James."

"Good night, Nell," he said softly.

Nell promptly left and ran toward her buggy, which was parked in the back lot several yards away from the building. She unhitched her mare, Daisy, then climbed into her vehicle.

As she reached for the reins, she watched as James headed toward his car. He stood by the driver's side and lifted a hand to wave. She nodded but didn't wave back. As she drove out onto the road, her thoughts turned to her family and most particularly her father, who wouldn't be pleased that she was late for supper.

She spurred Daisy into a quick trot and drove home in record time. As she steered the mare into the barnyard, her sister Leah came out of the house to greet her.

"*Dat*'s been wondering why you're late," Leah said as the two sisters walked toward the house.

"I was helping Dr. Pierce at the veterinary clinic." Nell stiffened. "Didn't Bob Whittier get word to you?"

"About a half hour ago."

"*Ach, nay,*" Nell said with dismay. "I didn't know he'd wait until that late. I called him hours ago."

"He sent word with Joshua Peachy but Joshua got sidetracked when he saw an accident on the stretch of road between Yoder's General Store and Eli's carriage shop. A truck hit a car and there were children..."

"I'm sorry to hear that. Is everyone all right?"

"Joshua didn't know."

"Is *Dat* angry with me?"

"*Nay*, Joshua told him what happened and why he couldn't get word to us earlier."

"But?"

"But he expected you sooner, and I don't think he was too happy that you stayed to help out James Pierce."

"Leah, you should have seen the waiting room. It was noisy and crowded, and there was no staff to help him.

Both Michelle and Janie were out and he was alone. I believe that God wanted me to help him."

Her sister smiled. "Then that's what you tell *Dat*. He can't argue with the Lord."

As she entered the kitchen, Nell saw her other sisters seated at the table with her parents. She nodded to each of them then settled her gaze on her father. *"Dat,"* she said. "I'm sorry I'm late. I didn't expect to be gone so long."

To her surprise, her father nodded but didn't comment.

Nell took her place at the table, and *Dat* led them as they gave thanks to the Lord for their meal. Nell's sister Charlie started a conversation, and all of her sisters joined in as food was passed around.

As she reached for the bowl of mashed potatoes, Nell caught her *dat* studying her with a thoughtful expression. She felt suddenly uneasy. Her father might have seemed unaffected by her lateness, but she could tell that after supper he would want to talk with her, and she had no idea what he was going to say or how she would answer him. The truth was, she had enjoyed her afternoon at Pierce Veterinary Clinic too much to be sorry that she'd decided to stay.

"Tell him what you've just told me," her sister Leah had advised her.

I'll tell him how I felt...that God had wanted me to stay and help James. Dr. James Pierce. She only hoped that *Dat* understood and accepted her decision as the right one.

Chapter Two

James admired the beautiful scenery as he drove his silver Lexus deeper into Lancaster County Amish country. Farmhouses surrounded by acres of corn dotted the landscape. Cows and sheep milled in pastures near Amish residences. Flowers bloomed in riotous color in gardens next to white front porches, while lawns were a splash of verdant green from the summer rains that had showered the earth recently. Familiar dark and solid-colored clothing flapped in the breeze, bringing back memories of James's teenage years living in an Amish community.

Seeing the Amish woman Nell again reminded him that it had been too long since he'd visited his mother and stepfather, so instead of going back to his apartment as he usually did, he turned in the opposite direction, toward the farm where he'd lived from the age of fifteen until he'd left Lancaster County at eighteen to attend college in Ohio.

His stepfather and mother's farm loomed up ahead. The beauty of it nearly stole his breath even while he felt suddenly nervous.

He didn't know why. He knew they both would be glad to see him. It wouldn't matter to them that he'd moved into the area over two months ago and had stopped by only once. He'd set up his practice here because he'd wanted to be closer to his family. Yet, for some reason he'd stayed away.

He drove over the dirt road that led to his stepfather's farmhouse and pulled into the yard near the barn. He didn't see the family buggy. He parked out of the way of the barn door, in case whoever had taken out the vehicle returned.

There was no sign of anyone in the front or side yard as James turned off the engine and climbed out of his car. He paused a moment with the door open to stare at the house that had once been his home.

It had been hard moving into this house after his father had died and his mother had married Adam. It wasn't that he didn't want his mother to be happy. But he'd missed his dad. Grief-stricken, he'd been a terrible son, bitter and angry and difficult to control. But Adam was a kind man, who seemed to understand what James was going through. Because of Adam's understanding, patience and love, James had grown to love and respect his stepfather.

James shut the car door. He was here, and he would wait for everyone's return, not run like the frightened teenage boy he'd been when he'd first moved into Adam Troyer's house. He wandered toward the backyard and saw a woman taking laundry down from the clothesline.

"Mom?" He hurried in her direction.

She stiffened, then with a garment in her hand turned slowly. She was too young to be his mother although the resemblance to her was striking. His eyes widened. "Maggie?"

"Ja, bruder." Her mouth firmed. "You finally decided to pay us a visit."

It had been too long since he'd seen his younger sister. He felt a rush of gladness that quickly turned to hard-hitting guilt.

"You weren't home when I last visited." He regarded her with affection. "It's good to see you, Mags."

"Nobody calls me that but you." She dropped a garment into a wicker clothes basket.

He grinned. "Yes, I know."

Warmth entered her expression. "So you really did move back to Happiness."

"I did—close to two months ago." He held up his hand. "I know. I should have come again sooner. I've been struggling to grow my veterinary practice but..." He sighed. "It's no excuse."

He gazed at his little sister who was now a woman. He regretted missing her teenage years. He hadn't been here for her while she was growing up. He'd left home, driven to follow in his late father's footsteps. He'd attended college in Ohio, then went to Penn Vet for veterinary school. "I'm sorry I wasn't here for you."

She dismissed it with a wave of her hand. "I have a *gut* life. *Mam* and *Dat* are wonderful and Abby—" Her eyes widened. "Have you seen our little sister yet? You won't recognize Abigail, James. She's eighteen now."

Regret overwhelmed him, and James closed his eyes. "I missed too much."

"You're here now," she reminded him softly. She was quiet a moment as she studied him. "You'll have time to see her now."

"And Matt and Rosie?" he asked of his stepsiblings.

Maggie smiled. "They are doing well. You wouldn't recognize them either." She studied him silently. "Matt is nineteen and Rosie's sixteen." She eyed him with curiosity. "Are you happy, James?"

Was he? No one had thought to ask whether or not he was content with his life—not even himself. He should be more than pleased with what he'd accomplished, but was he? He honestly didn't know.

"I enjoy helping animals, and my work reminds me of the time I spent with Dad. But happy? I'm working on it. What about you?"

A tiny smile came to her lips, and her green eyes sparkled. "*Ja*, I'm happy."

He stared at her, intrigued. He grinned. "You're being courted!"

She looked surprised and pleased that after all these years he still could read her so well. "*Ja,*" she confessed. "His name is Joshua Fisher. He's a kind man."

"How old is Joshua Fisher?"

His sister narrowed her gaze at him. "Why?"

He didn't answer her.

She sighed. "He's twenty-one."

"I'm pleased for you, Maggie." Warmth filled him as he studied her. "You like the Amish way of life." Like him, she was raised English until their father died and their mother had brought them from Ohio to live in his grandparents' home in Lancaster County.

Her gaze slid over him. "You didn't seem to mind our Amish life," she reminded him. "Once you'd adjusted."

It was true. He had learned to appreciate the life he'd once rebelled against. The quiet peace that came from working on the farm when he was a boy eventually had soothed his inner turmoil over losing the father whom he'd loved, admired and always wanted to emulate.

"Where's *Mam*?" he said, slipping easily back into Pennsylvania Deitsch, considering how long he'd been away.

Maggie eyed him shrewdly. "In the *haus*." She paused. "*Dat*'s there, too."

"He's done working for the day?" His stepfather was a hardworking man, just like his own father had been. Would Adam scold him for staying away?

James experienced a sudden onset of uneasiness. The man who'd married his mother had been a good father to him, and he'd repaid him by being difficult and mean during those first months…and then he must have hurt Adam, leaving home when he did to follow the path he'd set out for himself away from their Amish village.

"*Ja*, you came at the right time. *Mam* and Abigail are making supper. Will you stay?"

He felt his tension leave him as he acknowledged the truth. "*Ja.*" He knew this was an open invitation. It was the Amish way to be hospitable and never turn a single soul away. "Will they be glad to see me?" he murmured. He studied the house. "I guess I'll head inside."

"James!" his sister called as he started toward the house. He stopped and faced her.

Maggie's gaze was filled with warmth and understanding. "'Tis *gut* to see you. Our *eldre* will be happy that you've come. Please, James, don't stay away too long again." She pretended to scowl. "I've missed your ugly face."

James couldn't stop the grin that came with the lightening of his spirit. "You'll be eager to get rid of me now that I'm living close and can visit frequently."

She shook her head. "*Nay*, I won't." She regarded him with affection. "I'll always be happy to see you, big *bruder*."

They eyed each other with warmth. "I'd better go," he said. "You'll be in soon?"

"A few moments more and I'll be done here."

"I'll see you inside then."

Despite anticipating a warm welcome, James felt his

stomach burn as he crossed the yard toward the back door leading into his mother's kitchen. He drew a deep cleansing breath as he rapped on the wooden door frame.

The door swung open within seconds to reveal his stepfather, who blinked rapidly. "James?" Adam greeted softly as if he couldn't believe his eyes.

James offered a tentative smile. *"Hallo, Dat."* He watched with awe as happiness transformed his stepfather's expression.

"Come in!" he invited with a grin as he stepped back to allow him entry. "Your *mudder* will be pleased to see you." He regarded James with affection. "I'm glad you've come back to visit." His eyes brightened as if Adam fought tears. "You look well, *soohn*. Your clinic is doing *gut*?"

James suddenly felt as if a big weight had been lifted off his shoulders as he entered the house. "It's doing better now, *Dat.*" He needed this homecoming. Adam was still the warm, patient and kind man he'd always been, and James was so thankful for him. "It was hard to get started at first. I'm getting more patients, though."

Adam smiled. "I'm happy for you, James. I'm certain that you'll make a success of it." He gestured toward the kitchen table. "Sit, sit. I'll get your *mudder.*"

James sat, aware that the house held all the wonderful cooking smells reminiscent of those he'd loved and remembered from his childhood.

Before Adam could leave to find her, his mother entered the kitchen from the front of the house. "I thought I heard voices, husband. Who—" Her eyes widened as they filled with tears of joy. "James!" She beamed at him. "You're back."

James grinned. *"Hallo, Mam.* I'm sorry I haven't been back sooner."

His mother brushed off his apology. "You're here now. That's all that matters." She met her husband's gaze with a pleased, loving smile. "He's come home again," she whispered huskily.

Adam moved to his wife's side and placed a loving hand on her shoulder. His smile for her was warm. "*Ja*, he has." He captured James's gaze. "And he is happy to be here." His stepfather grinned when James nodded. "I know 'tis near suppertime, Ruth, but why don't we have tea first?"

James watched his mother put on the teakettle. He had to stifle the urge to get up and help, knowing that it would upset her if he tried. In her mind, a woman's work was in the house while a man's work was on the farm or at his business. Adam's farm was small but large enough to provide for his family. His stepfather made quality outdoor furniture for a living, and Adam was good at his work.

The teakettle whistled as *Mam* got out cups, saucers and tea bags.

"It's *gut* to be back," James said sincerely. It was good to see his family and the farm.

He made a silent vow that he would return more frequently to spend time with the family he loved and missed, he realized, during the years he'd been away from Happiness, Pennsylvania.

Her father came into the room as Nell was drying the last of the supper dishes. "*Dochter,* when you're done, come out onto the porch. I want to talk with you."

"I'll be right out, *Dat.*" She was putting away dishes when her sister pitched in to help. "*Danki*, Ellie." Nell hung up her wet tea towel on the rack when they were done.

"He'll not bite you," Ellie said softly.

Nell flashed her a look. "I didn't think he would."

"Then stop looking scared. *Dat* loves us." Her lips twitching, she teased, "Even you."

"I know, but I'm afraid he's angry that I didn't come right home from Aunt Katie's."

"He's not angry," Ellie assured her.

"Disappointed? Upset?"

"He was worried. Joshua didn't come until it was too late for him not to worry."

"I know. I'm sorry. I didn't know that Bob would send Joshua."

"Nor could you foresee the accident that would keep Joshua from getting to us sooner."

"Then why does he want to talk with me?"

Her sister shrugged. "Only one way to find out."

Nell nodded. "I guess I better go then."

She couldn't regret her afternoon at the clinic. She'd had a taste of what it might have been like if she'd accepted James's job offer as his assistant. She loved animals. She enjoyed spending time with them, caring for them, holding them. After her sister Meg became gravely ill, and Michael—the man she'd loved—had died, her animals had been Nell's only solace.

Working the afternoon at Pierce's Veterinary Clinic, she believed, was God's reward for doing the right thing.

Her father was standing on the front porch gazing at the horizon when Nell joined him.

"Dat?"

"Gut, you're here."

"Dat, if this is about today, I'm sorry that you were worried. I called Bob as soon as I knew that I'd be staying. I didn't know about Joshua and the accident."

"This isn't about today," he said, "although I was worried when you didn't come home."

"I'm sorry."

"You did what you should have. Joshua explained everything." He turned to stare out over the farm. "'Tis about something else. Something I've been meaning to talk with you about."

"What is it, *Dat*?"

"You're twenty-four, Nell. 'Tis time you were thinking of marrying and having a family of your own. Other community women your age are married with children, but you have shown no interest in having a husband. I'm afraid you're spending too much time with your animals."

Nell's heart lurched with fear. He'd talked previously of marriage to her but not negatively about her animals. "*Dat*, I enjoy them." She inhaled sharply. "You want me to get rid of them?"

He faced her. "*Nay, Dochter*, I know you care for those critters, and as unusual as that is, I wouldn't insist on taking anything away that gives you such joy. But having a husband and children should be more important. You're getting older, and your chances at marriage are dwindling. You need to find a husband and soon. If not, then I'll have to find one for you."

"How am I supposed to get a husband, *Dat*?" She'd loved Michael and hoped to marry him until he'd died of injuries from an automobile accident.

She knew she was expected to marry. It was the Amish way. But how was she to find a husband?

Chapter Three

Saturday morning found the five Stoltzfus sisters in the kitchen with their mother preparing food for the next day. This Sunday was Visiting Day, and the family would be spending it at the William Mast farm. Nell and her sister Leah were making schnitz pies made from dried apples for the gathering. *Mam* and Ellie were kneading bread that they would bake today and eat with cold cuts tomorrow evening after they returned home. Meg and their youngest sister, Charlie, were cutting watermelon, honeydew melons and cantaloupe for a fresh fruit salad.

"I'm going to Martha's on Monday," Meg announced as she cut fruit and placed it in a ceramic bowl. "We're planning to work on craft items for the Gordonville Mud Sale and Auction."

"What's so special about the Gordonville sale?" Charlie asked.

Ellie smirked. "She's hoping to see Reuben."

Meg blushed. "I don't know that he'll be there."

"But that's your hope," Nell said.

For as long as Nell could remember, Meg had harbored feelings for Reuben Miller, a young man from another Amish church community. She'd met him two years ago at their youth singing, after their cousin Eli had invited Reuben and his sister Rebecca, whom Eli liked at the time, to attend.

Reuben had struck up a conversation with Meg, and Meg immediately had taken a strong liking to him. Although the young man hadn't attended another singing, Meg continued to hold on to the hope that one day they'd meet again and he'd realize that she was the perfect girl for him.

Nell eyed her middle sister. "Meg, if you see Reuben and find out that he's courting someone, what are you going to do?"

Meg's features contorted. "I don't know," she whispered.

"You could be hurt, but still you won't give up..." Leah added.

Meg nodded. "I can't. Not if there is the slightest chance that he doesn't have a sweetheart. I know we spent only a few hours together, but I really liked him," she admitted quietly. "I still do."

"If you want a sweetheart, why not consider Peter Zook?" Nell suggested, anticipating Meg's negative response.

"Peter!" her sister spat. "I don't want Peter Zook's attention."

"Peter's a nice boy," *Mam* said.

"Exactly! He's a boy." She sniffed. "Reuben is a man."

Nell held back a teasing retort. Peter was the same age as Reuben. He was a kind and compassionate young man who'd had the misfortune of falling in love with her sister, who wanted nothing to do with him. In her opinion, Meg could do no better than Peter Zook.

If only she could find someone her age who was kind, like Peter, to marry. An Amish friend she could respect and eventually regard fondly as they built a life together.

"I hope it works out for you, Meg," she said as she squeezed her sister's shoulder gently.

Meg smiled at her. *"Danki."*

"Would you and Martha like help on Monday? I can make pot holders for the sale," their youngest sister offered.

"That would be nice, Charlie," Meg said. *"Danki."*

The day passed quickly with the sisters chatting about many topics while they worked, including their Lapp cousins and who they expected to visit tomorrow at the Mast home.

Sunday morning arrived warm and sunny. At nine o'clock, their father brought the buggy close to the back door. The girls filed out of the house with food and into the buggy. Nell handed them the pies she and Leah had baked before climbing inside herself.

"Dat, Onkel Samuel and *Endie* Katie are coming, *ja*?" Leah asked as *Dat* steered the horse away from the house and onto the paved road.

"Ja, so your *onkel* said," he replied.

"Endie Katie said the same when I saw her the other day."

"Will all of our cousins be coming with their *kinner*? Noah and Rachel, Annie and Jacob, Jedidiah and Sarah?"

"I believe so," *Dat* said.

Nell smiled. She enjoyed spending time with her male cousins and their spouses. And she was eager to see Ellen, William and Josie's daughter, who had come to her aid and taken her and Jonas to the vet the day Nell had rescued him.

Buggies were parked on the lawn to the left in front of the barn when *Dat* pulled in next to the last vehicle.

Nell got out of the carriage first. Seeing her, Ellen Mast waved and hurried to meet her.

"*Hallo*, Nell! How's Jonas?"

"He's doing wonderfully. His leg is healed, and he's gained weight. I'm about to start him on heartworm medicine."

The young blond woman looked pleased. "I'm so glad. I think it was a *gut* thing that you were the one to rescue him. I'm sure he's happy and well."

Nell beamed. "I'd like to think so." She and Ellen strolled toward the house as the other members of her family slowly followed.

Another gray family carriage parked next to theirs. "Look!" Charlie exclaimed. "'Tis the Adam Troyers!"

"Charlie!" Rosie Troyer called as she exited the vehicle. Abigail climbed out behind her and waved. The eldest sister, Maggie, and their brother Matthew followed and approached Ellen and the Stoltzfus sisters with a smile.

"I didn't expect to see you here," Ellie said with a smile. "I'm glad you could come."

"*Ja*, we thought our oldest *bruder* was coming also, but he was called out on an emergency," Maggie told them.

"*Hallo*, Ellen." Matthew turned to Nell next with a smile. "Nell, 'tis *gut* to see you."

Nell's lips curved. "Matthew."

Adam and Ruth Troyer approached. "Ellen, Nell. 'Tis *gut* to see you both. Ellen," Ruth said, "is your *mudder* inside?"

"*Ja*, I last saw her in the kitchen."

Loud, teasing male voices drew their attention. Nell's Lapp cousins Elijah, Jacob, Noah, Daniel and Joseph hurried out into the yard and gathered on the back lawn. Moments later, they were joined by her friend Ellen's younger brothers, Will and Elam.

Jedidiah came from the direction of the barn. "Found them!" he said, holding up a baseball bat and ball.

"Matthew! You going to play ball with us?" Isaac called.

"*Ja*, I'll play." With another smile in Nell's direction, the young man left to have fun with Nell's cousins.

"Nell, you watch the game and I'll bring your pies inside."

She smiled as she gave her pies to her friend. "*Danki*, Ellen."

Ellen entered the house, leaving her alone with Maggie.

"I didn't know you had another *bruder*, Maggie," Nell admitted, focusing on Maggie's revelation, as the baseball game began.

"*Ja*. He's a doctor and seven years older than me. He left our community when he was eighteen." Maggie's eyes filled with affection. "I've missed him so much. I was able to spend time with him yesterday but still…" She grinned. "Fortunately, he's moved closer to home, and we'll be able to see him more often. I'm sure you'll meet him eventually."

Nell didn't know why, but she felt an odd anticipation as if she were on the urge of learning something significant. "You said your *bruder* was called out on an emergency," she said. "What does he do?"

"He's a veterinarian. He's recently opened a clinic here in Happiness."

The strange sensation settled over Nell. Despite the difference in their last names, could James be Maggie's brother? If the young woman's sibling was a veterinarian, then she doubted that the man was a member of the Amish community. "What's his name?" she asked, although she had a feeling she knew.

"James Pierce." Maggie smiled. "He owns Pierce Veterinary Clinic. Have you heard of him?"

"*Ja*. In fact, 'twas your *bruder* who treated my dog, Jonas, after I found him."

"Then you've met him!" Maggie looked delighted. "Is he a *gut* veterinarian?"

Startled by this new knowledge of James, Nell could only nod at first. "He was wonderful with Jonas. He's a kind and compassionate man." She studied Maggie closely and recognized the family resemblance that she previously hadn't noticed between her and James. "How is he a Pierce and you a Troyer?"

"I am a Pierce." Maggie grinned. "Abigail is, too. But we don't go by the Pierce name. Adam is our stepfather, and he is our *dat* now. We were young when we lost our *vadder*. I was six, and Abigail was just a *bebe*. We lived in Ohio back then. After our *vadder* died, *Mam* moved us to Lancaster County where she was raised. She left Pennsylvania to marry *Dat* and start a life with him in Ohio. *Mam* was heartbroken when *Dat* died. She couldn't stay in Ohio without her husband and decided to return home to Lancaster County."

Maggie's eyes filled with sadness. "I didn't mind. I was too young to care, but James was thirteen and he had a hard time with the move. He loved and admired Dad, and he'd wanted to be a veterinarian like him since he was ten. James used to accompany Dad when he visited farmers to treat their animals. He was devastated by Dad's death, and he became more determined to follow in Dad's footsteps."

Nell felt her heart break for James, who must have suffered greatly after his father's death. "You chose the Amish life, but James chose a different path."

"And he's doing well," Maggie said. "My family is

thrilled that he set up his practice in Happiness, because he wanted to be closer to us."

"He missed you," Nell said quietly.

The young woman grinned. "I guess he did. I certainly missed him. I'm glad to have my big *bruder* back."

Nell couldn't get what she'd learned about James and the Troyers out of her mind. It didn't help her churned-up emotions when, later that afternoon, James arrived to spend time with his family.

She recognized his silver car immediately as he drove into the barnyard and parked. Nell watched as he got out of his vehicle, straightened and closed the door. James stood a moment, his gaze searching, no doubt looking for family members. She couldn't move as he crossed the yard to where William Mast and others had set up tables and bench seats. They had enjoyed the midday meal, but there was still a table filled with delicious homemade desserts, including the schnitz pies that she and Leah had baked yesterday morning.

She couldn't tear her gaze away as James headed to the gathering of young people, including his sisters Maggie and Abigail as well as their stepsiblings, Rosie and Matthew.

Nell found it heartwarming to see that all of his siblings regarded him with the same depth of love and affection. She watched as James spoke briefly to Maggie, who grinned as Abigail, Rosie and Matthew approached him, clearly delighted that he'd handled his emergency then decided to come. She heard the siblings teasing and the ensuing laughter. Maggie said something to James as she gestured in Nell's direction.

James turned and saw her, and Nell froze. Her heart started to beat hard when he broke away from the group to approach her.

* * *

"Nell!" Warmed by the sight of her, James smiled as he reached her. "I didn't expect to see you here."

Her lips curved. "I didn't expect to see you here either."

"So you know my family." He didn't know why the knowledge startled him. Not that he was upset. In fact, it was nice to know that before they'd even met, he and Nell had shared an undiscovered connection.

"I've known them a long time. I had no idea that your family is the Troyers." She shifted her gaze to his sister Maggie. "Then I recognized the resemblance between you and Maggie." She smiled. "I've always liked your sister. She's a *gut* friend, and I like her sweetheart, Joshua Fisher, too."

"Joshua is here?" James attempted to pick him out of the gathering.

"*Nay.* He couldn't come today. His *grossmudder* is ill, and he thought it best to spend time with her and his family."

He was pleased to hear that Nell thought well of the man his sister loved. "He's a good man," he murmured, his gaze on his sister's smiling face.

"*Ja*, and he'll make Maggie a *gut* husband."

James settled his gaze on Nell's pretty, expressive features. "I'm glad you think so. I haven't met him yet, but I trust your judgment."

Nell appeared startled. She blushed as if embarrassed by his praise. "I'm sure you'll meet him soon."

They stood silently for several seconds. James felt comfortable with Nell, and she seemed to have relaxed around him, too.

"Nell."

She met his gaze.

"I was going to stop by your house. I received a phone call from Michelle today. Her stomach virus has spread to her husband and children, and she won't be back for days. Perhaps even a week. Janie isn't due back from vacation for another week. Would you consider working at the clinic next week? I'll pay you a good wage."

She seemed suddenly flustered, but he could tell that she liked the idea. "I'll have to ask my *dat*," she said.

"May I talk with him? I may be able to help ease his mind."

"I don't know…" She glanced toward an area under a shade tree where a group of older Amish men were conversing.

"Are you afraid that he won't like me?"

"Nay!" she gasped, her eyes flashing toward his. She softened her tone. *"Nay.* It's not that."

"Then let me speak with him." He frowned. "Unless you don't want the job."

"I wouldn't mind working at the clinic again."

James grinned as he sensed the exact moment when Nell gave him permission to talk with her father.

He immediately knew who her father was when a man looked sharply at Nell and then him. "I'll be right back," James told her as he made his way to the man who'd left the group to approach.

"Sir," James greeted him. "I'm James Pierce. Your daughter helped me last Thursday at my veterinary clinic."

"Arlin Stoltzfus," the man said as he narrowed his gaze to take stock of James, "and I wonder how you know that Nell is my *dochter*."

"A *gut* guess?" James said, slipping into Pennsylvania Deitsch and noting the man's surprise, which was quickly masked by a frown.

"What do you want, James Pierce?"

"A favor," James said. He softened his expression.

"What kind of favor?" The man eyed him with doubt.

"First, would you feel better knowing that I've come to visit my family—the Troyers—and not Nell?"

Something flickered in the man's expression. "You're Adam and Ruth's eldest son."

"*Ja*, I have the *gut* fortune to have their love."

The concern eased from Arlin's expression. "I'm sure you are a *gut* man, James Pierce."

"James," James invited, and Arlin smiled. "But now that I've seen Nell here today, I'd like to ask your permission for Nell to work in the clinic next week."

The man lowered his eyebrows. "Why?"

"I have no staff next week. My receptionist is taking care of her sick family as well as recuperating from illness herself. My assistant is away with her husband and not expected back until a week from tomorrow. I would need her to fill in for one week only."

Arlin glanced toward Nell, who was talking with two young women. "Have you mentioned this to her?"

James shifted uncomfortably. "*Ja*, I wished to know if she was interested before I came to you."

"And she is interested," the man murmured, "which is no surprise, considering how much she loves caring for animals."

Nell glanced in their direction, then quickly looked away, but not before James recognized longing in her expression. She wanted the opportunity to work in the clinic if only for a short time.

Nell's father sighed heavily as he studied his daughter. His expression was light, and there was amusement in his brown eyes as he met James's gaze. "She can work with you. She'll be disappointed if I refuse permission."

James smiled. "And above everything, you want your *dochter*'s happiness." He watched with stunned surprise as Arlin waved at his daughter to join them. Nell approached, looking fearful as she glimpsed her father's stern expression.

"You want to work for him?" he asked sharply.

"*Ja, Dat*, but only if you give permission."

Arlin's expression softened. "He belongs to the Troyers. I give permission," he said, surprising James.

James grinned. "Monday morning, eight o'clock sharp. Can you be there?"

"I can be there," Nell said. She turned toward her father. "I'll have my morning chores done before I go."

"*Ja*, I have no doubt of that," Arlin said.

"Do you need a ride?"

Arlin narrowed his gaze. "She will take the family buggy."

He nodded. *"Danki,"* he said.

"James!"

He glanced over and beamed as his mother approached. "I'm happy you could make it," she said.

He regarded her with affection. "I'm happy I'm here." His gaze flickered over Arlin and Nell who were standing next to him. "My staff is out, and Arlin has agreed to allow Nell to fill in for them next week."

His mother's eyes crinkled up at the corners. "You can rest easily with this one," she told Arlin. "He's a *gut soohn*."

James felt a momentary unease. He didn't feel like a good son. He'd left his family and his community to attend veterinary school and had little contact in the years that followed.

As if sensing his discomfort, his mother squeezed his

arm. "He's moved back into the area to be closer to us," she said as she regarded him affectionately.

He did move to Lancaster to be close to his parents for he had missed his family greatly. The tension left him. Despite his past, he was determined that he would be a much better son and brother from this point forward.

Chapter Four

Monday morning, Nell steered her carriage down Old Philadelphia Pike toward Pierce Veterinary Clinic. She viewed the day with excitement. She'd learned a lot from just one day working with James. Imagine what she could learn in the next five!

When the clinic came into view, Nell felt a moment's dread. Learning from James was a benefit of working with the clinic, but working with the man could cause her complications she didn't need in her life. He was handsome and kind, but her attraction to him was wrong and forbidden.

Focus on what Dat *said.* Her father wanted her to marry. He'd find her a husband if she didn't find one on her own.

Nell knew that she just had to remember that although James had an Amish family, he was an *Englisher.* She couldn't allow herself to think of him as anything but her dog's veterinarian—and this week, as her employer.

When she pulled her buggy up to the hitching post in the back, Nell was surprised to see James's silver car parked near the back door. She'd arrived early. It was only seven thirty. She was sure she'd arrive before him and that she'd have to wait for him to show up.

She tied up Daisy, then went to ring the doorbell. Within seconds, the back door opened, revealing James Pierce dressed in a white shirt and jeans.

Nell stared and suddenly felt woozy. She swayed forward and put a hand out to catch herself on the door frame, but James reacted first by grabbing her arm to steady her. Seeing James looking so like Michael, her late beau, had stunned her.

"Nell?" he said with concern. "Are you all right?"

She inhaled deeply. "I'm fine." Like James, Michael, an *Englisher*, had favored button-down shirts and blue jeans. She'd met him in a grocery store before she'd joined the church and still had the option of choosing an English or Amish life. She'd chosen a life with Michael but she'd never had the chance to tell him before he died.

James still held her arm, and she could feel the warmth of his touch on her skin below the short sleeve of her dress. "Are you sure you're all right?"

Nell managed to smile. "I'm well. *Danki*." She bit her lip. "Thank you," she corrected.

James let go and gestured for her to come inside. "Is the day getting warm?"

"A little." But the heat wasn't to blame for her wooziness.

"Come on in. I'll turn up the air conditioner so we'll be comfortable."

The impact of the man on her senses made her feel off-kilter. Nell blushed at her thoughts as she followed him into the procedure area. Fortunately, by the time James faced her, she had her feelings under control again.

"I'm glad you came," he said. "We have a serious case today. Mrs. Rogan is on her way in with Boots. Her Lab's eaten something—she's not sure what, but she believes he has an intestinal blockage."

"Ach, nay!" Nell breathed. "What will you do? Surgery?"

His handsome features were filled with concern. "I'll do X-rays first to see if I can tell where the blockage is."

"How can I help?"

He studied her intently. "Are you squeamish?"

She shook her head. "I don't think so. Did I seem squeamish yesterday? If you're worried that I'll faint at the sight of Boots's insides, don't be. I was in the room when my *mam* gave birth to Charlie, my youngest sister." She smiled slightly; the memory wasn't the most pleasant. "No one else was home."

He raised his eyebrows. "How old were you?" he asked.

"Nine."

He jerked in surprise. "You were only nine when you helped your mother deliver?"

"Ja." Nell's features softened. "I was scared. I can't say I wasn't, but once Charlie was born, I felt as if God had given us this wonderful new life. Charlie doesn't know that it wasn't the midwife who helped bring her into the world."

"Why not?"

"It's not important. What is important is that she is a healthy, wonderful young woman of fifteen."

She wondered if James was doing the math to realize that she was twenty-four. She saw him frown. Was he thinking that at the age of twenty-four most Amish women had husbands and at least one child, if not more?

"I'm glad you're not squeamish," he said. "Boots will be here any minute, and I'm going to need you by my side."

Even though she knew she shouldn't, Nell liked the sound of his words, of her and James working as a team.

After hearing Nell's story about delivering her youngest sister, James quickly did the math and was relieved to know her age. Then he frowned. Why did he care how old Nell was? It shouldn't matter as long as she did her job, which so far she'd been doing well. He wondered why Nell wasn't married.

Or was she? He'd never thought to ask. To do so now would seem…intrusive. He feared there was a story there, and one he wasn't about to ask her about.

James found he liked the thought of having her at his side while he did the surgery. And why wouldn't he, when after only one day she already had proved her worth?

"I'll be ready," she said. "I'll hand you the instruments you'll need. Maybe you can show me what they are now before Boots arrives? I don't want to hand you the wrong thing."

"Certainly." He moved toward the machine on the counter. There were several packaged sterile instruments in the cabinet above it. "This is an autoclave," he explained, gesturing toward the machine. "I put certain metal instruments in here to sterilize them."

She nodded. "What are those?" she asked of the two packets he'd taken from the cabinet shelf.

James proceeded to tell her what they were—a scalpel and clamps. Then he pulled out a tray of other types and sizes of the same instruments as well as others. "You don't have to be concerned," he said. "I'll pull out everything I need, and then I'll point to the instrument I want on the tray. You don't have to know all the names, although I imagine you'll learn a few as we use them."

He had just finished explaining the tools when he heard a commotion in the front room. "Boots is here," he announced. He was aware that Nell followed closely behind him as he went to greet the concerned woman and her chocolate Lab.

Nell helped him x-ray Boots while the dog's nervous owner sat in the waiting room. It turned out that Boots had swallowed a sock. After James relayed his diagnosis to Mrs. Rogan, he and Nell went to work. He encouraged Mrs. Rogan to go home, but the woman refused to leave until she knew that her dog was out of surgery and in recovery.

"Do you have other patients scheduled this morning?" Nell asked as she watched him put Boots under anesthesia.

"Fortunately, no. Not until this afternoon."

He readied his patient. "May I have a scalpel?" He gestured toward the appropriate instrument. He needn't have bothered because Nell had already picked it up and handed it to him.

He smiled. "Perfect. Thanks."

She inclined her head, and they went back to the serious task at hand. It took just under an hour from the time they sedated the Lab until the time he was moved to recovery.

James went out to talk with Mrs. Rogan with Nell following. "Boots made out fine. We removed the sock, and there's been no permanent injury."

Edith Rogan shuddered out a sigh. "Thank goodness." She visibly relaxed as she glanced from him to Nell standing behind him. "Thank you. Thank you both."

"Boots may have to spend the night here," he said. "I'll keep a close eye on him today. If he does well, then you can take him home this evening. I'll call and let you know."

At that moment, the door opened and Mr. Rogan rushed in. "How is he?" he asked his wife.

"Fine," James said. "The surgery went well, but I'm afraid you may be one sock short."

The man shifted his attention from his wife to James. "You're Dr. Pierce?"

James nodded.

"Thank you, Dr. Pierce. Edith and I have grown very attached to him."

"He's our baby now that our children are married and on their own," Edith said.

"I understand," Nell said softly, surprising James. "I have a dog. I have several animals, in fact, and I would feel awful if anything ever happened to them."

Mr. Rogan studied her with curiosity. "You're Amish."

"I am?" Nell's brown gaze twinkled.

The man laughed. "Sorry. Sometimes I speak before I think."

"Well, you're right, Mr. Rogan. I am a member of the Amish church and community, and I had the privilege to work with Dr. Pierce during Boots's surgery." She paused. "He's a beautiful dog."

The man smiled. "That he is," he said.

"Edith, it's time for us to leave and let the doctor and his assistant get back to the business of saving lives and making our pets better."

"I'll call you later," James said as the couple headed to the door.

"I'll check on him often," Nell added.

The Rogans left, and suddenly James was alone with Nell. He was proud of the way she'd handled herself with

Boots's owners, and he was pleased with how she'd assisted during Boots's surgery.

He glanced at his watch to see how much time he had before his first afternoon appointment.

"A successful surgery calls for a special lunch." He grinned. "Hoagies!"

She laughed. "Hoagies?"

"Sandwiches."

"*Ja*, that sounds *gut*," she said. "But I'll be bringing in lunch for us tomorrow."

"Sounds *gut* to me." James smiled. "We should check on Boots again before I order lunch."

After ensuring that the Lab was doing well, they ate lunch, then went back to work. The rest of the day occurred without any major incidents.

By the end of the afternoon, James was tired. When he glanced at Nell, he saw that she looked exhausted, as well.

"Time to call it quits," he said.

She nodded and reached for the mop and bucket.

He stayed her hand. "We can clean up in the morning." He eyed her with concern. "Are you all right?"

She blinked. "*Ja*, why wouldn't I be?"

"You've been quiet."

"Just thinking."

"About?

"Boots."

James smiled. "He's doing well. I'm glad I called the Rogans. They're happy to come for him. He'll do fine as long as they keep him still, leave his collar on and give him his pain medicine on time."

"And bring him back to see you on Tuesday," Nell added.

"Yes."

"Do you need me to do anything else before I leave?"

James shook his head. "No, go on home." He paused and couldn't help saying, "Be careful driving."

She nodded and left. James was slow to follow, but he watched her through an opening in the window blinds. Once her buggy was no longer visible, he took one last look around the clinic to make sure everything was as it should be, then he left, locking up as he went.

As he slipped onto his car's leather seats, he thought of Nell on the wooden seats in her buggy. He wondered how she'd react if she had the chance to ride in his car. There might be a time that he'd bring her home. He scowled. Probably not, because her time at the clinic was temporary, until Janie came back from vacation.

Nell was a fine assistant, he thought as he put the car in Reverse. She would manage fine until Janie's return.

A dangerous thought entered his mind, but he pushed it firmly aside. He quickly buried a sudden longing for something—or someone—else in his life other than his work, which had been the most important thing to him for some time.

Nell answered the phone when James's receptionist, Michelle, called into the office the next day. "Pierce Veterinary Clinic," she greeted. "How may I help you?"

The woman on the other end sounded dismayed. "Hello? This is Michelle. Who is this?"

"*Hallo*, Michelle. It's Nell. I'm helping James in the office until you or Janie returns."

"That's wonderful, Nell," the woman said. "I was worried about him managing the office alone." The two women chatted for several moments more, catching up, before breaking the connection. Nell went back to work, relieved that Michelle was glad to learn that she was filling in.

"Who was on the phone?" James asked as he came out to the front desk.

"It was Michelle. She and her son are feeling better, but now her husband and two daughters are sick."

"I'm sorry to hear that. Was she surprised that you answered the phone?"

"Surprised but pleased. She's been worried about you." She and Michelle had become friendly since Nell's first visit to the clinic.

James smiled. "I hope you told her to rest, recuperate and take care of her family."

"I did."

"Good."

Nell glanced at the appointment book on the desk. "Boots Rogan is due any minute for his follow-up."

"I want to check to make sure he hasn't bled through his dressing," James said.

Boots's appointment went well, and the owner took him home to continue the dog's recovery.

The afternoon went by quickly, and before they knew it, they'd seen the last appointment. But then an emergency call came in from Abram Peachy, a deacon in Nell's church district. Their mare Buddy had been injured by another horse.

James grabbed his medical bag. "Nell, will you come?"

"*Ja*, of course I'll come." Nell locked the front door and turned off the lights before she hastened through the back door and met James at his car. She hurried toward the passenger side and hesitated, uncomfortable being in such close quarters with James. He was suddenly there by her side, opening the door for her.

Feeling his presence keenly, she quietly thanked him,

then slid onto the passenger seat. She ran her fingers over the smooth leather as James turned the ignition. The interior of the car smelled wonderful.

"Which way do I go?" he asked as he glanced her way.

She blushed under his regard and forced her attention ahead. "Take a right out of the parking lot," she told him.

As he followed her directions, Nell was overly aware how close they were in the confines of James's car. Did he feel it too? The attraction between them? Charlotte was waiting outside for them as he drove close to the house. She hurried toward the vehicle as Nell and James climbed out of the car.

Her eyes widened and a look of relief passed over her features as she looked from James to Nell.

"What happened?" Nell asked.

"Something frightened Barney," Charlotte said. "Joshua was getting Buddy out of her stall when Barney reared up and came down hard against her side." She addressed James directly. "She's suffered a large gash. Can you help her?"

"I'll do what I can. Show me where you keep her."

Charlotte led the way, and Nell followed them to the barn where they found Abram near Buddy's stall.

Abram looked relieved to see them. "I put her back in her stall."

James studied the horse. "Good. She's in closed quarters." He addressed Abram. "I may need your help to hold her steady as Nell and I ready her to stitch up the wound."

"She's a gentle soul, but she's hurting bad," Abram said after agreeing to James's request.

Abram's son Nate entered the building. "Can you help us for a minute?" James asked after a quick look in the young man's direction. "Do you have any rope? We'll need to secure it to the rafters and around Buddy to help keep her steady after I give her a sedative."

"Ja," Abram said. "Nate, will you get that length of rope from the tack room?"

Nate immediately obeyed then slipped inside the stall, being careful to skirt the animal until he reached the front right side. *"Dat?* You *oll recht*?" he asked.

"I'm fine. Be careful, *soohn*," Abram warned as Nate came up on Buddy's opposite side.

James grabbed the rope and with a toss of his arm, he threw one end over the rafter until it fell in equal lengths to the ground. "Nate, could you wrap this around Buddy? Abram, you don't have a wench or pulley, do you?"

The man shook his head. "We'll make do."

He addressed Nell, "Would you get me a syringe and the bottle of anesthetic?"

Nell handed him the bottle and the needle.

He took it without looking at her. She could feel his concern for the animal. She'd seen different sides to the veterinarian over the past week, each more impressive than what she'd seen before.

His face was full of concentration as he inserted the needle. The animal jerked and kicked out, her hoof making contact with James's shin. He grimaced, but that was the only sign that he'd been hurt. Nell worried about him when he continued as if the horse hadn't clipped him.

He stood back. "We'll have to wait a moment or so until the anesthetic takes effect."

His eyes met Nell's. She gazed back at him in sympathy, recognizing pain in his face. She wanted to take a look at his leg and help him, but she remained silent. It was clear that he didn't want his injury to detract from helping Abram's horse.

She felt a rush of something she didn't want to feel. This man clearly loved animals as much as she did.

They waited for tense moments until the horse seemed to quiet. Nell looked at Abram. "It's *oll recht*," she said. She watched as he and Nate released their hold on the horse.

"You might want to leave," James said. "This won't be pleasant to watch."

The two men left, leaving Nell alone with James. He met her gaze. "All set?"

"Ja," she breathed, ready to do whatever he needed.

"Come around to this side. Bring my bag. I'll tell you what I need."

Nell watched while James worked on Buddy. He sutured the mare's wounds, noting how gentle he was with the animal, soothing her with a soft voice.

After twenty minutes, James seemed satisfied that he'd done all he could for the horse.

"Nell, would you please see if you can find a container of antibiotic? I'd like Abram to give her a dose twice a day. He can sprinkle it on her food."

Nell understood when she found the bottle and saw that the antibiotic was actually granules instead of pills.

Soon they were driving away from Abram's farm, heading back toward the clinic. Nell caught James's wince more than once as he drove, but she kept silent. She couldn't offer to drive him since she didn't know how and wouldn't be allowed anyway because of the rules in the *Ordnung*.

James pulled into the parking lot and drove around to the back as usual. She saw him grimace as he climbed out, but she didn't say anything as she followed him inside the building. James went into his office while she went right to work restocking his medical bag with the supplies he'd used at Abram's. When she was done, she entered his office and confronted him.

"You hurt your leg," she said. She swallowed hard. "May I see?"

He gazed at her a long moment, and she felt her face heat, but he finally nodded. Fortunately, the legs of his black slacks were loose. James gingerly pulled up his pants leg.

Nell gasped. His shin was swollen and severely bruised. She eyed the black-and-blue area with concern. "You should see a doctor," she suggested softly.

"I'll be fine," he said sharply. She didn't take offense for she knew he was hurting.

"I'll get some ice," she said and went into the kitchen.

When she returned, his head was tilted against the chair back, his eyes closed.

"James," she whispered. His eyes flashed open. She held up the ice pack. "For your leg."

"Thank you." He shifted, straightening. His pants had fallen back to cover his injured leg. He tugged up the fabric again, and Nell bent to place the pack on his bruised skin.

"It looks sore," she said with sympathy as she knelt to hold it in place.

James gave her a crooked smile. "A bit."

She shook her head, trying not to be uncomfortable looking up at him from near his feet. "You should go to the emergency room—or a clinic." She rose, and her gaze traveled around the room.

"What are you looking for?" James asked.

"Something to prop your leg up on so you can ice it properly."

"No need." He dropped his pant leg and rose. "It's time to head out. I can ice it at home."

Nell saw him wince as he moved, but she held her tongue. "I'll check the reception area and make sure it's locked up."

"Okay." He waited while she hurried out to the front room to lock up and retrieve her purse from under the desk. She took one last look around, then returned to where James waited near the back door.

"Thanks for your help today."

Nell shrugged. "That's what you pay me for."

A tiny smile formed on his lips. "I guess I do."

They headed outside together. James pulled the door shut behind them and made sure it was secure.

Nell saw that he held the ice pack and was glad. She became conscious of him beside her as she waited for him to turn. "I will see you on Wednesday?" she asked.

He hesitated. "Yes."

"Is anything wrong?" she asked, sensing a shift in his mood.

James opened and closed his mouth, as if to answer but thought better of it. "It's late."

Nell experienced a burning in her stomach. "*Ja.* I should head home." She turned away. Something was definitely bothering the man.

"See you in the morning, Nell."

She paused but didn't look back. She was afraid of what she'd see. "*Ja*, I'll see you then."

Then she hurried toward her buggy, feeling edgy and suddenly eager to be away and at home.

James watched Nell leave, then followed her buggy in his car until their paths split. He continued straight until he reached a small shopping center with a bakery, a candy shop and a small gift shop. He drove around to the back of the building, got out of his car and went in a back entrance that led to his apartment above the bakery.

As he started painfully up the stairs, he caught the scent of rich chocolate. Usually, he'd head into the bakery to buy whatever it was that Mattie Mast was making downstairs. But with his throbbing shin, the only thing he wanted to do right now was put ice on the injury.

The trek up the staircase was slow, and he stopped several times. He breathed a sigh of relief when he finally made it to the top.

His one-bedroom apartment was dark as he entered. He threw his keys onto the kitchen table and went to open a few windows to let in the day's breeze. The delicious scent of baking was stronger upstairs than down.

He refilled his ice bag, then, ignoring his rumbling stomach, he plopped down onto the sofa in his small living room, turned on the TV and shifted to put his feet onto the couch. He carefully set the ice pack that Nell had made on his swollen leg. He gazed at the television, but his thoughts were elsewhere.

It was Tuesday. There was still the rest of the week to get through. Would the pain in his leg let up enough for him to leave his apartment in the morning?

Nell will be there. He would make sure he got to work. She was helping him out, and he needed to be there.

Stretched out on his sofa, he stared at the ceiling with the sound of the television a dull buzz in his ears.

The ice felt good against his swollen leg. James closed his eyes, and the day played out in his mind. Nell's calming influence as she worked by his side. Their trip to the Amish farm, treating the mare. Nell's assistance with Abram Peachy and his son Nate. Her calming way with their mare Buddy. His growing friendship with Nell.

He saw Nell clearly in his mind—her soft brown hair,

bright brown eyes and warm smile. She'd worn a green dress with black apron today, with a white *kapp*, dark stockings and black shoes. He smiled. He wondered how she'd look at home when she was at ease, barefoot and laughing as she chased children about the yard, with sparkling eyes and her mouth curved upward in amusement.

James wondered how it would feel to spend time with her outside of the office.

His eyes flickered open as shock made him sit up. He was more than a little attracted to Nell Stoltzfus!

James shook his head. He had no right to think about Nell in that way. He scowled. She was a member of an Amish community, a community like the one he'd left of his own free will to choose a different path in life.

He forced his attention back to the television. He began to channel surf to find something—anything— that would consume his interest other than thoughts of Nell Stoltzfus.

Nell's four sisters were in the yard when she returned home.

"We heard what happened!" Charlie said.

"At Abram's," Ellie explained.

"Nate said you were both wonderful. He said you worked efficiently and quietly by the veterinarian's side," Charlie added.

"Was it true that James got kicked by Buddy?" Meg asked.

Nell studied her sisters with amusement. "Do you want me to answer any of you, or would you prefer to provide the answers yourself?"

Leah, the only sister who hadn't spoken yet, laughed. She was the next oldest after Nell. "How did it go?"

"Well," Nell said. "It went well. James sutured Buddy and left her in Abram's care."

"Was it awful?" Charlie asked. "Seeing all that blood?"

"I felt bad for Buddy, but I was *oll recht*. I didn't think much about anything but what I could do to help James."

The sisters walked toward the house as it was nearing suppertime. There would be work in the kitchen as they helped their mother to prepare the meal.

"Only three days more, *ja*?" Leah asked when their sisters had gone ahead into the house.

Nell faced her sister as they stood on the front porch. *"Ja*, in a way I'll be sad to see it end."

"But 'tis for the better that it will." Leah watched her carefully.

"Ja." She leaned against the porch rail. "But until then, I'm learning so much. Things I'll be able to use in helping our friends and neighbors. I know I can't take the place of a veterinarian but I'll be able to handle more than I could before."

Leah regarded her silently. "What's he like?"

"James?"

Her sister nodded. Her golden-blond hair, blue eyes and a warm smile made her the prettiest one of all of the sisters, at least in Nell's eyes. Today, she wore a light blue dress which emphasized her eyes. On her head she wore a matching blue kerchief and she was barefoot. She had come from working in their vegetable garden.

"You saw him at the Masts'," Nell reminded her.

"But seeing him isn't working with him."

For a moment, Nell got lost in her thoughts. "He's a caring man who's compassionate with animals. He's a *gut* vet. You should have seen him with Buddy. He—" She bit her lip.

"He was injured today," Leah said. "Nate stopped while you were gone. He said Buddy kicked him while he was trying to sedate her."

"*Ja*, but you wouldn't have known it by looking at him afterward. He worked as if nothing was bothering him when his leg must have hurt terribly." Nell had been amazed—not only by his skill but by his attention to Abram's mare.

"You like him."

"I wouldn't work for him if I didn't like and respect him."

"I know that, but I think you feel more for him."

"*Nay*," she denied quickly. "He's *gut* at what he does, and I respect that."

Leah nodded. As they entered the house, Nell wondered if her sister believed her.

She'd felt awful when she saw the extent of James's injury. She'd been startlingly aware of him as she'd pressed the ice pack against his shin. The sudden rush of feeling as she'd held the pack against his masculine leg for those brief moments had frightened her. Caring for him in that way had felt too intimate. She'd risen quickly and searched for a chair or stool to prop up his leg. When James had declared that it was time to go home, she'd been relieved.

"Nell," her mother greeted as she and Leah entered the kitchen. "I heard you had an eventful day."

Nell nodded. "It was more eventful for Abram's mare."

"She's all right?"

"Buddy's fine. James stitched her up as *gut* as new. She'll be in pain for a while, but he left Abram medication for her."

"*Gut. Gut,*" *Mam* said. "Ellie, would you get the potato salad out of the refrigerator? Meg, you carry in the sweet and sour beans. Leah, would you mind getting your father? Supper is almost ready."

"What about me?" Charlie said.

Her mother smiled. "You can set the table with Nell."

Nell went to help her sister. She was home and felt less conflicted in this world she knew so well.

She might have imagined the strange tension between her and James. Tomorrow she'd put things in perspective and realize that the tenseness between them was just a figment of her imagination.

Chapter Five

Wednesday morning, Nell got up extra early to make her favorite contribution of potato salad for Aunt Katie's quilting bee. By the time her mother and siblings had entered the kitchen, she had finished cleaning the dishes she'd used. She automatically started to pull out the ingredients for the cake and pie that she knew that her mother wanted to bring.

"You're up early," Leah said.

"*Ja*, I thought I'd take a look at Buddy this morning before I head to the clinic."

"That's a fine idea," *Mam* said as she came into the room. "I'm sure Abram will appreciate it."

Nell ate breakfast with her family, then stayed long enough to clean up before she got ready to leave. She ran upstairs to get her black shoes. When she was done, she hurried downstairs to the barnyard. She chose to take the family pony cart and hitched up Daisy before she headed toward Abram Peachy's place.

She wondered what time James would arrive at the office this morning. Would she be able to reach him if Buddy suddenly needed additional medical care?

It was six thirty. She knew that Abram and his family most likely would be up and doing morning chores. No doubt Charlotte was already in the kitchen preparing food for this afternoon's quilting gathering.

The weather was lovely. Nell appreciated the colors and scents of summer. A bird chirped as it flew across the road and landed in a tree. The trees and lawns were a lush verdant green, moist with the morning's dew. There was no traffic on the roadway.

Nell steered her horse past Yoder's General Store, where she glimpsed the owner, Margaret Yoder, getting out of her buggy. Margaret made eye contact with her, and Nell lifted a hand in greeting. The woman smiled and waved back.

It wasn't long before she caught sight of Abram's farm ahead. She clicked on her directional signal and slowed Daisy to turn into the barnyard.

Nell saw Abram and Charlotte's eleven-year-old daughter, Rose Ann, as she came out of the house. Nell waved and climbed out of the open buggy and secured her horse.

"Nell!" Rose Ann cried. "Have you come to see Buddy?"

"*Ja*, Rosie. How is she doing?"

The child frowned. "I don't know. *Dat* won't let me near her."

"That's probably for the best. He doesn't want you to get hurt. Buddy's in pain and may kick out or nip you. You had best listen to your *vadder* and wait outside while I check on her."

Nate Peachy came out of the house. "*Gut* morning, Nell. Here to check on our mare?"

"*Ja*, Nate. I was telling your sister that it's best if she stays out here."

Nate smiled at his little sister. "Listen to her, Rose Ann. You know what *Dat* said."

"That I should stay out of the barn until *Dat*, you, Nell or James Pierce tells me I can visit Buddy."

"*Gut* girl," Nate praised. He led Nell into the barn. They eyed the mare silently for a moment before he turned to her. "You need anything?"

"*Nay*, if I do, I'll let you know." Nell smiled as the horse approached. "*Hallo*, Buddy," she greeted softly as the mare poked her head over the top of her stall.

"I'll leave you alone then," Nate murmured.

"*Danki*, Nate."

After Nate had left, Nell returned her attention to the horse.

"How are you feeling today, girl?" She reached toward the mare's head and stroked Buddy between the eyes then down her nose. "Are you in pain?"

She examined the area of the wound, where James had secured a bandage over the laceration. She was relieved to see that there was no blood seeping through the gauze. "Looks like you've not bled through. That's a *gut* thing."

Had James mentioned how long Abram should keep the bandage on? Nell frowned. Longer than one day, she was sure, but for how long? Had Abram given Buddy her medication?

"Did you eat breakfast, Buddy? Did you have your medicine?" She smiled when Buddy butted gently against her hand with her nose. "I'll have to speak with Abram," she told her. "We want you well and happy again." She spoke soothingly to the horse while she stroked her nose and the side of her neck.

She felt someone's presence in the barn before she heard a familiar voice.

"Nell."

"James!" She blinked and stared at him, taken aback by her stark awareness of him. This morning he wore a blue short-sleeved shirt with jeans and sneakers. She swallowed as emotion hit her square in the chest at the sight of him looking so tall, masculine and handsome. "I didn't expect to see you here."

"I see we shared the same thought." His warm smile made her heart race. "Buddy." His soft expression made her feel warm inside. "What made you come?"

"I was worried about her."

He approached, opened the stall and slipped inside. Buddy snorted and shifted uneasily. James set down his medical bag, then turned to the horse.

Nell watched as James spoke to the mare. She was amazed how well the animal responded to his deep, masculine tones.

He placed a calming hand on a spot not far from the wound as he bent low to examine the area around the bandage. "No infection to the surrounding tissue. She looks good." He glanced up at her when Nell remained silent. He searched her features as if he found something interesting in them.

Nell blushed, quickly agreed and glanced toward the horse.

"When does she need her dressing changed?" She kept her gaze on Buddy. The man's unexpected presence made her feel off-kilter.

"We probably should change it now since you're here and can assist. I'd like a closer look at her sutures." He opened the stall door to invite Nell inside. "Are you up for it?"

"Why wouldn't I be?" Nell asked, excited to learn something new.

The confines of the space seemed smaller than it had when she and James had come to take care of Buddy's injury the previous night.

As she stood by ready to assist, Nell was conscious of the man beside her as he worked. Fortunately, she was able to focus on the task and was ready with whatever he needed. Buddy shifted and snorted in protest as James carefully peeled back the bandage. Nell quickly stroked and spoke to sooth her until the mare settled down.

She watched as James checked the wound. He pressed gently on the surrounding area, and Buddy didn't seemed to mind. He stood back. "It looks great."

Nell silently agreed. She was amazed how well the sutures appeared. James had done an excellent job with them.

"Nell, would you please see if you can find the anti-septic ointment that's in my bag?"

She quickly found the tube and handed it to him along with a fresh dressing. He eyed her with approval as he took them from her.

"Thank you."

Nell nodded. She observed as James spread ointment on a clean square of gauze before he placed it carefully over Buddy's wound. She handed him the roll of surgical tape, and he secured the bandage in place.

James stood. "That should last until we see her next, unless a problem arises."

"I can stop by and check in a day or two," she offered.

He stared at her. "That would be helpful. Thank you."

They gazed at one another for several seconds. Nell felt a fluttering in her stomach. She looked away.

"Are you headed to the clinic next?" she asked as she left the stall with James following closely behind.

He glanced at his watch. "It's early, but I do have paperwork to catch up on." He smiled at her. "You're not due in for another hour."

"Is there something you need done?"

He hesitated. "Nothing that can't wait."

"I don't mind starting early," she said.

Something flickered in the depths of his dark eyes. "I don't want to take advantage, Nell."

"You won't be. If I can help before the clinic opens, I'll be happy to come." Nell headed toward her buggy.

James approached his car, which was parked several yards from her pony cart. "I'll see you there then."

She paused before climbing into her vehicle. "How is your leg?" she asked conversationally. She felt the intensity of his gaze and faced him. She'd seen him grimace when he'd stood after bending to examine Buddy and knew it had to be hurting him.

He didn't respond immediately. "Better today than yesterday."

"Gut." The realization that she had the ability to read him so well alarmed her.

"Nell—"

The ringing of his cell phone stopped his words. Nell waited patiently while James spoke to the person on the other end. When his face darkened, Nell became concerned.

"I'll be there as soon as I can," he said. He glanced at the thick-banded watch on his left wrist. "About ten, fifteen minutes." He listened silently. "Yes." He turned away from Nell, and she heard him issuing concise directions on what the caller should do until he arrived.

Suddenly feeling as if she was intruding on his phone conversation, she moved away to give him privacy.

James finished up his call and approached her with a look of apology. "Emergency," he said. "I guess I won't be doing paperwork this morning." He drew a sharp breath. "Want to come?" He explained about an injured dog that had been found on a man's back patio. "He's severely wounded."

"Ja," she agreed. "I'd like to help."

"It's not far."

Nell felt James's urgency as she left her pony cart and hurried toward his car. "Nate!" she called as she saw Abram's son coming around from the back of the barn. "We have to leave. Animal medical emergency. Is it *oll recht* if I leave my cart?"

"I'll drive it home for you," he offered.

She opened her mouth to object, but James said, "Thank you, Nate. I'll drive Nell home after work today."

Nell slid into the passenger side and buckled her seat belt as James climbed in beside her. He turned to face her in his seat.

"I should have asked you if it's all right if I drive you home," he said.

"'Tis fine," she assured him.

James gazed at her a long moment, nodded and then concentrated on putting the car into gear and driving off Abram's property.

James had visions of the injured canine as he drove toward Fred Moreland's farm. From Fred's description, the dog was covered with blood and in a terrible state. It was the reason he told Fred not to move the animal.

He was conscious of Nell beside him as he drove. Would she be upset by the sight of the injured dog? He frowned. He hoped not. She'd been of tremendous help to him and hoped to keep her working at the clinic for the rest of the week.

Fred waited for him at the end of his front yard as

James pulled into the man's driveway and parked close to the house. He got out of the car with his medical bag while Nell climbed out on the other side.

"Where is he?" James asked as Fred approached.

"In the back." The older man looked anxious.

He turned to Nell with concern. "Nell, this could be..."

"I'll be fine, James."

He set his medical kit not far from the little dog. He caught a glimpse of white fur beneath all the dirt and blood. He heard Nell's horrified gasp as she got her first look at the dog, but she didn't say anything as she quickly opened his medical kit and got to work.

"Is he yours?" James asked Fred.

"No. He's a stray. I don't have any barbed wire, but it looks like he got caught up in some. Not sure where."

The animal lay on its side on the concrete patio. He was breathing steadily, which was a good thing. James was prepared for the dog to snap and try to bite when he touched him. "Nell."

"I'm here," she said calmly. "I'll hold him while you give him the injection." She busily prepared the syringe that he would need as he studied her. He could see tears shimmering in her pretty brown eyes.

Nell handed him the syringe and vial of local anesthetic, then she hunkered down by the animal's head and placed her hands on an uninjured area of the small body.

As she touched him, the dog's eyes opened and he looked as if he would struggle to rise, but Nell quickly soothed him with soft words and a gentle stroke. James regarded her a few seconds, amazed by her ability once again, before he found a small area appropriate for the shot. Nell's soft soothing voice continued, and James found that it calmed him as much as it did the injured dog.

"Nell, get me that brown bottle, too, please. I think it will be best to lightly sedate him. It will make things easier for him."

Nell obeyed, and James gave the dog another injection.

"We'll wait a few moments, and then we'll clean him up and take care of his wounds." James eyed the dog, deciding how best to proceed. "Would you please get us a bowl of warm water and an old towel?"

"Certainly," Fred agreed and hurried to do his bidding.

James and Nell were left alone on the man's back patio with the injured animal. "Are you all right?" he asked.

"I'm fine." She hesitated as she studied the dog. "Do you think he got tangled in barbed wire or did someone abuse him?"

James regarded the animal with a frown. "I suspect he was abused."

"Fred?"

"No," he said. "Absolutely not. Fred is one of my clients. He's got a soft touch for all animals. I take care of his cat and dog. It's easy to tell that he loves them. His wife died recently, and his animals give him comfort."

James turned his focus back to the dog and wondered whether or not he should move him. Would it be better to treat him inside?

Before James could decide, Fred returned with an old but clean white enamel basin filled with warm water. He set it, a soft washcloth and towel within James's reach. He had draped a folded blanket over his arm.

"I thought you might want to move him onto this. It's soft and may be more comfortable for him." He dropped down on one knee and unfolded the quilt. "It's okay if it gets wet or dirty. I don't like seeing this little guy on the concrete."

"You found him here?" Nell asked softly.

"Yes. I came out this morning to have my coffee as I often do, when I saw him. That's when I called you, Dr. Pierce. I was afraid to touch or to move him. I didn't want to hurt him, and I didn't know if he'd bite if I tried."

"It was good that you let him be and called me, Fred." James eyed the unfolded blanket in Fred's arms. "You grab an end and we'll spread it out."

With Nell and James's help, Fred folded the quilt into quarters, then spread it over the concrete patio. James and Fred carefully eased the animal from the concrete onto the padded folds.

Nell grabbed the washcloth and dipped it into the warm water. She placed the towel within easy reach and began to clean the area about the animal's neck.

James went to work cleaning the actual wounds with antiseptic cleansing pads. He cleaned a wound on the side of the dog's belly. It looked as if he'd been burned as well as cut.

Nell met his gaze. "He *was* abused."

He nodded as he felt the anger inside him grow.

Fred had gone into the house for more linens. He came out in time to hear Nell's comment. "Someone did this to him?" He looked pale and upset.

"Yes, I'm afraid so." James didn't look up from his task.

"Whoever did this should be in jail," the older man said.

"If he's ever caught, he will be."

"Have you seen much of this before?" Nell asked, her voice sounding shaky.

"Too many times." He carefully washed each wound

while Nell cleaned the surrounding areas. "Did you see him walk?" he asked Fred.

"No. He was lying here. I supposed he was able to move well enough to get here."

James went on to check the animal's legs and was upset to find one that appeared to be broken.

"Fred, while he's knocked out, I'm going to take him back to my office. I want to do X-rays. One leg is broken, but until I see the extent of the damage, I won't know the best way to treat him."

"What are you going to do with him then?" Fred eyed the animal with longing. "Do you think I'll be able to keep him?"

"If the leg is bad, I may have to amputate."

He heard Nell's sharp inhalation of breath.

"Doesn't matter to me. Dogs can get by with three legs. I still want him."

"What about Max?" James asked of the man's other dog.

"This one will be fine with him. Max will like the company. I'll keep them apart until this little guy is well enough."

"If you're going to keep him, maybe you should come up with a name for him."

Fred thought for a moment.

"How about Joseph?" Nell suggested. "You can call him Joey." When Fred looked at her, she explained, "Joseph means 'addition,' and this little guy will be a new addition to your family."

Fred smiled. "I like it. Joey it is. Max and Joey."

Nell nodded, then returned her attention to patting dry the area she'd washed.

"We should move him while he's still sedated," James said. "I've got a small stretcher in the trunk of my car."

"I'll get it," Fred offered, and James handed him the keys.

The man was back in less than a minute. He set the stretcher on the ground, then the three of them took hold of the edges of the blanket and set Joey on the stretcher. James and Fred lifted the stretcher and carried it to the car, setting it carefully on the backseat. Without being told, Nell climbed into the back with Joey.

"I'll give you a call to let you know how he makes out," James said.

"I want him, James," Fred repeated. "No matter what."

James climbed into the front seat and glanced back to see Nell buckled into her seat belt and leaning over Joey while stroking his head tenderly. "Nell." She looked at him. "He'll make it."

"I hope so." She blinked rapidly as if fighting back tears.

James felt the strongest desire to take Nell into his arms to comfort her. But he ignored it and instead drove back toward the clinic.

He'd been thinking of Nell too much lately. He wasn't sure what to do, but he knew he couldn't risk hurting the young Amish woman who'd worked her way into his affections.

He reminded himself that he just had to make it through the end of the week. Once Michelle and Janie were back in the office, Nell would return to her Amish life and he'd be able to put her out of his mind.

At least, he hoped so.

Chapter Six

Nell felt her throat tighten and her eyes fill with tears as she gently stroked the injured puppy. Who could do such a thing to one of God's poor defenseless creatures?

She looked into the rearview mirror and asked James, "Do you think he'll make it?"

"He will if I can have anything to do with it."

She knew what he meant. James would do all he could, but ultimately the dog's recovery would be in God's hands.

Soon James was pulling into the clinic parking lot. He parked near the door, then got out to help with Joey.

Nell opened her door. "How are we going to do this?"

James eyed the little dog. "I'll carry him." He bent inside and, using the sides of the blanket, he scooped him up carefully. "Nell, would you get my keys? They're on the front seat."

One look at James's expression had her melting inside. The man was obviously as upset about Joey as she was. Enough that he'd forgotten to grab his keys.

James had straightened with the dog in his arms. "Would you open the door? It's the blue key."

She found the right one and hurried to open the building. She turned on the light and then held the door open for James.

James quickly went to the treatment area. He gently set Joey down on an examination table. "We have to x-ray him. I'm afraid he may have several broken bones—not just a broken leg."

Nell sent up a silent prayer, then whispered, "I hope not."

James checked the dog's heart and breathing with his stethoscope before he moved him over to the platform under the X-ray machine.

"Will he sleep for a while?" Nell asked with concern. She hated the thought that Joey might wake and be in pain. He might get scared and struggle, further injuring himself.

"Yes, long enough. He'll be groggy when he does finally come out of it."

Nell stood by ready to help as James prepared the machine. She helped shift the dog into different positions and then waited while James snapped the photos. Little Joey remained sedated while they worked.

Nell felt her nerves stretch taut as she waited for the results of the X-rays.

"He has a break in his hind leg," James said after reading the films for several long moments.

"Will he be all right?"

"I can't promise, but there is a good chance his leg will heal. We'll have to splint it. Unlike Jonas's injury, this little guy will have his leg bound for several weeks."

He stepped away from the X-ray light panel and moved toward Joey. "There doesn't appear to be any new bleeding, but I'm going to suture the worst of his wounds."

Nell kept her eyes on the little dog. She was feeling

emotional. The news that the animal's leg wouldn't need to be amputated had buoyed her spirits, but she still had a hard time accepting that someone could be so cruel to the little dog.

She knew others within her Amish community didn't understand her love for animals. They took good care of their horses, which they needed, and their other farm animals, but they didn't feel the same about dogs or cats. No one within her church community would intentionally hurt an animal, she didn't think. And they'd come to accept that her concern for animals made her a good person to call on when they needed help with them.

Working with James was teaching her how to better help her neighbors and friends…and gave her a sense of purpose.

She settled her gaze on James. His attention was on Joey, his eyes focused on the dog's little body as he meticulously stitched closed one wound before moving to another.

She concentrated on the work so that she could ignore her growing feelings for the man. She gasped, struck anew by how much she liked spending time with James.

James looked up at her, a frown settling on his brow. "Are you all right?"

She managed a smile. "*Ja*, I'm fine." She hesitated as he returned his attention to Joey. "How is he?"

"I think he'll make it, but seeing what was done to him—" She could feel his anger and understood it despite God's teachings.

"Will he have to spend the night?" she asked.

"I think it would be a good idea."

"I can stay," she offered.

He glanced at her then, his expression soft. "I appreciate it, Nell, but I'll stay. Your family will be worried about you, and I know what to do if something goes wrong."

She felt a sharp tightening in her chest. "Do you expect something to go wrong?"

"I don't know, but better to be safe than sorry." He grabbed a spoon splint and cut it to the correct size before he began to tape it onto Joey's broken leg. He paused to reach into his jeans pocket and pulled out a sheet of paper. "Would you call Fred and let him know?"

"*Ja*, of course." She took the phone number and abruptly left the room. After she told Fred how Joey was doing, she took a minute to compose herself before heading to the treatment area again.

James didn't look up as he continued to stabilize Joey's broken leg. "Did you reach Fred?" he asked.

"*Ja*. He was upset but eager for Joey to get well."

James straightened and turned to face her. A small smile hovered on his lips. "Fred's a good man. Joey will have a good home."

Nell's throat was tight, and she didn't want to break down in front of him. She didn't want for him to believe that she couldn't handle the work. The last thing she wanted was to lose this position.

"Now what?" she asked.

"We'll make him comfortable, and I'll see how he is when he wakes up. I'll move him into a kennel right now. We'll be able to keep an eye on him while we see patients."

She waited while he gently moved Joey and then headed back out to the front desk area where she pulled out the appointment book and prepared for the day.

It was seven forty-five when she unlocked the door. James's first patient with its owner was already waiting to come in.

The day went quickly because of their full patient schedule and their vigil of Joey. Soon, it was time for Nell to go home. James said that he would take her home, but she felt bad for making him leave Joey for even a few moments.

"I can call someone to drive me," she offered.

James shook his head. "No it's fine. I can take you home."

She waited while he checked on Joey one more time, and then they headed outside. He unlocked his car, then opened her door and waited until she was seated. His kindness made her feel both uncomfortable and somehow cherished.

The interior of the car seemed close, and she was overly conscious of the man beside her as he turned on the ignition, then backed away from the building.

She blinked back tears. What was she going to do? It was wrong to work with James when she had feelings for him. Yet, she couldn't leave the position. It would be unfair to force him to work alone in the practice, especially since she'd promised to help him. And he wasn't the one with the problem. She was.

Nell drew a steadying breath. It would be fine. She wouldn't let on how she felt. She'd finish the job and then get on with her life, taking with her new knowledge of animal care—and a longing for a life with someone she could never have.

James felt Nell's presence keenly as he exited the parking lot. "Which way?"

"Left."

As he drove, he remembered her making a left when she'd departed yesterday.

She was silent as he headed down the road. He flashed

her a quick look, wondering how she was feeling. She glanced toward the window but not before he saw her tears.

"Nell." Instinctively, he reached out and captured her hand where it rested on the seat beside her. He felt her stiffen and then look at him with brimming eyes. "He'll be all right."

She blinked rapidly, and he quickly released her hand.

"I'm sorry," she said.

He flashed her a startled glance. "What for?"

"I'm not a *gut* assistant if I cry about a patient, am I?"

"Nell, your compassion, your empathy makes you a great assistant."

"Then you're not disappointed in me?"

"For what?" he said. "For caring?" He paused. "Of course not." He drove past Whittier's Store and Lapp's Carriage Shop.

"Take the next left to get to our farm."

James made the turn and saw a farmhouse up ahead. "Here?" he asked.

"Ja."

Minutes later, he pulled into the barnyard. As he pulled the car to a stop, four young women exited the house. "Your sisters?"

She nodded as she opened the door and climbed out.

"How's the little dog?" a young redhead asked. "Will he be *oll recht*?"

"We don't know for certain, but we think so."

A dark-haired young woman bent to look inside the car.

"Hello," he said.

"You must be James," she said.

He inclined his head. "I am."

Nell quickly introduced him to her sisters.

"We did what we could for him. I'll know tomorrow morning." He glanced at Nell. "I need to head back."

"Let me know how he does?"

"I will." He gazed at her, interested to see her surrounded by her sisters. "I'll see you in the morning."

"*Ja*, I'll see you then."

James put the vehicle into Reverse and then turned toward the road. He saw that Nell's father and mother had joined her sisters in the yard. He waved at them as he drove off. He would have liked to stay, but he needed to get back to Joey. The last thing he wanted was for the dog to wake up and start to chew on his wounds.

Before he pulled onto the road, he took one last look toward the Stoltzfus residence. Seeing Nell with her family made him feel things he hadn't felt in a long time.

"How was your day at the clinic?" Arlin Stoltzfus asked Nell.

"I'd say *gut*, but we're treating an abused and severely injured dog. Seeing Joey suffer was anything but *gut*, *Dat*."

"Was that why Dr. Pierce left in a hurry?"

"*Ja*. Joey should wake up soon. James needs to be near when he does."

"He's *gut* at what he does," her father said.

"*Ja, Dat,*" Nell said. "He is."

"You have two days left in his employ."

Nell felt a sudden uncomfortable feeling inside. "*Ja*. Tomorrow and Friday—and I'll be done." She sensed someone's curious gaze and turned to see her sister Leah studying her closely.

"He seems like a *gut* man," Ellie said.

"He is," Nell admitted.

"An *Englisher*," *Dat* said as if he had to remind her.

"*Ja*, he is," Nell said, meeting her father's gaze directly. Arlin nodded as if satisfied by what he saw in her expression. "You know his family. You've spoken with him. He is an honorable man." She thought it wise to change the topic of conversation. "How is Jonas? Did he behave today?"

"He always behaves." Charlie's features softened with affection. It seemed that her sister loved the dog almost as much as she. Nell knew she could trust her youngest sister to take good care of him.

"'Tis hard to believe he'd injured his leg," Leah commented.

"I'm thankful that he fully recovered."

The family headed toward the house. "Anyone hungry?" *Mam* asked.

Nell looked at her gratefully. "I am."

"We all are." Ellie glanced back. "Meg? Why are you lagging behind?"

"I'm coming."

Nell waited for Meg to catch up. "Anything wrong?" Meg shook her head.

"Are you sure?"

Her sister smiled. "*Ja. Danki*, Nell."

"I'll be happy to listen if you need to talk."

"I'll keep that in mind." Meg ran ahead to join Ellie and Charlie who had climbed the front porch after their parents.

She and Leah followed more slowly as the others entered the house.

"Two days more and then you're done working for James," Leah said. She paused. "How do you feel about it?"

Nell shrugged. "Fine. I've learned a lot this week, but I have things here that need to be done."

Leah narrowed her gaze. "Like what?"

"Like care for my animals. 'Tis not fair that my sisters have to do the work."

"We don't mind. Charlie loves taking care of them, especially Jonas." Her sister reached for the handle and pulled open the door. "But I agree that you have something that needs to be done." When Nell met her gaze, she said, "You need to find yourself a husband before *Dat* gets impatient and finds one for you."

Nell experienced an overwhelming sorrow. If Michael hadn't died, they would have been married, and she would have had children by now. She kept her thoughts to herself. None of them knew about Michael and that was a good thing. She had the choice back when she'd met Michael. As a full member of the church, she no longer had the option of falling for an *Englisher*.

She still felt a tightening in her chest for her loss and what might have been had Michael lived.

Chapter Seven

After she'd enjoyed a delicious meal of fried chicken, vegetables and warm bread slathered with butter, Nell stood on the front porch and stared out into the yard. Her thoughts went to little Joey—and James. She had the strongest urge to ride over to the clinic and see how the dog was faring. But she couldn't. Thoughts of Michael made her particularly lonely this evening. It wouldn't be wise to see James, the only man she'd been attracted to since Michael's death.

She climbed down from the porch and crossed the yard to the barn, drawn once again to her animals for solace. James's attempt to comfort her earlier when she'd begun to cry had startled her. The warmth of his fingers covering hers had made feel things she had no right to feel about the *Englisher*.

She had just been upset over Joey, she reasoned. But was that it? She sighed. *Nay*, she'd felt an attraction to him well before they'd treated Joey.

Entering the barn, Nell went to the horses first. She rubbed Daisy between the eyes, then moved to pay similar attention to their other mare, Lily. She ensured each horse had enough water inside the barn and filled the trough in the pasture.

"Do you want to go outside?" she asked the horses when she went back inside. "'Tis a beautiful evening. You can enjoy it for a little while."

Daisy's stall was next to Lily's. She took her out of her stall and released her into the fenced area before she did the same for Lily. Nell felt her lips curve as the two mares galloped into the field. They chased each other in play before they settled down to leisurely munch on pasture grass.

Satisfied that the mares would be fine for a while, Nell stopped back in the barn to visit Ed, their gelding, and her dog, Jonas. Excited to see her, her little dog whimpered and jumped up on his hind legs. When he put his front paws on her skirt, Nell grinned, certain more than ever his leg was completely healed from the injuries he'd received when she witnessed some teenagers throw him out of their moving car.

"Let's not overdo it, Jonas." She gently repositioned Jonas's front paws onto the ground, then knelt next to him. The dog instantly rolled onto his back, exposing his belly. Nell laughed as she wove her fingers through his fur and rubbed.

"Nell?"

"In here!" she called.

Leah stepped into the light. "I thought I'd find you here." She opened the stall door and slipped in to join her. After closing the door carefully behind her, she squatted beside Nell. "Are you *oll recht*?"

"*Ja*, why wouldn't I be?"

Leah's expression turned somber. "What happened earlier?"

"What do you mean?"

"You were upset when James brought you home."

"Joey," Nell said. "What happened to him was heart-breaking."

"I'm sorry," Leah said softly.

Nell felt a clenching in her belly. "Me, too," she said. She continued to stroke Jonas, who clearly loved every moment of her attention. She bit her lip. "*Dat* seemed angry when James brought me home."

"I don't think he was angry. I think he was concerned."

"Why?"

"Because he's an *Englisher,* and he's handsome."

"*Ja*, he is," Nell murmured in agreement.

Leah stared. "Nell, are you falling for him?"

"*Nay,*" Nell said quickly. Too quickly. She had to admit that there was something about him that drew her like a moth to a flame. But she wouldn't give in.

They walked toward the fence to watch the horses. "Are you sure?" Leah asked.

Nell inclined her head.

Her sister sighed. "*Gut.*"

Ellie suddenly joined her sisters at the fence rail. "'Twas a delicious supper, *ja, schweschter*?"

Nell and Leah exchanged amused glances. "*Ja*, it was," Nell agreed.

"Will you bring the dog—Joey—home once he's well?"

Nell shook her head. "*Nay*, the man who found Joey wants him. He lives alone and dotes on his pets. Joey will have a *gut* home with him." She offered a silent prayer that Joey's condition didn't worsen.

"Come inside," Ellie urged. "*Mam* brought out dessert, and she and *Dat* are waiting for you."

"I'm not particularly hungry." But Nell knew her parents would be upset if she didn't return to the table.

"She made carrot cake," Ellie told her. "Your favorite."

"Sounds *gut* to me." Leah grinned.

"I guess I could eat a piece."

"Race you!" Ellie challenged.

The three sisters hurried across the lawn, up the porch and into the house.

James checked on Joey in his kennel several times during the evening. When he saw the little dog was resting comfortably, he relaxed and went to his office to do paperwork. He'd finished what he needed to for the day when he heard the dog whimper.

He hurried toward the treatment area. Mindful of the extent of Joey's injuries, James opened the kennel door and pulled him gently into his arms.

"Who did this to you, little one?" he whispered. He stroked the little dog's head as he moved toward a treatment table. If he ever discovered who it was, he'd call the authorities and have them prosecuted for animal cruelty.

He found some pain medicine and administered it to Joey. "This will make you feel better for a while, little one. I'll stay the night, and if you're better tomorrow, we'll call Fred and he can come for you."

He picked Joey up and held the dog close to his chest. Joey must have sensed that James wouldn't hurt him as the animal burrowed his head closer. James narrowed his gaze as he examined a small wound along the side of his neck. He didn't like the look of it. He grabbed a canister of antiseptic from a cabinet and sprayed it on the wound.

"Don't worry, Joey," he soothed when Joey struggled. "I won't hurt you. I'm here to help." What he wouldn't give to have Nell by his side assisting him. But it was late, and she'd already put in longer than a full day's work.

After setting Joey back in his kennel, James went to the refrigerator in the clinic's kitchenette, searching for some leftover pizza. When he was done eating, he went back to his office to make a few phone calls to check up on his patients. Afterward, he went into a storage closet and pulled out the cot he kept here in case he might need to sleep at the clinic.

He made up the cot, and then wondered what he'd do to fill the remaining hours until bed. He found the paperback book he'd started one afternoon before he'd moved back to Lancaster County and became engrossed in the story. He stopped once to give Joey another dosage of pain medication, then went back to the book.

The next thing he knew, he'd read through half of it, and it was late enough to sleep. He checked on Joey one last time. Satisfied the dog would sleep the night, James lay on his cot and closed his eyes.

Nell arrived for work at seven forty-five the next morning. James had been leaving the back entrance unlocked for her. There was no sign of him in the treatment room when she walked in. She peeked into an exam room but didn't see him. *"Hallo?"*

"I'm up front, Nell!" she heard him call out.

She made her way toward the reception area. As she entered the room, she caught sight of James bent over Michelle's desk, his eyes focused on the computer screen. As if sensing her presence, he looked up.

"Hi." He straightened. "Is it eight already?"

"It's a quarter to." She approached and placed her

purse under the desk where she sometimes stashed it. "What are you doing?"

"Updating health records on the computer," he said. "Not my favorite thing to do. Michelle usually does it for me. I did some of them last night but—" He keyed in another entry then stood, looking pleased. "There. I'm all finished. Michelle will be proud."

Nell felt a rush of pleasure upon seeing his grin. Mention of the previous night brought her thoughts back to their patient. "How's Joey doing?"

"He's doing well. In fact, I think I'll give Fred a call later today. I think it will be good for Joey to recover in his new home."

"I'm glad he's doing better."

"Me, too." James frowned. "I wish I knew who did this to him. Whoever it was should be held accountable."

"By whom?"

"Animal cruelty is against the law." He moved out from behind the desk, and Nell took his place.

She opened the appointment book to check on the number of scheduled patients. "There are only three appointments in the book today, and two are reschedules from Friday."

"Only three?" He sounded disappointed.

"We may have another emergency," she said. "Not that we want one," she added quickly, blushing. She knew he was working hard to grow his practice and realized that a schedule like today's wasn't encouraging. "Your first patient doesn't come in until ten."

"We'll check on Joey, then call Fred afterward."

The morning appointments went smoothly. Mrs. Rogan arrived with Boots, and a kitten in a cat carrier. Nell didn't have any experience with cats. She liked them, but they didn't have any on the farm. While they waited for James to finish up with Boots, Nell cradled the kitten in her arms, enjoying the way it purred and cuddled against her.

"She likes you," Mrs. Rogan said with a smile.

"She's sweet."

"Would you like to have one?" the woman asked. "Mimi came from my neighbor's cat's litter. She has three sisters and two brothers. They all need good homes."

Nell thought of how accepting her father had been of all her animals. But she worried if Jonas and a kitten would get along. If not, would *Dat* allow him in the house? She doubted it. She sighed. She really wanted a kitten. "Do Boots and Mimi get along?"

"Oh, my, yes, dear. Mimi even snuggles up to Boots to nap. He seems to enjoy her company."

"I'd like to have one, but I have a dog."

"I'm sure Jonas and a kitten will get along fine," James said. "When a cat is a kitten, it's a great time to introduce the two. Boots here likes Mimi, don't you, boy?" He smiled and rubbed the dog's neck.

"But Jonas lives in the barn," she said. "He does have his own stall. I fixed it up for him."

"I don't doubt that," James said, lending his support. "Nell is a wonderful assistant," he told Mrs. Rogan.

Nell blushed as the woman studied her. "I'm sure she is." She studied her kitten in Nell's arms. "I can bring you a kitten if you'd like. Any particular color?"

"The color doesn't matter."

"I'll pick one out for you then." She beamed at Nell. "Betty—my neighbor—will be so pleased that I've found a home for another kitten."

She checked the woman out at the front desk. "May I help you to your car?"

Mrs. Rogan looked pleased. "Thank you, Nell. You're very kind."

Nell took the kitten's carrier while Mrs. Rogan held on to her purse and Boots's leash. When the woman and her animals were settled in the car, Nell said, "Mrs. Rogan? Would you like to take a few of Dr. Pierce's business cards with you? He hasn't been in our area long. I'm sure he'd appreciate any referrals."

"What an excellent idea, Nell. I'll be happy to pass them to all my animal-loving friends. I've been extremely pleased with Dr. Pierce's care."

Nell hurried inside, grabbed a stack of cards and quickly returned. She handed them to Mrs. Rogan. "Thank you again."

"My pleasure."

Nell felt a sense of accomplishment as the woman drove away. Why hadn't she thought of this sooner? When she'd brought Jonas in originally to be treated for his injuries, James hadn't charged her. He'd asked if she'd spread the word about his practice instead. And she had, but not as much as she could have. James's concern over the number of patients made her realize that she could do more to help grow his practice.

He looked up with a heart-stopping smile. "Mrs. Rogan gone?"

Nell nodded. She hesitated and then asked, "Do you think I'm foolish for wanting a kitten?"

James blinked. "No. Why would you think that? The kitten will have a wonderful home with you"

She felt a rush of warmth. "I'll do my best," she said.

Surprisingly the phone rang moments after Mrs. Rogan left, and James answered it. "We have another appointment for tomorrow afternoon—Betty Desmond, a friend of Mrs. Rogan. Mrs. Rogan must have called her on her cell as she was leaving."

Nell hid a smile. "Did she say who she's bringing in?"

"A litter of kittens. You'll be able to pick out the one you want."

"I'd take all of them if I could. As it is, I'll have some convincing to do at home." But she wasn't worried. Her father was lenient when it came to her and her animals.

Nell turned away. "I'll set things up for tomorrow."

"Thank you, Nell."

She cleaned the exam rooms in preparation for the next day—her last one. There were now seven patients scheduled for tomorrow. Wearing protective gloves, Nell washed instruments, then placed them into the autoclave. She turned on the machine as James had taught her, then went to refill the disposables in the treatment room. One accidentally slipped out from her hand. She reached to retrieve it just as James bent to get it for her. They bumped foreheads as he rose with item in hand.

"Are you all right?" he asked with concern.

Nell felt her heart start to pound at his nearness. They were eye to eye, close enough that she glimpsed tiny golden flecks in his dark eyes.

She swallowed against a suddenly dry throat. "I'm fine," she said, aware of the huskiness in her voice.

James stared at her, a strange look settling on his features. "Nell."

Nell couldn't seem to tear her gaze away. She felt her chest tighten and an odd little tingle run from her nape down the length of her spine.

James's only thought was of how lovely Nell was both inside and out. He couldn't remember the last time he had feelings for a woman. And this one was more than special.

Suddenly he leaned forward and gently placed his lips against hers.

He heard her gasp, but she didn't pull away. His head lifted, and he searched her eyes. She looked thunderstruck and adorable. He bent again and took one last sweet kiss before he pulled abruptly away. "I'm sorry."

She gazed at him, apparently speechless.

"Nell—"

"I have to leave!" she gasped. "I'm sorry, but I won't be in tomorrow."

"Tomorrow is your last day, Nell," he reminded her. James felt a crushing sensation in his chest. "I promise it won't happen again—"

"*Nay*, I can't take the chance."

He studied her flushed cheeks, realized that she was not unaffected by his kiss.

"The office is ready for tomorrow. You should be fine without me. 'Tis only one day." She turned away and headed toward the front room.

"Nell." He saw her shoulders tense as she faced him. "I'm sorry if I've upset you, but I can't truly say that I regret kissing you."

She blanched, spun, then left in a hurry. He heard the front door open and shut. She had gone. Without saying goodbye.

James closed his eyes. What had he done? He should have known better. She was Amish; he was considered *English*. Their worlds were too different for them to be anything but friends.

He drew a sharp breath as the regret he'd claimed he hadn't felt suddenly filled him. His regret in chasing Nell away.

Chapter Eight

❧

Nell was rattled as she drove home. James's kiss had taken her totally by surprise. She should have pushed him away, and the fact that she hadn't done so scared her. What shocked her the most was that she'd liked his kisses.

It was midafternoon when she steered her buggy into the yard. She knew her family would wonder why she wouldn't be returning to the clinic. It would be easy enough to explain why she was home early this afternoon, for there were no patients scheduled. It made sense to call the day to a close.

But James had seven patients to see tomorrow, and while she felt bad that he would have to manage on his own, she wasn't about to go back. She had to avoid James. Her feelings for him were too powerful. And now that she knew he was attracted to her, too…

To her relief, her family didn't pry into her reasons for not going back to work. Her father seemed pleased that she'd be at home, and for that she was relieved and grateful.

As she washed the dinner dishes alongside her sister Charlie, she wondered if James had called Fred about

Joey. Then she mentally scolded herself. He probably had. Besides, Joey was no longer her concern.

That night as she went to bed, Nell couldn't help but recall the day's events. She sighed. There would be no returning to pick out a kitten. She could only imagine what Mrs. Rogan would think after she learned that Nell no longer worked there.

Moonlight filtered in through the sheer white curtains as Nell lay in bed and stared up at the ceiling. She couldn't stop thinking about James's kiss, his clean male scent with a hint of something. Cologne?

She was lonely. Was that why she'd reacted to James the way she had?

She became overwhelmed with sadness as she thought of Michael and the life she would have shared with him if he hadn't died. If she'd married Michael, she wouldn't be having these feelings about James.

She and Michael probably wouldn't have stayed in Happiness. They might not have moved far, but they would have lived perhaps within Lancaster City, in a small home surrounded by neighboring houses. They would have had children and been happy together...if only Michael hadn't died.

Grief struck her hard, and her eyes filled with tears. *Oh, Michael...*

Lonely and heartbroken, Nell sobbed softly. Unable to control her sorrow, she climbed out of bed and went to look out the window. It was on a night like this that she had left the house to tell Michael that she'd decided to accept his marriage proposal. The moon had been large in the dark sky, the summer air had been warm and balmy, a perfect night for meeting the man she'd loved.

Only Michael hadn't come.

She'd waited for him for over two hours until finally,

disappointed, she'd returned home. She'd reached the house and gone upstairs to bed. Then within an hour, her family had been on their way to the hospital after an ambulance had been called for Meg. Her sister had suffered excruciating abdominal pains.

Meg had been admitted to the hospital and spent several days in intensive care. A ruptured appendix had threatened her life.

Overcome with worry for her sister, Nell had attempted to put aside thoughts of Michael. But in those moments when she left Meg's hospital room to go to the cafeteria with her other sisters, Nell had suffered from more than concern.

What if Michael had come to their special spot the next night? What if he'd tried the following nights only to be disappointed when she didn't show?

During the afternoon of Meg's second day in the hospital, Nell had gone downstairs to buy a cup of tea, which she planned to take back to the room. Ellie, Leah and Charlie had gone home with *Mam* and *Dat* to pack a few items for Meg, to see to the animals and to get some sleep.

Mam and *Dat* had appeared to have aged since Meg was first brought in. The doctor had suggested that the family go home to eat properly and get some rest. Meg would need them at their best during her recovery. Nell had volunteered to stay until their return later that evening when she would head home for the night.

Nell had been returning with her tea when she'd heard loud sounds coming from inside a hospital room on Meg's floor. Without thought, she'd glanced inside and saw a man lying in the hospital bed, hooked up to oxygen and a heart monitor.

She could still recall with startling clarity the awful

moment when she'd recognized the patient. The horrible sounds that had come from the heart monitor and oxygen pump had turned her blood to ice.

Michael. It had been her beloved Michael. Her first instinct had been to go to him, but a nurse had stopped her.

"The patient isn't allowed visitors," she'd said.

Nell had wanted to cry out that she wasn't simply a visitor; she was the woman to whom he'd proposed marriage. The agony of seeing him in that bed, knowing that he was fighting for his life, was still painful to recall even after five years.

Her family didn't know about Michael. She and Michael had been meeting secretly as Amish sweethearts often did within her community. Only Michael wasn't Amish. He was an *Englisher*, but at the time, Nell could have left her community without reprisal. She hadn't joined the church yet, so she would have been free to leave.

The next day, after a night at home spent fervently praying, Nell returned to the hospital. She found Michael's bed empty as she passed by his room. Heart pounding hard, she'd asked at the nurses' station what happened to him.

She'd nearly fainted when she'd heard that Michael had died during the night.

In shock, Nell had gotten through each day focusing on her sister. She'd had no time to grieve or accept the fact that Michael was really gone. Afterward, she'd overheard the nurses talking. She learned that Michael's injuries had been sustained in a car accident when his vehicle was struck by a drunk driver's on the night they were to meet. She stared out into the moonlit yard and recalled the way she and Michael had met in a local grocery store. How they'd met up again in the same place on another day. Michael had been handsome and funny, and she'd fallen in love immediately.

After Meg recovered, Nell had decided to join the church. Couples usually joined prior to marrying, but Michael was the only man she'd ever love. There was no reason not to join the Amish church. She had lost Michael but she'd been grateful to the Lord for sparing Meg's life.

Nell turned from the window and went back to bed. And cried until she was so exhausted, she fell asleep.

The next morning, Nell climbed out of bed. She felt groggy from lack of sleep, but she knew she had work to do. She needed to feed and water the animals.

She smiled as she thought of her little dog. Nell was fortunate that her father tolerated her love of animals. After nearly losing her sister Meg, Arlin Stoltzfus had become lenient with all of his daughters.

She slipped out of the house and headed toward the barn. She took care of her pets and the farm animals, then returned to do her house chores. There was laundry to do, dusting to be done, and floors to be swept.

She entered through the kitchen and grabbed the broom from the back room, continuing her day with housework instead of enjoying her last day at the clinic as planned. Her sisters joined in to help, and their happy chatter and teasing helped Nell get through the day.

That afternoon, Nell heard the sound of a buggy as she swept the front porch. She paused to watch as it parked near the house. Matthew Troyer got out of the vehicle.

He waved. "Nell!"

"*Hallo*, Matthew." She smiled, for the young man always appeared to be in good humor.

"I've brought you something." He skirted the vehicle, then bent into the passenger side to pick up a cardboard box.

Curious, Nell set aside her broom and descended the porch steps. "What is it?"

"Come and see."

She approached and peered into the box. "A kitten!" It was a tiny orange tabby. "Where did you—" she began. She blinked back tears as she met his gaze. "James."

"*Ja*, he asked me to bring her to you. Said you were interested in owning a kitten. He thought you might like this one best."

Emotion clogged Nell's throat as she reached in to pick up the cat. "She's beautiful." Cuddling the kitten against her, she glanced at Matthew. "*Danki*, she's… perfect."

He eyed her with fond amusement. "James thought you'd say that."

Warmth infused her belly as she realized how well James knew her. "Please thank him for me."

"You can thank him yourself when you see him."

But would she ever see him again? Only if he came to a community gathering, which was entirely possible since his family belonged to her church.

Nell glanced back at the house for any sign of her father. She had to break the news to him that she now owned a kitten. "I need to make a place for him in the barn. He can share Jonas's stall."

Matthew blinked. "Wait! There's more." He reached into the back of the buggy for a bag of kitten food, a small scratching post and a small bed. "My *bruder* sent these, as well."

"He didn't have to do that," she said, but it didn't

surprise her that he had. James was an extremely considerate man.

"This is James. You've worked with him. This is his way."

"*Ja*, I know."

"Let me carry these into the barn for you."

Nell stroked the tiny cat's head. "*Danki*, Matthew." She was aware of the young man following her as she entered the barn and headed toward her dog's stall. Jonas whimpered and ran toward her as she pulled the door and held it open for Matthew. "You have a new friend, Jonas," she said. "You'll be nice to her, *ja*?"

She hunkered down to allow Jonas to sniff the kitten. She waited with bated breath to see how he would react to his new roommate. Nell grew concerned when Jonas growled and backed away. "Jonas! She won't hurt you. She's just a little thing. Come and meet her."

"He's growling at me, not her," Matthew said as he set the bed near Jonas's and the post in the opposite corner of the stall. "Where do you want her food?"

"You can put it there for now." She gestured toward a table in the back of the stall. "I'll move it later."

Jonas continued to growl, and Nell saw that Matthew was right. The dog was nervous of Matt, not the kitten.

Matthew crouched next to her and held out his hand. "Come. I'll not hurt you. I'm Nell's friend."

Nell flashed him a look, but Matthew was too busy trying to gain her dog's trust to notice her.

"Jonas! Come." The animal gazed at her with trepidation. "'Tis Matthew. He's James's *bruder*. You know James. He took *gut* care of you when you were hurt." She felt a pang in her heart as she mentioned his name.

Matthew didn't move. He waited patiently until finally Jonas inched closer. Although he and James were stepsiblings, they both shared the same patient and compassionate nature. Nell experienced a wave of affection toward Matthew.

The young man didn't speak. He simply stayed in his crouched position with his hand extended toward Jonas.

Finally, Jonas came close enough to sniff his hand then started to lick his fingers. Matthew laughed. "He's a *gut* one, isn't he?" he said with a smile.

"*Ja*, he is. And you were right—he was afraid of you, not this little one."

He regarded her with amusement. "Are you going to keep calling her *little one*, or will you be naming her?"

She made a face at him. "Any suggestions?"

"Kotz?"

"I'm not going to call her cat!"

He laughed, and the sound was delightful. "You asked for a suggestion," he reminded her.

"Not a bad one."

Matthew placed his hand over his heart. "You wound me, and I was trying to be helpful."

"Poor Matthew."

He grinned at her. "Nell?"

She set the kitten within distance of Jonas, who didn't seem to be alarmed or angry at its presence. "I think they'll get along."

"Nell." His tone had changed, become serious.

Frowning, she met his gaze. "Is something wrong?"

He shook his head. "I was wondering if you'd be attending the youth singing on Sunday."

"I haven't been to a singing in years."

"Would you consider it?" He paused. "I'd like to take you home afterward."

Her heart skipped a beat. Matthew was handsome and likable, and he would make some lucky girl a wonderful sweetheart. He was nineteen while she was twenty-four. Despite the age difference, she gave serious consideration to having a relationship with him until the fact hit home again that James was his *bruder*.

If Matthew courted her and they became serious with the intention of marriage, then James would be her brother-in-law, and she would have to see him often. She was afraid that her feelings for James would complicate her future, and Matthew would be the one who would ultimately suffer. While she'd suspected Matthew's feelings for her, she'd never thought he would make them known.

"I appreciate the invitation, Matthew," she said gently, because the last thing she wanted to do was hurt this kind young man. "But I think I should stay in. I wouldn't feel comfortable at a singing. I'm sure my younger sisters, Meg, Ellie and Charlie, will be going, but I feel as if the time for singings has passed me by."

Although he hid it well, she could sense his disappointment. "I thought you might like to get out a bit, but I understand."

"Matthew Troyer, you're a nice man and a *gut* friend," she said sincerely.

He gazed at her a long moment before his expression warmed. "Not what I was hoping from you, but I'll take it." He stood. "I should get home. James is staying for supper. 'Tis late. I didn't want to wait until tomorrow to bring your kitten." He brushed off his pants, then extended a hand to help Nell up.

Nell accepted his help and wished that things could be different for them. If she hadn't loved Michael and then met James, she might have given their relationship a chance. She was aware of the warmth of his fingers about hers as he pulled her to her feet. He released her hand immediately and stepped back.

"*Danki*, Matthew."

His smile wasn't as bright as previously. "You're *willkomm*."

Nell accompanied him to his buggy. "Matthew—"

"'Tis fine, Nell." Genuine warmth filled his blue eyes. "At least we are friends, *ja*?"

"Always."

"I'll see you at church service."

"*Danki* for bringing the kitten."

He laughed. "'Twas my pleasure."

As she watched him leave, she realized what Matthew had revealed—that James was at Adam Troyer's residence for supper.

Nell sighed sadly. James had brought the kitten with him to his parents' house. Apparently, he realized how upset she'd been by their kiss, so he asked Matthew to bring her the kitten.

She closed her eyes as she was overwhelmed. True to form, James remained ever thoughtful of her feelings. What was she going to do about this?

Chapter Nine

❧

"**W**ill you be coming to church service?" *Mam* had asked James last night during Saturday evening's supper. He had come for dinner the night before when his family had convinced him to stay the weekend. Upset over how he'd chased Nell away with his kiss, he'd been in need of some cheering up. And his parents and siblings' love and acceptance of him always made him feel better. So he'd spent last night, and this morning he'd promised to stay another. Therefore, he wasn't surprised when his mother suggested that he attend Sunday services with them.

"*Mam*, I haven't been to church in years," he'd confessed.

"All the more reason to come."

James had gazed at his mother, seen the warmth and love in her brown eyes and smiled. "I'll come."

Sunday morning he went to the barn to see to the animals. As he walked, he glanced down at his garments. On Friday, when he'd been asked to stay, he'd wanted to retrieve his clothing from his apartment. His stepfather had said there was no need. James and he were the same size, and so was Matthew. They owned enough garments to get James through the weekend.

Which is how James found himself wearing Amish clothing for the first time since he'd turned eighteen and left the community. To his surprise, he realized that he felt comfortable in them. It was like putting on a favorite T-shirt. They fit him like a glove and felt good against his skin.

He'd gotten up early and spent longer in the barn than he needed to. But it had felt good spending time with his stepfather's horses and goats. Usually the only animals he saw were sick or in need of medical care, except for the ones that only needed their vaccines and their annual exams.

He'd enjoyed the smell of horse and hay and the sound of the animals shifting in their stalls. The simple joy of just standing and watching kept him longer than he should have been.

But when was the last time he'd spent any amount of time in his stepfather's barn? The moment of peace wouldn't last long, he knew, so he stayed to enjoy it until, conscious of the time, he hurried back to the house. He entered the kitchen just as his mother announced that breakfast was ready. He joined his family at the table and thoroughly enjoyed the home-cooked meal.

"We have to leave for service by eight thirty," Adam said.

"Where is it this week?" Matthew asked.

"The Amos Kings." Adam turned to James. "You've seen the new *schuulhaus*?"

"*Ja*, I know where it is."

"It's on the Samuel Lapp property. The Amos Kings live across the street."

"The large farm?" James murmured. James suspected

that the man farmed for a living. Most members of the Amish community had smaller farms that provided food with only minimal cash crops. But he suspected that it was different with Amos King. His farm was larger than most in the area.

"*Ja*, Amos farms more than any of us. Samuel Lapp does some construction work for members of our community. He donated the property, and he with his sons built the *schuul*."

The school hadn't existed when James had lived here as a teenager. Back then, the school had been a small building in need of repair on the opposite side of town. James hadn't attended the school. Since he'd made the decision to become a veterinarian like his late father, his mother and stepfather had allowed him to attend public school.

"Do you have something I can borrow for church?" James asked. Amish dress for church was white shirt with black vest and black pants. He would have looked out of place in his Amish work clothes of a solid shirt, navy tri-blend pants and black suspenders. His mother left the room and returned within seconds. She carried a white shirt, black vest and black dress pants. She extended them to her son.

"I kept them in case you visited and needed them."

James felt his emotions shift as he accepted his former Sunday clothes.

"*Danki, Mam*," he said thickly. Emotion clogged his throat, making it difficult to swallow.

"Are you certain they will still fit?" Matthew asked.

"Matt."

"He's right, *Dat*. I'm a boy no longer. What if these don't fit?"

"Only one way to find out," Adam said.

James headed upstairs to change. To his amazement, the clothes fit as if tailor-made for him.

His mother smiled when he came downstairs wearing the garments. "I knew they'd fit."

"I don't have a hat," James said.

"*Ja*, you do," Matthew said. At *Mam's* insistence, Matthew must have retrieved the black felt hat James had in his youth.

James waited until he and his family were outside before he put it on.

Like the clothes, the hat fit perfectly.

"There you go. You've no worries. You look as Amish as the rest of us," *Mam* said.

James grinned. He couldn't help it. At one time, he'd objected to wearing Amish clothing, but now he appreciated how the simple garments made him feel as if he was a part of something big.

The first person James noticed as Adam steered his buggy onto the Amos King property was Nell Stoltzfus. He experienced a stark feeling of dismay as he saw that she was talking with a young handsome man closer in age to her than he was.

He knew he had no right to be upset. Despite their kiss, Nell and he didn't have a relationship. Given their life circumstances, they never would, but that knowledge didn't make the sight any easier for him.

Matthew jumped out as soon as the vehicle stopped. "Nell!" He hurried in her direction. *"Hallo!"*

James's heart ached as he climbed out more slowly and watched Matthew approach Nell. Unlike him, his brother hadn't hurt Nell or caused her discomfort and embarrassment.

He held out his hand to his sister Maggie. "That's the bishop," she told him as if she could read his mind. "His wife is over there." She gestured toward a chair in the sun. The woman looked frail as if she'd been ill.

"That's his wife?"

"*Ja*, Catherine. They have a two-year-old son, Nicholas. She's been under the weather recently, and we haven't seen much of her—or him. She must have felt well enough to come. If they leave right after services, then we know that she's not recovered as much as we'd like to think."

James met his sister's gaze. "And you're telling me this because…"

"Nell. I saw your face when you saw her with him, but you've no need to worry." Maggie studied him. "You know that she's a member of the church. Not like me and our siblings but as an adult member. She joined it five years ago, when they moved to Happiness after Meg recuperated from her illness."

"Young people don't normally join the church until right before marriage."

"*Ja*, that's true. But for some reason, Nell felt compelled to make the commitment. She can no longer leave the church without consequences."

James's stomach burned. "Being shunned by her family and community."

"*Ja*, James. She chose the path of the Lord when she was only nineteen. She'd had no sweetheart or prospects of marriage, but she made the choice anyway."

"I see." It was as bad as James had thought. There wasn't even the hope of a future with Nell, not with his life firmly entrenched in the English world while she lived happily within her Amish community.

"Nell!"

Nell turned and smiled. "*Hallo*, Matthew."

"Bishop John," Matthew greeted.

"Matthew."

"How is your wife?" he asked.

John gestured toward the woman seated in a chair in the backyard. "She wanted to come."

"That's *gut*. She must be feeling better."

The bishop eyed his spouse with concern. "*Ja*, she says she is."

But Nell could read his doubt.

"Where is Nicholas?" Matthew asked.

"Meg has him." She gestured toward the back lawn where the boy walked with her sister. "He's getting big, John. He's two, *ja*?"

"Almost three." The church elder smiled. "He's a *gut* boy. I can't imagine our lives without him."

"'Tis why the Lord blessed you with such a fine *soohn*."

Nell studied the small boy and wondered how difficult it must be for Catherine to care for him when she felt so ill. She had no idea what was wrong with John's wife, but she said a silent prayer that the woman would recover quickly.

"I'm going to check on Catherine," John said.

"If you need anything, please don't hesitate to let me know. I'll do what I can to help."

The bishop gave her a genuine smile. "*Danki*, Nell."

"How is the little one?" Matthew teased after John had left.

"You mean Naomi?"

"You named her!"

"Did you really think that I'd keeping calling her little one—or *kotz*?"

Matthew laughed. "Naomi, I like it."

"Like what?" Maggie said as she approached from behind. "*Hallo*, Nell."

"Maggie!" Nell greeted her with delight. She genuinely liked Maggie Troyer.

"I've brought someone with me." She stepped aside, and Nell found herself face to face with James.

She blushed and looked away. "James. Thank you for Naomi."

"Her kitten," Matthew explained.

A twinkle entered James's dark eyes. "I see. Do you like her?"

Nell stared. "What's not to like?"

His features became unreadable as he looked away.

She immediately regretted her behavior. "How is Joey?"

His face cleared and brightened. "He's doing well. Fred picked him up on Friday. I called to check on him yesterday. Joey's making great strides in his recovery."

"Any idea yet who hurt him?"

Maggie frowned. "Is this the little dog you were telling us about?" she asked her brother.

James nodded.

Matthew scowled. "Surely there is something that can be done."

"I called and reported it to the police. They're keeping an eye out. It's going to be hard because there are no witnesses to the crime."

Ellie approached. "'Tis time for service."

Immediately, everyone headed toward the King barn where benches had been set up in preparation for church. Nell entered and sat in the second row in the women's area. Maggie and Ellie slid in beside her and moments later, they were joined by Maggie's sisters Abigail and Rosie.

Nell watched as James took a seat in the men's area between Matthew and her cousin Eli Lapp. Soon all of the men were seated in one area of the room while the women and children were in another.

The room quieted as Abram Peachy, the church deacon, and Bishop John Fisher, who saw that his wife was comfortably seated next to Nell's aunt Katie Lapp, approached the pulpit area. Preacher Levi Stoltzfus, a distant relative of her father's family, led the service by instructing everyone to open the *Ausbund* and sing the first hymn.

The service progressed throughout the morning as it usually did. Abram spoke to the congregation first, then they sang the second hymn before Levi began to preach. Bishop John had a few words of wisdom for the church community, then the service was declared officially over.

Nell was conscious of James seated across the room. Dressed in Amish Sunday best, he was handsome, his presence a strong reminder of what recently had transpired between them.

Soon, everyone left the barn to enjoy a shared meal provided by the community women. After helping to serve the men, Nell gravitated toward her family with her own plate of food.

"Did you get any of Miriam Zook's pie?" her *mam* asked. Nell shook her head. "You should try it before there's nothing left to taste."

Nell got up from her family's table. "Anyone want something while I'm up?"

"A glass of ice tea," *Dat* said.

She nodded. "Meg? Leah? Do you need anything to drink?"

"We have lemonade," Leah said. "*Danki*, Nell."

As she wandered over to the dessert and drink tables,

Nell thought of James and wondered whether or not he'd left. She had her answer as she poured her father a glass of ice tea.

"Nell."

"James!" She nearly dropped the glass, but James quickly reached out to steady it.

"I need to talk with you."

"About what?" she said breathlessly.

"I wanted to apologize about the—"

"Don't say it," she gasped. "Please, James. Not here."

"Then will you understand if I just say that I'm sorry?"

"Ja," she said quickly and tried to dash away.

But James followed her. "Nell."

She sighed as she faced him. *"Ja?"*

"I'm glad you like your kitten. I saw her and thought immediately of you."

"That was kind of you."

"I don't feel kind." He took off his black hat and ran his fingers through his short dark hair. His haircut was the only thing that reminded her that he wasn't Amish. In his current garments, James looked as if he could easily fit into her world. The knowledge that his appearance was just an illusion upset her.

"James, I have to go."

"I miss you, Nell," he said.

"Don't!" She didn't need to hear how much he'd missed her. Or to have to admit the truth that she'd missed him, too. Despite his Amish relatives and appearance, James was an *Englisher*, and she had to get over him. She couldn't allow herself to care.

Nell worked to shove thoughts of James from her mind as she hurried back to her family. The afternoon passed too slowly as she felt the continued tension of James's presence.

"You're quiet," Leah said beside her hours later as they rode home in their father's buggy.

"Just tired."

She felt her sister's intense regard and turned to smile at her reassuringly. To her relief, Leah seemed to accept her explanation. "At least, 'tis Sunday, and we can read or play games if we want."

"Ja." Nell made an effort to pull herself from her dark thoughts. She would enjoy their day of rest and try not to worry about tomorrow and her need to find an Amish husband fast before her father decided to find one for her. Or she did something she'd forever regret, like giving into her feelings for James.

That night, Nell prayed for God's help in finding a husband, in doing the right thing as a member of her Amish community. She pleaded with the Lord to help her get over the *Englisher* who'd stolen her heart and threatened her future happiness.

Chapter Ten

"You like James," Leah said as she cornered Nell in the barn Monday morning.

"*Ja*, he is a fine veterinarian. I respect him."

"*Nay*, Nell. You *care* for him." She paused. "You love him."

Nell felt a flutter in her chest as her denial got hung up in her throat. "Why would you think such a thing?"

"I saw the way you looked at him."

"What do you mean?" She felt a sharp bolt of terror. "I don't look at him in any certain way."

"And he looks at you in a certain way," Leah said, surprising her. "He cares for you."

But Nell was shaking her head. She didn't need the complication of a forbidden relationship with the *Englisher*.

"Nell, you should think about marrying. Has *Dat* mentioned it to you again?"

Nell brushed a piece of straw off her skirt. "Yesterday after we got home from church. I explained that I've been trying. I considered Matthew Troyer. I know he likes me, and he's a *gut* man, despite the fact that he is too young for me."

"He's not too young. Many of our women marry younger husbands."

"*Ja*, but their young husbands are not *bruders* to a man you are trying to forget."

"Ha!" Leah exclaimed. "So you *are* attracted to James!"

Nell nodded, feeling glum. "I can't help it. And he likes me, which makes it all the more difficult." She sighed. "I care for him, but 'tis hopeless." She put Naomi into her bed and stood. "Do you know *Dat* wanted me to think about marrying Benjamin Yoder? He moved to Happiness recently."

"Isn't he in his sixties?"

"*Ja*, but that isn't the worst of it. Benjamin came here from Indiana." She shuddered just thinking about the man. "I'm sure he's nice but, Leah, he's never been married. Or had children. I can't imagine…" She blushed. "And what if after he marries, he decides he wants to go home to Indiana? His wife would be expected to go with him. I don't want to leave Happiness. This is my home, and my family is here."

"You won't have to marry him. We'll find someone else for you first."

Nell smiled. "We?"

"I'll help you. We don't want to set a precedence of *Dat* choosing our husbands."

"And at twenty-one, you'll be the next *dochter* our *vadder* will want to see married and with children."

Leah inclined her head. "*Ja*. I'll find my own man, and I won't marry for anything other than love."

"And if you take too long and *Dat* wants to interfere?"

"You mean, help me along." Leah grinned. "Then I'll expect you to step in despite the fact that you'll be happily married to your chosen man with your seven children clinging to your apron strings."

"Seven!" Nell couldn't control a snort of laughter. "How long do you think *Dat* will be willing to wait for you? Certainly not long enough for me to give birth to seven *kinner*?"

Her sister shrugged. "Not to worry. 'Tis all just a thought anyway. You'll find your own husband, and I'll find mine."

"Where?"

"Look around. There are a lot of young men in our community."

"Men like Matthew," Nell murmured. "I already told you why I can no longer consider him."

"Because of James."

"Ja." She sighed. "If only I'd met James years ago, before I'd met Michael, then we might have had a chance."

"Michael?" Leah frowned. "Who is Michael?"

James unlocked the clinic Monday morning and went inside. He turned on the computer at the front desk, then slipped into his office to work while he waited for his staff. He made a list of patients he needed to check up on, and just as he finished, he heard the opening of the front door and Michelle's voice.

"Good morning, Dr. Pierce!" she called.

"Good morning, Michelle."

The young woman appeared in his doorway. "You don't look well. Don't tell me you caught the stomach bug, too?"

"No, I'm fine. Tired but fine."

"I'm sorry that I was out sick so long. I knew with Nell here that you'd be able to manage." She frowned. "Is Nell coming in today?"

YOUR FAVORITE INSPIRATIONAL NOVELS!

GET 2 FREE BOOKS!

2 FREE BOOKS

To get your 2 free books, affix this peel-off sticker to the reply card and mail it today!

Plus, receive
TWO FREE BONUS GIFTS!

We'd like to send you two free books from the series you are enjoying now. Your two books have a combined cover price of over $10 retail, but are yours to keep absolutely FREE! We'll even send you two wonderful surprise gifts. You can't lose!

HEARTWARMING INSPIRATIONAL ROMANCE

Love Inspired

Her Single Dad Hero
Arlene James

HEARTWARMING INSPIRATIONAL ROMANCE

Love Inspired

The Deputy's Perfect Match
Lisa Carter

Each of your FREE books features unique characters, interesting settings and captivating stories you won't want to miss!

FREE BONUS GIFTS!

*We'll send you two wonderful surprise gifts, worth about $10 retail, **absolutely FREE**, just for giving our books a try! Don't miss out — MAIL THE REPLY CARD TODAY!*

Visit us at
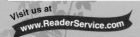
www.ReaderService.com

Books received may not be as shown.

GET 2 FREE BOOKS!

CLAIM NOW!
Return this card today to get 2 FREE Books and 2 FREE Bonus Gifts!

YES! Please send me the **2 FREE books** and **2 FREE bonus gifts** for which I qualify. I understand that I am under no obligation to purchase anything further, as explained on the back of this card.

**PLACE
FREE GIFTS
SEAL HERE**

❑ I prefer the regular-print edition
105/305 IDL GLUR

❑ I prefer the larger-print edition
122/322 IDL GLUR

FIRST NAME

LAST NAME

ADDRESS

APT.#

CITY

STATE/PROV.

ZIP/POSTAL CODE

▼ DETACH AND MAIL CARD TODAY! ▼

® and ™ are trademarks owned and used by the trademark owner and/or its licensee. © 2016 HARLEQUIN ENTERPRISES LIMITED. Printed in the U.S.A.

Offer limited to one per household and not applicable to series that subscriber is currently receiving. **Your Privacy**—The Reader Service is committed to protecting your privacy. Our Privacy Policy is available online at www.ReaderService.com or upon request from the Reader Service. We make a portion of our mailing list available to reputable third parties that offer products we believe may interest you. If you prefer that we not exchange your name with third parties, or if you wish to clarify or modify your communication preferences, please visit us at www.ReaderService.com/consumerschoice or write to us at Reader Service Preference Service, P.O. Box 9062, Buffalo, NY 14240-9062. Include your complete name and address.

LI-517-FMIVY17

READER SERVICE—Here's how it works:

Accepting your 2 free Love Inspired® Romance books and 2 free gifts (gifts valued at approximately $10.00 retail) places you under no obligation to buy anything. You may keep the books and gifts and return the shipping statement marked "cancel." If you do not cancel, about a month later we'll send you 6 additional books and bill you just $5.24 for the regular-print edition or $5.74 each for the larger-print edition in the U.S. or $5.74 each for the regular-print edition or $6.24 for the larger-print edition in Canada. That is a savings of at least 13% off the cover price. It's quite a bargain! Shipping and handling is just 50¢ per book in the U.S. and 75¢ per book in Canada. * You may cancel at any time, but if you choose to continue, every month we'll send you 6 more books, which you may either purchase at the discount price plus shipping and handling or return to us and cancel your subscription. *Terms and prices subject to change without notice. Prices do not include applicable taxes. Sales tax applicable in N.Y. Canadian residents will be charged applicable taxes. Offer not valid in Quebec. Books received may not be as shown. All orders subject to approval. Credit or debit balances in a customer's account(s) may be offset by any other outstanding balance owed by or to the customer. Please allow 4 to 6 weeks for delivery. Offer available while quantities last.

BUSINESS REPLY MAIL
FIRST-CLASS MAIL   PERMIT NO. 717   BUFFALO, NY

POSTAGE WILL BE PAID BY ADDRESSEE

READER SERVICE
PO BOX 1341
BUFFALO NY 14240-8571

NO POSTAGE
NECESSARY
IF MAILED
IN THE
UNITED STATES

▲ If offer card is missing write to: Reader Service, P.O. Box 1341, Buffalo, NY 14240-8531 or visit www.ReaderService.com ▲

He shook his head. "I don't need her now that you and Janie are back." It seemed a lie, telling Michelle that he didn't need Nell. But it was true that he didn't need her in the office. He needed—wanted—her in his personal life.

I shouldn't have kissed her, James thought when Michelle had settled in at the front desk. What on earth had he been thinking?

He hadn't been thinking. He only knew that at that moment he'd been unable to deny his growing feelings for her and he'd desperately needed that kiss.

A longing so sharp and intense that it made him groan and hang his head into his hands gripped him. He had a business to run, a goal to accomplish. It didn't matter how he felt about someone he had no right to love.

He straightened, threw back his chair and went to the window to enjoy the view of the farm across the road. He had done what he'd set out to do—become a veterinarian like his father.

James knew his father had never expected him to follow the same path, despite the fact that James had loved every moment he'd spent at his dad's side while his father had gone out on calls. James enjoyed his job, and he was sure John Pierce would be proud of the man he'd become and the vocation he'd chosen. But then, did he have moments like this when he'd felt empty inside?

He thought of his siblings. They were so happy and at peace with their lives. They didn't seem to be plagued by the same doubts and unrest that frequently overcame him lately. He felt torn between his chosen life and the life he'd left behind. Spending time with his family gave him a small measure of peace, something he hadn't experienced in a long time.

Suddenly he heard Janie in the treatment room, taking

instruments out of the autoclave and putting them within easy reach. They had a full slate of appointments today.

His assistant appeared in his doorway. "Your first patient has arrived. She's new—Mrs. Simmons with her Siberian Husky, Montana. I've put them in room three."

He turned from the window. "Thank you, Janie." He took one last look at the fields of corn that grew thick and lush in the distance before he left his office to see his first patient.

Though everything went smoothly, the day seemed to drag on. James had seen three new patients who told him how pleased they were with his care of their pets. They would tell others about the clinic, each one had promised.

While he knew that was good news, he couldn't seem to get excited about it. His business was growing, which was what he wanted. But then why didn't he feel good or complete? Why did he keep thinking about his family and the life he could have had if he'd stayed within the community? Why couldn't he stop envisioning a different choice which could have given him what he needed and wanted most…a loving relationship with Nell Stoltzfus?

Janie approached him in the treatment room. "Dr. Pierce, I've cleaned the exam room and mopped the floors."

He glanced at her with surprise. His assistant had never cleaned the floors since she'd started work at the clinic. "Thank you, Janie."

"Is there anything else you need?" she asked.

James glanced at his watch. It was already well past closing time. "No, you've done enough, and I appreciate it. Go on home. I'll see you tomorrow."

The girl hesitated as if she had something to say. "Dr. Pierce?"

He looked at her with raised eyebrows. "Yes?"

She shook her head. "I just wanted to thank you for letting me take two weeks' vacation. It meant a lot to me. I know it couldn't have been easy for you while I was gone. Especially with Michelle out sick."

He smiled. "I managed to find some help. But I won't have to worry now that you're back."

"Good night, Dr. Pierce."

"James," he said. "Call me James. We've worked together long enough, don't you agree? Even Michelle calls me James."

Janie grinned. "Good night, James. I'll see you in the morning."

The office was quiet. He enjoyed the silence after hours of tending to his noisy patients. Normally, he'd reflect on his day's work and experience satisfaction. But not today. In fact, he hadn't felt satisfied since the last day Nell had worked at the clinic.

He checked to ensure that the clinic was locked up before he headed home. The sun was bright in the sky, but it looked like there might be rain in the distance to the east. He would miss the longer daylight hours once fall came. The thought of staying alone in his apartment made him ache.

He felt a tightening in his chest that didn't go away as he reached his apartment and climbed up the stairs. By the time he entered his home, there was a painful lump in his throat and his tired eyes burned.

He threw his keys on the kitchen table, then collapsed onto his sofa. He stared at the ceiling, angry with himself for loving Nell—and for driving her not only out of his office but out of his life.

They could have remained friends if he'd controlled his growing feelings for her. But he'd had to go and kiss her—and ruin their friendship, the only thing he was permitted to have with her.

Four more days of work before the weekend. He had a standing invitation to stay at home. After long years away, he felt compelled to spend as much time on the farm as possible. It wasn't only his mother who was glad whenever he stayed. His stepfather, sisters and stepsiblings were happy to see him, too.

He knew Adam kept busy trying to keep up with his lawn furniture business. His stepfather had added children's swing sets to the list of items he could sell to his customers. If Adam would allow it, he'd like to help with the furniture. He was good with his hands and had learned from his stepfather when he was in high school. He could work with Adam on Saturdays unless he received an emergency call about a patient. He was busy at the clinic during the week and work was not allowed within the Amish community on Sundays.

He envisioned cutting wood, bolting long heavy boards together to form the legs of a swing set. It was something to look forward to—helping Adam with his business and on the farm.

James smiled and closed his eyes. And couldn't block the mental images of Nell that sprang immediately to mind. Only they weren't images of Nell walking away after he'd kissed her.

They were of her walking toward him on their wedding day.

Chapter Eleven

Nell pulled the buggy into the barnyard a little after one in the afternoon. She'd made beds, done the laundry and shopped for her mother. Instead of feeling as if she'd accomplished something, she felt totally out of sorts. Once again, she went to seek comfort from her animals, most particularly Jonas. When she'd returned from the store, she'd put away *Mam*'s groceries, then went directly to the barn.

Jonas greeted her enthusiastically, and she felt her mood lighten as she slipped inside his stall. His happy cries and kisses as she sat down beside him were just what she'd needed. Her fierce longing for a man she couldn't have upset her. She'd never expected to love again, and that she loved James made it hard.

She didn't know how long she sat playing with Jonas, but it must have been some time. Jonas finally exhausted himself and curled up to sleep in her lap. Nell studied him with a smile. Then her eyes filled with tears. It had been Jonas who had first brought her into contact with James Pierce.

Nell lay back against the straw and closed her eyes. It was how her sister Leah found her several minutes later.

"Nell."

She opened one eye. Leah's concerned expression wavered in her narrow vision. She opened her other eye and sat up. "Leah. I'm just having a rest."

Her sister regarded her with worry. "Are you ever going to tell me about Michael?"

Nell had put her sister off after she'd made the mistake of mentioning Michael's name. She'd had no intention of ever telling her family about him. Michael was dead, and there didn't seem to be any reason to resurrect her feelings for him—and her grief.

Jonas stirred in Nell's lap as Leah slipped inside and knelt in the stall beside her. "He's a *gut* dog." She reached to stroke the dog's fur.

Nell smiled. "He gives me comfort."

Leah looked at her. "Why did you need comfort? Because of Michael?"

Nell stiffened. "Leah…"

"You should just tell me. I won't tell anyone if you don't want me to." Leah studied her with compassion. "What happened, Nell?"

Nell felt her face heat up.

"Nell—"

"James kissed me."

"What?"

"He kissed me. He didn't grab or hurt me. It was an innocent kiss that happened after we accidentally bumped heads."

"Nell," Leah whispered.

"*Ja*, I know. That's why I didn't go back to work for him at the clinic."

Leah eyed her with sympathy. "Although you loved the job."

"I only had one day left. Why should I risk it?"

As Leah remained quietly beside her, Nell finally gave in to the urge to tell her about Michael. "Leah, I've kept something from you and our family. It happened right before and then during the time Meg was ill."

Leah shifted to sit. "Michael?"

"Ja," Nell said. "He was an *Englisher.* I fell in love with him and we used to meet each night in secret. Our meetings were innocent, but he was handsome and kind, and I loved him."

Leah gazed at her with confusion. "Michael left you?"

"Not exactly. One night he asked me to marry him. I told him I would think about it, although I knew what I was going to tell him the next day. That I would leave the community to be his wife."

Her sister frowned. "I don't understand."

"That night I waited for Michael, and he didn't show—it was the night that Meg became ill. I went to our special spot, ready to give him my answer. I knew he loved me, and when he didn't come, I thought he'd been detained for some reason. I waited for hours, then finally I went home. I went right to my room and cried and prayed and hoped that I hadn't been a fool for loving him."

Tears filled Nell's eyes, and she couldn't hold back a sob. "Then Meg got sick, and we all went to the hospital. I couldn't think about Michael, Meg needed me— she needed all of us."

"You were the strong one, and *Mam* and *Dat* needed you, too," Leah murmured, her blue eyes filled with emotion.

"The next day I was coming back to Meg's room after getting tea from the cafeteria, I heard a terrible loud beeping. It was in a room on the same floor as Meg's.

I looked inside as I walked past and that's when I saw him. It was Michael, hooked up to life support.

"At first, I felt faint, but then I wanted to run to him. I needed to scream and cry and beg him to get better. I started into the room, but his nurse stopped me. She told me that I was in the wrong room, that Meg was in another. She said that this particular patient—Michael— wasn't allowed visitors." Nell wiped away tears. "The nurse looked at me and saw Amish. No one would have believed me if I'd told them we were in love."

She felt Leah's touch on her arm. "What happened to him?"

Nell's eyes filled with tears as she was overcome by her memories of that day. "I later learned that he'd been in a car accident. He was driving to meet me when a drunk driver struck him." She stood and turned away as her tears trailed down her cheeks.

She hugged herself with her arms. "Michael died from his injuries the next day. I wanted to rail against God, but in the end I put myself into His hands instead. I prayed for Meg to get well. I had already lost Michael, and I couldn't let myself grieve. I knew I'd fall apart and completely lose it. The only thing I could do was to pray for Meg's recovery."

Nell offered Leah a sad smile as she continued, "When Meg got better, I was so relieved. I'd made a promise to God, and I kept it. I joined the Amish church less than three months later."

Leah drew a sharp breath. "That's why you didn't wait until marriage. You'd lost the only man you'd ever love—or so you thought, and you thanked the Lord for Meg's recovery by fulfilling your promise to Him."

"Ja," Nell whispered. Her tears trickled unchecked. With a cry of sympathy, Leah hugged her. "Leah, you

can't tell anyone. Please. You can't tell *Dat* or *Mam* or our sisters. Meg especially must never know."

Leah opened her mouth to object.

"*Please*, Leah."

"I promise that I won't tell them, but only if they don't ask. If one of them learns the truth, I won't lie."

She released a sharp breath. Nell was sure that after all of this time no one would find out. *"Danki."*

"But now you're in love with the *English* veterinarian. But this time the choice of whether or not to leave is no longer yours."

Nell inclined her head. *"Ja,* 'tis not."

"You've joined the church, and there is no obvious way for you and him to be together."

"Ja."

Leah stood abruptly, held out her hand and pulled Nell to her feet. "You've done the right thing. Avoiding him."

"But it still hurts."

"I know," Leah said. "Come. Let's go into the *haus.* It's near suppertime, and you must be famished."

Nell stared at her sister. She had no idea that by simply telling Leah about Michael she'd feel a lightening of her burden. "I *am* hungry."

Leah grinned. "Let's hurry in before our younger sisters decide to eat everything and leave us nothing."

When they entered the kitchen, it was to find their other three sisters and their mother working together to prepare a meal.

"Nell, I wondered where you'd gone to," *Mam* said. *"Danki* for doing the wash and all the housework."

"I didn't mind. I like being busy."

Her brow furrowing, *Mam* glanced her way. If she'd noticed Nell's red-rimmed eyes, she didn't mention it. "How's your kitten, Naomi?"

"She's fine. *Dat* was *gut* about allowing me to keep her."

"Because he knows that you won't leave her care to your sisters, and you prefer to take care of her yourself."

Dat came in when the meal was ready. He gave the prayer of thanks. Conversation during dinner was loud and filled with feminine laughter. Nell smiled at Ellie as she regaled them with a story about the one family she cleaned for. Meg offered comments on how Ellie should handle the husband the next time he left food on dirty dishes on his night table.

Nell became aware of her father's gaze as Charlie joined in with the outrageous solution of putting the food in the man's bed and the dishes in his bathtub. As her father watched her, she saw something in his eyes that gave her concern.

"I'll lose my job if I do that." Ellie laughed.

"Husband," *Mam* addressed him. "Chocolate cake for dessert?"

Dat nodded to *Mam,* a soft expression on his face.

Once the leftover fried chicken was put away, *Mam* brought out the cake and sliced each of them a nice-sized piece. When they were done with dessert, Nell and her sister Leah rose to clear the supper dishes while Charlie and Meg filled up the sink basin and started to wash. With five daughters in the house, there was always plenty of help, so when her father beckoned to her, Nell did whatever any good daughter would do. She handed Ellie her dish towel and followed him out into the other room.

She felt edgy as she waited for her father to speak. She had a feeling she knew what he wanted to talk about.

"Have you given it any thought?"

"It?"

"Marriage. A husband." Her father studied her thoughtfully.

She relaxed and smiled. "*Ja, Dat.* I haven't found the man I want to marry yet, but I will. I just need a little more time."

Dat sighed. "You can have more time, but not too much." Then he hesitated as if he had something else on his mind. "Nell, I know how much you enjoy your animals. You've got a certain way with them, everyone says so. But you have to face the fact that your husband might not care for them as you do."

Nell gazed at him with a little smile on her lips. "Then I'll find a man who does love animals as much as I do."

He narrowed his gaze. "You're asking a lot of the man who hasn't married you yet."

"I'll find the right man, and he'll understand how I feel."

"You need to find him quickly, *dochter.*"

"How can I rush this? I'll not marry for anything but love."

Her father's jaw tightened. "Are you disrespecting me with your tone, girl? I'm still your *vadder.*"

She sighed. "*Dat*, I mean no disrespect. But this isn't easy for me. I thought I might be a *schuul* teacher until I meet a man I can love and who loves me, too."

"'Tis past the time to be thinking about becoming a *schuul* teacher. 'Tis time you took a husband."

"You think I have nothing to offer the *kinner*?" she asked softly. She was hurt by his dismissal of her skills. Was she that old that all he could think of was marrying her off?

"You could still marry Benjamin Yoder. He's single and never been married."

"*Nay!* I'll not marry a man older than my own *vadder*!"

Her father swallowed. "In truth, I don't want that for you either."

"I didn't think you wanted me to be unhappy."

His lips firmed. "Of course, I want your happiness. 'Tis my fondest hope that all of my girls will be happy in marriage, but time is passing you by, Nell. You have to take your chance soon."

Tears filled her eyes, and she tried to blink them away. She thought of Michael and then James. She could love James, marry him if he were a member of the Amish community. James loved animals as much as she did. Her heart ached, for she knew she would never have a life with him.

"Nell…" Her father's expression softened. "Know this. I do want you to be happy."

"*Ja*, I know."

"You deserve to have a husband, a family. You'll make a wonderful *mudder*."

"*Dat,* I'll try harder to find someone I can love. But *please* don't arrange a husband for me. I can't…*please*."

He nodded. "You will be open-minded? Give up this notion of being a *schuul* teacher?"

"*Ja, Dat.*"

The man looked relieved. "*Gut.*" He smiled. "How is Jonas?" he said, quickly changing the subject. The little dog had worked his way into her father's heart, it seemed.

"He's doing well. Have you been to visit him?"

A slight tide of red crept into her father's cheeks. "This morning."

"He's a wonderful pet." Nell gazed at her father with fascination. "And Naomi? Have you visited with her, too?"

He looked embarrassed. "Neither one works or provides a service," her father pointed out.

"*Ja*, they do. They give unconditional love."

Her father laughed. "That they do, so I guess that is something."

Friday morning, James woke up with a stiff neck, a sore back and with the television murmuring softly. He must have finally fallen asleep on the sofa and left it on. Unable to sleep for hours last night, he'd alternately stared at the ceiling and the TV.

He couldn't get Nell out of his mind. How could he have been so foolish to give into his feelings? If he had controlled himself, he might have been able to spend more time with her.

He glanced at the clock on the cable box: 6:45 a.m. He had to get moving, or he'd be late for work. He sat up quickly and groaned at his aching muscles. There were consequences for sleeping on his old sofa five nights in a row. He'd fallen asleep to the noise from the TV, so tired each night that he'd been unable to find the strength to go to bed.

He grabbed the remote and turned off the TV. For a moment, his apartment was blissfully silent. He closed his eyes and drank the quiet in.

But then his thoughts filled with Nell again, and his brain buzzed with regret. James stood and headed to get ready for work. The only bright side was that it was the weekend, and he'd be spending it with his family. And there was a possibility that he might see Nell again on Sunday.

When he saw her, he vowed, he wouldn't joke or smile or cause her discomfort. He would be polite so that she didn't feel threatened. He wanted her in his life, even if only from a distance.

"James?" Janie poked her head into his office where he'd sat down between appointments. "Your next patient is here."

"Who is it?"

"Mrs. Becker and her dog Melly."

"Thank you. Would you please put them in exam room two?"

She nodded and left. James sat a moment longer.

The day went by quickly, for he had enough patients to keep him busy. He'd seen a record number of patients this week.

Janie was cheerful and clearly happy to be back at work in the clinic, but she wasn't Nell. Still, the tech's mood became infectious, and there were moments during that day that he smiled and laughed. Maybe he could do this after all, James thought. Maybe he could get past his feelings for Nell even if he couldn't ever forget her.

But then right before closing, Nell came to his office.

"Hi," he heard Janie say. "Welcome to Pierce Veterinary Clinic. Oh, poor baby, is this the little one who needs medical attention?"

He became alert as he heard Nell's voice, but he couldn't make out her words. He waited patiently for his assistant to come for him, although he was eager to see Nell and help.

"Come on back to exam room one," he heard Janie say. "You'll find it on the left as you go down the hall."

James had to smile. Nell knew exactly where the exam room was, where everything was in the clinic, but he doubted that Nell would say anything about having worked here while Janie was on vacation.

Janie entered his office. "You've a patient in exam room one. A little dog with a bee sting."

James was instantly concerned. Jonas got stung? He hurried into the exam room, where he found Nell with Jonas in her lap. She was hugging her pet against her. The dog was whimpering, and Nell was doing her best to soothe and comfort him. She must have sensed his presence because she looked up, happy to see him.

"James!" She rose quickly, mindful of her dog. "Jonas got stung by a bee. I put vinegar on it. I didn't know what else to do."

"You did good, Nell," he said quietly. "Vinegar helps draw out the toxin." He softened his expression as he held out his arms.

Nell didn't hesitate to hand him Jonas, and James experienced a deep sense of joy that she trusted him.

"Let's see, Jonas," he murmured as he placed him on the metal exam table in the room. "What have you done to yourself?" He examined his little swollen nose.

He heard Nell sniff, glanced over and saw her tears. "I only let him outside for a moment," she told him, "and I kept him on his leash."

"Nell," he said kindly, "dogs get into things. If they didn't, there wouldn't be a need for veterinarians like me." He used a magnifying glass to study the dog's nose more closely. "Ah, I see the stinger."

He reached into his pants pocket for his wallet. He flipped open the billfold and removed out a credit card.

He leaned close and scraped across the tip of Jonas's nose with the edge of the plastic card. "Got it!" he exclaimed. He displayed the tiny black object on his thumb. "Bee stinger." He smiled. "He should recover quickly." He handed her a tube of ointment. "For the itch," he said. "He's liable to keep scratching at his nose before it heals completely." He opened a bottle and shook out a pink pill. "Benadryl. And make sure you use the plastic collar I'm going to give you. He will try anything to get at his nose."

Nell nodded, and he knew that she recognized the bottle from her time working here. "I'll give him a Benadryl now. It doesn't appear that he's allergic, but I'll send you home with the liquid form anyway. It may help with some minor reactions. If his nose starts to swell or he becomes lethargic on the Benadryl, please bring him back. Better yet, call me immediately." He jotted his number on a Post-it note. "It's my cell phone. Don't wait if there's a change in him. All right?" He locked gazes with her.

"Ja," she promised, and he felt something tight ease within his chest.

Janie called out that she was finished for the day and was getting ready to lock up. He went to the door with Jonas in his arms to acknowledge his assistant's departure. "We'll be leaving in a minute. Good night, Janie. See you on Monday."

"James, *danki* for seeing him at such short notice," Nell said as he brought Jonas back to the table.

"Always," he said as he grabbed a collar from a cabinet and handed it to her. "Whenever you have a problem with Jonas or Naomi or any of your animals, come right in. You don't have to call. You don't need an appointment. Just come."

He saw her mouth open and close as she tried to process what he'd said. He watched her physically gather her composure. *"Danki."*

He glanced down at Jonas and smiled. "Back to your *mam*," he murmured as he lifted the little dog and placed him into Nell's waiting arms. His arm brushed Nell's, and for a moment, their eyes locked and tension arced between them.

He headed toward the door, waiting for her to follow him. "If he is still bothered by the sting, try using a cold pack on his nose. You can use ice in a plastic bag. Put it on his nose for short time intervals—about ten minutes on and fifteen off." He opened the door. "Make sure it's not too cold for him. If it is, wrap the bag in a dish towel."

He gestured for Nell to precede him into the front reception area. "Take care of yourself, Nell—and Jonas."

"James, I need to pay you."

"Not necessary." His tone was insistent but gentle. "I still owe you for your help here in the office."

Nell sighed. "I… *Danki*."

He smiled and waited while she went out the door. Then he quickly closed it behind her before he called out to her or did something that he would regret. Like kiss her or hug her.

When she was gone, James locked up the office and drove to his family farm. Fifteen minutes later, he took a duffel bag from his trunk and headed toward the house. He entered through the kitchen.

"Hallo, Mam."

"James!" she gasped with pleasure. "It's late. I thought you'd changed your mind about spending the weekend."

"Not a chance. I had a late appointment." After setting his bag by the door, he pulled out a kitchen chair and sat down.

Her brow creased with concern. "Everything *oll recht*?"

"Dog with a bee sting. I was able to get out the stinger. I was concerned because he got stung on the nose, but I believe he'll be fine."

His mother looked relieved, and something startling

occurred to him. "*Mam*, how many times did Dad talk with you about his patients?"

Mam smiled. "Quite a few. He needed to talk, and I liked listening to him." She opened a cabinet door and pulled out two cups. "Coffee or tea?"

"Tea, please." He'd always found comfort in tea whenever he was sick or wanted to remember his time at home. His mother didn't say anything as she put on the kettle and took cookies out of the pantry. She set them within James's reach and then fixed their tea.

"What about dinner?" James asked.

"There's time. I was going to have tea myself," she assured him as she sat down across from him.

She prepared her tea the way she liked it, took a sip, then looked at him.

"Tell me what's wrong." Her warm brown eyes held concern.

"Nothing that can be fixed." He swallowed hard. "But I feel better now that I'm here."

Her expression grew soft. "James, this will always be your home. I love that you enjoy being here. Come whenever you want. You don't have to ask first."

James realized he'd said the same thing to Nell about the office. And he'd meant it. He smiled at his mother as a huge burden was lifted from his shoulders. *"Danki."*

He glanced toward the kitchen window as they finished their tea. "I parked behind the barn."

"Don't want anyone to know you're here, *ja*?" *Mam* teased.

"It doesn't seem right to park a car in your driveway."

She shook her head but a smile played about her mouth. "'Tis fine. You can park it wherever makes you feel better."

James reached out to clasp his mother's hand. "I love you, *Mam*," he said.

"I love you, *soohn*. I wish I could help with whatever is bothering you."

"You already have, *Mam*," he whispered.

"You'll be staying in Matt's room again," *Mam* said as he stood and retrieved his duffel.

He didn't mind. He and Matthew had become close since he'd moved back to Happiness. His brother seemed to enjoy his weekly visits almost as much as he enjoyed staying the weekends in his parents' house.

He carried his belongings upstairs and into Matthew's room which had two single beds. He put the duffel bag on the bed he'd been given the last time, then moved to look through the window at the farm fields below.

The crops Adam had planted were green and thriving. James smiled. He enjoyed the view. It brought back childhood memories of living in Ohio with his parents and of his home here in Pennsylvania with his mother and stepfather.

"Come downstairs after you get settled," *Mam* called up. "You can keep me company while I make dinner. *Dat* and Matt are at your *onkel* Aaron's. Maggie, Abigail and Rosie have gone to the store but will be home soon. They'd planned to stop to see the Stoltzfus girls on their way back."

James felt a jolt. He wasn't surprised that his sisters knew the Stoltzfus girls. They belonged to the same Amish church community. But he hadn't realized that the girls were friendly.

Seeing Nell in his office this afternoon, knowing that she'd come to him for help, warmed him. He couldn't have Nell Stoltzfus as his sweetheart, but perhaps there was still hope that they could be friends.

His stepfather and brother arrived home an hour later, surprised to discover that James had gone to the barn to check on the animals.

"James!" Adam exclaimed. "*Gut* to see you again, *soohn*." He grinned. "Can't manage to stay away from us, *ja*?"

"Ja," James said soberly. "I enjoy spending the weekends with you." He swallowed. "If it's not too much trouble."

"You can stay every weekend—and every weekday if you'd like. We love having you here." He narrowed his gaze. "Where is your car?"

"Behind the barn." James spied his stepbrother, Matthew behind his father. "Matt, I hope you don't mind sharing again."

Matthew grinned. "I don't mind as long as you keep to your own side of the room."

James grinned. "You always know how to put me in my place, little *bruder*."

"As you know how to put me in mine, big *bruder*," he teased.

"Our animals *oll recht*?" Adam asked.

"They are fine." He met Adam's gaze. "They look well fed and healthy." He paused. "Are you having any problems with any of them?" Adam shook his head. *"Gut."*

"We're going inside," his stepfather said. "Coming?"

"Ja, Mam has a *gut* supper simmering on the stove. Chicken potpie." James regarded his brother with amusement. "You staying behind?"

"And have you eat my share of supper?" Matthew smiled. *"Nay."*

"You don't seem upset to have a roommate again,"

he told Matthew as they followed their father toward the house.

Matthew shrugged. "I've gotten used to you."

"Ja?" James smiled.

"You grew on me. It seems I've missed my older *bruder*," he confessed.

"Danki, Matt," James said softly. "I've missed you, too."

"Are you hungry?"

"Starved." James stared at his brother's garments. "I've brought my own clothes, but may I borrow some of yours?"

"Missing our suspenders, are you?" Adam teased. He turned to his other son. "Matthew, do you think you could find some clothes for your *bruder*?"

Matthew sighed. "If I must." But then he grinned. "I'm sure I have a few things that will fit him despite the fact that he's an old man now."

"Don't be smart, youngster," James said with a laugh. "I'm not an old man, and you know it."

James changed into the Amish garments that Matthew got out for him. He was standing with his brother by the pasture fence when his sisters arrived home with their purchases and news from Whittier's Store.

"Did you see Nell and Charlie?" Matthew asked.

"Nay, we didn't have time to stop. We saw Daniel and Isaac Lapp, and we got to talking with them. I wanted to give Leah some quilting fabric. I'll have to bring it with us tomorrow." Maggie glanced at her older brother. "Nice to see you at home again, *bruder*."

"Nice to be home again, Mags."

His sister growled playfully at his use of the *English* nickname.

"Supper!" their mother called.

"We'd best hurry. She may be needing help before we sit down to eat," Maggie said.

The sisters rushed on ahead of them, and the men followed. James felt an infusion of good humor. It was good to be home.

Nell's sisters were laughing. The five of them were in their family buggy taking a drive to visit their cousins.

Aunt Katie and Uncle Samuel would be hosting Visiting Sunday, and the girls wanted to help out in any way they could. With seven sons, more than half of whom were married, and Hannah, her eight-year-old daughter, Aunt Katie had less help than their *mam* did in the Stoltzfus house. Nell knew that Katie's daughters-in-law had offered to come, but they had children to take care of, and Katie thought it best if they stayed with her grandchildren. It was only natural for the Stoltzfus sisters, Katie's nieces, to help out instead.

Nell, who sat in the front passenger seat while Leah steered the horse, heard laughter from her sisters in the seat behind them. She glanced back. "Charlie, I don't know why you insisted on bringing Jonas. You don't have to watch him. His nose is fine. What will we do with him while we work?"

"I brought his kennel," Charlie said with a chuckle. "Stop, Jonas!"

"Nell, he's trying to give puppy kisses," Meg said with laughter.

"Trying and succeeding," Ellie said. "I just got licked in the face."

"Eww!" Meg said, and she roared with delight when she received a doggy kiss of her own.

"Look!" Charlie reached over Nell's shoulder to point

to a farmhouse on the right. "There's Matthew Troyer. He's waving to us."

Nell glanced over with a smile that promptly froze on her face when she saw the man standing beside Matthew. She knew immediately who wore the Amish solid shirt and tri-blend denim pants with black suspenders. It was James. "Who's with him?" Ellie asked. Her voice held interest.

"You've met him," Meg said.

A car came up from behind them, and Leah slowed the buggy, steering it closer to the side of the road.

"'Tis Matthew's *bruder*, and he's someone too old for you," Charlie told her.

"Ha! As if any eligible man in our community is too old for me," Ellie said. "He may be too old for you, Charlie, but not for me."

Nell couldn't keep her eyes from James. Her heart thumped hard as she recalled her time with Jonas in his office yesterday afternoon. He'd been kind and patient… and too professional.

Matthew leaned in to say something to his companion, and James turned, giving Nell a full view of his handsome features. The shock of her continued attraction to him hit her hard. It didn't matter if he'd been professional and friendly. As she met his gaze, she immediately recalled their kiss.

As if sensing Nell's disquiet, Leah looked over and frowned.

"James," Nell murmured. She gestured toward the man in Amish dress, and her sister's eyes widened.

Matthew waved at them to pull into the driveway. She and Leah exchanged glances. They had come for fabric. She could get it from Maggie and then leave immediately. Nell felt her pulse race as Leah turned on the blinker, then pulled onto the Troyers' dirt driveway.

"*Hallo*, Nell," Matthew greeted with a smile.

"Matthew," she greeted pleasantly. She flashed James a look. "James."

"Where are you headed?" the younger brother asked.

"Aunt Katie's," Leah said. "But Maggie has some fabric that she was going to drop off today if she had the time."

"I'll get her for you," Matthew offered, drawing Nell's attention. She looked away as he entered the house, leaving the sisters alone with James.

"Will you be coming to visit at the Lapps tomorrow?" Charlie asked from the backseat.

"I don't know yet," James said.

Nell locked gazes with him. "You should come," she urged and was rewarded by his look of surprise.

"I'll consider it if my family goes," he said.

Nell blushed and was unable to look away.

Matthew exited the house with his sister.

"Sorry we didn't stop by this afternoon," Maggie said as she handed Nell a plastic bag.

"We could have gotten them from you tomorrow, but since we were on our way to Aunt Katie's anyway…"

After their initial eye contact, James seemed to be avoiding Nell's gaze.

There was no logical reason why she should feel hurt, Nell realized. Unless it was because, wrong or right, she wanted his attention.

"We should go—" Leah began.

Nell took the hint. "*Ja*, we need to go. It was *gut* to see you," she said. She started to turn away until James called out to her.

"Nell?"

She froze then glanced back.

"May I speak with you a moment?"

She nodded and followed him to where they could talk privately. "Is something wrong?"

James gazed at her warmly, his intense focus making her wish for things she couldn't have. He didn't say anything for a long moment, as if he were happy just to have her attention.

"James?"

His gaze dropped briefly to her mouth. "How's Jonas?" he asked.

She swallowed hard. "He's fine. Doing well. *Danki*."

"Nell, I miss you."

"James, we can't do this. *I* can't do this."

"What exactly is this?" he asked quietly. "The fact that we like each other but shouldn't?"

"*Ja*, we shouldn't," she said and started to turn.

He captured her arm. "Nell, I'm sorry. I know I have no right to ask anything of you, but please…consider us being friends if we can't be anything more."

"I don't know if I can," she whispered.

"Can't be friends?"

"'Tis too risky. I want more, but it will never happen. So I'm sorry, James, but we can't be friends. Ever." With that last remark, Nell hurried back to the buggy where her sisters were chatting with Maggie and Matthew while they waited. Nell saw that their sister Abigail had joined them.

"*Hallo*, Abigail," she greeted, then she leaned into her sister and said, "Leah, we have to go. *Now*."

"Matthew, it was nice to see you," Nell said with a smile. "Nice to see you again, James," she said politely. She drew on all of her skills to hide the fact that she remembered his kiss and how much she'd enjoyed it. "Enjoy your time with your family."

James looked at her. "I will. *Danki*, Nell."

Leah climbed into the front seat of the carriage while Nell got in on the passenger side.

"Have a *gut* evening," Leah said.

"Bye, Nell," Matthew said. "I hope to see you at the Lapps' tomorrow."

Nell nodded. She had no choice but to go. Would James be there, as well?

Her glance slid over him briefly before she stared ahead as Leah steered their buggy toward Aunt Katie's. She shouldn't want him there, but she did. Nell closed her eyes. She was a fool for loving him. But she couldn't seem to help herself.

She needed to find an Amish husband…soon.

Chapter Twelve

Katie Lapp came out of the house as Leah steered the family buggy into the barnyard and parked. Nell climbed out and waited for Leah while their sisters ran toward the Lapp farmhouse.

"We've come to help, *Endie* Katie," Charlie cried.

"Wunderbor, g'schwischder dochter." Wonderful, *niece*, they heard their aunt exclaim. "I'm so glad you could come—all of you! Come inside!"

Leah hitched up the horse before she turned to Nell. "What are you thinking?"

Nell frowned. "I'm wondering why I can't forget him. He makes it hard, staying with his Amish family, dressing like them."

"He's still an *Englisher*, don't forget. He made the choice to leave our way of life." Leah fell into step beside her as they slowly made their way to the house.

"I know."

"But you still love him."

Nell met her sister's gaze with tears in her eyes. *"Ja."*

Why doesn't he wear jeans? Nell thought. He could have worn jeans, and she'd be unable to forget that he was *English* and unavailable to her. But would it have helped even to see him like that?

Nay, she thought. James in jeans was just as devastating to her peace of mind. Although seeing James in Amish clothes gave her a fierce longing for something she could never have.

Nell preceded Leah into Katie Lapp's house. "*Endie* Katie. Where would you like us to start?"

"Charlie and Hannah are in the kitchen. It would be helpful if you could work in the great room?"

"We'll start there then," Leah said.

Grabbing cleaning supplies and a broom, the sisters entered the large great room, where the family often gathered for late evening and Sunday leisure time.

"What are you going to do about your feelings for him?" Leah asked as she dusted the furniture.

"What can I do? 'Tis not like it matters one way or another how I feel. I have to marry within the Amish faith." Nell swept the floor with long, even strokes of the corn broom.

"You're upset," her sister pointed out. "And hurt. I don't know how to help you."

Nell blinked to clear her vision. There was suddenly a lump in her throat. "No one can help me."

"Matthew cares for you," Leah said. "You could still marry him."

"*Nay!* He'll still be James's *bruder.* And it will seem as I'm deliberately trying to hurt him."

"Matthew?"

"*Nay,* James."

"If he's staying the weekend, James may come visiting tomorrow."

"I know." Nell felt a burning in her stomach. Odds were that he'd come.

"There will be plenty of opportunities to have a word with him and clear the air." Leah paused in her dusting and touched her arm to draw her gaze. "You could check on *Onkel* Samuel's farm animals. 'Tis possible he'll follow you."

It was true. He might follow her because of the nature of his profession. "And if he does, what am I supposed to say to him that I haven't already said?"

"You'll think of something."

"You're not afraid I'll do something terrible, like run away and marry him?"

Her sister's blue eyes widened. "You're not actually considering it, are you?"

Nell's face heated. *"Nay."*

"Then we have nothing to worry about. Just tell him to leave you alone and be done with it."

Nell doubted that it would be so easy. She loved James too much to be cruel. But being cruel might be the only way for him to get on with his life without her.

James liked working side by side with Adam and Matthew. The manual labor on the farm felt good, and it gave him an outlet for the frustration of struggling to make a success of his practice. He also enjoyed helping Adam in his small furniture shop attached to the barn.

The only concession he allowed himself during these weekends was to keep his cell phone with him. He needed to take calls in the event of an emergency. Fortunately, there had been no such calls.

His thoughts focused on Nell as they did often during each day. The image of the young Amish woman constantly hovered in his mind. He'd seen her this afternoon, and he missed her already.

He sighed. There was no chance for them. Why couldn't he put her out of his mind?

Then there was Matthew. It was clear that his younger brother had feelings for Nell. It would be acceptable for Matthew and Nell to have a life together. Acceptable to the community, but not to him.

He heard a bell from the direction of the house.

"Dinnertime," Adam announced, glancing toward his sons who were fixing the fencing on the far side of the property.

"Thanks be to *Gott.* I'm as hungry as a bear." Matthew straightened and leaned on his shovel. The two brothers had just replaced a rotten fencepost.

"You're always hungry," *Dat* said.

"How do you know about a bear's appetite?" James teased. "They hibernate through the winter and don't eat while they're sleeping in their den."

"The animal expert," Matthew groused, but the grin on his face told James that he was teasing back.

"Wonder what *Mam's* fixed for supper?"

"More than you eat on your own, James, I'm certain."

James stretched, reaching over his head until he experienced the sharp pull of his arm muscles. He felt good, better than he had in a long time.

"Thanks—I mean, *danki* for allowing me to stay the weekend again," James said, regarding the two men beside him with warmth.

"Come every weekend. I'm always happy to share the work," Matthew joked.

Adam gazed at him with affection. "We enjoy having you, *soohn.*"

The dinner bell resounded again, and the three men started toward the house.

"You want to see my place?" James asked his brother. "I live over Mattie Mast's Bakery."

"You do?" Matthew's eyes had widened. "Must smell *gut* in your *haus*."

"Most days. Monday through Saturday, it's a sure bet. I particularly like Tuesday's when Mattie makes her special chocolate cake."

"*Mam* made a chocolate cake this morning," Matthew said.

"She did?" The thought made his mouth water.

"She said something about it being your favorite," Adam interjected.

James suddenly felt emotional. "It is."

Adam regarded him with a knowing look.

Matthew, on the hand, appeared puzzled. "*Ja*. Why are you surprised?"

"I haven't been home much these last years." James paused. "I haven't been the best son."

"You're a fine *soohn*, James, and don't you forget it. As for not coming to visit much, you're home now, and you moved to Lancaster County to be closer to us, *ja*?" Adam said.

James nodded.

"Then stop fretting. Be welcome. Come and stay anytime you want. Move in if you'd prefer. We love having you here." He hesitated.

"Thank you, *Dat*," he said softly.

"Let's eat," Matthew rumbled. "I'm as hungry as a b-boar!"

James laughed, and Adam joined in. Matthew glanced at each of them sheepishly until he began to giggle himself.

They could smell *Mam's* cooking through the kitchen window. It was a warm day. In sweltering temperatures, the shades would be drawn and windows might be open or closed depending on whether or not there was a breeze.

James entered the house, stepping into the kitchen behind Adam and Matt. One look at the table laden with an Amish feast made everything worth it. He had missed such meals with his family. From the pleased look on her face as she noted his happiness, his mother had missed having him home, too.

Sunday morning Nell woke up early. The rest of the family was sleeping in. Since it was Visiting Day, they didn't have to be at the Lapps' until nine thirty or ten o'clock. She slipped downstairs, taking extra care to be quiet, and went into the barn to feed and water the animals.

Nell heard Jonas's excited barks. She hurried to his stall with a smile.

"*Hallo*, little one. Would you like to go outside?" She snapped on his leash and led him out of the barn. She walked about the property for a while, then took him back inside. Her gaze settled on Naomi's bed, and Nell was overwhelmed with sudden tears. James had known just what she would want—something for her new cat.

She crouched down and picked up Naomi. She was so tiny. The kitten was eating well, no doubt because James knew exactly what her cat would need. She grabbed a little toy, held it to Naomi's mouth. The kitten batted at the stuffed mouse playfully.

Nell put her down and watched for several moments, feeling a longing so intense that it nearly stole her breath. James. Why did she have to fall in love with an *Englisher*?

Nell was sure that Leah was correct. James was an

Englisher with a stepfather, mother and siblings who were Amish.

She knew that she would have to talk with him, no matter how hard it would be to listen, and to step back after they'd parted friends.

She didn't want to be friends with James, but it was her only option. She poured dog food into Jonas's bowl and refilled his water dish.

James and she had a lot in common. They both loved animals. They enjoyed each other's company and got along well. But the most vital thing that was different about them was their chosen way of life.

Nell had chosen God's way through the Amish church, while James had made the choice to leave the community and become a veterinarian, with a life with TV, radio, cars and computers. She couldn't help the small smile that formed on her lips. *Maybe not computers.* He didn't like using the one in the office. He left that up to Michelle to handle.

I'm sorry. His words came back to haunt her. What exactly had he been apologizing for? She'd thought it had been because of the kiss, but what if it was more?

Her mind replayed every day since her first meeting with James. From his tender care of Jonas, his compassion and concern for Joey, his patience and intensity while caring for Buddy and the other animals he treated in and outside of the practice. She sat, stroking Jonas, watching Naomi play, giving equal attention to both her beloved pets.

"Nell!"

"In here, Charlie!"

"We made breakfast. How long have you been out here?"

Nell shrugged. "What time is it?"

"Nine thirty."

She felt a jolt. "It is?" How had three hours passed so quickly? Had she been so wrapped up in her thoughts of James and what she was going to say to him that the minutes had flown by?

"*Ja*, come and eat. *Mam* and *Dat* will want to be heading to Aunt Katie's soon. There are muffins and pancakes, ham and bacon—and cereal if you want it."

"I'll be right there." Nell pushed to her feet. "Bye, little ones," she whispered.

Charlie waited for her outside the barn. "Who do you think will come visiting at *Endie* Katie's today?"

"I have no idea. The Kings and the Hershbergers, most likely."

"And the Masts and Troyers."

"And all their children and spouses and their grand-children," Nell added.

"I wonder if the boys will play *der beesballe*."

"What else will they do on a nice summer's day?"

"*Ja*, they'll play baseball, and I'll get to watch." A mischievous look entered Charlie's expression. "Maybe I'll convince them to let me play."

Nell laughed and hugged her sister before they climbed up the front porch. "I have no doubt you'll be playing baseball today. You are *gut* at convincing people to do what you want."

Charlie paused and frowned. "Is that a bad thing?"

"*Nay*, sister, 'tis a *gut* thing," Nell said as they entered the house.

He wasn't here. The Troyers had arrived an hour ago, and there was no sign of James. Nell stood at the fence railing and overlooked her uncle's pasture.

I should have stayed and talked longer with him at the Troyers' yesterday.

But she hadn't. She'd become upset at seeing him there, at him being Matthew's brother, that she'd been eager to get away. And just when she'd made up her mind to tell him to leave her alone, he didn't show.

Nell heard laughter behind her. Elijah, Jacob, Jedidiah, Noah and Daniel, Aunt Katie and Uncle Samuel's sons, were playing baseball. Isaac, another son, stood near the house talking with Ellen Mast, the girl who'd loved him forever.

Ellen was a good friend, and Nell hoped that her cousin saw her in the right light—and soon. It was obvious to her that Isaac had similar feelings for Ellen but was, for some reason, holding back. She wondered if it had something to do with the trouble he'd gotten into two years back. Nell had never believed that Isaac had been responsible for the vandalism at Whittier's Store—none of them did. But Isaac had never defended himself or confessed the truth, and so he suffered because of it.

Her gaze followed the horses in the pasture. The mares were running through the open space, beings of pure beauty in energy and form. Closer to the fence, goats munched contentedly on the grass. To the left were the Lapps' two Jersey milk cows.

She heard hens clucking from a pen near the barn. She smiled, wishing she'd brought Jonas. Naomi was too little to expose to curious eyes and small hands.

"Nell."

She stiffened. Why was she imagining his voice? It hurt that she was so caught up in her feelings for him that she pictured him everywhere.

"Nell, I have to talk with you." His touch on her arm convinced her that the voice was real.

She turned, locked gazes with him. There was a depth of emotion in his dark eyes that quickly vanished as they stared at one another.

A quick study of him revealed that he'd changed clothes. Gone were the Amish garments he'd worn yesterday. Today he was back to wearing jeans and a blue button-down, short-sleeved shirt.

"What are you doing here?" she demanded, all thoughts of her desire to talk with him gone in the reality of his presence.

"I was on my way home, but I wanted to talk with you first."

"Why?"

"To explain about my family."

"What?" She bit her lip and blinked rapidly. Why did being near him upset her so much? "I know about your family. Your sister told me."

"I'd like to tell you why I kept the Pierce name." He leaned against the fence rail beside her, his tall form seeming bigger and more present than ever before.

"James." She gestured to the gathering in the yard behind them.

He didn't seem to care that someone might be watching, listening. "My mother was raised in an Amish household. When she met and fell in love with my father, John Pierce, she made the choice to leave her community and marry him. They moved to Ohio where my dad set up his veterinary practice. They were happy. I was born a year and a half later, and years later, my sister Maggie was born."

"Maggie Troyer."

"Except she was Maggie Pierce. Then Abigail came into our lives. When she was just a small child, my father died when he was on a vet call. He'd had a massive heart attack. He was forty."

"I'm sorry." She gazed at him with sympathy. She could see that the loss still deeply affected him after all these years. "How old were you?"

"Thirteen."

"A time when a boy needs his father."

"During the weekend, I used to accompany him on calls. I was sick that Saturday and couldn't go. I had a cold. He told me to stay home." He paused, closed his eyes then opened them. "I should have gone. I might have been able to do something."

"Nay!" Nell cried. "What could you have done?"

"Called the ambulance. Something."

She drew a deep breath as she fought the urge to pull him into her arms and offer comfort. "Didn't someone call the ambulance?"

"The homeowner. But Dad was in the barn tending to a cow when he keeled over. By the time the man found him, it was too late."

"I'm so sorry," she said softly, reaching to touch his arm. "That must have been difficult." She no longer cared that they were standing in full view of everyone near the fence. Her concern was only for James. "Then your *mam* came home to Pennsylvania with you, didn't she?"

"Yes, she was suffering, grieving. I didn't want to leave Ohio. It had been my home. My father was buried there. I'd gone to school there, and my friends were there, but I didn't say a word. Mom was hurting so badly. I understood her need to be with family. But to leave the English world to live with my Amish grandparents was more than I could handle. I was a sullen, angry teenager, and I didn't make things easy for anyone once we'd moved back. Suddenly, not only had I lost my dad but also my life and my identity."

Nell studied him. He stared at the animals in the pasture, and she watched as, miraculously, a small smile came to his mouth.

"This view reminds me of one at my grandfather's. *Grossvadder* was a kind and patient man." He closed his eyes, shuddered. "I still miss him—both of them. My grandfather and grandmother."

He opened his eyes and fixed her with his dark gaze. "One day, I became so overwhelmed with grief that I broke down and cried. I sobbed as if I was a baby and I'd lost sight of my mother. *Grossvadder* saw me crying and nodded as if I had done the right thing to break down. He'd moved on without a word, but I could read his thoughts even as I cried. Afterward, we talked. He said it was good to be strong, but that it is a stronger man who allowed himself to cry and to heal. He taught me about God and love, and because of him, I learned to settle and enjoy my life at the farm until Adam's wife died. *Mam* took my sisters with her every day so that she could take care of Adam's two children while he grieved. Matthew was three and Rosie was a newborn. Adam's wife, Mary, died after giving birth to her."

Nell knew what it was like to lose someone you loved. Lately she'd seemed to be moving past her grief until she mostly thought of Michael with simple affection. Only on occasion did the pain rear up and strike her when she least expected it.

"You didn't like your *mudder* helping Adam?"

James shook his head as he faced her and he met her gaze head-on. "I didn't mind that. I minded that she and Adam later fell in love and married. I felt as if their love was a betrayal to my father. It was wrong, but I was fifteen—what did I know about love? I'd had a girlfriend in high school—but it wasn't anything serious and our relationship didn't last. When Dad died, I made a vow to honor him by following in his footsteps. I would become a vet. I'd always thought I wanted to be one anyway, but my goal became more of an obsession after losing Dad."

He glanced back toward the yard and stared at her cousins playing baseball. His lips curved. "I used to play baseball in Little League and in school. I loved it."

He drew a sharp breath, then released it. "I attended public, not Amish, school. By the time we moved here, I was already finished with eighth grade. *Grossvadder* approved of me continuing at the closest high school. Mom understood. She had loved my father. I'd known that. I'd seen and felt their love. Mom knew that continuing my education was the only way I could become the vet I was determined to be."

"And you did," Nell said with warmth. She paused. "What happened after your *mudder* married Adam?"

"We moved to live with him, of course, and I became a nightmare. I acted terribly toward Adam. I was difficult, and I rebelled the only way I knew how by being cold, unfeeling and nasty to him."

Nell saw regret settle between his brows. This James she was learning about was even more appealing and more attractive to her. She bucked herself up with the reminder that the most they could ever be was friends—and that it would be wiser for her to keep her distance from him.

"I take it things eventually changed between you and Adam."

James flashed her a grin. "No thanks to me. I give Adam all the credit. The only time I ever behaved was at school. I studied hard because I was determined to get into a good college."

Nell was curious. "How did Adam change your relationship?"

"One day he'd had enough. It was late during my sophomore year. He took me aside, and we had a talk. Well, he talked, and I listened. He told me that he loved my mother and my sisters and that he loved me no matter how difficult I acted toward him. That his love won't stop because I wanted it to. He said that he wouldn't replace my dad and that he didn't want to. A dad's place in a son's life is important. He simply wanted to be my friend and to be there whenever I needed him."

"Oh, James… Adam is a *gut* man."

James blinked, his eyes suspiciously moist. "Yes, he is. He then told me that I needed to be a man, not a boy."

Nell raised her eyebrows, hurting for the boy he'd been and the man he was. "I doubted that went over well."

"Actually, it did. I understood what he was saying. I realized that God had given me Adam after He'd taken my father."

"James…"

"I'm not angry with God, Nell, but I do think that He took Dad home for reasons of His own."

"Matthew and Rosie might believe it's because they needed a *mudder*—your *mam*."

He smiled. "She loves them like her own." He slipped his hands into his front jeans pockets. Suddenly, he seemed uncomfortable as if he might have revealed too much of himself. "Adam became a father to me, and I let him. He's never been anything but fair and understanding, even when I chose to leave the community to attend Ohio State, my father's alma mater. And later when I left for Penn Vet—the University of Pennsylvania's Veterinary School. Even when I stayed in the Philadelphia area afterward and worked for six years in an animal hospital there."

"But then you decided to move back to Lancaster County."

"To be closer to my family," James said. "I realized that I was working all the time. I wasn't really living. My father would have hated that. He loved being a vet, but he loved his family more." He removed a hand from his pocket to run fingers through his dark hair. "I missed *Mam*, *Dat*, Maggie, Abby, Matt and Rosie."

She held back a smile as she noted how he'd slipped into his former Amish life pattern with the Pennsylvania Deitsch names for his mother and father.

"So now you know."

Nell didn't know how to respond. Why had she chosen to believe ill of this wonderful, kind man? Because she didn't want to have these warm and affectionate feelings for him.

"I should go," he said as he straightened away from the fence and faced the yard. "Work tomorrow." His brow furrowed. "I'll miss you, Nell. You were the best assistant a man could have."

Emotion rose as a knot in her throat. "I'm sure Janie is better," she said hoarsely.

"I doubt it." He looked up and apparently saw something that made him separate himself from her not only emotionally but physically, too. He drew back a few feet from her. "Matt," he greeted.

Nell smiled at James's brother. "*Hallo*, Matt. Tired of playing baseball?"

"*Nay.*" He glanced from her to James and back. "Did you like working for my *bruder*?"

"Ja," Nell said, "I learned a lot from him. You know how I love caring for animals."

"I do." Matthew's expression had turned soft.

"I need to go," James said.

"I'll walk you to your car," Matthew offered.

"You just want to take another close look."

Matthew laughed. "Maybe."

James turned to Nell. "Goodbye, Nell. Thanks again for filling in at the clinic when I needed you."

"Thank you for Naomi and taking care of Jonas when he needed you."

"You're *willkomm*." James gave her a sad smile.

Then Nell watched him walk away, and her heart ached for what she couldn't have and what her life would never be.

Chapter Thirteen

It was late. Darkness had settled over the land. Nell had brought in the horses when she heard a car rumble down the driveway. James. He came to mind immediately. She closed the back barn door and hurried through the building to meet him out front. But it wasn't James who was getting out of his car. It was their *English* neighbor, Rick Martin.

"Nell," he said soberly when he caught sight of her. "I have bad news. Catherine Fisher was rushed to the hospital a few minutes ago."

"Ach, nay!" she breathed. "And Bishop John?"

"He went with her to the hospital. I've brought their son, Nicholas. Catherine asked if you would watch him."

Nell swallowed. "She mentioned me?"

"Yes, by name." Rick opened the back door of the car. The little two-year-old lay on the backseat. Curled up in sleep, the boy looked like a little angel. "He doesn't know what happened. He was upstairs napping when Catherine collapsed."

"I'm sorry," she murmured. She reached inside the car and lifted baby Nick into her arms. He cuddled against her, and she sighed. "Thank you for bringing him, Rick."

"I'll find out how she is and let you know."

Nell nodded. "I'm going to bring him inside and put him to bed before he wakes up."

She turned toward the house with the bishop's son in her arms. She didn't wait for Rick to leave as she entered the house. As she headed toward the stairs, she met her mother.

"Nell."

"'Tis Nicholas Fisher, *Mam*." Nell shifted to bring the child closer. "Catherine is in the hospital. John went with her. Rick brought him. Before the ambulance took her away, Catherine asked that I watch him."

Her mother's expression softened as she studied the sleeping child in Nell's arms. "You'll put him in your room?"

"Ja," Nell said. She eyed the child in her arms with warmth. "I wonder why Catherine asked for me?"

"Everyone has seen how you are with their animals, Nell. If you have enough love and compassion for animals, imagine how much you have for a little boy?"

She widened her eyes. "You think that's why?"

"I do." *Mam* smiled. "You're a kind and loving woman, and everyone sees it."

Nell started up the stairs then stopped. *"Mam?"*

"Ja, Nell?"

"What if someone loves the wrong person? Someone who isn't right for her?"

Her mother looked at her with love and understanding. "Does this someone recognize that it's best to avoid the wrong man?"

She nodded.

"Then you have your answer, Nell. Although God the Father might not disagree. The Lord wishes us to love all men."

Her heart was heavy as Nell climbed the stairs with the small boy in her arms. She felt terrible for Catherine and John. She was worried about little Nick, who would awaken in the morning looking for his mother.

With Nicholas in one arm, she pulled back the top layers on her bed. She laid the boy gently on the mattress and covered him with the sheet and quilt. Then she pulled up the chair that she'd kept in the corner of her room and sat—and she watched him until exhausted, she climbed onto the double bed next to him. She offered up a silent prayer that Nicholas would have his mother and father home by tomorrow morning. With that good thought, Nell was able to close her eyes and sleep.

"Catherine Fisher died during the night," *Mam* told James and his siblings at breakfast on Sunday morning. "John was by her side."

"When did you hear this?" Adam asked.

"Just a few minutes ago. Nell's *mudder* stopped by. It seems that Catherine's last words were that Nell take care of their little son, Nicholas, while she was in the hospital. She didn't realize that she wouldn't be coming home again."

James's thoughts went immediately to Nell. "Where is Nicholas now?"

"He's still with Nell. John's still at the hospital, making the final arrangements for his wife."

"What's going to happen now?" Matthew reached for a muffin and put it on his plate.

"Nicholas no longer has his mother. John will need to marry again and quickly for the sake of his son."

"Who would want to marry a grieving widower with a young child?" James really wanted to know.

"Nell might," *Mam* said. "She's single and well past

the age of marrying. It would be a *gut* arrangement for the both of them."

"*Nay!*" James exclaimed. When his mother stared, he blushed and looked away. "It makes no sense for them to rush into marriage. I know too many people who married in haste and then suffered afterward."

"But these people you know—they weren't of the Amish faith, were they?"

James shook his head. "No. But why would that make a difference?"

"It's not unusual for a man to take a wife simply for the sake of his motherless child. The couple will find love and respect with the passage of time," Adam explained.

Feeling a hot burning in his gut at the thought of Nell marrying another man, James couldn't let it go. "And if John…"

"Bishop John," his mother said.

"And if the bishop doesn't accept his new wife as someone he could love? What will that mean for the woman?" For Nell, he thought.

Adam looked sorrowful. "Only the Lord knows the answer to that question, James."

James looked from his stepfather to his mother. "*Dat*, you didn't," he reminded. "It wasn't until you fell in love with *Mam* that you asked her to marry you."

"*Ja*, 'tis true. I couldn't at first. I was grieving too much, but then your mother entered my heart like sunshine on a dark, stormy day. It was then that I asked her to marry me. I'd had an inkling that she had similar feelings for me."

"How?" James asked. "How did you know her feelings?"

Adam gazed at his wife with soft eyes. "She told me."

"She *what*?" It was Matthew who had spoken.

Mam laughed. "Not in words, *soohn*," she assured Matt, "but in looks and my caring for you and your sister."

Matthew joined in her laughter. "It would be fine if you'd told him, *Mam*, right off."

"Right for you," James said with good humor. "I would have been a nightmare worse than I already was if you'd married right after Mary died."

"I would have been right with you," Matthew admitted with a grim smile.

"Is there anything we can do?" Maggie asked. She'd been listening quietly up until now. "Nell may need some of Nicholas's things. We could get them for her."

"I'll go with you," Abigail offered.

"James?" Rosie said. "You know Nell. Maybe she'd like you to bring her little Nick's things?"

He looked at his stepsister and sisters. "I don't know—"

"That's a fine idea, James. You have a car. You can drive over to the bishop's house and gather what Nell will need."

"I could get there faster," James agreed. "What if John isn't home? How will we get in?"

"The bishop doesn't lock his house," Maggie said. "He trusts that God will protect his family and his home."

James frowned as he stood. God hadn't kept the man's wife from death's door. Not that he thought less of God. Life and death were simply the way of a person's existence. "Rosie, it was your idea. Would you like to come with me?"

Rosie stood and carried her breakfast dishes to the sink. "*Mam*—"

"Go, *dochter*. James needs your help as much as Nell is going to need his."

* * *

Leah sneaked into Nell's room where Nell lay awake next to the bishop's sleeping child. She motioned for her sister to step outside.

Nell frowned as she stood in the hallway.

"Nell, Catherine is dead." Leah flashed a look of concern toward the boy in Nell's bed. "She died during the night. There was something wrong with her heart."

"John—"

"Is devastated. He'll not be thinking of his son at a time like this. It could be the reason why Catherine asked you to care for him…because she knew she wouldn't be coming back."

Nell's eyes filled with tears. "But why me?" She drew a shuddering breath. "What am I going to tell that little boy? Nicholas, your *mam* is dead, but it's okay because she is with the Lord?" She lifted a hand to brush back an escaped tendril of soft brown hair. "He'll never understand that. He's too young to know about God and death…and losing his *mudder*."

"Get dressed," Leah said. "We need to figure out a way to get more of Nicholas's things."

"*Ja*, Rick only brought Nicholas. He had no clothes, no diapers." Nell grimaced with wry humor as she glanced toward her bed. "I'm going to need clean sheets, I think."

Leah chuckled. "A wet bed is the least of your worries." She moved into the room. "I'll sit with him. *Dat* wants to see you. He's waiting for you downstairs."

Nell raised her eyebrows. "What could he possibly want—" Her eyes widened. "*Nay,* surely he won't suggest that I step in and marry John?"

"Only one way to find out."

"Fine. Let me change clothes, and I'll go down to see what he has to say."

"Remain calm," her sister instructed. "Don't lose your temper. If you stay calm, you'll retain the upper hand."

Dressed and ready to face her father, Nell went downstairs, pleased that Nicholas continued to sleep for now.

Arlin Stoltzfus was at the kitchen table. Her sisters and mother were absent. Having no one in the room was a sure sign that her father had something serious to say to her.

"Dat?" She entered the room as if she wasn't concerned with what he might say. She poured herself a cup of tea and then held up the teakettle. "Would you like some?"

Her father shook his head. *"Nay,* I've had my morning coffee. Sit down, Nell."

Nell sat, pretending an indifference that she was far from feeling. "Doughnuts! I love doughnuts. And there are powdered and chocolate glazed. I'll have one of each!" She knew she was rambling, but she couldn't seem to stop herself.

"Nell."

"Ja, Dat?"

"We need to talk about Nicholas—and John."

"Nicholas is still sleeping, poor *boo."* She took a small bite of her powdered doughnut, chewed and swallowed. "I imagine John is devastated over losing Catherine. And Nicholas—how is he going to react when he learns that his *mudder* isn't coming home to him?"

"Nicholas will be fine once he gets another *mudder."*

Nell stared at him. "Another *mudder*? No one can replace his *mudder."*

"He can, if you marry John."

"Dat, the man just lost his wife. The last thing he'll want is to marry me—a stranger. I'll be happy to care

for Nicholas until he has his time to grieve, but to even suggest that he marry so quickly…"

"You *will* marry him."

"I—*what*?"

"This is your opportunity for marriage. John is a fine man. He'll make you a *gut* husband. Nicholas is a sweet little *boo* who needs a mother."

Nell gazed at her father in shock. "*Dat*, surely you don't believe that God wants me to be Nicholas's mother?"

"There are many young women within our community, *dochter*. If God didn't want this, then why did Catherine specifically ask for you?"

"*Dat*," she whispered. "*Nay*." But what if the Lord did want this for her? What if this was the answer to her prayers regarding her forbidden love of James? If she married John, then she would have to get on with her life without James. It was something to think about. "I'll consider it, *Dat*."

Her father looked pleased. "Do that, but do it quickly. John is a practical man. He will want to marry again soon for the sake of his *soohn*."

Nell opened her mouth to object. She didn't believe for one second that John would be in a hurry to marry. Not when he was still grieving over the loss of his beloved Catherine.

With Rosie's help, James entered John Fisher's house and found clothes, a blanket and a basket of clean cloth diapers for Nicholas. They left as quickly as they'd come, and James drove right to the Stoltzfus farm so that he could hand over the boy's belongings to Nell.

His heart was pounding hard as he drove up to the

Arlin Stoltzfus residence. Rosie opened her car door first and reached into the back for the basket of diapers. James carried the rest of the items—the boy's nightgown, some socks, shoes, little shirt and pants—and cute little straw and black felt hats.

His sister waited for him to join her before they climbed the steps to the large white house. James glanced at his sister and nodded. Rosie raised her hand and rapped her closed fist on the doorframe.

The screen door opened immediately, and James found himself face to face with Nell's sister Leah. "I— we've—" he said, including his younger stepsister, "picked up a few of Nicholas's things from the house."

Leah glanced from him to his sister. Rosie held up the wicker basket. "I have clean diapers."

"I brought his blanket and his garments—and his hats." James smiled as he studied the hats that lay on the pile of clothing in his arms.

"That was kind of you," Leah finally said. She opened the screen door and stepped aside. "Come in. Please."

James followed Rosie into the house.

"You must have gone early," Nell's sister said.

"As soon as we heard," he admitted.

"Let me get Nell. You may take a seat if you'd like. There are doughnuts on the table and fresh coffee on the stove."

"Thank you." James exchanged glances with Rosie, then together they set the items they carried close by and sat down.

Nell came into the room less than a minute later. "James! Rosie, Leah said you brought Nick's clothes."

James stood as she walked into the room. "Yes, we thought you could use them, considering what happened."

The young Amish woman's eyes filled with tears. "He's going to need them."

"*Mam* said that Catherine asked for you to take care of him."

"*Ja*, I was surprised. I didn't know Catherine that well." She bit her lip, looked away. "*Dat* believes God has a plan."

"What kind of plan?" James asked. He had a bad feeling about Arlin's belief in a plan that somehow involved Nell with the bishop's son.

Nell shook her head. "It doesn't matter."

"Nell," he began. "Can I do anything for you? Something? *Please*, I want to help."

He saw her swallow hard. "You've already done a lot by getting Nicholas's things for him," she said.

"Nell!" Leah called. "He's waking up!"

"I'm sorry," Nell whispered. "I have to go to him." Her gaze went to Rosie but settled longer on James. *"Danki."* She blinked back tears. It was as if she were saying goodbye. To him.

They didn't stay for doughnuts and coffee. James drove back to the house with his sister.

"What do you think Nell meant when she said that her *vadder* thinks that God has a plan?" Rosie asked, breaking the silence in the car.

"I don't know." But then he realized that he did. Arlin Stoltzfus had been wanting his daughter to marry, and with Catherine's death, Bishop John would be seeking a mother for his child.

No! James thought. He couldn't allow her to marry John Fisher. John would never love Nell like he did. But what could he do?

He was powerless to stop them from marrying. An *Englisher*, he had no right to marry Nell or to stop her from heeding her father's wishes.

Chapter Fourteen

Her *dat* was right. Bishop John was grieving but he would marry again for the sake of his young son. Nell herself was exhausted. She'd gotten little sleep since her *dat* had made the suggestion that she become John's new bride. And while it was true that she'd not found a man to marry on her own, Nell knew that she'd never find the love she'd once hoped to find in marriage. Not when she loved James, who could never be her husband.

Little Nicholas had taken to Nell as if she was the one who'd given him birth. Nell found out the reason why after learning just how ill Catherine had been since giving birth to her son. She'd been unable to take care of him except for short periods of time. Nicholas had spent time in several different neighboring households who cared for the little boy while Catherine had attempted to rest and recover. Only she never had.

The night she realized that she would soon become John Fisher's wife, Nell dreamed of Meg's hospital stay, of going for tea and hearing the beeping of life-support machines…and looking into a room and getting the shock of her life. Only it wasn't Michael in the room in her dream. The man in her dream was James, and when she saw him hooked up to machines, Nell cried out and fell to her knees. *"Nay! Nay!"* she screamed.

She woke, gasping for air, her heart pounding hard with the sudden concern that something had happened to her beloved James. She might not be able to have a life with him, but that didn't mean that she wouldn't think of him, worry about him, every single day for the rest of her life. Whether she was the bishop's wife or not.

Nell recalled little Nicholas and wondered if her screams had frightened him. She looked next to her to the empty space and remembered that Leah had taken him to sleep with her for the night. Nell had suffered from lack of sleep since learning of the child's mother's death. Leah had suggested that if Nicholas was with her, Nell might be able to rest without worry and with the possibility of sleeping late.

She rose and went downstairs. Her head hurt. Her heart ached. She didn't know how she was going to go through with the wedding. Because of Nicholas's age, *Dat* thought she and John should marry quickly. Nell wanted to wait until November, after the harvest, when it was wedding time.

"There is no reason to wait, Nell," her father had said time and again. "John's a widower. Widowers don't have to wait until the month of weddings."

"I want to wait," Nell insisted. "Unlike John, I have never been married. Don't I deserve a wedding like the other young women in our community."

"Nicholas needs you."

"I need the time. I'm happy to care for Nicholas before the wedding. There is no reason to wait for that."

And so her father had relented. Even John, Nell realized, seemed relieved. What kind of future would they have if both of them married only for the sake of a child?

An unhappy one, Nell thought, but then she didn't expect to be happy without James Pierce in her life.

The number of appointments had increased in Pierce Veterinary Clinic. James tried not to think of Nell's upcoming marriage to the bishop as he kept himself busy seeing patients during the week and worked hard in Adam's furniture store on Saturdays.

He was amazed at the change in his business. He'd gone from worrying about his finances to raking in money. He should be glad. It was what he'd always wanted, but he realized that he was never going to feel successful. Because he was missing something— someone—vital in his life. *Nell.*

Two weeks had passed since he'd given her the child's belongings he'd retrieved from the bishop's house. He wondered if she was happy. Was she looking forward to her marriage? Did she love the thought of becoming Nicholas's mother for real?

He wondered how her dog, Jonas, was faring. If she had been one of his *English* clients, he would have called and found out if Jonas had suffered any ill effects from his bee sting. He could have stopped by the house and visited Naomi, seeing if there was anything Nell needed in the way of shots or food or cat toys.

"Last patient before the weekend, Dr. Pierce," Janie said as she entered the back room. "Exam room four."

"Thank you, Janie."

The last patient was a simple checkup with shots. He was tired when the day ended.

He came out to the front desk to hand Michelle the last patient's summary.

His receptionist eyed him intently. "Have you heard from Nell?"

He shook his head. "No. She's busy taking care of Nicholas Fisher. She's going to marry the boy's father."

"And you're going to just let her?"

"What else am I supposed to do? She belongs to the church. I'm considered an *Englisher*, and she can't marry me without serious consequences."

A small smile curved Michelle's lips. "So you've thought of marrying her," she said with satisfaction. "You love her." She shut down the computer and stood. "You should talk with her. Tell her how you feel."

He frowned. "You're awfully bossy lately." He sighed. "I appreciate the thought, but it won't help. I wouldn't hurt her with my love. If she marries me, she'll be shunned by her family and friends."

"If you were an *Englisher*."

He stared at her, puzzled. "I am English."

"But your family isn't."

"Yes, but…."

"Think about it, Dr. Pierce." She picked up her purse and went to the door. "I'm going home. I'll see you on Monday."

He couldn't help smiling at Michelle's attempts to throw him into Nell's path as he locked up and left. Even though there was no hope of that happening. Still, he drove out of the parking lot in the direction of the Stoltzfus residence. It wouldn't hurt to check on Jonas and Naomi…and to see Nell one last time before she became another man's wife.

"Hello! Is Nell home?"

Startled, Nell dropped a garment and spun. "James!"

"Nell, I didn't realize it was you. You look different with your kerchief." He smiled. "I hope you don't mind, but I stopped by to check on Jonas and Naomi."

"That's kind of you." She felt self-conscious in his presence. Wearing her work garments and taking down clothes didn't make her feel any less conspicuous and dowdy.

"Come and I'll show you where I keep them." She waved to her sister Ellie who was leaving the barn. Nell approached her, aware that James followed. "Ellie, would you please finish taking down the clothes?"

Ellie glanced from Nell to James and back. "*Ja*, I'll be happy to." She smiled. "Come to see her animals, I take it."

"I haven't seen Jonas since his bee sting, and Nell hasn't brought Naomi into the office yet."

Ellie met Nell's gaze. "I didn't feed either one. Wasn't sure if you wanted me to."

"That's fine, Ellie," Nell said. "I'll feed them. *Danki.*"

She was overly conscious of the man beside her as they walked into the barn. "I did what I could to make them comfortable."

"Stop fretting, Nell. You love them. I know they're well cared for."

She stopped, looked at him and was shocked to see sincerity in his dark gaze…a small upward curve to his masculine mouth.

Nell heard Jonas's excitement as they drew close to his stall. He always seemed to know when she came to visit him. He'd bark and whimper and rise up on his hind legs as soon as he saw her.

"Jonas!" she crooned as she opened the stall door and went in. James followed behind her. "Guess who's here, buddy? 'Tis James."

"Hey, Jonas," he said softly. "May I examine you?" He bent and sat on the straw.

To Nell's delight, Jonas immediately crawled to James.

He curled onto James's lap and looked up at him with big brown eyes. "How's your nose?" James bent and examined the injured area. "It looks good. All healed, huh?"

"*Ja*. He's suffered no ill aftereffects."

"Good." James smiled. "I brought you an EpiPen to keep on hand in case it ever happens again. I know Jonas wasn't allergic, but that could change if he gets stung again. Also, if he ever gets stung in his mouth, don't wait, Nell. Bring him in immediately. Okay?"

"I will," she promised, frightened by the thought. "I've kept him away from our flower beds."

James looked approving. "Unfortunately, you can't always avoid bee stings. Sometimes bees show up when you least expect them. Oh, and, Nell?"

She met his gaze. *"Ja?"*

"The same goes for hornets or wasps. Hornets and wasps will keep stinging. A bee loses its stinger, but they don't."

"I've never been stung," she admitted.

"I have, and it hurts terribly. Putting vinegar on it was the right thing to do. Remember that remedy if it happens to you or to Nicholas."

Tension rose between them at the mention of Nicholas.

Nell's kitten, Naomi, woke up and clambered over to James's side, easing the strain of the moment. She tried to crawl onto his lap beside Jonas. Nell saw that James looked surprised when Jonas allowed it. He shifted a tiny bit so that the kitten could snuggle against both of them.

Drawn to be included, Nell sat next to James. She could feel the heat of his skin when his hand accidentally brushed her as he moved Naomi into a different position.

"I'll take her," Nell said.

He handed her the kitten, his eyes never leaving hers. She experienced a flutter in her chest as she carefully took Naomi and held the cat to her cheek. "I love how she purrs."

"Like a motorboat," James agreed. "A soft one."

James gazed at the woman before him and experienced a painful lurch in his chest. He cared so much for her that it was a physical ache in his gut. The thought of her married to another man agonized him.

He realized that he should leave, but still he lingered. He shifted Jonas a little and reached for his medical bag. He quickly found what he was searching for and handed it to her.

"The EpiPen."

Nell looked at the pen, then accepted it. "How would I use it?"

He showed her how it worked. Then he placed Jonas carefully in his bed and stroked him one last time before he pushed to his feet. "I should go."

He had plans to be with family again this weekend. Nell surely had plans with the bishop and his son.

She set Naomi down and started to rise. James held out his hand and after a brief hesitation, she accepted his help. He released her hand as soon as she stood. He stepped back.

"Remember you don't need to call first if either of them is having an issue."

She murmured her agreement, and he followed her as she led the way out.

Emotion got ahold of him, and he stopped. "Nell."

She halted and turned. *"Ja?"*

"I—I care about you." He tried to gauge her reaction. "A lot." He heard her intake of breath, the way she released it shakily. "I know that you're going to marry the bishop, but—"

"James—"

"I know."

She seemed to struggle with her thoughts. "I care for you, too. But you know it won't work. I'm a member of the Amish church. I joined years ago. I can't leave, or I'll lose my family."

"I know," he whispered. "I won't say any more. I won't tell you how I wish you were mine."

"'Tis better this way. With you, I'd be shunned."

He felt a sharp pain. "I know. I'd never want that for you." He stiffened his spine, lifted his head and managed a smile. "I should go."

She nodded, turned, and continued on. James gazed at her nape beneath her kerchief and the back of her pretty spring green dress and tried not to feel devastated. Why did he have to fall in love with someone he couldn't have?

Always polite, Nell walked him to his car, and waited while he got in and turned the engine.

"Take care, Nell. Please don't let what I said stop you from seeking my veterinary services. I just had to say it one time. I won't make you uncomfortable again."

"Goodbye, James."

"Have a happy marriage, Nell."

He shifted into Reverse, backed up a few feet and made the turn toward the road. He pulled onto the pavement and saw the car too late to avoid it. The impact jerked him forward painfully, then forcefully bounced him back against the seat. And then he felt nothing.

Chapter Fifteen

Nell watched James drive away with a sinking heart. She knew he was upset. She would be marrying John, and there was nothing either of them could do but accept it.

She saw the flash of his car's right blinker, watched as his dark head swiveled as he checked both ways before he pulled out onto the road. She turned away, unable to watch the final moments of his departure. Then she heard a high-pitched squeal of tires, followed by a loud crash.

Nell took off running. There was the sound of a skid, then she saw the blur of a white vehicle as it whizzed past. Gasping, she reached the street and saw James slumped over the steering wheel of his Lexus.

As she ran forward, she glimpsed the pushed-in left front of his car, the tangle of broken fiberglass, metal and glass. She realized that James was sandwiched between his seat and the air bag. And she screamed.

"James!" Frantic, she ran to his driver's side. "James! James!"

"I'm all right," he muttered.

"*Nay*, don't move! You'll hurt yourself!"

"Nell! We thought we'd heard something!" Leah and her other sisters rushed to help.

"We need someone to call 911! We need to call 911!" Nell was beside herself as hysteria threatened to overwhelm. "How do we get to a phone?" The closest phone booth was down the road. "James needs help now! What do we do? What can *I* do?"

"I have a cell phone," Ellie said, pulling it from beneath her apron.

Nell stared, hoping she wasn't imagining things. "You have a cell phone?"

"What?" Ellie said defensively. "I clean for *English* families. They have to be able to reach me. The bishop approved it." She tugged on a pocket sewn to the underside of her apron.

"Thanks be to *Gott!*" Nell exclaimed. She didn't care that the phone and Ellie's pocket were deviations from the *Ordnung*. Pockets were fancy, but Nell didn't care. She was too happy, so very happy that her sister possessed both.

"Please, Ellie," she whispered. "Call 911." Close to James's window, she leaned in, mindful of the glass. "We've called for help."

James was barely able to nod. The air bag had deflated and finally she could see him. "Nell," he murmured.

"Don't talk. Don't move! Please, James!" She sounded high-strung, but she didn't care. This was James, the man she loved. Her recent nightmare about him in a hospital room came back to taunt and scare her.

Please let him be all right, she prayed. *Please, Lord. He's a* gut *man. Please help him. Please help me.*

It wasn't long before the ambulance arrived along with a local police officer. The EMT examined James, and as a precaution, the man used a brace to secure James's neck. Nell had to stifle a cry at the sight of it. She didn't want to upset James, who already had suffered enough.

The men carefully extracted him from the vehicle. They placed James gently on a stretcher, watchful of his condition and any unknown injuries.

The officer questioned Nell. "Did you see what happened?"

"I didn't see the accident. I saw James look both ways before he pulled onto the road. I turned to go back inside when I heard the sound of the impact, then of another car speeding away."

"Sounds like a hit and run," the officer said.

"Is James all right?" Nell asked anxiously.

"They'll be transporting him to the hospital to make sure," the technician said. "Things could have been worse."

Ja, he could have died. Nell couldn't keep her gaze off James who lay on the stretcher, looking frightfully vulnerable. She addressed the EMT. "May I talk with him a moment before you take him?"

"Not for long. We need to transport him—and the sooner the better."

Nell flashed her sisters a look. "Go," Leah said. "You don't have much time."

She was trembling as she approached the stretcher. "James," she whispered. "Are you *oll recht*?"

"I'll be fine, Nell."

"Your nose is swollen. You're going to have two black eyes." But she still thought of him as the most handsome man she'd ever known.

"The air bag," he breathed with a weak smile. He closed his eyes and exhaled.

"May I call the hospital to see how you are doing?" she asked, feeling suddenly shy.

He opened his eyes and focused his dark gaze on her. "Yes, if you want to."

"Do you want me to tell your family?"

He gazed at her with pain-filled dark eyes. "Yes, please. They'll be worried when I don't show. I planned to spend the weekend with them again."

"I'll go to them as soon as you leave," she promised, glad that she could be of help. "What about Michelle? Would you like me to call her, too?"

"No need. I'll give her a call if needed. I hope that I'll be examined and then released in a few hours."

Nell nodded, but she sincerely doubted that James would be staying anywhere but the hospital for a while.

"Time for him to go, miss," the technician said.

Nell stepped away, but she couldn't stop looking at him, caring…loving him. She shed silent tears. It didn't matter if she shouldn't care or love him. The only thing that mattered—and hurt—was that when he was well again, she would no longer have an excuse to see or talk with him. Her tears fell harder.

Her sisters joined her, standing around to offer her comfort as Nell watched the ambulance workers pick up James's stretcher and load it into the back of the vehicle.

Nell wiped away her tears and hurried forward. She needed to see him one last time. "James!"

"Nell." He gave her a genuine smile. "Don't worry."

She swallowed hard as she fought unsuccessfully to stop crying.

"Nell," he groaned.

She blinked, managed a grin. "I will talk with you soon."

And then they took him away. Nell stood a moment and as the ambulance drove away, her tears fell, streaking silently down her cheeks.

Leah slipped an arm around her waist. Ellie hugged her shoulders. Charlie stared a moment at the disappearing vehicle before she turned to Nell. "Let's get going. You need to tell the Troyers what happened."

Nell strove for control, drew herself up. "Will you take care of Nicholas for me?" she asked Leah. She heard a sound behind her and saw that Meg had readied the carriage.

"We'll go with you. I'll tell *Mam*. She'll be happy to watch him."

"All of you want to go?"

"I'm happy to watch Nick, but what will the Troyers think if all five of you drop in to give them the news?" *Mam* said, coming up from behind.

Blushing, concerned with how things might look to her parents, Nell said, "It might cause them more worry."

"Leah, Ellie, you go with Nell," *Dat* said. "Meg, you can help with Nicholas. Charlie, you can help your *mudder* with supper." His gaze was shrewd as he studied Nell. "He will be fine, Nell, but we will pray for him."

"Danki, Dat."

Within minutes, Nell and Ellie were in the family buggy as Leah drove at kicked-up speed toward the Troyers'.

Nell was still shaking. She stared ahead with her hands clenched in her lap. All three sisters were in the front seat. Ellie placed her hand over Nell's.

Nell blinked and turned her hand to squeeze Ellie's. "I'm glad you're coming," she admitted.

"We're sisters, and we are always here for you."

Nell thought that she might need her sisters more than ever in the coming weeks and months. During James's recovery. During her marriage—if she could go through with it—to John Fisher.

"Nell!" Matthew Troyer greeted them as they pulled into the yard.

Nell climbed down from the buggy with her sisters following. "Are your *eldres* home?"

He nodded. "What's wrong? Has something happened?"

"I'd like to tell all of you," she said quietly, but then she relented. "James was in an automobile accident." Her voice broke on the last word.

His face blanched. "Come inside."

They hurried toward the house while Nell's sisters waited outside.

"Mam! Dat!" he called as they entered the main hall.

"In the kitchen, Matthew!" his mother responded.

They entered the room to find the family getting ready to sit down to supper.

"Nell," Ruth greeted warmly.

Nell was unable to manage a smile. "I'm afraid that I have serious news. James was in an automobile accident this evening. He's in the hospital. He spoke with me before the ambulance took him. I think he'll be all right."

"Nay," his mother whispered as she rose, swaying. Adam immediately got up and put his arm around her.

Nell heard his sisters cry out, and she felt for them. She loved James, too, and knew it hurt to hear such terrible news.

A knock on the back door heralded her sister Ellie. Matthew opened it and invited her in. "I called Rick Martin," she said with the cell phone still in her hands. "He's on his way. He'll take you to the hospital."

"Danki," Ruth and Adam said at the same time.

The whole family was obviously devastated by the news.

"What happened?" Adam asked.

Nell explained that James had stopped in to check on Jonas and Naomi. "He told me before he left that he planned to spend the weekend with you."

"Ja," Matthew said. "He likes to visit on weekends and help with the farm work." He blinked rapidly, then drew himself up. "We like having him."

"We just got him back," his sister Maggie cried. "We can't lose him now."

Nell inhaled sharply. She didn't want to think about James dying, she didn't want to think about anything except for him to be walking through that door and awarding her his wonderful smile.

Impulsively, Nell reached out and gently squeezed his sister Maggie's hand.

Rick Martin arrived, and Nell watched as the Troyers piled into the car and left.

Nell returned to the buggy with her sisters. Ellie and Leah gave her a hug.

"He'll be *oll recht*," Ellie said.

"I hope so." Nell climbed into the buggy. She closed her eyes and offered up another silent prayer. *Please, Lord, allow James to heal. Please let him be well.*

At home, Nell and her sisters got out of the carriage and went into the house.

"How are the Troyers?" *Mam* asked as they came inside.

"Understandably upset," Leah said.

Nell wasn't hungry, but she knew her parents would worry if she didn't eat.

"Dinner is ready," Meg declared.

Nell sat at the table with her family, but the sick feeling in her stomach made it difficult to eat.

James had a doozy of a headache. His nose hurt, and his face, shoulders and chest felt like they had been beaten with a piece of wood. But all in all, considering what could have happened, James felt fortunate. He was alive and eventually would heal. Unless there was some injury the doctors hadn't discovered yet. Soon he would know.

He thought back to the moment of impact. A white sedan had been speeding in the opposite direction when James had made the right turn. For some reason he couldn't begin to fathom, the car crossed into his side of the road, only pulling back at the last second, crashing into the driver's side of his Lexus. If it wasn't for the air bag deployment, he figured he'd have been hurt a lot worse.

What had shocked him, however, was that the driver of the car had taken off. He'd been stunned and unaware of himself for a moment, but that lasted only several seconds. The next thing he heard was Nell's scream.

"Mr. Pierce," a nurse said as she entered his emergency room cubicle. "Your family is here."

"Are they allowed back?"

"Not all at the same time. Who would you like to see first?"

He immediately thought of Nell, but of course she wouldn't be with them. Would she?

"I'd like to see Adam please. Adam Troyer, my father."

The nurse left and moments later returned with Adam.

Adam came to the side of the bed, his expression worried, his brow creased with concern. "James, *soohn*, are you *oll recht*?"

"I'll live. I'm waiting for them to take me to X-ray." He managed a smile for the man who'd had nothing but love and patience for an angry teenager. "Is *Mam* ok?"

"She's worried as we all are. She'll come in next." He

gazed at James, no doubt noting his swollen face, cut forehead and bruised nose and black eyes. "When your *mudder* sees you…" Adam began.

"*Ja*, I know." James shifted slightly and grimaced. "I needed to see you first so that you can prepare her."

"I will. I'm glad to see you awake and talking. We imagined the worst when we heard the news from Nell."

"Is she all right?" James asked quickly.

"Shaken up, but she gave us the message. Tried to ease our fears, but that's hard to do when you envision your *soohn* in a car crash, hurt, unconscious. Bleeding."

"I'm sorry, *Dat*."

Adam waved his apology aside. "You did nothing wrong." He paused. "Nell…she must care for you a great deal."

"She does?" James asked with hope. But his hope died a quick death. Nell was going to marry the bishop.

"How do you feel about her?" Adam asked.

"I…" He looked away, stared at the curtain surrounding his hospital bed.

"You love her."

"Which is why I should stay away from her. Nell is a member of the church. There can be no future together for us." Although he'd like nothing more.

"What makes you think you can't have a future with her? You have the power to change your situation. Nell doesn't. You could come home, join the church and marry Nell."

For a moment, an idea that Michelle had given him appealed. "I can't." He sighed. "I spent all of my dad's money to become a veterinarian. I wanted to follow in his footsteps."

Adam pulled a chair closer to the bed and sat down.

"And you went to school, worked hard, became a veterinarian and from what I hear from others, you are a *gut* one."

"Business is picking up."

"But why does having one thing negate having another? Members of our Amish community need basic veterinary care for their animals. It would be a simpler life, 'tis true. You wouldn't have your fancy car."

"The totaled car?" James commented with amusement.

Adam's lips twitched. "*Ja*. But James, I may be wrong, but you seem happier and more at peace when you stay at the farm. 'Tis almost as if you've missed the life."

James didn't say anything as thoughts ran through his mind. "I am happier there." He grew silent as realization dawned. "I do miss it."

"So? Why can't you return to the Amish life and still be a veterinarian? You'd be more of a country vet than a city one. It would be different, but it would be just as rewarding."

"It's something to think about," James agreed. Life in the Amish community with Nell as his wife? It sounded like the closest to heaven that a man could ever come to. If he still had a chance and Nell chose not to marry John.

Adam stood. "Your mother will be fretting. I'm going to leave and tell her to come in."

"Danki, Dat."

Adam placed a gentle hand on his shoulder. "We can talk later."

"You won't tell *Mam*? Or anyone about my feelings for Nell?"

"For now. But if I were you, I'd talk about them with

your *mudder*. She loves you and can offer a woman's side of things."

James nodded. He watched the curtain close behind Adam. Moments later, it opened again, and his mother walked in.

Nell didn't feel well. The food she ate settled like a lump in her belly. She knew she wasn't good company and that she should be spending more time with Nicholas. While her family moved to the great room after cleaning up after supper, Nell put Nicholas to bed, then went to sit on the front porch. The day lengthened, and darkness fell.

Was James all right? How was his family? The worry about James consumed her to the point where she felt physically ill. She loved him. He was an *Englisher*, and she had no right. He had obviously made the choice to leave the community and she couldn't ask him to change. She thought he had some affection for her. But love? His loving her would only complicate matters.

Nell heard the sound of a buggy—the clip-clop of a horse and the noise of metal wheels rolling over gravel before she saw the lights of the vehicle. As the carriage drew closer and stopped, she saw a flashlight flare, and someone stepped out, illuminated by the golden glow. It was James's sister Maggie. She realized that James's family was in the buggy behind her.

Nell felt instant alarm. "Is James *oll recht*?"

Maggie smiled. "He'll be fine, Nell." She approached and placed her hand on Nell's arm. "*Danki* for all you did for him."

Nell exhaled with relief. "Is he home?"

"*Nay*. He's still in the hospital. They want to keep

him overnight and maybe one more day. He's battered and bruised, and he broke his collarbone. He won't be working at the clinic for a while, I'm afraid."

"Ach, nay!" Nell couldn't imagine James not working at the clinic for any length of time. Recalling how much being a veterinarian meant to him, she knew it would upset him to stay away.

"Danki for stopping by and telling me." It was late. His family didn't have to go to the trouble of letting her know, but she greatly appreciated it. She wondered if she would have been able to sleep if she didn't.

"We didn't just stop for that," James's sister said. "James wants you to use this until he gets out of the hospital."

It was his cell phone. Maggie extended it toward her, and Nell accepted it, her mind reeling from his thoughtful concern for her.

Maggie smiled. "He'll call you. Said he wants to talk with you himself."

She swallowed hard. "That's kind of him."

The other young woman nodded. "I should go."

Nell walked her to the buggy and the rest of the family who had remained inside. "I'm glad that James will be *oll recht*," she told them.

"We are, too," his *mam* said, echoed by Adam and his other siblings.

"Danki for what you did," Matthew said quietly.

"I did what I needed—wanted—to do. No thanks necessary."

Once Maggie was settled in the vehicle, Nell stepped back, clutching James's cell phone against her.

"Nell!" Maggie called as the buggy moved. "James said you can charge the phone at the clinic."

Nell hadn't thought about the phone battery dying. What if there wasn't enough charge left to answer James's phone call?

The Troyer family left, and Nell went back to the house. She entered the great room. "I think I'll head up to bed. Nicholas hasn't woken up, has he?"

"Nay," her mother said. "He's sleeping soundly." She smiled. *"Gut* night, Nell."

Her siblings echoed her mother's good-night. Her father eyed her carefully. If he noticed the cell phone in her hands, he didn't comment. "Sleep well, *dochter.* You did well today."

Blinking back tears, Nell murmured good-night, then quickly spun and headed toward the stairs. James's phone felt warm to the touch. It felt like she was holding his hand. She sighed, feeling close to him. She couldn't believe he'd sent her his cell phone.

After reaching the top landing, Nell walked the short distance down the hall to her bedroom. She looked inside, but didn't see Nicholas. She paused. Did Leah put him in her bed again?

She checked and found him sound asleep just as her mother had said. She was surprised to see that someone had brought in a crib for him. Why they'd put it in with Leah, she had no idea. She would ask them in the morning, not tonight. Not when she was expecting James to call at some point.

She hit a button on the phone, saw the face light up and was relieved to discover that the phone was fully charged. She set it carefully on her night table. James would probably call her tomorrow. She could rest easy tonight at least. She looked forward to talking with him. Just to assure herself that he is all right, she thought.

A short while later, Nell fell asleep and slept through the night until the soft ringtone of the cell phone next to her bed woke her the next morning.

Chapter Sixteen

"James?"

"Yes, Nell."

Nell closed her eyes. The sound of his deep familiar voice moved her through an ever-changing realm of emotion. "How are you feeling?"

His slight chuckle quickly died. "Like I've been run over by a truck."

She inhaled sharply. "I'm sorry."

"What for?" His genuine puzzlement filtered through the phone connection. "You have nothing to be sorry about." He paused. "Thank you for coming to my rescue."

"I didn't do much."

"Nonsense. You did a lot. You got me help. Told my family. Cared."

Nell's heart started to thump hard. "I did what anyone would do." But it was more. She loved him, but she shouldn't. Still she couldn't hang up the phone.

A few seconds of silence. "Maggie said that you'll be staying another day in the hospital."

"Yes. Unless they decide to release me sooner. I have some bruising they are concerned about…and my head.

I think once they see I'm all right, the doctor will allow me to leave."

Nell couldn't forget the awful image of him trapped in his car behind the airbag. Her mind switched to her awful dream, and she gave a little sob.

"Nell? What's wrong?"

"You were in a car accident."

"I know, sweetheart. Believe me, I know."

He said it with such dry humor that Nell couldn't help but laugh. She missed this man. How was she going to live without him? His endearment warmed her as much as it frightened her. She had to believe that it was his condition and pain medication.

"*Danki* for giving me the use of your cell phone. I was worried about you. 'Tis *gut* to hear your voice."

He didn't immediately reply, and a tense awareness sprang up between them. "I feel the same. It's good to hear your voice. It's not the same in the office without you." She heard him draw a breath. "I miss you."

"James—"

"Nell, it's okay. We're just talking."

He was right. "*Ja*, just talking," she agreed. "Maggie said you won't be able to work in the clinic for a while. What will you do?"

"I'm going to call an old college buddy of mine. We both attended Penn Vet, and we both took our first jobs at the same animal hospital after graduation. I left the practice, but he still works there. I'm hoping that he'll be able to get away for a time and fill in for me."

And if he doesn't, Nell wondered, *then what will you do?*

"If it doesn't work with Andrew—that's his name, Andrew Brighton. He's English." He chuckled. "To you, we're all English, but Drew is truly an Englishman. He's from Great Britain."

"He has an accent?" she asked, and her lips curved into a reluctant smile.

"You like men with accents?" He made a growl of displeasure. "Ignore me. I'm hurting, and it's almost time for my pain pill."

"I should let you go."

"Yeah. The nurse is here to take my vitals." A voice asked him something on the other end of the line, and Nell heard James mumble something in reply. She wished she could see him. It was reassuring to hear his voice, but she wanted to see him so she could gauge with her own eyes how he was faring.

"Nell, are you still there?"

"*Ja*, I'm still here."

"May I call you again?"

How could she say no? *"Ja."*

"I'll call you after lunch—about one?"

"I'll be here." She should remind him about Nicholas, that the little boy might need her, but she didn't.

"Have a good morning, Nell."

"Feel better, James."

"I already am…after talking with you."

And with that, he hung up.

Nell stared at the phone, wondering what she was doing—what they were doing. She was going to marry the bishop! She shouldn't be talking with James. It was wrong. Just as wrong as it was to love James.

She tried but couldn't convince herself to return James's phone to Maggie. No, she needed—enjoyed—talking with him too much.

One o'clock came and went, and Nell grew worried. What if James's condition had taken a turn for the worse?

She started to panic. She flipped open the phone, pressed some buttons. She read the word *Recents* on the screen. She saw the time next to the number. Was that his hospital room telephone number?

She was behind the barn in the pasture. Leah was in the house with Nicholas. *Mam* and her other sisters had gone into town. Her father was at Aunt Katie's with Uncle Samuel. He had said he wanted to ask her uncle about adding on to the house.

Dare she call that number? She was concerned. If he didn't call soon, she would call the hospital…

The phone vibrated in her hands as she heard the familiar ringtone. She didn't know what the tune was. The only music the *Ordnung* permitted was the hymns from the *Ausbund* that they sang during church services.

The music continued, and Nell broke away from her thoughts to answer.

"Nell? Are you there?"

"*Ja*, James. Are you *oll recht*? I was worried."

"I'm sorry. I know it's later than one, but the doctor was in my room, and I couldn't call."

She experienced a knot in her belly. She had a mental image of him in bed, ill, sore, hurting. She closed her eyes, tightened her grip on the cell phone.

"What did the doctor say?"

"That I'm doing well. I'm being released this afternoon."

"You're going home?"

"Not to my apartment. I live over Mattie Mast's Bakery. The doctor wants me to avoid stairs."

Where would he stay? "You'll be staying with your family," she guessed. It made sense. He'd be comfortable, cared for, and he already enjoyed his weekends there.

"Yes, I'll stay with my mother and Adam. I've called

Rick Martin. He's going to come for me when the paperwork for my release is ready."

She heard movement as if he were shifting the phone. "Will you come see me?" he asked.

Dare she?

"You can bring me back my cell phone."

"When?" she asked as she felt her face heat. Fortunately, he couldn't read her thoughts or see her blush.

"I'll borrow Rick's cell to call you once I get to the farmhouse."

Silence reigned between them for several seconds, which seemed longer. "Nell? Will you come?"

"*Ja*, I'll come." She could sense his relief that she would be visiting. "I know that you're eager to get your phone back."

"No, Nell. I'm eager to see you."

"The nurse will go over your instructions, then you'll be able to leave," Dr. Mark Keller said.

"Thanks, Doc."

The man smiled. "I'm glad it was nothing serious, James. It does upset me to think that I'll need to find another vet. I like you and so does Fifi." He grimaced as he said the name. "Frankly, I'm not particularly happy with my wife's name choice for our miniature French poodle."

James grinned. "Maybe you can tell her that it's too common for French poodles, that yours is special, and she needs to come up with a name that is unique."

Dressed in green scrubs after having been on call for most of the night, the man looked like the competent and confident surgeon and internist that he was. However, his expression lacked confidence as he talked about dealing with his wife about their dog. "Any suggestions?"

James gave it some thought. "None that immediately

come to mind." He grinned. "Check the internet. Find some fancy French name."

The Kellers had come into his office a while ago with their miniature poodle that was just old enough to be taken from its mother. They had brought her to him straight from where they'd gotten her. This was their first puppy.

"The internet." The doctor laughed. "I'll do that."

James felt dizzy as he swung his legs off the side of the bed.

"Remember to take it easy. Don't go into the office for any reason for at least two weeks." He paused. "You have a broken collarbone," he reminded him.

James sighed. "I know."

"It will be longer before you can see patients—about six weeks. What will you do?"

"I called a friend of mine to cover for me."

"Is he good?"

"Yes, he's good," James assured him. "We went to school together, worked in the same practice outside Philly."

The doctor looked relieved. "Maybe we'll get lucky and won't need a vet before your return to work." He looked over his shoulder at someone James couldn't see. "There is an officer here to speak with you. Says he found the hit-and-run driver."

James closed his eyes as another wave of dizziness swept over him. "Okay. Send him in."

"James—or should I say, Dr. Pierce?"

"James is fine." He managed a smile. "I'm your patient. You're not mine."

The doctor's mouth curved briefly in response. "Do you need another pain pill?"

"No, I already feel as weak as a baby lamb."

"Nevertheless, I'll send a prescription home with you. Given where you're going, I'll also have it filled in the hospital pharmacy. I'll ask the nurse to wait until it's filled before releasing you."

"Thanks." James stopped the doctor as he started to leave. "What about *Abella*?"

The man looked thoughtful, then his features brightened. "I like it. Now I just have to convince my wife."

Dr. Keller left, and the police officer entered the room. "Mr. Pierce," he greeted. "I'm Officer Todd Matheson. We found the person who hit you…"

James was told it was a teenager. A seventeen-year-old girl. James experienced a myriad of emotions as he listened to what Officer Matheson was telling him.

"She saw a rabbit on the road. She swerved to avoid hitting it."

James could understand the quick reflex that would have someone trying to preserve an animal's life. Who would understand better than he about valuing an animal?

"What will happen to her?" James asked. "You won't press charges, will you?"

"It's complicated. She did surrender herself at the station." James was surprised to see concern flicker across the officer's features. "I think there's more to it," the man said. "She was sobbing, crying hysterically, when she came in. She kept saying, 'Don't tell them. Please don't tell them.'"

"Who?" James asked.

"Apparently, she's in the foster care system. She didn't want her foster parents to know. It was almost as if she is terrified of them."

James frowned. "Does she have reason to be?"

"She was driving their car. Maybe she was afraid she'd get in trouble."

"Do you believe that?"

Officer Matheson shook his head. He looked quite intimidating in his police uniform, but there was something about him that told James the man was more compassionate and caring than most.

"Can you find out?" James hated the thought that a young girl had made one mistake that could make her life more miserable than it already was.

"I'm certainly going to try."

Later, as he sat buckled carefully into the passenger seat of Rick's car, James thought about the girl who had hit him and run. His mind naturally veered to Nell. What if it had been Nell who was the seventeen-year-old driver? Of course, she'd had a much better upbringing than Sophie Bennett apparently had. And she was Amish and would never get behind the wheel of a car. *Sophie.* That was the girl's name.

"You feeling all right?" Rick asked.

"Sorry. Preoccupied with what I learned today." He saw the man's curiosity and decided to satisfy it. Rick Martin had been a godsend to his family. Telling him about Sophie was the least he could do.

"The police found the hit-and-run driver." James went on to tell him about the girl, the officer's suspicions and James's own concern for a teenager he'd never met.

"I hope they go easy on her," Rick said. "Sounds like they might need to find her a safe home with loving foster parents who will take good care of her."

"Yeah." James couldn't agree more.

A few minutes later, Rick pulled the car into the Troyers' driveway and drove close to the house.

"Thanks, Rick." James reached gingerly into his front

pocket, trying not to wince at the ensuing pain. He pulled out a few bills that he'd taken from his wallet earlier. He'd put his wallet in the bag with his medication and paperwork.

"No." Rick placed a hand on his arm to stop him. "No payment. I won't take it. You helped our guinea pig, Tilly. Our daughter was beside herself until you took a look at her." He continued, "You wouldn't let us pay. Said it was nothing. But it was something to Jill and to me. So, no, I will not take your money—ever."

"Rick—"

"Ever, Doc. Or you or your family won't get another ride from me."

James stared at him in shock. Then he saw the tiny grin that hovered over Rick's lips. "Oh, I get it." He smiled. "Thanks."

"You're welcome."

"Does this mean that I can borrow your cell phone if I need it?"

He handed James his phone. "What happened to yours?"

"A friend has it."

James quickly made the call, was glad when Nell picked up after the first ring. "I'm home," he said. "Just arrived."

"How are you feeling?" Nell asked with concern.

"Fine."

"When do you want me to visit?"

"Now?"

"I'll be there soon."

"Okay. I'll see you soon."

James ended the call and handed Rick back his phone, grateful when the man didn't ask him who he'd been calling. "Thanks."

"The phone call will cost you," the man joked.

James laughed. The door to the Troyer house opened, and every member of his family came hurrying to see him.

"Gang's all here."

"Nice gang," Rick commented.

James agreed. "Yes, the best."

The door opened, and Adam reached in to help him rise. His mother and sisters fussed over him while Matthew stayed behind a few moments, apparently to discuss something with Rick.

Once inside the house, with his mother on one side and his stepfather on the other, James was escorted to the great room where he was lowered into a comfortable easy chair.

"We've set up a bed in the sewing room for you. You'll have plenty of space. We didn't want you to go up and down the stairs. This way you'll be comfortable, and we'll be close if you need us."

"Danki, Mam. Dat." His gaze swept over his siblings, including Matthew who was carrying the plastic bag from the hospital. "All of you."

"You look pale," Maggie said. "Do you have your medicine?"

"It's in here," Matthew said as he approached and handed it to *Mam*.

His family all stood around him, making him feel slightly uncomfortable. He stared back at them. "What?" he finally asked.

"Your poor face."

"It's bad?"

"Could be worse," Matthew said.

They all laughed, and the tension that had crept into the room dispelled.

"Tea!" *Mam* exclaimed.

"Mam?" James called her back. "Make enough for one more?"

She gave him a curious look.

"Nell is coming. She likes tea, I think." He tried to keep his thoughts private and quickly said, "She's bringing back my cell phone."

Mam nodded, and she along with his sisters headed toward the kitchen while discussing what food they'd serve once Nell got there.

She came within the hour. James heard her voice as she entered through the kitchen. He suddenly felt like a nervous schoolboy. Ever since he'd talked about her with Adam, he couldn't get the possibility of her in his life out of his mind.

Dr. Drew Brighton would start on Monday. Much to James's delight, when he'd talked with his friend this morning, he'd learned that Drew was tired of his job at the animal hospital. He'd grown up in a rural area, and the city life was starting to get to him. "I'd love a chance to help you out," the man had said in his thick British accent.

And that got James to thinking. He wouldn't mention it to anyone. Not until he knew if it would work or not.

Nell walked into the room, stealing his attention immediately. She was a vision of loveliness in her purple dress and black apron and prayer *kapp*. He gazed at her as she approached, holding his cell phone. She seemed shy. He heard her inhale sharply as she drew near.

"James," she gasped, "your injuries!"

"I look like a bit of a monster, don't I?"

"Nay, not that." She took a chair next to his. His family, James noted, had thankfully made themselves scarce. "I'm sorry for your pain."

He regarded her with affection. "I'm fine."

"You don't look it!"

"You sound as if you care," he teased. He saw something in her expression that gave him pause.

"I care. We're friends, *ja*?" She stared at him, looked away. "Have you forgotten about John?"

"How could I forget?" he said. "Although I'd like nothing more."

Nell was more than a friend, and he figured she knew it. But for now, she believed that she would be marrying the bishop, unless he could figure out a way to convince her otherwise.

"*Mam's* making tea. Will you stay for a cup?" he asked.

She nodded and happened to glance down at the phone in her hands. "Here." She extended it to him. *"Danki."*

He accepted it and placed it on a nearby table. "You figured out how to work it easily enough." He should be thanking her for letting him call her. She could have refused the phone, and he would have had no way to talk with her. It was her voice that brightened his day, made the pain of his injuries more bearable. *Nell soothes me as she does the animals.* His lips twisted. What did that say about him?

"*Ja*, it took some learning, but it wasn't as hard as I thought. It's not what they call a smartphone, is it?"

He shook his head, unable to pull his gaze from her face. "No. It's just a flip phone. I don't like fancy technology. It's wasted on me." He loved the color of her hair…her warm brown eyes. The warmth of her smile when she was amused. The rich vibrancy of her laughter… He sighed, glanced away.

She chuckled. "Like your office computer." Her brow furrowed. "What's wrong?"

"Nothing. Everything's fine." He returned his focus to

her with a smile, drinking in the sight of her as a thirsty man longs for a glass of cold water.

She stayed just long enough to finish her tea and have a piece of cake. It seemed like she'd just arrived when she stood and said she had to leave.

"Stop by again, Nell," Maggie invited.

His sister Abigail had collected the dishes and stood with a pile in her hands. "*Ja*, Nell, come see us." James's mother, Ruth, and sister Rosie echoed his other sisters' sentiment.

James watched Nell interact with his family. They liked her, a genuine like and respect that told James that Nell could easily become a member of the family.

Nell turned her attention his way. "Take care of yourself, James," she said. "Feel better soon."

"Will you come see me?"

"I don't know." She blinked, looked away, then glanced back. "I will if I can."

The fact that he couldn't get her to agree worried him. What if he was wrong about Nell's feelings for him? What if she wanted to marry John and be a mother to his son, Nicholas? He watched helplessly as she paused in the archway as she was leaving and met his gaze.

And then he held on to hope. Joy filled his chest, stealing his breath as he saw a longing that mirrored his own. If he could have risen without aid, he would have gone to her. For now, he could only keep his feelings to himself and watch her leave, until he knew whether or not all would go according to plan.

Chapter Seventeen

James had called Michelle and Janie after he'd confirmed with Drew that his friend would cover for him while he was recuperating. Michelle had been extremely upset to learn about his accident. When she'd asked how it happened, he told her that someone hit him on the road near Arlin Stoltzfus's place.

"I'm glad Nell was there for you," she'd said softly.

Janie was more matter of fact about his injuries. "I'll help Dr. Brighton get situated in the office." Then she'd wished him a quick recovery.

Midmorning on Monday, James called the office to speak with Drew. "How are things going?" he asked.

"Fine. You've got a busy practice," Drew said. "I never imagined you were this successful."

"Ha! Didn't think I had it in me, huh?" James couldn't bring himself to confess how hard things had been before they'd suddenly got better. "Does it bother you to be working in a successful practice?"

Drew snorted. "No, not at all. In fact, I'm enjoying myself." He hesitated. "Take all the time you need."

"I will." James had a sudden thought. "Drew, stop by the house on your way home tomorrow, will you?"

"Be happy to. Haven't seen you in a while. I'd like to get a glimpse of how ugly you've gotten with that banged-up face."

Drew had been staying at James's apartment since Sunday night. The arrangement worked well for both of them. It was nice to know that someone he trusted would be living in his apartment while he stayed with his mother and Adam.

"Funny," James said with a laugh.

As he closed his cell phone, he got more comfortable in the chair and shut his eyes. He must have dozed, because the next thing he know it was late afternoon.

He blinked and focused as someone came into the room.

"*Gut*, you're awake. You've skipped lunch. I'll make you a snack."

"*Mam,*" he said as she turned to go back into the kitchen. "I've asked my friend Drew to stop by."

"The one who is running the practice while you're recovering?"

"Yes."

"Does he like tea or coffee?"

James chuckled. "The man's a Brit—from England. He's a tea man all the way."

His mother eyed him with amusement. "Will he be happy with zucchini cakes and lemon squares with his tea, or do I need to pull out my recipe for scones?"

"I'm sure whatever you have will be fine."

Just before suppertime, Drew appeared and stared down at him aghast. "You look like a Sasquatch attacked you, James."

"Sasquatch?"

"The huge, hairy caveman people say they've seen living in the woods. You look dreadful."

"Thanks, Drew. I appreciate the sentiment."

The British man grinned. "All right, that might have sounded a bit dramatic."

"You think?"

"But seriously, James, you look awful."

"So I'm told." He studied his old friend and realized that he missed Drew's dry sense of humor and quick wit. "I've got a proposition for you."

Drew folded his long body into a nearby chair. "Do tell."

And so James did.

Drew cocked his head as he listened. "Seriously?" he asked. "Wow, I never thought this of you."

"When you know, you know." James stared at him. "Do we have a deal?"

Drew smiled slowly and stuck out his hand. James grabbed it and they shook it twice, then again. "Deal."

James beamed, feeling hopeful for the first time in his life.

Nell steered her buggy into the clinic parking lot and to the back of the building. A black SUV was parked in James's spot. For a minute she stared, recalling the wonderful times she had working with James, learning about the man, falling in love with him.

But now it was over, and she'd never again have a reason to spend time with him. She would consent to marry John as soon as possible. She would only allow herself one more visit this afternoon to see how he was faring.

With a silent sob, she got out, hitched up her horse then circled the building to enter through the front door.

Michelle sat in her usual spot behind the desk. "Nell!" Her eyes widened with delight as Nell approached.

"Lunch?" Nell asked of the girl she'd gotten to know

since she'd first brought Jonas to the clinic. The two women had shared an instant connection.

"Definitely!" The other woman stood. "Janie just showed in the last patient. I'll tell Drew that I'm leaving and ask Janie to handle the last check-out."

Nell sat while Michelle went into the back room. The woman returned within minutes and smiled. "Last patient is almost done. Do you mind waiting?" She lowered her voice. "I'd rather check out the last one myself since it's so close."

"I'll be happy to wait."

Michelle grinned.

Nell picked up a dog magazine and leafed through it. She looked up when she heard voices and watched as a tall, handsome blond man in a lab coat escorted a woman with a cat carrier to the front desk. Nell felt a jolt. She recognized the cat owner.

"You have nothing to be alarmed about, Mrs. Rogan. Your kitten will be fine. I suggest you keep her away from Boots for a while…or at least Boots's food." The man was obviously British. His richly accented tone was pleasing to her ear. *James's friend Andrew Brighton.*

"I will," Edith Rogan promised. The older woman turned, saw her sitting in the waiting room. "Nell!" she greeted with obvious delight. "How are you?"

"I'm well, Mrs. Rogan."

"I miss seeing you in the office."

Nell smiled. "I enjoyed working here."

"Why are you here? Is something wrong with kitty?" Mrs. Rogan asked.

"Nope," Michelle piped up before Nell could answer. "She's my lunch date."

"Naomi is wonderful," Nell assured.

Mrs. Rogan looked pleased. "Enjoy your lunch, Nell. It was nice seeing you again."

"You, too, Mrs. Rogan."

Nell rose as the woman went to the door. Mrs. Rogan halted and turned. "I was sorry to learn what happened to Dr. Pierce."

"*Ja,* it was terrible."

"He doing all right?"

"He'll be fine. I thought I'd stop by and visit with him later today."

"You give him my regards."

"I will, Mrs. Rogan. Thank you."

"Aren't you going to introduce us?" a rich British voice asked.

Nell turned and met the man's curious gaze.

"This is Nell Stoltzfus," Michelle said. "Nell, Dr. Andrew Brighton."

"It's nice to meet you, Nell," he said with gray eyes that regarded her warmly.

She felt her face heat. "Nice to meet you, too."

Michelle watched the exchange with amusement. "We're going to go, Drew. I'll be back in an hour."

"Take as long as you like," Drew said, withdrawing his gaze from Nell.

"I'll take the rest of the day," Michelle teased.

"Better not," the man quipped. "It seems Nell here has plans for the afternoon."

Michelle grabbed her arm and escorted her to the front door. "Come on, Nell. Don't let this Brit embarrass you."

"Embarrass her!" he exclaimed. "That wasn't my intention!"

Michelle grinned as she shut the door, blocking out his words. "He is just too easy to tease!"

Nell laughed. "You are terrible."

"I know. Don't you love it!" She pulled Nell toward her car. "No offense, but I'm driving."

"Where are we going?"

"I know a little place," Michelle said.

Ten minutes later, they were seated in Katie's Kitchen in Ronks, sipping on fresh-brewed ice tea and enjoying their delicious yeast rolls with the restaurant's signature peanut butter spread. Nell had been there before and enjoyed their food.

"So you're going to see James today," Michelle said after the two had caught up on news of their families.

"*Ja*. I haven't seen him since the day after it happened."

"You visited him in the hospital."

Nell shook her head. "*Nay*. At his family farm where he's recovering." She took a sip of her ice tea. "Have you heard from him?"

Michelle finished chewing a bite of roll before answering. "Yesterday. He called to speak with Drew." She smiled. "He sounded good. Said he was feeling better."

"He was really hurt, Michelle. His face…" Nell blanched as she recalled the accident.

The other woman reached across the table to squeeze Nell's hand. "You were there. It must have been awful."

Nell released a sharp breath. "You have no idea." She shifted uncomfortably when Michelle's gaze sharpened.

"Dr. Brighton is working out?" Nell said, changing the subject.

"Oh, yes. He is wonderful. He's like James in many ways. Both are kind and compassionate men with a deep love for animals."

Nell smiled. "I'm glad James was able to call on someone to help so quickly."

"Yes. You won't believe how busy we've become!"

Nell was glad. She'd done all she could to help James build his practice, handing out his business cards, getting others to hand out cards and recommend the clinic... spreading the word throughout her Amish community.

All too soon, Michelle's lunch hour was up, and they were heading back to the clinic.

"We'll have to do this again," Michelle said with warmth as she pulled into the lot and parked. The women got out and met in front of the vehicle.

"*Ja*, I'd like that."

Michelle encircled her with her arms. "Great to see you. Take care of yourself."

"I will. You too."

Michelle went inside, and Nell suddenly experienced nervous excitement as she unhitched Daisy and climbed into her buggy. It was time to see James. She both yearned for and dreaded the visit.

Last time. Soon, James would be well and back to work, and except for the rare occasion when she might need to call on him for her animals' medical care, she wouldn't have much opportunity to see him.

Losing Michael had been devastating, because Michael had died while he'd been on his way to her. But losing James would be different. She was older now, and she'd had a chance to mourn Michael's death.

When she left James this afternoon, she knew she would feel destroyed. She was glad that James would be out there in the world, doing what he loved to do. It was her only comfort. But him being so close yet out of reach was going to hurt her like nothing else ever had.

James was still sore but feeling better. He knew his face was black-and-blue. His sister had used his battered looks to coerce him into staying put in the chair. But he could no longer remain inactive. He knew he looked terrible, but thanks to ice and time to heal, the swelling around his nose had gone down. The ache in his muscles had become bearable with no need of medication to help him with the pain.

He knew he'd been given orders to rest for the next two weeks, but he was going crazy. Maybe if he just went outside for a little while. Surely, he could sit on the front porch and read or something. Anywhere but the inside of the house which he loved but had had enough of for now.

He stood and went into the kitchen. His mother and sister Abigail were at the table, snapping green beans they had picked from their vegetable garden.

"You should have called out if you needed something," *Mam* said.

"I had to move. Seems like I've been sitting in that chair for months."

His sister smirked. "James, 'tis only been five days."

He sighed. "I know. I'm not used to the inactivity. I want to be outside helping *Dat* and Matt."

"We can't allow you to do that."

The kitchen windows were open, and a light breeze blew into the house helping with the heat.

"'Tis a while before supper. Do you want something to eat?"

"If I eat any more, I'll gain ten pounds."

His sister ran her gaze the length of his lean form. "Doubt it."

Her dry tone made James smile. "I'll have an ice tea." When his sister started to rise, he said, "I can get it."

He saw his mother put a hand on his sister's arm as if to stop her from objecting. James moved stiffly to the refrigerator where he took out the pitcher. He shifted more slowly closer to the cabinet where the glasses where kept. "Do either of you want a glass of tea?"

"I'll have a glass," Abigail said strangely. James flashed her a glance and saw an amused look on her pretty face. She looked so much like their mother, but her hair was blond while his mother's hair was a sandy brown.

"In the cabinet," James teased, filling his own glass before setting down the pitcher. He felt slightly unsteady as he moved toward the table and pulled out a chair.

"If you sit here, we'll put you to work."

By this time, James was feeling awful. "I think I'll go sit in the other room."

"Don't spill that tea," Abigail taunted with a laugh.

"Brat!" James chuckled as he carefully returned to the great room and took a seat.

A window on the one side of the room was open and faced the driveway. James sat and closed his eyes while wondering what Nell was doing. She had said she would visit again, but it had been four days since he last saw her and he missed her like crazy.

He heard the sound of buggy wheels as a vehicle came down the driveway. *Dat* and Matthew must be back after going to the store to pick up chicken feed and a few other supplies.

He leaned back, closed his eyes. He heard the kitchen screen door slam shut, but he didn't move. Then he sensed someone enter the great room and stare at him. And he knew immediately that it wasn't his father or Matthew.

His eyes flickered open and he thought he was imagining things because he'd wanted so badly to see her. "Nell."

She hesitated in the doorway between the hall and the great room. "James."

"Come in and sit." Then it occurred to him that she might have come for some other reason than to see him. He frowned. "If you have other business and don't have time…"

She came forward and took the chair across from him. "I came to see you."

He couldn't help the grin that burst across his lips. "I'm glad. I've been wanting to see you. Talk with you."

She looked surprised. "You were?"

He picked up his glass. "Would you like some ice tea?"

"That would be nice."

"Abigail!" he shouted. He met Nell's beautiful brown gaze with an amused smile.

"Already got it, *bruder*," Abigail said curtly as she handed Nell a glass. "I don't mind waiting on her."

His sister stayed in the room and hovered.

"Abigail, *danki*. Now please leave us to visit alone," James told her. "I don't need you hovering."

With a sigh of exasperation, his sister left. Nell had a strange look on her face as she stared at him.

"I'm sorry," he said, worrying what Nell was thinking.

"I'm not."

"What?"

"You and your sister…you're just like me and mine."

He released a sigh of relief. "I love her."

"I can tell."

"I love you."

She froze. "What?"

"I said I love you."

She seemed shaken as she looked away. "James, you shouldn't say that. You know I'm marrying John."

"My friend Drew is joining the practice. He's staying."

Nell looked confused. "That's nice. I heard that business is up. You'll need his help."

"Thanks to you." He had learned recently just how much Nell had worked to grow Pierce Veterinary Clinic.

She blushed, looked away.

"Drew is going to be working at the clinic while I work from home."

Nell arched her eyebrows. "You're going to work out of your apartment?"

James gazed at her, watching every nuance of her expression, hoping for a glimpse of her thoughts, something that told him she cared for him more than as a friend. He had told her he loved her, but she hadn't reciprocated. Or did she brush off his feelings because she was Amish and he was English and she was afraid to acknowledge them?

"For a while I'll be living here. *Mam* and *Dat* assured me that it would be all right. Matthew doesn't mind sharing his room for a while." James reflected how his relationship with Matthew had greatly improved since he'd begun to spend time at home.

"You're going to be living here," Nell said. "Why?"

"I'm rejoining the community. I plan to join the church come November."

Nell's mouth opened and closed as if she didn't know what to say.

"I don't understand…"

"If you'd listened to what I said, really listened, you'd know."

Nell stared at the man she loved, unsure of what he was saying. She was afraid to hope, afraid to love, but at the same time, she was terrified of no longer having him in her life.

Now he was telling her that he'd be moving back to the Amish community. Had she only imagined that part because she'd wished for it?

"Nell." He rose from his chair, crossed the distance between them and sat down next to her.

She met his gaze with longing and hope…and everything she was afraid he'd see in her expression. "Why are you telling me this?"

He took hold of her hand, capturing it between his larger ones. His dark eyes held a sudden intensity that stole her breath. He looked vulnerable with his twin black eyes and bruised face, but she could feel his strength. Dressed in a solid maroon shirt and tri-blend pants held up by black suspenders, James looked as if he had always been Amish, that he'd never left the community. He'd shaved recently, and his firm chin was smooth and drew her attention. What would he look like in a beard as a married man? She gasped as hope reared up, enthralling her.

"James—"

"I love you, Nell. I want to marry you if you'll have me. Will you forget John and become my wife?"

"But, James, you've been *English* for so long."

"That's true. I worked hard to be what I thought my father wanted for me. I went to school, became a veterinarian, worked near a city…and opened a practice here. But you know all that."

Her heart was pounding hard. James was offering her most secret desire—to be his wife, to live with him, have his children…to love him until their lives ended.

"I haven't been happy, Nell, in the *English* world. Not until you stepped through the door of my clinic with

Jonas in your arms. You calmed me like you did him. I knew I had to get to know you. I figured right then that I wanted you somehow in my life."

He was running his fingers gently over the back of her hand. His caress tingled and thrilled her.

"Nell," he went on. "I'm happiest here in the community. When I told Adam about my feelings for you—"

She felt a jolt. "You talked with Adam about me?"

His features were apologetic. "I needed his advice. I loved you and thought I didn't have a hope of having you in my life. Adam told me that above everything else, my father wanted me to be happy." He paused, and his hand cupped her face. "That I could easily be a country veterinarian working in our community." He drew a deep breath, released it slowly. "You make me happy. I love you. Please allow me to love you. Marry me."

Tears trickled down her cheeks as she gazed at him. "I said that I'd marry John."

"Does John really want to marry you because you're you? Or because he needs a mother for Nicholas?"

"He wants a mother for Nicholas," she admitted.

"Then it doesn't have to be you. Another woman will do."

She recognized love in his dark eyes. "I'm afraid."

He jerked. "Of me?"

"*Nay.* Of backing out of marrying John, of telling my father of my true feelings." She blinked back tears. "But most of all—what if you aren't happy with being Amish? I want you to be happy," she sobbed. "I don't want you to ever regret the choice you made. I don't want you to be sorry that you married me."

"Sweetheart." He wiped away her tears with his fingers. "I will never regret marrying you. Don't you understand? I love you—so much. Not having you in my life will kill me. You mean that much to me."

"I do?"

He nodded.

"Oh, James, I love you so much it scares me."

"Then you'll marry me?"

"I want to—"

"But?"

"We can wait. I need to know if you change your mind."

"Never! I will never change my mind." He drew her closer. "Nell, let me court you. We have until November before we can marry. Let me prove to you that this life—and you—are what I want more than anything in the world. So, Nell, sweetheart, may I court you?"

Basking in the radiance of his love, Nell felt warm and tingly...and so much in love. *"Ja."*

James groaned, and suddenly he was kissing her, a gentle kiss that made her feel special. He pulled back, his eyes glowing, his mouth curved in a tender smile. "I'm afraid it may be weeks before I can court you properly."

"I can wait."

"But you'll come visit me."

"Ja, James, I'll come," she promised. "Every day."

"And you don't love John."

"Nay, I love you. Always have. Always will."

"And you're going to marry me, not him."

"Ja, I'm going to marry the man I love."

She watched as his eyes closed as she heard him murmur, "Thanks be to *Gott*."

And Nell had never felt happier. She loved this man, and she would pray every day that God would bless their marriage.

Epilogue

Summer slid into autumn, the months flying by so quickly that Nell wondered where the time had gone. As promised, James had moved all of his things into the Troyer farmhouse. Nell visited him every day while he healed, and afterward, the man spent every moment that they were together proving how much he loved and valued her.

It had been difficult for her to tell her father that she wouldn't be marrying the bishop. Telling the bishop himself had been easier, for as she'd thought, he wasn't done grieving for Catherine. He wasn't ready to marry again.

As for Nicholas, there were plenty of community women who were happy to help with the little boy's care. But as time went by, John kept the boy close with him more often than not.

The fall harvest had come and gone. James had purchased a small piece of property, and the community had worked during the last months building a home for the soon-to-be-married couple.

The house was perfect, at least to Nell. There was a room for James's satellite veterinary office and plenty of space for the children she and James both hoped to have one day. James asked her to be his veterinary assistant. Nell quickly accepted the position.

Dr. Andrew Brighton was doing well at the clinic. Since Drew would be the only one working in that office, James had insisted that the clinic be renamed to Brighton Animal Hospital, but Drew had disagreed. The friends had compromised by adding Drew's name first to its current name, making it Brighton-Pierce Veterinary Clinic.

Their wedding banns were read in church. James had fit right back into the community, and each passing day had convinced Nell that he truly was happy and belonged.

The morning of their wedding finally arrived. Her parents' house had been transformed to allow for the wedding feast, and the wedding ceremony was at Aunt Katie and Uncle Samuel's.

After riding together while holding hands, Nell and James arrived at the Lapp farm, eager for the services, the ceremony, that would join them as man and wife.

Afterward, they got into the buggy driven by their attendants—Nell's sister Leah and James's brother, Matthew. Leah and Matthew were chatting about the ceremony, the day and celebration to come.

James leaned closed to Nell, his breath a soft whisper in her ear. "I love you, wife."

Nell smiled as she regarded him with love. "I'll love you forever, husband."

And then her husband of less than an hour leaned close and gave her a tender kiss that stole her breath, her heart—and bound her to him forever. James's head lifted; his dark eyes glowed. His face had healed, and he looked as if he'd never suffered in the accident. Her new husband was easily the most wonderful and handsome man Nell had ever laid eyes on.

She had everything she'd ever wanted—James, the man who loved her, her life's partner. *Thank You, dear Lord, for blessing us with Your love.*

* * * * *

If you loved this story,
check out the books in the author's
previous miniseries
LANCASTER COUNTY WEDDINGS:
NOAH'S SWEETHEART
JEDIDIAH'S BRIDE
A WIFE FOR JACOB
ELIJAH AND THE WIDOW
LOVING ISAAC

Available now from Love Inspired!

Find more great reads at www.LoveInspired.com

Dear Reader,

Welcome back to the Amish community of Happiness in Lancaster County, Pennsylvania. If you have read any of my Lancaster County Wedding series, you would have met and read about the Lapp brothers, sons of Samuel and Katie Lapp. In *A Secret Amish Love*, Nell Stoltzfus is one of five sisters who are cousins to the Lapp siblings. Although there are still two Lapp brothers who haven't found their true love, I thought them too young to have their own story yet.

Their cousin Nell, on the other hand, is long overdue for marriage. Unfortunately, she finds herself falling for someone she shouldn't. James Pierce, an English veterinarian, is forbidden to her, a young woman who had already joined the Amish church. The fact that James is drawn to her as much as she is to him becomes a problem for the both of them. While her father urges her in one direction, Nell can't keep herself from longing for her forbidden love.

I hope you enjoy Nell's story and your return trip to Amish country in Lancaster County.

Blessing and light,
Rebecca Kertz

COMING NEXT MONTH FROM
Love Inspired®

Available July 18, 2017

A GROOM FOR RUBY
The Amish Matchmaker • by Emma Miller

Joseph Brenneman is instantly smitten when Ruby Plank stumbles—literally—into his arms. The shy mason sees all the wonderful things she offers the world. But with his mother insisting Ruby isn't good enough, and Ruby keeping a devastating secret, could they ever have a happily-ever-after?

SECOND CHANCE RANCHER
Bluebonnet Springs • by Brenda Minton

Returning to Bluebonnet Springs, Lucy Palermo is determined to reclaim her family ranch and take care of her younger sister. What she never expected was rancher neighbor Dane Scott and his adorable daughter—or that their friendship would have her dreaming of staying in their lives forever.

THE SOLDIER'S SECRET CHILD
Rescue River • by Lee Tobin McClain

Widow Lacey McPherson is ready to embrace the single life—until boy-next-door Vito D'Angelo returns with a foster son in tow. Now she's housing two guests and falling for the ex-soldier. But will the secret he's keeping ruin any chance at a future together?

REUNITING HIS FAMILY
by Jean C. Gordon

Released from prison after a wrongful charge, widowed dad Rhys Maddox wants nothing more than custody of his two sons. Yet volunteering at their former social worker Renee Delacroix's outreach program could give him a chance at more: creating a family.

TEXAS DADDY
Lone Star Legacy • by Jolene Navarro

Adrian De La Cruz is happy to see childhood crush Nikki Bergmann back in town and bonding with his daughter. But he quickly sees the danger of spending time together. With Nikki set on leaving Clear Water, could their wish for a wife and mother ever become reality?

THEIR RANCH REUNION
Rocky Mountain Heroes • by Mindy Obenhaus

Former high school sweethearts Andrew Stephens and Carly Wagner reunite when Andrew's late grandmother leaves them her house. At odds on what to do with the property, when a fire at Carly's inn forces the single mom and her daughter to move in, they begin to agree on one thing: they're meant to be together.

LOOK FOR THESE AND OTHER LOVE INSPIRED BOOKS WHEREVER BOOKS ARE SOLD, INCLUDING MOST BOOKSTORES, SUPERMARKETS, DISCOUNT STORES AND DRUGSTORES.

LICNM0717

Get 2 Free Books,
Plus 2 Free Gifts—
just for trying the Reader Service!

Love Inspired®

YES! Please send me 2 FREE Love Inspired® Romance novels and my 2 FREE mystery gifts (gifts are worth about $10 retail). After receiving them, if I don't wish to receive any more books, I can return the shipping statement marked "cancel." If I don't cancel, I will receive 6 brand-new novels every month and be billed just $5.24 for the regular-print edition or $5.74 each for the larger-print edition in the U.S., or $5.74 each for the regular-print edition or $6.24 each for the larger-print edition in Canada. That's a saving of at least 13% off the cover price. It's quite a bargain! Shipping and handling is just 50¢ per book in the U.S. and 75¢ per book in Canada.* I understand that accepting the 2 free books and gifts places me under no obligation to buy anything. I can always return a shipment and cancel at any time. The free books and gifts are mine to keep no matter what I decide.

Please check one:
- ☐ Love Inspired Romance Regular-Print (105/305 IDN GLWW)
- ☐ Love Inspired Romance Larger-Print (122/322 IDN GLWW)

Name _____ (PLEASE PRINT)

Address _____ Apt. # _____

City _____ State/Province _____ Zip/Postal Code _____

Signature (if under 18, a parent or guardian must sign)

Mail to the **Reader Service:**
IN U.S.A.: P.O. Box 1341, Buffalo, NY 14240-8531
IN CANADA: P.O. Box 603, Fort Erie, Ontario L2A 5X3

Want to try two free books from another line?
Call 1-800-873-8635 today or visit www.ReaderService.com.

*Terms and prices subject to change without notice. Prices do not include applicable taxes. Sales tax applicable in N.Y. Canadian residents will be charged applicable taxes. Offer not valid in Quebec. This offer is limited to one order per household. Books received may not be as shown. Not valid for current subscribers to Love Inspired Romance books. All orders subject to approval. Credit or debit balances in a customer's account(s) may be offset by any other outstanding balance owed by or to the customer. Please allow 4 to 6 weeks for delivery. Offer available while quantities last.

Your Privacy—The Reader Service is committed to protecting your privacy. Our Privacy Policy is available online at www.ReaderService.com or upon request from the Reader Service.

We make a portion of our mailing list available to reputable third parties that offer products we believe may interest you. If you prefer that we not exchange your name with third parties, or if you wish to clarify or modify your communication preferences, please visit us at www.ReaderService.com/consumerschoice or write to us at Reader Service Preference Service, P.O. Box 9062, Buffalo, NY 14240-9062. Include your complete name and address.

LI17R2

SPECIAL EXCERPT FROM

Love Inspired.

Ruby Plank comes to Seven Poplars to find a husband and soon literally stumbles into the arms of Joseph Brenneman. But will a secret threaten to keep them apart?

Read on for a sneak preview of
A GROOM FOR RUBY by **Emma Miller,**
available August 2017 from Love Inspired!

A young woman lay stretched out on a blanket, apparently lost in a book. But the most startling thing to Joseph was her hair. The woman's hair wasn't pinned up under a *kapp* or covered with a scarf. It rippled in a thick, shimmering mane down the back of her neck and over her shoulders nearly to her waist.

Joseph's mouth gaped. He clutched the bouquet of flowers so tightly between his hands that he distinctly heard several stems snap. He swallowed, unable to stop staring at her beautiful hair. It was brown, but brown in so many shades…tawny and russet, the color of shiny acorns in winter and the hue of ripe wheat. He'd intruded on a private moment, seen what he shouldn't. He should turn and walk away. But he couldn't.

"Hello," he stammered. "I'm sorry, I was looking for—"

"Ach!" The young woman rose on one elbow and twisted to face him. It was Ruby. Her eyes widened in surprise. "Joseph?"

"*Ya.* It's me."

Ruby sat up, dropping her paperback onto the blanket, pulling her knees up and tucking her feet under her skirt. "I was drying my hair," she said. "I washed it. I still had mud in it from last night."

Joseph grimaced. "Sorry."

"Everyone else went to Byler's store." She blushed. "But I stayed home. To wash my hair. What must you think of me without my *kapp*?"

She had a merry laugh, Joseph thought, a laugh as beautiful as she was. She was regarding him with definite interest. Her eyes were the shade of cinnamon splashed with swirls of chocolate. His mouth went dry.

She smiled encouragingly.

A dozen thoughts tumbled in his mind, but nothing seemed like the right thing to say. "I…I never know what to say to pretty girls," he admitted as he tore his gaze away from hers. "You must think I'm thickheaded." He shuffled his feet. "I'll come back another time when—"

"Who are those flowers for?" Ruby asked. "Did you bring them for Sara?"

"*Ne*, not Sara." Joseph's face grew hot. He tried to say, "I brought them for you," but again the words stuck in his throat. Dumbly, he held them out to her. It took every ounce of his courage not to turn and run.

Don't miss
A GROOM FOR RUBY
by Emma Miller, available August 2017 wherever
Love Inspired® books and ebooks are sold.

www.LoveInspired.com

Copyright © 2017 by Emma Miller

LIEXP0717

book
you!

Earn points from all your Harlequin book purchases from wherever you shop.

Turn your points into *FREE BOOKS* of your choice
OR
EXCLUSIVE GIFTS from your favorite authors or series.

Join for FREE today at
www.HarlequinMyRewards.com.

Harlequin My Rewards is a free program (no fees) without any commitments or obligations.

MYR17

Inspirational Romance to Warm Your Heart and Soul

Join our social communities to connect with other readers who share your love!

Sign up for the Love Inspired newsletter at **www.LoveInspired.com** to be the first to find out about upcoming titles, special promotions and exclusive content.

CONNECT WITH US AT:

Harlequin.com/Community

 Facebook.com/LoveInspiredBooks

 Twitter.com/LoveInspiredBks

LISOCIAL2017